killoyle

killoyle

Roger Boylan

 Dalkey Archive Press

Boylan, Roger, 1951-
Killoyle / Roger Boylan. — 1st ed.
p.   cm.
1. City and town life—Ireland—Fiction.   I. Title.
PS3552.0915K55   1997   813'.54—dc21   96-51796
ISBN 1-56478-145-3

This publication is partially supported by a grant from the
Illinois Arts Council, a state agency.

Dalkey Archive Press
Illinois State University
Campus Box 4241
Normal, IL 61790-4241

*Printed on permanent/durable acid-free paper and bound in the
United States of America.*

killoyle

1

Like Castle Dracula, or the Bates mansion in *Psycho*, Spudorgan Hall stood out in stark relief atop its looming escarpment,[1] lit up in the lightning glare that alternated with the barrel-hollow grumbling and asthmatic throat-clearings of distant (but approaching) thunder. It was a quite entertaining phase of the autumnal equinox,[2] especially if viewed from behind twitching lace curtains, or trembling roller blinds—at any rate, more edifying than the telly for the guests at the Hall, as it was for all the snug homebodies and smug early-to-bedders throughout Killoyle City and southeastern Ireland and out to sea almost as far as Wales. Decidedly not entertained, however—although likewise sporadically illuminated—was homeward-bound Milo Rogers, Spudorgan Hall's headwaiter and his own occasional poet and dreamer extraordinaire. Nearing the topmost corner of Uphill Street (a real slog, in that wind), he took a cigarette out of his coat pocket and cursed the fates that (a) allowed his last fag to be waterlogged, (b) did likewise to his matches, and (c) ordered the pubs closed at such a sodbuggering early hour—and on his

---

[1]The Micheal MacLiammoir Overpass, just across from the railway station if you're coming in that way (CIE spur line twice daily Cork–Killoyle, three times on Sunday, no returns), or a brisk walk from the bus stop if that's your fancy (CIE Express, Green Line #15A: CORK Central–Cobh–Youghal–Killoyle–WAXFORD East).

[2]Autumnal equinox? Your granny. A spit of rain, nothing more and nothing less; natural as your morning stool, especially in this place (SE Ireland) at this time of year (October).

night off, for the love of God.[3]

"Ballocks," he howled. The thunder burped, sarcastically.

Of course, there were the after-hours clubs on Parnell Parade, where for a cover charge that would buy you a weekend on the Riviera, including airfare and several Blue Ribbon dinners, you could sit until 2 a.m. and guzzle yourself into oblivion and beyond; but Milo, shameless Saturday night inebriate that he was, nevertheless retained enough self-respect to avoid clip joints of that class. Imagine expecting the likes of him to part with good money to buy vintage "champagne" for some raddled slut he'd probably see Monday lunchtime coughing into her fried cod at the Crubeeneria[4] down the street! Moreover (crucially), Milo was nearly penniless, this particular Saturday being equidistant between fortnightly paydays at Spudorgan Hall. In any event (i.e., conclusively), he was already standing at the intersection of Uphill Street (Ir. *Sraid Uphail*)—alias the N6 Waxford-Dublin dual carriageway[5]—and the T45 Killoyle–Cork ring road,[6] half a mile and more from Killoyle town centre—comprising O'Connell Square, Parnell Parade, Pollexfen Walk, Brendan Behan Avenue, St. Derek's (C. of I.), St. Oinsias' (R.C.), SS. Peter &

---

[3]Not anymore, thanks to Gar Looney's Fine Whiskies coalition government and the new All-Night Licensing Act they managed to get passed last Wednesday—and was that ever a squeaker, twenty minutes before the pubs closed and guess whose belly was pressing against the bar at Neary's a scant five minutes later, that excellent establishment being a judicious six minutes fifteen seconds on (fleet) foot from Leinster House, in normal traffic? Ten out of ten if you guessed your man Gar himself (unrecognized by one and all).

[4]*Do* you mind? Tam-Tam's, on Haughey Circle; oh, their crubeen's all right, and I quite fancied their fillet of plaice in aspic, and wait till I tell you about their toasted cod on barley—you'd think Heaven itself was the next stop! But the squid courgettes I had there once, and the grape-free vinegar they serve with everything . . . *UGGGGHHHH*, if you follow my drift.

[5]Jewel carriageway, indeed! Four lanes for as many miles, then back to the old one-two, if you ask me. What a country.

[6]Leading from the shopping arcade on Parnell Parade to Cork, via Skibbereen, bold Gougane Barra and (on a clear day, mind) parts of North Tipperary (Ryan country—brrrr!).

Laurence O'Toole's (R.C.), and the lower approaches to King Idris Road (E. & W.)—and mere seconds away from the front door of his house at no. 7b, Oxtail Yard—well, "house" is perhaps putting it a bit strongly. The "b" in the address pretty much sums it up.

Still (he thought), things could be worse. Reassuringly, they were, as soon as the storm hit Killoyle proper instead of loitering timidly on the outskirts like a country cousin, but by that time Milo had bowed to the inevitable and regained his domain to enjoy the dubious delights of television from Wales—beamed weakly across St. George's Channel from the Principality itself[7] —and his own Three-Star Home Brew, a guaranteed tummy-tickler.[8]

"Blow, wind, and crack your cheeks," muttered Milo, as the gale raged outside. On the screen flickered a flick featuring big-nosed Spencer Tracy, like his erstwhile character Daniel Boone wearing a coonskin hat, itself sporting a coonskin tail. Caucasian extras, clumsily made up to resemble Red Indians, huddled together in the damp forests of Upstate New York (in reality the San Fernando Valley, plus decor), plotting evilly against fork-tongued Paleface (Messrs. Boone/Tracy). Arrows flew; a cannon barked; death was shammed in awkward poses athwart the studio floor. The heroic music of Erich Korngold[9] overflowed the

---

[7]Harlech TV, of course, at its best on Saturday nights to lure Taffy home from the bloody local (if his area's wet; if it's dry, well, that's another set of bloody problems entirely, isn't it, boy *bach?*): reruns of traditional Welsh dramas, e.g., *Dai of the Tryffyds*, *Rhondda!* and *Cwm Cymru*; the occasional game show/quiz, usually hosted by Geraint ap Rhys, raven-haired Schwarzenegger of North Gwynedd; a war film now and then, invariably starring Dickie Jenkins from Abergavenny, he whose Swiss tombstone reads "Richard Burton, 1925-1984."

[8]And occasional bowel-reamer.

[9]More Korn than Gold, as the old Da used to say. Ah, wasn't he the sharp one, and didn't all the neighbors call him Wally the Wag, and isn't he where he always wanted to be, up there at the right hand of God—or was it the left? One or the other, anyhow (or both, unless he's taking the Mystery Tour of Purgatory, and just between you and me I wouldn't put anything past him, sure now wasn't he the sharp one, etc.)!

soundtrack, flooding broad-nostrilled Spence as he shared the pipe of peace with an obvious Nordic (indeed, Celtic) specimen daubed a sporadic shite-brown color that inexplicably left patches of European pallor exposed: one by his left earlobe, another on his neck, a third up by his daringly low hairline[10] . . . it was ludicrous, absurd, a disgrace!

The thunder crackled, snored, eructated hugely. Rain lashed the windows with pent-up sadism. The gas fire was burbling comfortably, releasing frequent hiccups in sympathy with the wind. Past time for a refill, said Milo to himself. He made this declaration aloud, although to the best of his knowledge there was no one in any of the bungalow's three rooms to hear him.

"Time for a refill, eh, me man?" he repeated. His voice boomed hollow in his empty glass. Nodding in self-agreement, he squeezed his generous bulk out of his armchair and swept majestically from the parlor into the vestibule and thence to the kitchen, abode of (reading from left to right):[11] a Frigidaire, vintage 1962; closets dating from the founding of Oxtail Corners, *circa* 1976, which year also saw the razing of a dwelling from the Georgian period and in its place the raising of no. 7b, a lopsided bungalow better suited to the Curragh,[12] or infamous holiday camps on England's South Coast . . . next, the microwave (Hatichi, '87), head cheerleader among the bachelor's friends, always on hand to dish up a lukewarm snack of boxty, or colcannon

---

[10]This thespian poltroon later became (hold on to your hats) president of the United States, prehensile forehead and all; known to posterity as the Dozer, he wasn't bad, actually, despite *his* grandpa's being born in Ballyporeen, not a million miles away from storied Killoyle (but not far enough, in them days).

[11]Your left, his right, unless you're standing on my left, then his left's your right and vicey versa, at least from where I sit.

[12]Renowned for the nags, of course, as well as that nasty old army jug the lads sprang Johnny Owen from back in '79—he's in L.A., now, doing the heavy lifting for some Asian crowd. Johnny, we'd hardly know ye: as a law-abiding Californian, he's into organicism and multitasking, but—poor homesick gurrier that he is—he showers down with Irish Spring, and doesn't the scent of his freshly scrubbed oxters remind him of the Vale of Avoca on a soggy day!

and broth; the sink, with refitted taps, hot, cold and in-between; above the sink, a window, at that moment framing a pinkish-white face with anxiously wandering eyes; next to the sink, a broom closet, rarely entered, containing dusty pails, a dryish mop, and three yards of twine, but nary a broom in the two years and a bit Milo had been *in situ* (he Hoovered instead, at an incredible rate); a mid-sixties Hoover, leaning drunkenly against the kitchen's pièce de résistance: the stove. A real turn-of-the-century masterpiece, this beauty was hammered out of a single sheet of drop-forged steel back in 1896 (or was it '97?) by MacSweeney of Chicago and miraculously salvaged from the other house[13] just in time to be connected to existing gas mains under the thick macadam of Oxtail Terrace (adjacent to the Yard).[14] Intended for display rather than use, it squatted across from its distant descendant, the Hatichi microwave, which gazed back, exuding the callow superiority of its generation.

The floor featured tiles, hexagonal in shape, some with intriguing whorls of ancient grime embedded in the fading interstices.

Milo turned on the light in the kitchen. Out of a charitable impulse to amuse the solitary spectator he took at first to be his

---

[13]Known in Killoyle's teeming places of refreshment as "De Udder House (hic)," q.v. Maher, *infra.*

[14]As Milo wrote in his diary: *Prodigious and giantlike is Milo's stove, boasting six coal-black burners, four in back, two in front, each wide enough to service a pot of porridge for six, and they with the hunger of unfed men; deep as the pockets of Dail Eireann its oven, and broader than the broad sands of Magilligan Strand; higher and loftier its bulk than the golden-stoned majesty of Joyce Castle, dominion of the Ondt and industrious Gracehoper; louder roar the six flames of its burners than the massed throats of the warriors of Meath, and they without drink taken this fortnight past; sweeter sings the gas through its nozzle of brass than the purling of the tern in the soughing reeds of Inishbofin; heartier than burly pub-crawlers the soups and stews fermented there, and ranker than the summer sweat of panting lovers the lingering aftertaste thereof; smooth as Chinese silk the porcelain hull, and of a sheen brighter than Lough Neagh in the gilt of a springtime dawn!* In a word, it's a corker. Good thing Milo never uses it: who knows how fast the market value might depreciate?

own image reflected in the darkened windowpane, he fell into Quasimodo pose—one shoulder upraised, knuckles of opposing hand grazing the floor, facial distortion[15] accompanied by hoarse cackling—and lurched towards the sink, beneath which a little brown jug of fresh home brew awaited his attentions. Before he could proceed further, however, he froze, rooted to the spot. Electrified insects danced along his spine; sweat teased his palms; his intestines shrank in on themselves in the immanence of fear. It was no reflection after all: *there was a face at the window!*

It was only Murphy, but still . . . !

"What the blazes are you playing at?" inquired Milo, unheard through the closed window. Once open, it admitted a swaggering gust of midnight storm, as well as a few stray leaves and, one leg nimbly preceding him: Murphy, Peter X. of that name, fellow Dubliner, fellow Northsider and chief barman at Spudorgan Hall. Milo repeated his question.

"What am *I* playing at?" echoed Murphy. With meticulous irony, he briefly but masterfully aped Milo's apish gait. "You're well away, aren't you, Milo. Could I, ah . . . ?" He straightened his back and shot a significant look toward the sinkside home brew. "As long as you're having one, like."

When interrogated on his unorthodox method of entry, Murphy turned out empty pockets to denote the absence of money and/or keys to his basement flat across the Yard.

"I was on me way to meet a woman but it started pissing down, so here I am. Are you deaf? I knocked on your door until my knuckles were black." He displayed a chapped fist as evidence.

They repaired to the parlor, beakers brimming. As soon as Murphy crossed the threshold, he broke into a run. The man's eyes were rolling like the eyes of the horses of Tintoretto (or even Rosa Bonheur), thought Milo, an aficionado of the plastic arts.

"I bags the sofa," gasped Murphy, and lost no time in arranging himself in the attitude of the Strong Man at Ease: supine, feet

---

[15]One eye shut, the other roving wildly; tongue lolling dogwise from mouth; nostrils flared; exaggerated overbite.

raised, one arm cushioning his head, drink squarely planted on midriff. Meanwhile, Milo found himself occupying the entire space between the two arms of his chair. His bum anchored his bulk downward, while his legs, swelling like engorged goitrefish with the beer and the wind, buttressed the upper part, being firmly placed side by side and tapering into feet shod in running shoes of imported Bessarabian oryx hide.[16]

There followed a traditional, if somewhat shopworn, scene of Irish hospitality: without, the throbbing gale; within, the lowering of ale.[17]

"That was a rotten day, let me tell you." Murphy received no more than a coarse slurping sound in reply as Milo applied himself to his fresh drink, while out of habit gazing over the rim of his glass at the television. Color faded in and out of the screen image of Tracy/Boone's profile silhouetted against sunlit mountaintops. A woman wearing a bonnet entered stage left and flung herself into Boone/Tracy's arms. They embraced, tightly, as Korngold swelled and credits rolled, then it was back to Cardiff and an update on the day's rugby (New Zealand 9, Wales 0).

"What a load of shite," snarled Milo. This was misinterpreted by Murphy as an overdue response to his complaining about the day's doings and led to a heated exchange, sadly typical of bachelor friendships,[18] before Milo explained himself, his manner mellowing at the sudden recollection of Murphy's former membership in the All-Ireland Middleweight Boxing Team. He even sealed his peroration with a smile. Murphy relaxed, mollified.

----

[16]Will you get out of that right now! With oryx hide loafers going for fifty quid the pair at Boylan's? And your man without the means to buy an extra pint after-hours of a Saturday night? Listen here, Mister Know-It-All: if that's oryx hide, I'm a Dutch person called Joop den Uyl.

[17]Straight out of James Stephens, or J. M. Synge, or another of the Holy Ireland crowd, the ones you'd find lurking in the cool Celtic twilight and forever peopling the place with silver-tongued hags and toadstool-dwellers and harpists with arse-length hair; to hell with that lot, the Clurichauns are the men to look out for (have you checked your cellar lately?)!

[18]I.e.: faces glowing in mutual contempt; bared teeth on display; words unsuited to decent company swatted about like shuttlecocks.

Still toying with the rotten day theme, he lay back again and gazed at Milo's well-stocked bookshelves,[19] although reading for anything other than titillation was a phenomenon foreign to his tastes; in fact, he hadn't opened a book since the Easter weekend, when Doreen Grey, a girl he went out with now and then, loaned him the latest Michelle Stoane bestseller—*Slut*, or *Chick*, or something along those lines[20]—but he'd chucked it after about page 10. Murphy, like most young men, was more interested in sports, wheeled vehicles, TV glamour, technological gimmickry

---

[19]I saw them once, as I shudder to recall. All right, if you insist. Here's a random sample: *Encyclopedia of Irish Farm Animals* (Cork: G. Nackert, 1965); *Mother Arafat's Arab Kitchen* (Redgrave House, 1980); *Freight Trains of Canada* (Winnipeg: C.N. Rail, 1949); *¡Nalgas! 101 Rear Views of Cuban Women in Swimsuits* (Miami: Anon., 1989); *Fifty Pee a Pint: The Later Verse of Jasper Hoolihan* (Athlone: O'Duffy Press, 1980); *Two Bob a Pint: The Complete Early Poems of Jasper Hoolihan* (Athlone: Blueshirt Press, 1966); *Four Great Irish Recipes* (Sligo: Stubble House, 1982), etc. The remainder of Milo's collection consists mostly of collections of verse—many of them by the aforementioned Hoolihan—and a few classics (Scott, Dante, Kavanagh, et al.) guiltily nicked from Fred Hanna's in Dublin in college days gone by: an unambitious display, and yet! Somewhere deep inside Milo Rogers there squirms a nascent bookworm (or is it tape-?)!

[20]*Wench*, actually, number one on the *Sunday Post* best-seller list for thirty-seven weeks. Ms. Stoane's latest blockbuster is the story of Tess, unwanted illegitimate daughter of the Duke of Whipminster. Raised by Rosie, the head chambermaid—who later dies of tuberculosis in an alleyway as the German panzers roll into Paris—Tess discovers her true identity in the brutal arms of Thatcher, the wine steward. Determined to claim her rightful inheritance, she fights and claws her way from the low groggeries of Cheapside and the belowstairs brothels of Houndsditch to the salons of Mayfair, the Left Bank, and Monte Carlo, until finally—as the German panzers roll into Paris—she acquires the rank and title she has so long sought; but her happiness is short-lived. Soon afterwards, she loses her polo-playing Argentinian fiancé Apollo Belvedere in a freak horse collision at Auteuil; two days later, lesbian fashion plate and would-be suitor Caca Chamois, jilted by Tess, commits suicide with an elegant silver-plated handgun in the Bois de Boulogne as the German panzers roll into Paris. Disguised as an oberst in the Wehrmacht, Tess flees to Hollywood, where she meets and marries aging Dutch-born matinee idol Joop den Uyl.

and, of course, most of all: GIRLS.

"They're terrible men for the teasing," he said.

Milo blearily awoke from his contemplation of inner space.[21]

"Who?"

"The girls, of course. Take that Doreen creature, now—you know the one I'm talking about, a right flirt so she is, works down at Woolworths?"

"That's the one you're on your way to see, is it?"

"No, not that one. Doreen. Ah, come on, you know the girl," coaxed Murphy. "Reddish hair, or is it brownish-red, or brown altogether, or almost black, would you say . . . ."

"I'd not know her from Eve. When was the last time I went into Woolworths, for God's sake?" spluttered Milo. He was rocking back and forth in an effort to dislodge himself from the armchair and extinguish a cadaverous television face lecturing him in Welsh.[22] Beer spillage was considerable, impregnating his shirtfront with a tart aroma. Finally, after seesawing violently five or six times, Milo put down his drink, took a firm hold of the armrests and—with a mumbled "one-two-heave"—he propelled himself forward at a sufficient velocity to change channels, switch off the light and slam the door shut, all without the use of his hands.

"There." He looked around the room, a smile crumpling his whey-white face. "That's better." The shadows danced on the wall in the gas fire's cheery glow as, contrapuntally, the cheerless wind keened through the chinks. "Sure that's very nice. It is that."

"Turn on the feckin' lights," said Murphy, stridently.

Milo obeyed, but as he did so, he muttered imprecations sotto

---

[21]Dense, mealy, dark; something like the home brew he's working on, or a pint of stout.

[22]Knowing the men of Harlech as I do, I'd say it was probably old Dafydd Jones ap Jones, the Nonconformist minister who gets three minutes' free airtime every Saturday night just after closing time to scold the ladies for letting their menfolk relive the pukey heaven of Stag Night once a week (except in south Powys, and the drier parts of Dyfed).

voce having to do with Murphy's lineage and general morals. If his friend heard, he gave no sign; instead, a sloppy grin spread across his face and his eyelids slowly drooped. Light tenor snoring announced sleep. This suited Milo. He thought Murphy was a grand old hoor, but a man needed a moment or two to himself now and then to reflect on things, just. Milo's morale was at low ebb, anyway, what with the job, the weather, thwarted ambitions, the rent, enforced chastity (leading, sadly but inexorably, to onanism), etc.—of course, with this last item, we find ourselves on the familiar, dangerous ground so well-trodden by blue-jowled clerics and Mother Church on one side and Austro-American psychoanalysts and the Hollywood crowd on the other: sex, in a word, always a guaranteed ticket to the shakes. Milo's experience of the matter was short but broad, somewhat like his person. In his final year at Trinity, he'd met a honey-skinned Frenchwoman named Martine, an encounter that led, in panting single file, to your standard tongue-tied, red-faced, knock-kneed wanker's courtship—oddly successful, perhaps owing to Martine's being from the great and sophisticated city of Lyon.[23] In urban France, that kind of thing is generally over and done with by age ten, or twelve at the latest, so to see it in full bloom in an allegedly full-grown man of twenty-three was no doubt such a novelty to the woman that she gave in just for the laugh that was in it. Anyhow, the affair lasted for the balance of

---

[23]There's the place for us, son, a gracious town of a million or so—about Dublin-sized, and the air's a bit close in winter months, so they've their fair share of bronchial hackers and round-the-clock bottle men, but the grub's in a different class altogether. The only Liffeyside eatery that comes close is Le Phacochère in Harold's Cross, and guess who runs it? You're right: a man from Lyon (Jean-Claude)! Seriously, now, what I can't understand is how the locals can take the pace—you know, every single blooming day God sends they're off to Bocuse's, or the Bouton d'Or, or the Trèsgros Brothers, or *chez* Alain Blanc, shovelling in the *cassoulet au vin blanc* and the *caille aux raisins noirs* and (as if that weren't enough) washing the whole caper down with a Beaujolais, or a smart palate-tickler from the Rhône valley! Civilisation, that's what it is, boy; that, and no mistake. There's nothing like it for prolonging life.

Milo's undergraduate career, and pretty well scuttled his degree: come June, there he was in the exam hall, facing the European History final,[24] with any real chance of passing it well behind him. Only Martine existed in Milo's mind, and she'd gone back to Lyon, unresponsive to his moist missives and telephonic pleading. Eventually, marriage claimed her, followed boringly by maturity and maternity and the creeping dowdiness of domestic life. Meanwhile, Milo, short one degree (B.A., no honours), found fewer and fewer opportunities for his unlicensed genius. After a year in London pulling pints for the Kilburn crowd, and six months' illegal building work in New York, rooming with a crazed Brit-hating rebel from Co. Queens, he drifted back to Ireland like ash on the wind and softly fell to earth in the cozy confines of Spudorgan Hall, "the Ritz of the Southeast." There were unfriendlier places to be, and he'd had a worse time of it in New York, but on the loneliest nights the memory of Martine returned and no time was worse than poor Milo's present,[25] and if he was behind with the rent into the bargain, life was hardly worth the effort. At two hundred and fifty punts a month, the rent bit hard into his waiter's wages, so hard that sometimes (as now) he was forced to reconnoitre every street corner before venturing round it, lest his landlord, Tom "the Greek" Maher, loom into view. Outwardly bluff and jovial, given to affecting Aran sweaters and a Donegal tweed cap, the Greek, paradoxically, struck Milo as the most diabolical man he had ever met.[26] In his eyes—blue as speedwell, with flecks of feral yellow—there twinkled the spirit of Himmler and de Sade, or so Milo claimed,

---

[24]"Was the Treaty of Timisoara of 1867 the sole cause of, or merely a contributing factor to, the Balkan crisis of 1848? Discuss."

[25]Sniff, sniff. Suitable accompaniment would be mumbling chords in D minor, e.g., cello or double bass, with violins waiting in the wings, just in case.

[26]And he'd met a few, that galoot in New York, for one: as a staunch fifth-generation Irishman, his declared mission in life was to assassinate the British prime minister. Once, overloaded with Budweiser, he practised on Milo, using steak knives. Not surprisingly, it was their last night as roommates.

perhaps fancifully; certain it was that inexplicable things tended to happen when the Greek's tenants lagged in the payment of their rent. On each of the past four days, for instance, Milo had spoken to telephonic whisperers variously claiming to be a Church of Ireland minister, a travel agent named Bob, the R.C. Bishop of Monaghan and finally—ominously—a Russian tourist with a message from "The Big Guy." As if all this weren't enough to drive the sanest of men to the very brink of madness, on the following Monday, ten days into arrears, Milo was settling down to watch the repeat of *Strumpet City* on RTE 2 when a stench as of the overworn underwear of an entire boarding school rose from beneath the floorboards and rapidly permeated the bungalow. Driven from his home, Milo made for Mad Molloy's, there to while away the evening making loud noises of protest over a series of whiskies paid for by none other than the Greek Maher. The same Greek sat next to him the whole time he was there, murmuring age-old clichés of sympathy: "now, now"; "there, there"; "I never"; "ya ballocks," etc., accompanied by nudges in the ribcage and, once, a mock left hook to the jaw fuelled by gusts of laughter and resonant slaps on the back. Never once during the entire evening did the man take off his Donegal cap, or pronounce the word *rent*. This confirmed Milo's fears. He spent the rest of the night behind the reception desk at Spudorgan Hall, only returning to his bungalow in the early morning. The smell was gone, but on the front doorstep was the decomposing body of a mongrel dog known to all of Oxtail Yard as the agent of many a sleepless night when the rutting season was on.[27]

---

[27] God, that reminds me of something I read in the *Press*, a while back: "The Odorous Overcoat of Sandymount Strand." That was a story and a half. Wait till I tell you. James Barnacle, solicitor's clerk and aspiring playwright—i.e., a perfectly respectable class of person—found himself being overcome by fumes every morning as he put on his old Burberry mac. In chronological order, your man slid heavily to the floor after (a) kissing the wife, (b) adjusting his tie in the hallway mirror, and (c) reaching for the dreaded coat; then, of course, he needed prompt reviving with smelling salts and turpentine to be on time for the 7:41 at Sandymount Station, a terrible drain on the family finances. After several weeks of this, and poor old Jembo beginning to topple over as if

An especially discordant note in the storm's diminishing song jolted Milo back to so-called reality.

"It's true that the mysteries of life are deep and various," he said to himself, staring at his own face staring back from the now-blank television screen, "but that one took the grand piano."

And so to bed, not including three visits to the jakes and one to the front door (exit Murphy, groggily).

---

banjaxed at both ends of the day inclusive—incurring serious risk of concussion, with that raised footrail at the Parnell Mooney's—Father Joyce, the Television Exorcist, performed a TV exorcism in the dead of night, hoping to catch the evil visitor napping, so to speak. Confident in the powers of Good, next morning, regular as one-two-three, Jembo put on his coat with a light Dublin air on his lips—and whammo, there he was, measuring his full length at the wife's feet, exorcism or no exorcism. This can't go on, says the missus (a woman of firm opinions), it's him or me, I'm off to stay with my sister in Longford. Arrangements were accordingly made, dress clothes brushed, shoes polished to a high gloss, parcels containing personal belongings entrusted to the mails—and wouldn't you know it, she mailed her sister the wrong parcel, containing you-know-what (meanwhile, Jim's falling fits stopped altogether—very suggestive, if you ask me)! Naturally, once Sis caught a whiff of it, the coat went straight from her house to the laundry, but no sooner was the wrapping paper off than the laundry crew passed out as promptly as if they'd been bashed on the noodle one at a time with a blackthorn stick, or billy club. They survived, thanks be to God, and shortly thereafter the townsfolk torched the Burberry in a traditional Longford auto-da-fé, so we'll never know the whole truth; but, haunted or not, that old mac was a godsend to Jim, if you want my opinion. Last we heard, his play *The Haunted Overcoat* was in its forty-fourth week of rehearsals at the Peacock Theatre (or was it the Abbey?).

2

The storm spat out its ultimate bile in a choreographed triple assault, comprising a blinding flash of lightning with God on the kettledrums and a gale-force blast of wind off the sea. Trees yawed and shook, telephone lines sagged and soared, rain hissed and spat, micturative drunks huddled in doorways upstream from themselves, newspapers careened through the empty streets like misshapen ghosts;[1] outside a circa-1900 redbrick villa at no. 117, King Idris Road (West), the gnarled branch of an elm tree broke away from its parent and smashed into the windscreen of a late model Rover 3500BTS belonging to the occupant of the redbrick villa, who was watching from her front window.

"Shite and rubbers," she expostulated. "There goes the insurance."

Katherine MacRory Hickman was the expostulant's name, the

---

[1] Quite a meteorological carry-on, I hear you muttering: what's the point (you quaver, querulously)? The point, Jacko, is this: remember the Great Storm of '87? England got it worse, but we weren't spared either. My Auntie Nuala, for one (and be janey was she a handsome piece in her day), found herself laid up in the Mater with two severely sprained calves. She was on her way home from the South Leinster Bingorama—navigating pretty well exclusively by nose, in that wind—when a small tree uprooted itself as she walked by and gave her the holy terror of a shellacking across the backs of her legs. Lucky it didn't hit higher up, she wisecracked, lying prone in her hospital bed surrounded by flowers and doting admirers admiring the tapered shoulders and pert bum of She Who Once Ruled Him Who Ruled Ireland (but more of that later).

MacRory being hers by right of birth and the Hickman a token of her former married state. Not a beauty of the sort to grace the covers of the magazine that employed her—*Glam*, a glossy fashion monthly—she was handsome enough, at thirty-nine (just), to warrant the occasional double-take: straight-nosed as a Norman, flaxen-haired as a Saxon and Celtically freckled on the cheekbones, with the ample build of a country girl (ex-Ballykilloran, Co. Louth) clothed in the undemonstrative style of a one-time city dweller (Dublin, London, New York for a bit, then a bit of a ramble around Europe, then Dublin again en route to Killoyle) with some education (M.A., UCD, '79). She was a widow. Her late husband, Phelim, a crusading reporter and novelist and one-time editor of *Glam*, had drowned off the Blaskets a year previously, after setting off with his Irish terrier Strongbow to circle Ireland in a coracle, as Saint Oinsias of Dingle, hero of Phelim's novel *The Loves of Oinsias*, is said to have done with an anonymous dog in the sixth century A.D.[2] Strongbow, a strong swimmer, had survived—indeed, at that very moment he was

---

[2]In fictionalized form, Hickman's book deals with the life and loves of Killoyle's patron saint, and believe me it's a hoot (of course, if you've already read it, you can skip this part): born in Gaul of Romanized parents, young Oinsias fled to Ireland at the age of six, becoming in short order (a) Bard of the *Ard Rí*, (b) Baron of Dingle, (c) Jousting Champion of Meath, and (d) a Christian, this last cancelling out all the preceding. After rapidly circumnavigating the island in a coracle by way of testing his faith—thereby providing old Phelim his last inspiration, at a remove of fourteen centuries—he retired into a bed of reeds on the edge of Lough Dough, Co. Killoyle, and meditated for seventeen years on the ardours and vanities of men; then, suddenly, he fled to Gaul, becoming in short order (a) Troubadour-in-Chief to Duke Carapace II, (b) Baron of Normandy, (c) Tug-of-War Champion of Picardy, and (d) a Gnostic, this last in contravention of the One True Faith and its several legitimate heresies. By special dispensation of Pope Septus VI, he was granted permission to be hanged, drawn and quartered on his birthday (2 Sept. 599); actually, according to contemporary eyewitness reports, he thoroughly enjoyed his martyrdom, shaking the hands of the faggot-bearers and treating the audience to a baritone recital of their favorite Norman ballads while accompanying himself on the serpent. His last words, "O, optimum est," now form the official motto of Killoyle City.

cowering under the sofa, interpreting the sounds of the storm as
Judgement Day for dogs—but his master, a nonswimmer, lay
somewhere on the ocean floor between the Great Blasket Island
and Massachusetts. Although naturally shocked by the peremp-
tory nature of Phelim's disappearance, Kathy had mourned him
with restraint. After all, his journalist's zeal had spawned illegitimate issue in Europe and North America but no legitimate heirs
at home, even after ten years of marriage, so once she was shut of
the old philanderer, she was free to enjoy what he'd left behind:
the house, the car, and—sales of *The Loves of Oinsias* having been
boosted by its author's well-publicised demise—a hundred grand
in royalties in the Peninsular Counties Bank. This gave her the
time to examine at leisure the verities of her existence. These
were three: that the writing of magazine articles was a tedious
task and one unnecessary to the survival of wisdom; that love was
on everyone's lips but in precious few hearts; and that the
weather of Ireland was one of God's greatest gifts to that long-
suffering country, despite appearances.

"Tomorrow the clouds," she murmured, "then, again, the
rain; then the sun turning cartwheels of gold through the grey
curtains of heaven . . . oh Jesus, that's pretty, that is. I wonder if
it's poetry." Knowing full well it was,[3] she put down her coffee
(Franco-Brazilian, stone-ground) and hurried across the short
hallway to her study, once the GHQ of Phelim's freelance empire. Forgetting her wounded Rover and the storm's frenzied
final act, she sat down in front of her word processor, but by the
time the machine had squawked and grumbled and booted itself
awake, she was drifting away to Poesy's neighbouring dimension,
that of Love, where only Love itself was lacking, a lack made
up for by her lofty dismissals of it (or reductive comparisons to
sex) in unwanted conversations that she writhed to recall. She'd
always found it hard to disagree with others face to face, making

---

[3]Or at least as much as the constipated groanings of so many, e.g.,
Jeansberg, Gumm, Bedwetter & Co. I disdain to mention the latest
crop of gibberers from Eastern Europe, with their leather jackets and
Marlboros and mispronounced adoration of Western pop ("pap"), jazz
("chess"), sex ("sax"), etc.

her unfit for any really go-ahead job in politics or business or the higher reaches of journalism (as Phelim had pointed out often enough), so too often she found herself agreeing with fools just to avoid the unpleasantness of conflict. When she did disagree, she preferred to register it in heavy irony that generally went straight over her interlocutor's head (blank stare, then "well, as Oi was saying") or was misinterpreted as sincerity (forced smile, then "ach come on, you don't honestly mean that, do you?"). Having to mingle in uncongenial company was one of the penalties of her job. Since the success of Phelim's book, and her subsequent appearances in widow's weeds on two breakfast shows in London and *The Late Late Show* in Dublin—each time for no longer than two minutes, between breaks—men had naturally come calling, most of them unattached, but there were a few would-be adulterers among them, and one or two of those were flagrant indeed, but instead of telling that ilk to bugger off, she overdid the irony, trying to be subtle. This only made matters worse and forced her to such crustacean measures as returning letters unread and going ex-directory, a course of passive resistance despised by her rebellious MacRory blood, hence the nightly aperitif or so to jolly things along and other small luxuries, such as a satellite dish for the television and the overpriced Provençal Grand Pagnol cigarettes she subscribed to in monthly installments of eight hundred, via airmail from Toulon to Cork and thence by van to Killoyle through the good offices of Mr. Gallogly, the tobacconist on Parnell Parade. The fags came in four cork-lined tin amphoras of two hundred smokes each, roughly working out at four tins per month at Kathy's rate of consumption, higher in widowhood than formerly: as Phelim had been a nonsmoker and something of a bore on the subject, her pleasure was doubled by this posthumous scoring off her late lamented, although inevitably guilt lurked somewhere, ready to clutch at her with yearning nonsmoker's hands. It was too late, anyway, to deodorise the house, now fully redolent of French tobacco. The smell clung to the curtains, burrowed into the carpets and hovered in the air. Sometimes, after a long day's work on her column, her study smelled like a Marseilles café, down to the French coffee she drank now and then, from nostalgia if not taste; for Kathy, as for so many members of her race, the south was a place of escape and adventure, or had been, before life's disillusionments—before her marriage, that is, when she was a staff writer at a London women's magazine where "the girls" organised annual excursions to Provence with the unspoken purpose of ecstatic couplings beneath the starry firmament.[4] One such had occurred, in her case, not with a dark and dashing Frenchman but with a lobster-red journalist from Drogheda, Phelim Hickman, the rest being history, his and hers becoming theirs, then hers alone. In fact, the cigarette pong that would have had Phelim doing his nut was also a homage to their past together and the way they'd met, at the Grasse wine festival in the summer of '81, with the melancholy tootle of accordions in the olive groves surging above the boisterous vomiting of other Irish tourists, tums tenderised by the local cuisine.

Glancing at her watch, Kathy turned off the word processor and crossed the darkened hallway to the sitting room, preceded by the firefly-glow of a fine Grand Pagnol. The receding storm fired a parting lightning-shot, barked once in response to barking Strongbow, and subsided into the banal pattering of rain on October leaves. Kathy opened the door and inhaled air unmixed with smoke. As if on cue, a man lurched up the garden path: Murphy, late as usual.

"Punctual, aren't we?" Kathy recoiled from his beery scent.

"What do you mean, punctual? I'm late. The storm, woman," he said. "I was on me way but I had to take shelter somewhere, so I stopped in at Milo's."

---

[4] Aye, and we all know where that sort of carry-on leads, don't we? Take Maura Finnegan, down the street: ten days in Cyprus and she came back with that bearded dwarf on her arm, some sort of Arab by the look and sound of him—well, didn't I see him coming out of the Star of Kashmir on the Terenure Road the other day, and isn't that proof enough? Anyhow, five years and three dusky brats later, Maura's moved to England and the wee black fella's going great guns with his kebab shop on Baggot Street (and, some say, after-hours brothel in the basement flat, ring twice and ask for Omar); as for the kiddies, sure aren't there fine opportunities for stowaways, over by the North Wall: Liverpool, the Isle of Man, Greenock, the South China Sea . . . !

"The wine bar?"

"What are you on about. Milo's place. You know, the gloomy wee fella that serves the food up at the Hall, sure you've seen him often enough."

"Oh, you mean the waiter. The fat one with the eyes."[5]

Murphy snorted, positioning himself dorsally. She slewed around, but he had her in a fleshy place. A slap rang out. Strongbow emerged from under the sofa, issuing throaty warnings.

"Call off the feckin' hound, will you."

In due course the dog was in the kitchen and Murphy was where many a better man had never been (as guilt, in Phelim guise, hissed reproaches in Kathy's ears).

---

[5]Fat one with the eyes? That's no way to describe "one of the most promising poets of his generation" (Ned Kelly, the *Independent*), or "Ireland's answer to Villiers de l'Isle-Adam" (Homer MacBee, *The People's Friend*)—but I'm getting a little ahead of myself. She'll learn, you just wait and see.

3

Guilt-ridden, too, was Wolfetone Grey, but no more than usual. In fact, he was having a relatively good time of it that Saturday night, with the kettle singing on the hob and a sweet-drawing pipe in his gob[1] and the murmur of the dying wind outside. Mrs. Grey was upstairs in bed, and that was no abuse to his peace of mind, nor was the absence of their daughter Doreen (she'd insisted on moving into a bedsit in the town the month before, "just to be on me own, like"—aye, she'd find out what *that* meant, soon enough). Television had never appealed to Wolfetone Grey, and reading was a bore, with few exceptions (e.g., anything by, or for, God), so the inner life he depended on was, by necessity, rich and varied, like the lush forests of New Guinea. As in those jungles, beauty and strength were combined with the objectionable quirks in Nature's humour: man-eating savages in the case of New Guinea, a passion for quasi-religious texts and anonymous phoning in Wolfetone's. Even now his hand reached for the telephone, stayed only by the thought of God, with Whom he was in regular communication—not by telephone, but via the prayer waves that emanated heavenward

---

[1]Kettle on the hob, you say? Pipe in his gob, is it? God save us, that wouldn't be a wee cottage somewhere in a wee corner of the darlin' land of the bogs and the little people, would it? You can count me out of this caper, Patrick my man. Hob, indeed. And through the tiny wee winda wisps of peat smoke and the trackless Twelve Pins, I suppose? Get out of that. Housing estates and heavy metal and bumper-to-bumper on the Ring Road, that's more like it these days.

from the Grey house (suitably grey in colour, with white edgings) on Lostwithal Road, several times weekdays and Saturdays and twice, loudly, on Sundays, in unison with the other congregants at St. Oinsias' in the town. At church, his prayers were generally bland, hewing to traditional themes: bless those we don't know— help us along a bit—give us a boost now and then—sorry we're such sinners, etc. There was rarely time to allude to the phoning in those group chats with Him, but at home—one-on-one, as it were—Wolfetone was more direct, going boldly on the attack in anticipation of the Divine School-master's displeasure. There was nothing intrinsically wrong with calling up people he didn't know, he argued, not per se, like. Sure, it gave most of them the bit of a thrill, something to talk about the next day over the fence or the office desk, that kind of carry-on: no harm there, eh? On the other hand—yes, he was forced to admit (reluctantly) that the impostures taken on by his telephonic personality were some-times a bit much, sailing a little too close to the wind—all right, tantamount to deception if you wanted to be legalistic about it, i.e., lying, cheating, and other naughtiness. The Sweepstakes promoter, for instance, flirted with outright fraud; he knew that, but he was the first to admit it, wasn't he? Anyway, hadn't he sent them both return bus tickets, at no small cost to himself (he might add)? All quite human, though, he reassured himself, jollily, before turning as in remorse to the Almighty and grovel-ling a bit—after all, He *was* the Almighty.[2]

Interjection: Wolfetone Grey was a model citizen and pro-vider in all other realms of his existence.

"I work my arse off, begging your pardon," he bellowed into the ruffled night. "A rise of 11 percent last month and that's more than anyone else makes at the Hall bar that old coot Power—not as if he was underpaid, that's certain," modulating the volume somewhat. God listened; go on, He said, nudging.

---

[2] Well, now, in my day, you'd have had a right old barney on your hands trying to get this kind of thing past the Censor's Office—but maybe that's the point! Aha! *Mutatis mutandis* and all that, eh? I'm onto you now, boyo.

"Well, you remember when they suspected that O'Moon character of cooking the books? Given the look on his face and his general morals—not that I'm in any position, oh you're right enough, but still, with a map like that I could hardly blame 'em, but I knew he never went near the bloody account books, except to make the odd entry at month's end. Not to mention the fact that they've got most of the stuff on the computer now, anyway. The point I'm making is this: was O'Moon grateful?"

Somewhat sanctimoniously, Wolfetone went on to lay out the extent of O'Moon's ingratitude: a snub in public on Parnell Parade; surly backchat in the anterooms of the Hall; overheard mockery of his, Wolfetone's, mannerisms and style of dress; general insolence, in short, that many a lesser man would have allowed to get right up his nose. He didn't, but. Not for a good wee while, anyway. Then came the day when his phone directory fell open at:

O'Moon, Kenneth — 45 Sea Lion Drive — Killoyle E. 12-34-56

Quite honestly now: who could resist?
In the event, it went like this, verbatim:
"Hello? Mr. O'Moon? Mr. Kenneth O'Moon?"
"Is that you, Grey?"
"I beg your pardon? No, sir, my name is Owen Roe O'Neill and I'm with the Munster Sweeps, which, as I'm sure you know, is the third biggest sweepstakes organisation in Europe, after the Swiss and French lotteries, total annual revenues well into the seven digit range, with the bulk, as you know, going to benefit the poor kiddies with Lautrec Syndrome . . . ."
"What are you blethering about? What the flamin' heck's Low Track whatsit?"
"A terrible disease, sir, striking young and old alike—have you never seen the legs of a Lautrec victim, Mr. O'Moon? Well, thank the blessed saints above for the favours they so sparingly bestow. In Lautrec Syndrome, you see, the shins are suppressed and the ankles spring directly from just below the knees, transforming the victim's forward locomotion into an awkward scuttling gait, not unlike the French painter Henri de Toulouse

Lautrec, hence the name, as you will readily surmise."[3]

"I never heard such a load of bumf. You listen to me, Grey."

"O'Neill, sir. Now, according to our records, last month you were the lucky winner of the Bonnie Bachelor contest, grand prize a weekend in Lisdoonvarna at the—and our records never lie, Mr. O'Moon, I want no doubts on that score—at the Spa Hotel with the middle-aged TV beauty of your choice, contest not open to employees of RTE-TV or radio or the Munster Sweeps organisation or their families."

"What's middle-aged?"

"Oh, anywhere between thirty-five and fifty, give or take."

Lewd smacking of lips, then:

"Now listen here. If I've really won this thing, and if it isn't a cod . . . it better not be, or I swear to God I'll have your gonads for breakfast, Grey, if it is Grey . . . ."

"O'Neill, sir."

"Whatever you call yourself. I'd fancy a weekend with Maire O Baoigheallain."

"Would you, indeed. Who might that lady be, sir?"

"Who might—don't you watch the television, man? The gell who reads the news in Irish on RTE 1—well, I call her a gell, but she's a good thirty-five if she's a day. Unmarried, too. I know that because she let it slip once during the show, like."

Unctuous sniggering followed, and Wolfetone knew the slob was on board. It was so easy to get the poor eejits to believe, and sex was at the bottom of their yearnings, nine times out of ten. Of course, O'Moon was known as the class of man who'd get up on a cracked plate, or his own dying grandmother herself, so Wolfetone was happy to part with nineteen quid seventy-five pee for the bonus pair of bus tickets to Lisdoonvarna: one for Ken-

---

[3]Oh, come on now. I mean, blasphemy's one thing, but making fun of those poor tykes hopping about like that—it's beyond the pale, if you'll pardon the expression. I'd write to my late lamented Blessed Uncle Francis if he were still with us. Many's the time he took his hairbrush to my backside when I was the odd bit obstreperous, or dallied too late in the nightclubs. Aye, he'd straighten youse out and no mistake. Bloody shower.

neth and one for Shelagh Kellaway, Wolfetone's former landlady from Killoyle West, a big-busted lass of some forty-six summers. Booked into neighbouring rooms (it was the off-season, and Wolfetone could have had an entire floor if he'd wanted it), they could hardly fail to strike up an acquaintance, but whether O'Moon noticed that Shelagh wasn't Maire O Baoigheallain, or whether Shelagh claimed to be Maire O Baoigheallain, as instructed, and whether Kenneth fell for it, or not (probably not, in light of subsequent developments) Wolfetone never knew for sure; in any event, the next time the two men encountered each other on Parnell Parade, O'Moon made up for his former snub by having at Wolfetone with twirling fists, and it was only after a long day in the dentist's chair that Wolfetone Grey's shadow fell across his own threshold again.

"Oh, that was a right cock-up, I won't quarrel with you there," he declared over his third cup of black tea, staring into the embers of his pipe as into the eyes of God. "And wouldn't they have made the charming couple. Still, there's always another time, and while I'm about it, there's no time like the present—oh, come on," to an imagined tsk-tsk from the Heavenly Head. "This time it'll be as moral as all get out, just you wait and see." The fever of forbidden desire swooned through his frail frame as, with sweating palms, he picked up the telephone. On his lap was the directory, well-thumbed in the Killoyle area. Finger poised above the dial, he cleared his throat of tobacco oysters ten or a dozen times, then dialed a number, only to be accosted by an answering machine, bane of these nighttime japes. He tried again, and again, with the same result. It was nearly half-past eleven before an actual human voice spoke the magic word.[4]

"Hello?"

---

[4]Just as well, if you ask me. While we're on the subject, that brings to mind something that happened to my Auntie Nuala, a while back—that's right, the one poleaxed by a tree in the Great Storm of '87—when she was the Taoiseach's mistress and living in comfort in a mews off Fitzwilliam Square. One morning, or early afternoon as it might be, she answered the phone in her boudoir to hear nothing but heavy coughing on the other end of the line. Hello, she says, waiting for the poor

"Mr. Power? Mr. Emmet Power?"

"Is that you, Grey?"

"I beg your pardon? Mr. Power, this is Father Patrick Mac-Carthy of the Society of Jesus and the Redemptorist Mission. I do apologise for the lateness of the hour, but the hour is late in more ways than one, if you catch my meaning."

"Bloody nonsense," blustered Power, but the hook was in, the catch was thrashing its last.

---

bleeder to get a hold of himself and state his intentions, like; but no sooner does he draw breath than he's off again, coughing and wheezing like the business end of a bus, and it due for the scrapheap. Well, says Auntie Nuala to herself (being a woman of firm opinions), this is no sort of conversation at all, and damn near hangs up the phone when something in the other party's coughing makes her pause, a kind of roaring high note you'd hope never to hear this side of a bullpen in the mating season. Suffering Jesus, says Aunt Nuala, the poor fella's in a bad way, and wasn't that the God's own truth! Before she could fasten her corsets it was all over, in a regular crescendo of hacking and spewing. Next thing Nuala knows there's a policeman on the line asking her if she's the one who left the open packet of twenty Players Full Strength by your man's bed! I ask you. Well, take my word for it, she hung up quicker than you can say Seoirse O Suilleabhain—which, coincidentally, was the dead man's name. You remember him: leader of the Fir Bolg parliamentary splinter group back in the late . . . ? or was it the early . . . ?

4

Discontent traced a southerly path across Emmet Power's broad Northern face as he put the phone down, muttering. He never liked being in the dark about things, as he was now literally, it being almost bedtime, and figuratively, with echoes in his head of the voice that sounded so much like Grey, the Head of Catering—not that he'd spent enough time with him to be sure, they worked most days at opposite ends of the Hall, but there was that cheesy quality in it, like export Harp—while seeming to be very confident of being Father Patrick MacCarthy, S. J., of the blooming Travelling Redemptorists or what have you; of course, most voices sounded slightly off, coming over the wire, and whoever he was (or wasn't), he'd stirred up the jitters in Emmet Power's soul.

"Bloody nonsense," he repeated to himself, but his conscience droned dully on, oblivious, presenting him with a list of sins that seemed petty unless you lumped them together: the imitation marmalade he'd had the guests served all last week without one of them complaining, except the Colonel in 16A; the extra charges he sometimes added to the bills of the overly affluent[1]

---

[1]Japs, Yanks, French, and Germans, mostly, with the odd Italian or Belgian throwing the moolah around. We Irish, being a soft-hearted lot (bar the hard men), generally take pity on the British, Old Oppressor turned Poor Relation, with their Vacuum Savings Plan and the Minor Exchange Rate, pegging the pound to the Portuguese escudo. Thank God for Gar Looney and his Greater West Eurasia Co-Prosperity Sphere, strapping the old punt securely to the yen and the upcoming Hong Kong yuan!

when they were in a hurry to catch the Heathrow or Paris flight out of Cork International; the lies he told his wife on a regular, indeed compulsive, basis ("I only had the one pint, dear," meaning two or three; or, "that's a low blow, acushla, the very idea of me skelping off to the races, haven't I avoided the ponies for donkey's years," meaning he'd watched the 3:30 at Leopardstown in Muldoon's betting shop at the far end of the town, sacrificing his monthly commission at the altar of the also-rans—this leading inexorably to the additional, redundant lies of "What monthly commission?" and "I never," etc.); that vague sense that came with being human of somehow having been there when Adam wiggled his eyebrows at blushing Eve and heard the divine thundering from on high—in other words, up popped all the failings that the priests were so good at reviving just when a man thought it was coming on time to relax and grow turnips in the back garden or buy a new car and drive to Italy for a holiday in the sun! None of that, mister-me-man! Truly, once the padres had you by the goolies, they were hard to shake off. In the words of the poet, "their vulture's eye / covets the soul of the secular man."[2]

And he a dues-paying member of the Leinster and Munster Knights of Oinsias, freethinkers all!

---

[2]Misquoted, for a start, and not too well paraphrased, if you ask me. It's from Jasper Hoolihan's "Dreaming of the Martello Tower on Killoyle Strand, Winter 1899, from Ossining Prison, New York State while serving time for breaking and entering" (1898), one of my least favourites—but Milo likes it, so here goes:

> Like a biscuit tin looms she high
> Darkling in the day's nude night
> Midst virgin white and royal blue:
> Is't paradise, or just a view?
> As chiaroscuro's dun-grey gown
> Cloaks, below, the drizzly town
> (Seen, alas, from exile's dream,
> Where things are seldom what they seem);
> As the vulture-priest wheeling above
> Covets my soul, that secular dove,
> So my foolish heart reaches beyond
> For Killoyle—home, abode, earthly bond!

Emmet Power quietly returned to the sitting room and low-ered himself into his leather armchair, facing his dozing wife. She was curled up on the sofa, in a quasi-fetal pose. Now and then a fierce, boarlike snarl escaped from her open mouth, jar-ring her awake. At such moments, with loud snorts, she would cast her head to the opposite angle and subside once more into sleep, paying no more attention to her husband of twenty-three years than to the potted fern on the sideboard, or the fading mezzotint on the far wall (Addingley Hall, Essex, 1811). This process consummated itself three times, until, roused to half-wakefulness, she let out an incoherent noise of inquiry at the sight of Emmet staring into the mock flames of the electric fire.

"Whaa maaa?" she yawned.

"Never mind," said Emmet. "Go on up. I'll be along."

She went, leaving him to face himself in the mirror of his soul. What he saw there was this:

Emmet Power of the Tribe of the Gaels, Manager of Spud-organ Hall, husband to Roisin Power (née Gavin of the Mayo Gavins), father of three sons (one in the Maze, two in the States), autodidact (i.e., graduate of no college save that of Life), ex-bi-cycle repairman, ex-Greco-Roman wrestling champion of South Armagh, lifelong skeptic, lifelong Nationalist, lifelong reader of periodicals (e.g., *Glam*, *The Bell*, *Quorn*),[3] and biographies (e.g., Childers, Connolly, de Valera),[4] recent convert to the doctrine of

---

[3] Ah. I'm glad you asked that. *Glam* we know, thanks to our brief glimpse of Ms. Hickman *chez elle*; however, *The Bell*, a politico-social review, raises our chum Power to quite an elevated—say, higher middlebrow—level. Founded back in the '40s by O'Faolain, Cronin, Ryan, & Co., it rang the changes many times before a slightly cracked note in the upper registers drove readership into the sewer-pipe; in fact, only E. Power, Esq., remains steadfast, as the old rag folded up fifteen-odd years ago. What about *Quorn*, you ask? Well, let me say if I caught my lads reading that kind of hoity-toity horsey rubbish, I'd make them wear a harness for the rest of their lives and no mistake.

[4] Three outstanding quondam schoolboys, all Irish, even de Valera (born in New York of an immigrant Irish seamstress and an itinerant Spaniard): in adulthood, they brayed exhortations to an oddly respon-sive nation, one (Connolly) paying for it with a bullet through the chest,

Letting Others Do It For You (e.g., buy the rounds, deliver the groceries, pay the doctor's bills), connoisseur of fine stout and oysters, admirer of a well-turned ankle and a well-tailored suit; all in all, in his opinion he'd done pretty well, for a publican's son from Keady, Co. Armagh (The Shandon Bells, on the Monaghan Road). They spoke highly of him, so they did, not only the staff up at the Hall,[5] but people around the town and elsewhere besides. He was known, he was appreciated, and he was well-liked, and that was more than many could say, and less than most desired.

"But is it enough?" he wondered aloud to the falsely flickering electric fire. The ceiling, beneath Roisin's bedward tread, creaked in the ominous key of C minor, causing Emmet to momentarily catch his breath and swivel around, alert to he knew not what . . . Marley's Ghost? A burglar? The revenant Captain D'Alton, found black and dead in this very room on Michaelmas morning in 1886?

THE SHANN VAN VOCHT?[6]

None of the above, God be thanked. Breathing easier, Emmet sat back and lifted his gaze from the electric flames to the family portraits on the mantelpiece. Arranged in rough chronological order, they displayed: himself, aged twenty-six, newly arrived in Dublin, unjaunty for one so young (hands clasped, schoolmasterish scowl); Roisin, about the same age, with her sister who'd emigrated to Australia and spoke over the tinny long-distance wire with an aggressive Aussie accent; the three boys, ranging in age from five to nine, posing in the garden of their old house on Elbow Road, with a pile of unrepaired bicycles visible against the pebbledash wall in the background; Emmet and Roisin's wedding, 1969, with the Georgian elegance of St. Oinsias' Church behind them, on their left Roisin's parents, standing to attention like soldiers on parade, to their right Emmet's Da, relaxed and beaming like the bottlenose he was, to his right the priest, plain-

---

the other two (the dismounted horse-Prod, the half-Irish hidalgo) dying cozily in their beds.

[5]That's what he thinks. Just goes to show, doesn't it?

[6]Read your Yeats, boy—W. B., that is.

spoken Father Doyle, nemesis of the liberal class . . . the old vulture-priest himself! Emmet chuckled. If anyone knew whether a Father so-called MacCarthy of the Society of Jesus might be present among the forty thousand souls in Killoyle parish,[7] that person was Father Philip Doyle—why, if it weren't so late, he'd call him now, tomorrow being Sunday, when he'd naturally be on the job—but then (Emmet reminded himself, his disgruntlement taking wing and becoming near-elation) Father Phil usually dropped in at the Hall for a quick one between Masses, didn't he?

"Aye. He'd know, so he would," said Emmet. Relieved, he dismounted heavily from his chair and trudged upstairs, there to doff his dressing gown and align his body roughly parallel to his snoring wife's before plummeting like a rock into sleep's dark pool.[8]

---

[7] Living souls, I'd guess. If you added the dead, sure wouldn't Killoyle be the size of Tokyo, or London itself, what with centuries of bloodshed of one kind or another: the MacMurroughs, the MacCarthys, the Normans, the Tudors, the Stuarts, the Oranges, the Hanoverians, and the Saxe-Coburgs, going right on up to Lloyd George and his diabolical Tans; then of course you had the Civil War until '22 (or was it '23?) and the odd shoot-out since then, and the way they drive these days on the MacLiammoir Overpass . . . !

[8] Ir.: *Dubh Linn.*

5

Father Doyle tossed and turned, to no avail.

"Baldy ballocks," he said. The storm had passed, but the rain was still drumming on the skylight through which, in his spare moments, he stared at Heaven. A curtain covered it now, but the noise was only getting worse. Father Doyle sat up and turned on his bedside lamp.

"Sod it," he said, in the unadorned way for which he was famous throughout North Killoyle parish and suburbs. "We'll have a wee drop, just." A dry chuckle completed this wet thought. He peered at the alarm clock. A quarter past one, and he was due in church for Matins at six. With stylish insouciance, he gave a Gaelic shrug, thus mentally dismissing his parishioners, then rose from his bed, naked but for a pair of blue Y-fronts: it was Venus on the half-shell, minus the beauty. His face was long and pale, with a fringe of beard and sporadic hair; his limbs were stick-thin, with liver spots stamped here and there on the chalky pallor like mud bespattering snowdrifts; his chest varied from hollowness to concavity under the on-and-off pressures of exist- ence and the only bad habits he dared indulge; inside, his lungs rattled and wheezed and fired off salvos of phlegm, frequently discharged (as now) out the window. His joints, too, wowed and woofed in the autumn damp, and there were times in the vestry when he thought he'd be needing a permanent hip-flask implant. In short, his body distracted him somewhat from the spiritual side of things, as bodies do. Still, he *was* sixty-eight, he'd not had the easiest of lives, the priesthood was a heavy burden and there were younger men worse off than he, Monsignor Stripling down at SS. Peter and Laurence O'Toole's for one: not a day over fifty and look at him, rigged up to a bloody forest of tubes at the Star of the Sea Hospital ever since they'd found him hanging halfway out his bathroom window with cotton balls in his ears, driven stone mad by voices only he could hear . . . !

Father Doyle threw on his nightshirt and sat down at his writing desk, humming bonhomously as he poured out an approximate gill's measure of whiskey into a tooth glass from the pint bottle of Jameson's he kept in his desk drawer, accompanying it with a Craven "A" from the same hiding place. As he luxuriantly drew on the cigarette to coughing point (but not beyond), he was suddenly and loudly afflicted with flatulence, producing a sound that, in musical terms, was like a breve tied in a long slow loving phrase on, say, the clarinet, over five bars times its equivalent in semiquavers.[1] In the silence that followed, the priest exhaled sibillantly and reflected on the indignities of old age and the promise of the Eternal, as seen through the fog and cigarette smoke of mortality, a vision something like that of the painter Raphael of Urbino, with yawning cerulean blue above and Grecian buildings in ideal geometric order and groups of wise men in robes, many with beards (here Father Doyle fondled his own modest whiskers), mingling with the fiery-eyed Fathers of the Church—Jerome, Augustine, Ambrose, et al.—and lesser luminaries from two millennia of Church history, right on down to Father Philip Doyle of North Killoyle parish, waiting humbly on the fringes, drinking in wisdom and sanctity with every uncon-

---

[1] In what key? Anyway, that reminds me of a concert at the National Concert Hall, back in the '80s. Norman Ornstein's Clarinet Sextet, it was, the one with the duet part for uillean pipes and French horn. Jimjam O'Donnell was pumping the old elbow, and Jean-Pierre Purée was taking care of the French side of things: man, they made music like the lambs of Inishmore. The only other time I can remember sleeping so soundly was back when I was a Young Pioneer on a Health Walk in the Knockmealdown Mountains, sixteen hours' march straight up a cliff and running in place for another eight—believe me, friend, I was ready for me kip after that (but not before a good old singalong around the campfire)!

gested breath. There were those, of course, who said the whole thing would be a bit of a bore, just standing about in robes all the time with harp music in the background and the ceaseless drone of interpreters interpreting Amharic and Greek and Aramaic and the hundred and one other languages of the Bible (or was it a hundred and two? Leviticus would know), but it was a vision of serenity and calm compared to the life he'd spent in the service of the Church, and it *had* been a long haul, seen from the summit of his sixty-eight years. Back in the late '40s Philip Aloysius Doyle of Derry was one of only eight seminarians from Maynooth to spend a year at the Gregorian University in Rome.[2] What a time he'd had, between the Trastevere trattoria and the Gregorian Library and long walks through the haunted nighttime streets, before the Church in its wisdom packed him off—"a brash young Turk, or do I mean berk?" in the words of his cousin, Bishop Teddy "Two Dinners" Glaghan—to the island of New Nubia in the Western Antilles, a hellhole of back-alley beggars, clouds of mudflies everywhere except in hurricane season, ruddy English colonials presiding over the simultaneous dissolution of the Empire and their own livers, and a Catholic population smaller than that of North Killoyle parish, most of them half-breeds with wits to match. The only soul he saved there was his own, by getting out, first to Canada (Lachine, Quebec: long winters and ear infections) and finally, thank God, Teddy Glaghan put off his fatal heart attack long enough to intercede for him and get him sent back to Ireland for the salvation of darkest Sligo and the Donegal townlands of Muff and Moville and, ultimately, North Killoyle, plum of southeastern parishes with its moneyed retirees and seaside promenade and Shrine of the Invisible Virgin at Ballymahone . . . in some ways, he couldn't have done better if he'd

---

[2]Now *that* was a time to be in Ireland! If you haven't read Ryan and Cronin on the period, don't; try Ulick O'Connor's biography of the boisterous Behan, or Pat Kavanagh's letters to his brother. God, I could go on. The steaks were that thick, boy, you needed both hands just to make an incision in the top layer, and as for the stout and salmon, well, calling them nectar and ambrosia would be erring on the side of caution, if you don't mind me saying so.

been made a cardinal. Not that he didn't wonder, now and then, if it hadn't been a total waste of time, despite (or maybe because of) his early ambitions, going back to the halcyon days in Rome, Gregorian University and the wine of the Trastevere taverns and the purer intoxication of Aquinas over alcohol; not that doubts never surfaced, less about whether God existed (how could He not?) than about whether He was aware of Philip Aloysius Doyle's existence, or cared (why should He?); not that (especially) the life of the flesh—i.e., sowing one's wild oats, then swelling the numbers of the human race with a kid or two and having a bouncy wife for the rest of your natural to comfort you and do the laundry—never raised its scaly head, oh definitely not the latter, not after a couple of years in the Caribbean where nubile New Nubians were two bob a toss (three to his credit, or eternal disgrace)!

Doyle had doubts; Doyle was human.

"I doubt, therefore I believe," he declared to his second glass of Jameson's, blurring the light of his desklamp with further exhalations of smoke. He even permitted himself a snatch of song: "Arrividerci Roma," rendered wordlessly in a whiskery countertenor.

"Arree-vee-derchy Ro-o-o-maaah," he bawled, between coughs.

Loud pounding on the wall and shouts of "not now" measured the extent of his housekeeper's disapproval.

"Fuck off," barked Father Doyle, but the coughs were taking over anyway, so he merely hummed and coughed his way through the remaining refrains, while perusing memory-shots of the Eternal City and the young manhood he'd left there. Dear old Rome! With a good enough excuse, he might make it back one more time, he thought, perhaps even manage to die in one of the Franciscan guesthouses in the lee of the Gianicolo, with the umbrella pines shading his face under the Roman sun (ah, there'd be umbrella pines in Heaven—in fact, if Heaven wasn't more than a bit like Italy, He'd missed a bet)[3] and the tired old Tiber at his feet wending its weary way to Ostia, *Cloaca Maxima*, and so to the sea, *Mare Nostrum*, and from there—like Saint Umbragius of Corinth—di-

---

[3]More like Blackpool, I'd reckon, with all that jabbering and milling about—or Lourdes, in peak season.

rectly to Heaven to kiss the hem of Our Mother, *Regina Coeli!*[4]

When Father Doyle fell asleep, at two o'clock, it was with an empty tooth glass in one hand and the serene smile on his face of a Raphael saint, very likely the same expression he would wear in death, if he died in the Rome of his dreams.

---

[4]Ah, that's more like it: Queen of Heaven, unsullied in body and soul. We were all Mariolatrists in our family, you know, going back to the Penal Law days and my great-great-uncle Eusebius, "The Unsung Martyr of the Hedgerows," as the sharp tongues had it.

6

Killoyle City (Ir. *Cuìll gHuaìll*, Church of the Flail), pop. (1990) 41,545, lies 19 miles SW of Waxford, 41 miles SE of Cork, 22 miles NSW of Weterford, and 121 miles SW of Dublin, on the stretch of Munster coast known as the Irish Algarve for the three blanched-concrete Martello towers on Killoyle Strand that from a distance are said to resemble the whitewashed windmills of the Lusitanian holiday Mecca.[1] Killoyle port is the deepest natural harbour between Waxford and Youghal, with a docking capacity of up to 100,000 metric tonnes dead weight. This was proven in late 1975 when the world's second biggest oil tanker, the 99,000 tonne *M/S*

---

[1]Lucy my arse. Those Martello towers look about as much like Portuguese windmills as my old man resembled Kirk Douglas—in other words, if you were talking to him over the phone, you just might be taken in enough to say (ignoring his powerful Northside accent and shrill Woodbine wheeze that used to set all the neighbourhood dogs to barking like billy-o): it's never Kirk Douglas, God bless and protect us? Likewise, one of those Martello towers might do a very respectable Portuguese windmill impersonation from a distance, but on seeing any of them close up (the Martelloes, your old fella) you'd be hard pressed to detect the first shadow of an atom of a resemblance, as the Da always used to say—only now that you mention it, he *was* driving his bus (the 12A to Donnybrook, back in the good old Cuba Car days) along Dame Street one fine morning when a lady passenger did a double take and asked him quite politely if he hadn't been in the film *Spartacles*, and could she have his autograph? No, but you can have my phonograph, said the Da. God bless him anyway, and wasn't he the two ends of a wag altogether, and didn't his passing mark the end of an era (or is that Eire?) itself?

Alcibiades Junior, flagship of the Onarchos Line, forced her way
through the port's narrow aperture with Pheidippides Onarchos
himself standing on the bridge, an event that brought the townsfolk out in gawking droves. Onarchos was magnanimous and,
for once, quite sober. Having taken a liking to the unctuous but
efficient harbourmaster, Thomas Maher, who cleared out half
a dozen fishing trawlers to make way for mighty *Alcibiades*, the
great man tossed him an imitation-gold Dupont cigarette lighter
(with handy PVC carrying case) and instructed him to trace his,
Pheidippides', Irish ancestors, without delay (under the dual
influence of aged whiskey and his third wife, American-Irish
actress Mavourneen O'Shillelagh, the shipping magnate had
become persuaded of Celtic forebears, adducing the evidence of
his sea-blue eyes and wide-winged nose). Maher promptly set to
work, getting himself the sack for his efforts. These included
sending a £5 note through the mail to the Heraldry Office at
Dublin Castle, along with a letter promising the Chief Herald
"the same or more" if he came up with an O'Narchos line traceable to Kings Brian Boru and/or Cormac Mac Art. The Herald,
Gerald Spole, LL.D., F.R.I.C.S., rejected offer and bribe out
of hand, and threatened to go to the papers. Publish and be
damned, said Maher scornfully, and threatened in turn to frac-
ture Dr. Spole's jaw. The newspapers took Dr. Spole's side, as
might be expected, and an extensive array of connections and
old-boy networks extending from Dublin Castle to the offices of
Killoyle Corporation (45 Pollexfen Walk, second floor) ensured
that the post of harbourmaster was soon vacant once again, as
it had been so often before.[2] Undaunted, Tom Maher laboured
through many successive nights on behalf of the still-resident

---

[2]Quite right too. I remember old Dr. Spole, he lived down the street
from us when I was growing up. He became a regular caller at our house
after Da died, ostensibly to share the family's grief as well as any grub
that was going, but different motives revealed themselves when one day
after the roast he suddenly sank to his knees and proposed marriage to
my poor widowed mother. Whether his offer was motivated by genuine
affection or was merely an excuse to justify his unexpected votive pose
we never ascertained, although the fact that he was already married and

Aegean Bluebeard to draw up a fictitious family tree, in coloured crayons, linking the O'Narchos sept of Western Roscommon to Niall Nine-Hostager and the doughty Mahers of Glen Glum, Co. Antrim, claiming blood ties thereby and, in consequence, a share in the family fortune—no more (he hastened to add, modestly) than, say, one-fifteenth, or £15,000,000, payable in fifteen annual installments of a million each, approximately—starting sooner, rather than later, say within the week? Tom Maher was a broad-shouldered lad and an easy mark for no man, but by the time the *Alcibiades* crew rolled their sleeves down and swaggered away, his own wife, passing by on her way to the shops, failed to recognise him; on the contrary, she mistook him for "another blasted pot-swilling layabout taking money out of honest people's pockets" and gave him a sound kick in the goolies as he lay groaning on the oil-slicked cobblestones. "Efharisto poli," bayed the bruisers (or words to that effect) from the stern of the departing *Alcibiades Junior*, bound for France, home of the De Narcus clan and Pheidippides' new girlfriend, rising starlet Babette Fessay.

The experience transformed Tom Maher from dreamer to man of action, determined never again to be at another's beck and call. Before his wife could apologise for unwittingly mugging him, he'd taken her life savings off her hands and built twelve bungalows on a narrow tract of land overlooking the sewage works, the sight and smell of which, he predicted accurately, would guarantee a rapid turnover of tenants and correspondingly rapid rent increases. More purchases followed, including that of a fine old Georgian mansion, the Udder House, demolished within a matter of days to make room for another dozen balsa-

---

the father of four daughters inclined us to the latter explanation; furthermore, when the family gathered round and interrogated him on his bank balance, we discovered that, although sound enough, it was well below the mother's expectations. Dr. Spole never came calling again, and subsequently always pretended to be a foreign tourist whenever we saw him on the street. Mother's expectations proved thoroughly justified, by the way, when she met my stepfather Mr. Duddy, the stock investor and train-spotting enthusiast (we never learned his first name, or even if he had one).

dash bungalows grouped around newly rechristened Oxtail Corners, "a housing estate for our time," according to the publicity brochures. By the end of the decade Tom Maher was the coming man, landlord of a goodly part of central Killoyle, loved by few and feared by many; under the sobriquet "the Greek," he became a familiar figure throughout the town, with his trademark Donegal tweed cap (concealing a dent inflicted on his cranium by the stalwart seamen of *M/S Alcibiades*) and Aran sweater (to enhance his chest expanse for purposes of intimidation, i.e., evicting tenants, outstaring rival landlords, looming over bailiffs, etc.).

Sunday mornings usually found him late abed, cap on head, having a smoke, and the Sunday morning after the storm was no exception, only this time his tea was late and his stomach was clamouring for its breakfast ration of rashers and toast.

"Wet the tea, woman," he roared, with no real hope that his wife could hear him, as she was in all probability a mile and a half away, at St. Oinsias' Church; still, the Greek was never shy of his own voice and gave the view-halloo another try, but to no avail. Sunday was, after all, Sunday, he reminded himself, so he swung his legs out of bed and went downstairs to the kitchen, where—fag glued to lower lip, cap rakishly askew—he puttered about, assembling the elements of breakfast. Thick black smoke soon filled the kitchen and billowed out the open window into the soft morning light as the Greek pampered himself with an extra rasher, extra-streaky, rewarding Superman the cat, too, with a dish of cream and a gristle or shard. After gobbling the last remnants of his breakfast off the heel of a stale loaf dripping with egg yolk, the Greek sat back and smoked in full-bellied ease, digesting audibly. From afar the liquid Sunday sound of church bells floated down the wind, bringing thoughts of idyllic retreats and soughing pines and empty mountainsides and all the holiday homes a man might build, say in a place the Irish holidaymaking punter would go to, like Italy,[3] with the right backing and enough cheap labour— Poles ideally, or Protestant Ulstermen. Southern Italy was the

---

[3]With land prices the way they are over there? You're joking. Even Sean MacBride had a rough time of it buying his 230-hectare spread near Rimini, and him with his impeccable Italian accent! Ah, I know

coming place, right enough, he'd heard that once or twice . . . as
if struck by a thought, he sprang to his feet, went into the hallway and picked up the phone directory, muttering to himself.
In the kitchen, Superman paused in his ablutions to listen to
the growling man-tones from the hallway, but—cat that he
was—human words conveyed nothing to him, except the key
ones that sounded like "Superman," or "Chuck-chuck," or "Din-
dins,"[4] and indeed it did seem to him, fleetingly, that all three of
these sounds were pronounced in the course of the man's solilo-
quy, but as nothing materialised in the way of snacks, leftovers,
dairy products, etc., he resumed licking his midriff with feline
precision and utter indifference to the doings of humanity.

---

what you're going to say: what price an Italian accent in English if the
locals don't understand a single blasted syllable of English to start with,
isn't that it? Musha, you have a point there, Eamon, there's no denying
that. By the way, according to those in the know, Sean's accent in Italian was pure West Cork, with a hint of Carlow.
[4]Not quite the vocabulary the old man was given to use, in addressing
his cat Theobald. Wordless was their dialogue, with mimickry of the
simian orders thrown in: AAAARRGH from the Da, EEEEYEW from
persnickety Theo, or vice versa when human foot trod feline tail.

7

Milo awoke in the sweaty panic of the overslept wage slave.

"Oh Jesus," he said. "Oh God Almighty."

Sunlight through uncurtained windows slapped him in the face as he tumbled from bed, to be instantly set upon by the elves of Hangover armed with anvil and churn.

"Bloody hell," he said. The journey to the bathroom that followed was a giddy one, consummated in such a paroxysm of vomiting that his eyes made briefly as if to uncork themselves from their sockets. Running water improved things somewhat, but the face that stared back from the shaving mirror was a sickly parody of itself: grey fading into fishbelly white, with eyeballs and lids of matching pink.[1]

"Holy Christ," groaned Milo. Hurried scraping with a blunt-

---

[1]Sounds rough, right enough. I once saw a face like that, and I only wish I could say it was my own, but wait till I tell you. I was staying in a small hotel south of Strangford Lough, back in my travelling days—God, how time flies. Anyhow, I'd turned in after a hard day on the road, you know, ready for a good old sleep I was, when suddenly I came over all tingling like, and opened my eyes just in time to see a face rising up from the end of the bed, underlit in a kind of greyish green glow, with pinkish eyes, like your man's! Well, I don't mind admitting it, for once in my life I was struck dumb, tongue-tied as a deaf-mute. I lay there gawking like an eejit while the face floated about the room, inspecting my belongings, looking out the window, admiring itself in the mirror . . . then, as God's my witness, it wheeled about, opened its mouth and spoke to me in a hoarse whisper, with a pronounced Belfast accent. "Are

ish razor, and another dash or two of cold water, restored him to partial well-being, although the butterflies in his stomach were beginning to feel more like wheeling birds—Texan buzzards above the Edwards Plateau, say, or the carry-on of carrion crows eyeing the incarnadine splashes of afterbirth in the springtime farmlands—or even ravens, ravenous for remains.[2] Breakfast, he decided, would have to wait, as would the usually jolly morning cigarette. Just getting there in one piece would be challenge enough. Stoically, he fought down resurgent retching and dressed in haste, double-checking to ensure proper closure of flies, pockets, etc. A brisk comb through lank hair created a pompadour effect with a cowlick on the right that made him look like an embalmed 1950s crooner, he thought, assessing his mirror image with reluctance.

"You're a misery, my man," he blurted, brutally. On his way out, assailed by sudden thirst, he risked a swallow of orange juice. It smelled a little off, but it was wet, at least, and it quenched him for the time being, even raising his spirits a touch. He whistled a token tune as he stepped into a chirping world of sunbright puddles and autumn leaves and slammed the front door behind him in fine, manly style, reminding himself that things had been worse, much worse, and not long ago, either: last Monday week, for one, when that perishing stink had invaded the place, or last Friday, when he'd smiled at that really not-bad Kathy gal—the female journalist Murphy was after in his unsubtle way—then turned bright red when he realised his nose had been quietly blowing itself all the while: hell, in short, made more hellish by

---

you a fockin' Roman Caffleck?" it said, before vanishing into thin air. Boys, it gave me the jitters, I can tell you. Nothing for it but half a dozen double whiskeys at the double—fortunately I'd remembered my Jameson's samples—and even then I hardly closed an eye for the rest of the night. Mind you, next day I found out from the landlord that Sammy Marx, a former UVF brigade leader on the run from his comrades, had hanged himself in that very room, so at least I knew I wasn't going completely round the twist. As to where Sammy came from, and where he went to—well, that's not for you or me to decide, is it, at all? [2]Thank you *very* much. I don't know about you, but my dinner's sitting less easy after that. YECCCHHH, if you take my meaning.

Murphy looking on, shoulders heaving in silent mockery . . . ach well, mused Milo. It's a long road that has no turning, as the saying went, and he reckoned he was about due for a turn, preferably good—although this was by no means certain, of course.

"Of course," Milo repeated to himself, bitterly. With a conscious muscular effort, he imposed order on his intestines, at least until he was in the vicinity of a bathroom.

Bathrooms abounded in Spudorgan Hall, and much else besides. Built on Killoyle's highest point in 1894 as the secondary residence of an earl whose primary mailing address had been the Hôtel du Casino at Divonne-les-Bains, it was auctioned off by his profligate lordship in 1926 and had been a hotel of varying quality ever since, reaching a low point in the late '70s when it was known as "The Rat Palace"; however, recent high ratings conferred by the pundits of the travel industry reflected the sound renovating job undertaken in the mid-eighties by its current owner, Fred Carfax the jockey.[3] Mr. Carfax, a resident of Disney Beach, Florida, left daily management in the hands of a team headed by the Administrative Manager, Emmet Power; the Catering Supervisor, Wolfetone Grey; an Entertainment Coordinator named Una; and the Cork law firm of MacSmarmy, MacSweeney, and Gallowglass, solicitors. In this hierarchy, Milo Rogers was about two-thirds of the way down, just below Petey Murphy the Head Bartender but distinctly above Leo Gomez the Stairwell Cleaner, not to mention Ragu Gupta, the stooped Indian woman who pushed an enormous mop through the public rooms several times a day.

On the wall behind the reception desk in the panelled lobby

---

[3] A** in the 1989 Mault-Giroux International Travellers' Companion; a small French country house flanked by a rosette and two sets of crossed knives and forks in the Michelin of the same year; "The Ritz of the Southeast: outstanding by Irish standards," in the words of Barry Vorster of Vandervalk's Double-Dutch Guides. I stayed there once, on expenses. It's not bad, but the wallpaper . . . ! As I said to the night manager, Mr. Fowlkes, "Either that wallpaper goes or I do." He promptly asked me if I had anything to declare, upon which I naturally responded, "Only my genius!" Poor man: his hair turned quite gold with grief.

was an oil painting depicting Mr. Carfax in his jockeying youth, crouching atop a horse with cheering crowds in the background and many-coloured flags straining at their ropes under the scudding clouds of a west of Ireland sky.[4] Standing in front of the painting on any normal morning would be the manager himself, Mr. Power, ready with a quip for the guest and a frown for the tardy underling, but that morning, as Milo hurried up to sign the time sheet with telltale March Hare glances at his watch (a Swass in blue plastic), he was greeted by Murphy's beaming face.

"May I help you, sir?"

"Power's off, I suppose," said Milo.

"No, sir. The lights are on, as you can see for yourself."

"Get off my arse, Murphy. What are you doing behind the front desk?"

"And I could ask you what you're doing in front of it."

"Out of that. I'm late already. Give me the time sheet."

"It's Sunday, boy. You don't come in till four."

Odd, thought Milo. It didn't feel like a Sunday, probably because he'd managed to wake up, get dressed, and come to work in half the time it normally took him to scratch himself. He stared at Murphy for a few seconds until the full force of the revelation hit him: *it was Sunday!*

HE COULD GO HOME!

Or have a hair of the dog.

(Or both.)

With a facial expression inspired by the School of El Greco (eyes uprolled, lips puckered) he raised and lowered an invisible drink in his right hand.

"Forget it, Milo. Bar's closed until lunch, as you well know. Go on home and sleep it off."

Sweet reason, however, was a foreign tongue to hungover Milo Rogers. From nausea and headache he had progressed to the third phase of the condition, at least his mutation thereof: all-devouring lust, expressed in slick palms and rapid heartbeat. As a bachelor, his frustrations were normally given vent in the

---

[4]Try the other coast. The horse was Temeraire; the race, the Tom Moore Cup; the place, Punchestown; the year, 1964.

comfort of home, in bed or bathroom, amid visual aids, but at the Hall things had to be managed more tactfully. He knew there was a stash of well-thumbed back issues of imported glossy magazines, most of them in the vicinity of Leo Gomez, and the stalls of the gents' WC across from the main dining room were quite accommodating for brief stays of five to ten minutes, as long as one muffled one's voice and kept the rustle of pages down to a minimum.[5]

Wasting no time, Milo rode the lift down to the cellar, a dimly lit warren of corridors and alcoves favoured as a trysting place back in "Rat Palace" days but now mostly empty and echoing with the dark vastness of the years. The vintage mags were in their usual dishevelled piles next to the door in Leo's broom closet, not only *Crusader* and *Leather Mistress*, as expected, but also back issues of *Dominatrix* and *Quest*, as well as *El Caballero* and *Desnudissima* from Leo's lately re-sexualised homeland. With expert fingers, Milo winnowed erotic wheat from pornographic chaff, flipping through the topmost issues in the pile and discarding those with displays of group sessions or implements. He held no great brief for couples, either, or seaside spreads posing as aerobics. Indoor *déshabillé* was what he was looking for, and he found it in a 1983 edition of *Quest* devoted, serendipitously, to "The Country Girls: Irishwomen in England."

In the gents' upstairs, a tiled realm of plashing peace and oak partitions, Milo settled himself to study his acquisition at leisure. The Irish girls of the cover story were quite pretty, in an un-made-up kind of way, fair-skinned and inclining to plumpness, some with naively pouting expressions, others with the brittle smiles of London careerists willing to do anything short of actually breaking the law to get ahead—hard faces but softer contours, he was pleased to note. Odd, he also noted, how so many of these pinup girls seemed to resemble one another, facially as well as anatomically: Fiona, the Archway barmaid, for instance, looked quite a lot like Sheila, the Birmingham hairdresser, and Rosie, the Dan-Air stewardess, was the spitting

---

[5]Right, well, I'm scrubbing round this for the time being. Let me know when the coast is clear.

image of the St. Anselms go-go dancer, Sinéad. As for Kate, the editorial girl Friday, she evoked a resemblance that clamoured in Milo's brain, distracting him from the erotic essence of his research: blonde, long-limbed, endowed a shade too generously for modern tastes (but not for Milo's), biggish nose—just who was it that she brought to mind? Or was it another version of herself she resembled, an earlier incarnation come upon in another glossy centrefold, on another hungover Sunday, or solitary weeknight's alternative to television programmes about dung beetles or starving Africans . . . when the answer finally roared to the surface of Milo's mind, he dropped the magazine in astonishment, then snatched it up again to double-check the facts.

"Kate's a real country colleen," burbled the rag. "Raised among sheep and goats on her father's farm, she's known Nature's way ever since girlhood. Her own way led her out of the unforgiving hills over the sea to forgiving London and a job she loves in the editorial department of *Fave*, the society mag, where the greatest part of the job is the fascinating people she meets.[6] Men? Lots, she says, but none too seriously (seriously, folks!)—at least not for the moment. Eligible Kate wouldn't give us her phone number, but here are some other equally vital statistics to be going on with: 35-28-36!"

It was unmistakable, thought Milo. The undressed Kate of *Quest*, June 1983, was the well-dressed Kathy of today's Hall lounge bar, the lady journalist he'd quite fancied from the very first, the one whose hubby had fallen off a cliff or something while doing research for some best-selling novel or other! Raised among sheep and goats, was she? Lots of men, our girl Friday,

---

[6]Not a bad publication, really, if you'll excuse the observation—didn't they break the Mike Halle-Princess Khasbin scandal? I used to subscribe because they ran a raffle in every issue. We won a RailPass to the Benelux countries—ah, the Ardennes! Ostend! Esch-sur-Alzette! Our guide was a gent named—hang on, it's on the tip of my tongue—Joop den Uyl, that was it. Nice old party, but more than a little deaf. Whenever we asked him a question, he'd stick his fingers in his ears and shout "Waat?" He got stroppy, too, sometimes; once he even made a face at us behind our backs, the old daredevil! Still, he was a kingly man, and it is not in my lifetime nor yours that we will look upon his like again.

and none too serious? Over the sea to *Fave*? Milo explored the pictorial details with relish. As he did so, his mouth went dry and his breathing grew shallow, and for once he thought soft-focus was a bad idea.[7]

His exit from the cubicle was heralded by the camouflage sounds of voluminous flushing and throat-clearings of consequence, but they went unnoticed in the Sunday torpor that was otherwise broken only by the Hindi muttering of Ragu as she plodded through the empty public lounge in the wake of her mop. Secondary waiters flitted silently about the main dining room, ignored by Milo, ignoring him in turn.

Murphy was still behind the reception desk, but his energy was on the wane.

"God, that was a rough night," he said, through the tears of a withheld yawn, inviting comment. Milo sidestepped the invitation.

"Oh, I don't know. Once the rain stopped I slept like a dead man."

"Aye. Dead drunk, you mean. I, on the other hand . . . well, let's just say I was up late." His eyebrows semaphored significance. Milo gave in.

"All right, all right. Who was the lucky gal, then?"

Murphy leaned forward.

"Between the two of us, mind that, Milo. It's a rotten lousy friend you'd be if you opened your trap on me."

"Ach, get on with it."

"You know Kathy Hickman, the journalist gal? The one with the big house?"

The house isn't all she's got that's big, thought Milo, diluting the bitterness of bachelor's envy (Murphy had got a bit further along than he'd suspected, the scheming rat) with the smug

---

[7]The softer the better, if you ask me. Sure, all they're about is sex, pardon me speaking plainly. Obsessed is what they are, with their fallen arches and cheap makeup. You see them by the dozen along the Grand Canal (the irony is, most of them are over from Liverpool, dropping their English knickers for Irish nicker, as the Da always said, late Saturday nights when he'd a drop taken).

knowledge of his secret as he suddenly realised, after intending to pull the magazine out of his inside pocket and show it to Murphy (his gob already half open to announce the discovery), that he would do no such thing.

"You don't say. Well, well, I can't say I'm surprised," lied Milo. "Didn't I always detect a certain gooey-eyedness on your part whenever she was around?"

"Gooey-eyed yer backside. Notice how often Milady drops by these days, and not just for the view."[8]

"Ah, you're the cute fella, Murphy. You are that, entirely."

Murphy gloated. Meanwhile, Milo inhabited two minds, each containing an alternative. The more devious, Faustian approach would be to use his secret information to his own financial advantage by insinuating, via notes anonymously penned, or casual allusion, or sly flirtatiousness, that his discretion could be bought like any other commodity, say five hundred quid in tenners tucked into a shoebox—no, better make it a round thousand in twenties (or a rounder two?), dropped into the blue dustbin on the corner of Oxtail Yard and Uphill Street at 5 a.m. on Sunday morning—no, that was no good, crowds were your best protection, the films always said so: change that to 12 noon on the corner of Parnell Parade and King Idris Road West (and make it five thousand—in for a penny, after all!).

Sweat was already beading his brow at the mere thought of the logistics involved. The easier alternative was to forget the whole ludicrous business, return the magazine to Leo's cubbyhole, and carry on as usual. Both options were intrinsically good and bad at the same time,[9] the active one promising adventure and cunning but pointing the way down the low road to vice and moral

---

[8]Truly *magnifico*, especially over a slap-up breakfast of scrambled tripe, boiled hermit crabs and meat-free diet bacon (with a cup or two of detanninized Darjeeling to wash it down): to your right, the six hills of Killoyle, crowned by the granite spire of St. Oinsias' Church (1172, revisited 1833); to your left, the Queen Anne jetty (1711) extending to the Con Leventhal lighthouse (1904); farther to your left, the sea, the sea (and Wales, somewhere thereabouts).

[9]A bit like life itself, if you'll pardon my French.

degradation and prison sentences, while the passive course had the virtue of not making things worse but doing damn-all to improve them.

It was a dilemma custom-made for ditherers, and Murphy's next remark only made things worse.

"Solo flying's all right for a while, mister-me-man, but before long you forget the rules of the game," he said, with near-insufferable superiority of tone. "You should get yourself a woman." He completed this statement with a jaw-cracking yawn.

"You're the sharp one, Murphy. Wasn't I just saying the very same thing to myself?" Milo gave a woozy smile to match his innards.[10]

---

[10]Honestly, there are times when I wish Milo had been indoctrinated more, indulged less! Now, if (for example) my Uncle Francis had stood *in loco parentis* to the lad, believe me, the outcome would have been quite different, and we wouldn't be witnessing this spectacle of human degradation and moral diarrhea; but *c'est la vie*, if you follow my drift.

8

As the mechanic studied the damage to the Rover's windscreen, he thoughtfully probed each nostril with a motor-oiled forefinger. Bold smudges adorned the flanges of his nose when he turned to face Kathy with his verdict.

"Two hundred's the job."

"Two hundred? Good heavens. I'd expected half that, at most. Two hundred, is it? I see."

"Right. Like I'm after tellin' ya, missus, ya won't find another garage in Killoyle willin' to do repair jobs on a Sunday, but if ya hand over yer two hundred, cash or charge, I'll have it done for ya by teatime, true bill."

"Holy bloody smokestacks. What if I bring her in tomorrow?"

"Ah, well, now, we're closed Mondays, like, and God bless ya, on a Chewsday ya'd think it was the Hurling Final itself, the mob scene's that desperate, so 'tis."

He sniffed the air urgently, doglike—like Strongbow the terrier, in fact, engaged at that moment in exploring urinary corners, nosewise. Kathy cursed, once silently ("Bugger!"), once aloud ("Blast!"), then handed the man her credit card.

"Robbery is what that was," she explained to Strongbow as they left the garage. Unmoved, the dog paused to lift a leg on an overturned dustbin, gazing at his mistress with equanimity. She was lighting a cigarette and inhaling busily, as indifferent to him as she was to the view of Killoyle stage-managed by the collaboration of Parnell Parade and King Idris Road (W.), a prospect captured on many holiday postcards ("Greetings from Killoyle" captioning huddled rooftops, six spires, the silvery strand).

Human anxieties that Strongbow could never divine bedeviled Kathy's mind, starting with the two hundred quid for that bloody windscreen, a write-off as far as the insurance boys were concerned, she was sure of that, with a driving record like hers (three New Years' accidents in a row), never mind half the country bearing witness to the storm that was the real culprit . . . oh well, turn the page, she told herself. It wouldn't be the first write-off, and anyway there were murkier, Murphier things to be thinking about. God knew she wasn't a snob, but bedding a barman was a bit much, not at all the done thing, not where she came from, anyhow[1]—or was it Murphy himself, just? The predictability of him, Paddy rampant that he was, eternally smelling of beer, ambitious only for his wee house and car and his six to eight pints of a Saturday night and good crack in the pubs and a woman to adorn the imitation-leather banquette (red or green) next to him: a woman to fondle, a woman to impress, but ultimately—inevitably—a woman to forget? There was too much of her late husband in that, and Phelim had been harder-headed, and a sight sharper. Murphy was a dreamer, not a doer, like her own three brothers, and that was why that lot were still lounging about Ballykilloran, Co. Louth, while she'd seen a bit of the world, if not yet the whole.

"He's a waster, and that's the truth of it," she confided to solemn Strongbow. Oh, Murphy was ruttish enough between the sheets, and that wasn't necessarily a part of your average Irishman's birthright, but a waster he was, nevertheless.

Woman and dog proceeded down the road, braced by lashings of sea breeze and sharp ozone in the air. A bluish mash of cloud fringed the tea-dark waves, and the sun's fried egg glistened in

---

[1]Not the done thing, is it? In Co. Louth? My own native land? Are you joking, so? Wait till I tell you. Seven barmen there were in Colmcross townland where I was bred, and seven faithless wives to keep them company of a weekend night, and seven cuckolded husbands intoxicating themselves in the seven pubs of the seven barmen, seven nights a week; and not in seventy times seven nights did any of those culchies ever awake to the horns on his head, which made the wives happy, until the next lot came along. Believe me, this kind of thing happens every day in the blessed hinterland.

the inverted pan of Heaven. Somewhere out there was Wales, and somewhere else—France! Nearer at hand, however, was Parnell Parade, sloping gently downward from King Idris Road West along the unpeopled Strand. Benches sat stoically facing the sea, positioned at strategic intervals of seventeen feet or more, decked with seaweed blown in by last night's storm. Abutting the Queen Anne jetty was a bronze statue of General Michael Collins swearing an oath to the Republic indivisible, one hand tucked Napoleonically into his vest, the other pointing toward the Con Leventhal lighthouse and beyond, to the cosmos.

Adjacent to the Big Fella, extending lengthwise in both directions on the landward side of Parnell Parade—at the foot of the churches and MacLiammoir Hill—were the shops,[2] each proudly boasting a shopwindow. In one of these, Kathy assessed herself: windblown, coat collar upturned, cigarette dependent from lower lip in the manner of a French cabaret singer. Her appearance suited her somewhat unsettled, liverish mood. It was partly the late night, of course (and as if that weren't enough what did Murphy do afterward but insist on pouring them both a double Bushmills on the rocks) and partly the smoking; whenever she went beyond her usual arbitrary limit of twenty per diem she regretted it the next day, and the day before she'd had twenty-five at least (then there'd been Murphy's ghastly Gold Flakes to round things off, or poison the well for good!).

Then there was her mood, just. Things wouldn't do, the way they were, it was as simple as that. This little weekend romance with Murphy had to be called off and replaced with something more ambitious, or nothing at all. Yes, she'd rather be entirely on her own again if the alternative was feeling like a barman's floozy, and anyway enforced solitude might be just what she needed to sort things out. *Glam?* The house? Killoyle itself? All

---

[2]Known locally as "The Shops." My favourite's Beano's, with the year-round koala display. Try their nuts sometime—they're out of this world! Hundertwassers, next door, make unforgettable hats to go with that diamond tiara you just picked out at Van Veen and 'ter Horsts, and if you need restoring after all that shopping, there's Pico's the Hib-Mex cantina and La Grande Salade, the famous Provençal steakhouse: confidentially, I don't know of a better deal this side of Kowloon.

negotiable, as far as she was concerned. Two things weren't: Strongbow, God bless him, and her ambition to be, one day (near or distant), a woman of substance, someone not to be dismissed lightly, a Serious Person—a poet?

Anything was possible, within limits.

"Ach, not again," said Kathy presently, as Strongbow straddled a grassy verge. Nearby was a sign reading *Keep off the Grass— Absolutely No Children, Games, or Dogs.* Kathy glanced around apprehensively for accusing onlookers, but the street—Brendan Behan Avenue, joining the lower reaches of the Parade to Pollexfen Walk and the Mid-Upper Town—was astir only with the church-bound, travelling in twos and threes to heed the brazen summons of Mad Begg, the great bell of St. Oinsias'.[3] Small groups stood outside the church, awaiting the stroke of ten, when Father Doyle, or his curate Father Skelly, or both, would emerge from the presbytery and stride across the intervening lawn, head (or heads) bowed, chasuble (or chasubles) flapping gently in the breeze (or wind). Kathy winced as age-old guilt hissed Shirker in her ear. When she was growing up in Ballykilloran, Sunday Mass had been an inflexible routine for the culturally deprived, and for those starved not only of culture but also of companionship— widows, widowers, sixty-year-old bachelor brothers and their

---

[3]Forged out of a set of pure bronze fire irons by D. Hampster of Durham in 1642, mighty Mad Begg struck its first note at the restoration of Charles II and hasn't stopped ringing since, in a manner of speaking—but wait till I tell you. One Sunday in March 1837, the citizens of Killoyle (then called West South) were startled out of their beds by the distinctive sound of their beloved bell ringing an augmented fourth, in direct contradiction to the conventional wisdom of the age that totally ruled out any augmented half notes for church bells weighing more than 750 lbs! Of course, human nature being what it is, there were those who denied it had ever happened, and in October of the following year riots broke out and the Town Hall of West South was set on fire by a crowd of Anti-Augmented Fourthists calling for the immediate execution of the Lord Mayor, Sir Jocelyn De Beef, an ardent member of the Pro-Augmented Fourth Party. Eventually the army had to be called out of Kneeland Barracks, but their intervention came too late to save Sir Jocelyn, who was lynched by the crowd on Michaelmas Day, 1838. His last words were, allegedly: "You f—ing d—heads."

own bachelor uncles and cousins—daily churchgoing had been
the norm, followed in most cases by a visit to the back room of
Milligan's Distillery next door, where ex-officio Sunday tastings
were as much a part of local ritual as weddings and burials—for
the men, that is, not for women, and certainly not for girls.
Young Kathy, like her peers, could only watch and wonder as the
men came and went, variously sozzled, uniformly foul-tongued,
in church devout as saints, blatant sinners outside, happily trans-
gressing the priest's (i.e., God's) injunctions, preaching their
own form of Reformation while urging the girls and young
women of Ballykilloran to learn their catechism—go to Mass—
give generously—at table, keep eyes lowered, hands above—pray
to the Sacred Heart—adore the Infant of Prague—hope for
husbands of strength and Christian virtue (or, failing that, a fella
with twenty acres and a car). These voices were readily summoned from the long-ago by Kathy's church-bell-troubled conscience:

Old Mrs. Boyle from next door—"Ach sure, there's no harm in
the one drink atself, but wasn't Mrs. Farrell telling us Father had
an extra twelve last night after his tay?"

Bachelor Uncle Tim—"Aw, it's a world of book learnin' they
possess, the fathers, right enough, but God bless and save 'em
they're no better than the pigs in the yard when it comes to
settin' a young gossoon to rights."

Her father—"Shut yer gob."

Her mother—"Gowan, ya slob, divil the man in these parts
who'd marry ya even if yer backside were paved with rubies,
they're in that deep with the priests, so they are. It's Dundalk for
ya, my girl, or Dublin atself."[4]

Eventually the contradictions outnumbered reasons to believe

---

[4]Double-check your folklore, mister, this rendition sounds more like
Monaghan than Louth, at least to my ears—sure and amn't I the fussy
one, I hear you saying! Well, so would you be if you'd grown up in a
patch of tatties six yards wide by three deep with only the snails and the
dung to keep you company through the long winter nights! No wonder
the others got out while the getting was good: Terence to Delaware,
Uncle Mike to Ceylon, the Brannigans to Innisfree's bee-loud glades.

and Kathy stopped going to church altogether. Six months later, with her reputation preceding her and Ballykilloran's ill wishes in her wake, she moved to Dundalk, rebel town of the borderlands; there she found jobs to pay the rent and learned the craft of survival in a world bounded by the eager hands of men. In her growing maturity and desire for wider horizons she moved again, southwards this time, and put the lessons of grasping Dundalk into practice in Dublin's firm embrace.

Yet even after all these years and a lifetime's moving hither and yon, here she was, still beleaguered by her own unbelief!

"Jimminy, I'd go in to Mass, so I would, if it weren't for you," she muttered accusingly to Strongbow, but, his duty done, the dog yearned onward. Kathy made a face and with a Kleenex did her own duty as a civic-minded Killoyler. Blessed at least with that virtue which is next to godliness, as well as a now-scampering excuse not to cross the church's threshold, she allowed herself to be guided away from the metallic harangue of Mad Begg and down sloping Behan Avenue toward the tea shops of Parnell Parade.

9

Catering meals for hotel guests was a dull and thankless job, fit only for fools, simpletons and failures, as Wolfetone Grey remarked often enough to God, when He was within earshot; to others, however, he expressed delight in his line of work, claiming peace of mind and contentment in that longed-for still place between ambition and death. The truth lay elsewhere, as it nearly always does. In most respects, Wolfetone's job was like any other, absolute in its demands and relative in its benefits, although of course the routine was soothingly unchanging, and the fortnightly deposit of four hundred pounds into his account at the Allied Irish Bank on Pollexfen Walk was welcome—indeed essential, if the Greys' mortgage stood any chance of being paid off before the turn of the century. The sooner it was over and done with, the better, as far as Wolfetone was concerned, because life was a haimes unless you owned property. He was tormented by the very notion of having to pay the maintenance bills on their wretched barracks of a house, what with the national economy, telephone answering machines, the new stairway tax, sullen womenfolk, overpaid swine-faced superiors, etc.!

Sundays were usually a welcome respite from all this, but Wolfetone was in something of a wax that particular Sunday morning, after a night of shallow sleep and deep nightmares. In the *Weekly Harbinger* was a review of *Up and Down and Out* by the Russian spirit-sleuth Leonid Glossovich.[1] Wolfetone had read

---

[1] Blank Books, Ltd., Wolverhampton and Ulan Ude, entering its

it eagerly, wantonly, despite his better judgement; years of the finest Comprehensive education notwithstanding, he had once—and not so long ago, if the truth were known—allied himself to Glossovich's thesis, as described in the Slavic sage's previous book, *Up and Down and Round We Go*, that a small, select part of the world's population (including the author) would soon disappear into thin air—*but not really!* According to Glossovich, what we call "thin air" or "air" is really no more than an impermeable curtain of marsh gas that renders invisible the "Near World," or "Next Door," of "Great Ones" or "Big Guys," beings like ourselves, only better (he points to the "Golbkiy'," or will-o'-the-wisps, so common in the Volga and Dnieper deltas), i.e., the chosen, or "Favourites," of God (or "Him")—God's booking agents, in a word—through whom (or which) enlightenment is available "beyond the curtain" to an elite group of 104,000 mortal humans bearing surnames beginning with *G*: Glossovich, Goethe, Gandhi, Grey....

Wolfetone put aside the paper, took a final draw at his pipe and exhaled irritably. Yes, he was in a right old stew, and he didn't care who knew it. Mrs. Grey did, certainly. She was an expert in recognising the symptoms. When sudden pinkish blotches appeared on her husband's prominent nose and cloven chin, and belly-deep chortling noises and moist belches (pipe-induced) resonated in the air; when, especially, the wretched fellow indulged in the unappealing habit he'd refined over the years of leaning forward as in meditation and, seemingly unawares, emitting a steady floorward drool of tobacco-coloured saliva—at such times Mrs. Grey withdrew, with disapproving harrumphs.

"Time for church," she said, over her shoulder, a staunch non-goer herself. Bells rang in concurrent concord, without. Wolfetone looked at his watch.

"Golly, you're right," he said, brightening at the prospect of change, however predictable.

---

seventy-ninth week on the *Sunday Post* best-seller list as we went to press. Glossovich has some interesting theories, certainly, but did you know he spent fifteen years alone in a yurt in the mountains of Tadzhikistan? He calls it enlightenment, but I reckon you or I might have a different word for it. Makes you wonder, anyhow.

Twenty minutes later he was standing in his usual pew at St. Oinsias'. Father Doyle was well into the reading of the Epistles, with the sermon to follow; a frightful bore, thought Wolfetone. Still, it was High Mass, after all, and nothing could be omitted, least of all his customary report to the Almighty, detailing last night's telephonic missions.

"I called the bugger and put the fear of—well, Your fear, in him, so I did," said Wolfetone, to himself (and God). "All on Your behalf, too! Wait till you see the class of jigs that throws him into. Actually, I'm surprised he's not here today."

From his vantage point at the back, he surveyed his fellow parishioners. Emmet Power was nowhere to be seen, but it was a good turnout, anyway, Wolfetone observed contentedly, as pleased as if he had sent out the invitations himself.[2] It always looked better to have a full house. Prosperity hung thereby, and government grants, and the promise of future generations. Speaking of prosperity and government, Benedict Ovary, the Lord Mayor, stood with his family in the front row, his two young daughters as pretty as pictures in their blue-and-gold denim gowns, the Mayoress stunning in cashmere and lace, His Worship declaiming the responses in an officious baritone. Chief Superintendent of the Gardai and Mrs. Nugent and their five strong sons occupied the next row behind them, and across from the Nugents stood Conan the grocer, a pious widower, next to the pharmacist, Mr. O'May, married but a notorious philanderer; even now, his eyes were roving the assembly in search of likely prey. His gaze alighted, gleaming with concupiscence, on the Lord Mayor's wife.

"That's bloody disgusting, so it is." Wolfetone's voice brought heads smartly about in the next row. He muttered apologies and piously attended to the reading of the Epistles.

"And may ye walk with Him that is the Anointed of God, saith

---

[2] I should think so, too. Last time I checked, our congregation back in Colmcross was down to the three Calloon brothers, Seamus, Petey, and Jean-Christophe, and they freely admitted they'd only come because St. Ferdinand's had the best Communion wafers in Co. Louth (naturally, being Pioneers, they weren't too keen on the wine).

Paul to the Corinthians," brayed Father Doyle. Sunlight, filtered through the stained glass of the Non-Norman Altar Windows into rays of blue and red, illuminated his balding pate, atop which unkempt hairs waved languidly in the draft, like sea anemones.[3] Serving Mass with him were Father Skelly, the curate, and Jim Pat O'Moon, nephew of Wolfetone's one-time victim and subsequent nemesis, Kenneth O'Moon. An awkward youth of thirteen or so, Jim Pat already stood an inch taller than Father Doyle, and the sleeves of his altar boy's gown extended no farther than the middle of his wrists, giving him a gangling, Frankensteinian appearance that matched his character (and his uncle's), in Wolfetone's opinion.

"Why Father Doyle asked a half-witted galoot like that one to serve Mass is a total mystery to me," he mumbled, put in mind of the time young O'Moon had driven a moped through the back door of the Grey residence and straight down the hallway through the front door and into Lostwithal Road and back again, not once but several times, unbeknownst to Wolfetone and his wife, sleeping upstairs; only the sharp eye and tongue of Mrs. Cane next door had saved the Grey residence from further incursions. In the event, it had taken three weeks and a gallon of Swipe to get the tire tracks out of the hallway.

"A lout is what that Jim Pat O'Moon is." Wolfetone stoked retrospective fury in declarative tones. "A good-for-nothing lay-

---

[3]Leaded, stained, and installed in the original non-Norman—i.e., Hiberno-Romanesque—church by the Master of Ouest Sud, c. 1299, the Non-Norman Altar Windows were stored in the cellars of Mad Molloy's tavern from 1794 (when the old church was sacked by visiting French tourists) until the new St. Oinsias' was inaugurated in 1833. They depict famous non-Norman events of medieval history, from the occupation of Antwerp by Burgundian forces under Duke Heston IV in 1015 to the signing of the Bull of Promulgation by Pope Boniface VIII in 1298, through the assassination of William Rufus in the New Forest in 1100 and the death by hernia strangulation of the Umbrian painter Dino of Umbria, in 1206. Lord Clark, the art historian, said of the Killoyle windows, "They're unbelievably awful, a world-class disgrace, stained-glass bum fodder, God they make me sick"; so look sharp, next time you're visiting.

about lout of a hoor he is, and a thundering great horse's arse."

"Shut your noise," said a stout lady in the adjacent pew.

"Aw, go knot your knickers," said Wolfetone. A scuffle ensued, resulting in flushed cheeks, heavy breathing, and tousled
hair, as after lovemaking. Father Doyle went behind the pulpit
and banged his fist.

"Whisht! Will you quit your brawling during Mass, for the
love of God?" he shouted. "There'll be none of that in my church.
Be quiet, the lot of you, or I'll be asking Chief Superintendent
Nugent to take down your names."

He returned to the altar after escorting the ructions through
the church and out the door, upon which Jim Pat dropped the
paten with a resonant clang, raising sniggers.

"Peace be upon you," commanded Father Doyle, echoed by
the congregation, Wolfetone among them. He felt braced by the
morning's events. A good old barney was as good as the phoning
to get his blood up—of course, it was unfortunate it had to be in
the house of God, but that was the way most people were, quite
frankly (and come to think of it, didn't that Jim Pat article have
his own phone listing in the directory . . . ?).

"For thine is the kingdom, the power, and the glory, for ever
and ever, amen," chanted the congregants, none more lustily
than Wolfetone Grey.[4]

---

[4]Now hang on a second there, boy, is this a Catholic Mass or the bleeding C. of I.? That response sounds dead Prod to me, even with the
wreckage of Vatican II floating all around us—I mean, the Pope says
he's a traditionalist and all that, but only last week I heard the shortage
of priests in the Gambia had become so severe that they were planning
to fly witch doctors to Rome for a crash course in Christening and Extreme Unction. Just goes to show, doesn't it? Robbing Peter to pay
Paul—or should that be John Paul?—when the left hand doesn't know
what the right hand's doing, and so on. What a sell.

10

"Say when, Father," said Emmet Power. Without the slightest interest in its contents, he gazed abstractedly at the just-opened bottle of Bushmans Black Bull. In this he was the opposite of Father Doyle, sandpapering eager hands while ogling the alluring amber of the water of life.

"Not quite a double, Emmet, but near enough, that's right, ah—when! When! Good man yourself." The priest supervised the pouring with micrometer judgement, but once the whiskey was ready and waiting, palpably *there*, he rearranged himself on the barstool and casually glanced around the room, lighting a debonair cigarette with his back to the drink, as if nothing could interest him less. This sham indifference was a sure sign of the boozer deluxe, as Emmet Power knew from a lifetime's observation of the genus, notably his own father, who—although theoretically still alive—had been thoroughly pickled these forty years. Father Doyle was a less acute case, as befitted a still-active priest, but one would get you ten, self-wagered Emmet, that there was always an open bottle on the presbytery sideboard.

"And how was Mass this morning, Father?" said Emmet with the faintest curl of his upper lip, like a vegetarian among meat-eaters. Father Doyle feigned surprise at the sight of his whiskey.

"Ah, there it is." He raised the drink to the light. "Mass? I'm not so sure I should tell you, Emmet. It's my opinion that you'd come along in person if you were that interested—which you're not, also in my opinion." His eyes were eloquent as he took his first swallow, but he said nothing, and emitted only the faintest sigh of satisfaction. Oh, go on, at least smack your lips, Emmet urged him, mutely; but Father Doyle was obstinate, and chose to play the charade to the end.

Of course, self-denial's all in a day's work for the clergy, reflected Emmet.

"However, since you ask. I read Paul's First Epistle to the Corinthians and showered the congregation with confetti from the gospels of Mark and Luke relating to the abuse of power, which Ben Ovary showed no sign of appreciating, then I administered the responses in fine voice and chastised one or two rowdies in the back rows—that's where they always are, in school the bullies were always in the back rows too, as I recall—and finally I delivered myself of a long-winded sermon on the beauty of the appropriate death that drove a good 20 percent of 'em out the side door before the end." Here he coughed, vigorously. "I propose to put the wind up the next lot with precisely the same sermon and if they don't like it, they can come in for one of Skelly's droning old yarns about risen angels and fallen women. Frig 'em, anyhow." He hoisted his glass in a mock toast, and this time his Adam's apple bobbed three times before he lowered the glass.

"What's the appropriate death, exactly?" asked Emmet. Father Doyle gave a conspiratorial glance from side to side, taking in glass-polishing Murphy yawning at the far end of the bar and three other preprandial customers, two with visible shakes, heads bowed over their drinks, in reverence, or drunkenness.[1]

"The appropriate death is the greatest gift of all," he said. "It means snuffing it when you've made your peace with God and Man, and if you're lucky, with Woman too. A tall order, eh?"

Emmet grunted. Sod the priests, after all, he said to himself. They always had to have the last word.

"By which I don't mean ascending to Heaven on a cloud with a choir singing the Ave Maria," continued Father Doyle. He stared fixedly at Emmet, filling him with the fear of sin. "Although that would be a grand old lark. No, I'm talking about a conjunction of things we don't commonly have: the right people, the right place, and the right faith."

"Sounds like a bloomin' self-help programme on the telly,"

---

[1] Or both?

growled Emmet.

"Aye. Well, it could be, so it could, self and all. Of course, being who I am, I'd naturally believe all the help we need comes from God, originally, only you and I are responsible for the details, like supporting ourselves and/or family, preserving health and sanity"—here, shockingly, he gave a hiccup loud enough to startle the two shakers ("Mother of God," said one, "a priest!")—"and living a fulfilling existence while obeying the law, God's law, that is, as well as Man's." He groaned passionately, quelling further upsurges. "The common response to which would be, show me a man who conforms to all that and I'll show you a saint or a liar."

"More riddles, eh, Father?" said Emmet, on top of the situation again. This was more like it; this was like Sunday school. "You're terrible ones for the riddles, you ecclesiastical gentlemen."[2]

"No riddle at all. That's just a nonbeliever's easy way out. The Christian moral code is the best prescription for a moral life, bar none, even if you're a bloody Buddhist. I believe there are more people who lead lives of simple decency than cynics like yourself, begging your pardon—for you're an excellent host, Emmet, and a better man than you think, I'll go bail—there are more such people, as I was saying, than you cynics—or should I say free-thinkers—are willing to admit."

"And the appropriate death?"

"Believing you're where you want to be even if you aren't. Having one last look at the miserable arseholes you've had to put up with and finding a reason to delight in their company, even if it's only to laugh at them. Remembering lost loves, if you're alone. Thinking back over a lifetime's doubt and sin and realising you always had faith in spite of everything. Then cutting loose and heading home," with a soaring upward—heavenward—motion of his hand.

Emmet pondered, fighting off a sinking feeling.

------

[2]Here's one for you: what if the Almighty Boss turned out to have the sense of humour of your typical boss or office supervisor, i.e., *absolutely none?* Not a pleasant thought, I agree, but one worth considering, in view of things in general, and so on.

"Very likely, Father. A trifle esoteric for a humble hotelkeeper to apprehend, mind you."

"Esoteric? Don't be talking, man. It's plain as cowpiss. Half the world's problems would go away if we all accepted God and, having accepted Him, admitted that we'd been looking for Him all along."[3]

Oh dear oh dear oh dear, was Emmet's reiterated cry of distress to himself; then, remembering the phone call of the night before, he tried to steer Father Doyle into less eschatological regions.

"You may well be right, Father. By the way, I had a question for you."

But Father Doyle was remembering a shady street between the Via del Corso and the Piazza Navona (Garibaldi? Cavour? one of those), the one with the ecclesiastical outfitters' shop next door to the trattoria where young Phil Doyle, that total stranger from a hundred or more years ago, first met slightly younger Tancredo Barberini, now a monsignor in the Vatican Overseas Secretariat —a French specialist, if memory served (twenty years in Paris, ministering to ministers)—the encounter taking place over a chilled bottle of Frascati on a mild May day with the wisp of a breeze off the Tiber and the snarling of Fiats and Vespas in the street outside; a toothaching gelato and supercharged cappuccino to follow, of course, then a final youthful outburst of optimism at the world and God and the future's winding path toward righteousness and reward before returning to the Gregorian and an afternoon of Canon Law or Dogmatic Theology . . . .

"He said he was a Redemptorist, I believe, a Travelling Redemptorist or something along those lines."

. . . *buon giorno, Roma!*

"A commercial traveller selling redemption, eh? Don't tell

---

[3]Hear, hear. Just what my Uncle Francis used to say—Auntie Nuala's husband? the Cardinal's secretary? that's the one—aye, he used to say something very like that when we kids were getting up to a bit of no good. Oh, he was moral, all right, was Uncle Frank, at least everybody thought so till they discovered those Wank-o-Rama videos in the garden shed. He repented after six weeks at Lough Derg, and Aunt Nuala got the shed and the videos as part of the out-of-court settlement (then the fun really started, but that's another story).

me—a Yank, was he? One of those Mormons?"

"No, no, no," said Emmet, peevishly. "You weren't listening, Father. I'm after asking you if you know anyone called Father Patrick MacCarthy, who says he's a Jesuit with the Travelling Redemptorists Mission or Redemptorist Travelling Mission or the Pisherogue Music Band or whatever the hell he called it."

"Do calm yourself, Emmet. A Jesuit, is it? You're taking a chance, asking a secular like me. They're the hard men, the S. J.s. How many divisions does the Pope have, quoth Uncle Joe. Count the Jesuits and multiply by ten, was Pius's reply.[4] Patrick MacCarthy? A common enough name in these parts—no, I don't think so, unless you're talking about Pat MacCarthy, the ultra-traditionalist over at Youghal. He might be a Jesuit, or he might not. Then there's Paddy MacCarthy, the Ballymahone man, but he could never be one, not with the way he has of giggling like a mental case if you so much as raise an eyebrow at him. There's always Padraig MacCarthy, of course, the dear old Bishop of Derrymoyle, but if he's a Jesuit, I'm Mr. Universe. I doubt His Lordship can even unzip himself without getting permission from his housekeeper, God bless him. Well, that's the list *in toto*, unless you include P. J. MacCarthy the Chinese missionary out by Slaneford town, old Missionary Position as we called him—I don't *think* he was ever defrocked, but don't quote me on that, Emmet. Someone told me he was once a monsignor, but I wouldn't swear to it."

"Slaneford, you say?" Emmet's tongue tiptoed from tooth to tooth in vivid token of his concentration as he wrote down names and addresses in a notebook, like a traffic warden. "But none in Killoyle itself, now? Is that right?"

"MacCarthy, MacCarthy. Let me see. No, that's all I can re-

---

[4]Yes, but then (and this is borne out by eyewitness accounts and an editorial in *L'Osservatore Romano*) Pius covered his face with his hands, burst into tears, and rushed madly from the room uttering a thin wailing sound that many of those present mistook for a Stuka, or a prototype V-1, hiding therefore behind the Bellini tapestries and planning to emerge when the danger passed, which it never did: seven died, asphyxiated (no S. J.s).

member. Unless—why, of course, how could I forget young Canon Patric MacCarthy (that's Patric with a *c*)? He was over in France, last I heard—he's quite a bon vivant—but he might be back. He can usually be found in the former bishop's residence at Ballyduff, not a bad billet, between you and me—it's some kind of college now, you know, or seminary—and let me tell you, in my opinion he's the most likely of the whole shower to be a Jesuit. Come to think of it, I believe he is. Actually, I could've been one myself, you know, if I'd wanted."

"Blast it, Father, that's five names you've given me now," said Emmet. "In as many parishes. Is that the lot?"

Father Doyle ignored the question, distracted by his own mental image of the zealous Philip Doyle of the Society of Jesus who never was (but who might have been), renowned for his quick wit and glittering eyes, fluent in many languages, lean and muscular in physique, ascetic in his habits (gazing through the smoke of his cigarette at the whiskey in front of him: oh yes, that would have been the best part, no fags and one chaste glass of wine a day), concert-level violinist, champion polo player and cricketer (better for the image than Gaelic football or hurling),[5] intimate of princes and prelates—private confessor, in fact, to the Orsinis or the Colonnas (or both)—and, last but not least, author of half a dozen or more trenchant works on belief, dogma, and the post-Vatican II Catholic weltanschauung! A Renaissance class of fellow, all in all, and the funny thing was, he was convinced it really could have been that way, with a touch more belief, and a lot more effort—but no more than the kind of effort any young man can make, if he's ambitious enough, which he'd never been (New Nubia, indeed!).

Tears threatened. It was time for the one o'clock Mass.

"Cheers, Emmet."

Emmet's farewell was barely civil. He was staring at the list in front of him.

"Five Paddy MacCarthys," he said. "It'll take all bloody week."

"Whiskey priests getting on your wick, Emmet?" said

---

[5] Whose image? The G. A. A. bends the knee to nobody, boyo.

Murphy.

"You keep out of it. The afternoon crowd's on its way, so look lively."

"Jawohl, mein Kommandant."

Emmet went home. Once there, he sat in his armchair and stared at the undulations of the electric fire and weighed Mac-Carthys in his mind.

"What's the matter?" His wife patted down her hat and coatsleeves, on her way to the one o'clock Mass at St. Oinsias'.

"Nothing," said Emmet.

She left. He brooded. Father MacCarthy or not (and Father Phil could bugger off, never mind his "you're a better man than you think you are": thanks for nothing, padre), there were other things he'd never mentioned to his wife, and foremost among them, taking precedence even over the odd flutter at Muldoon's and those extra pints of an evening, was the never-to-be-forgotten near-adultery of '89, when—en route home from the World Hoteliers' Congress in Lausanne—he'd been stranded in Geneva's snowed-in Cointrin Airport in the company of a hundred or more other passengers, among them Fiona O'Malley, manager of the Edward M. Kennedy Hotel and Inn in Westport, Co. Mayo: ah, Fiona!

Bloody hell, what a close call that had been, fretted Emmet, running his fingers through his ever-thinning hair; and yet what a truant thrill it still gave him to dwell on the possibilities! Yes, addresses and significant glances *had* been exchanged, along with superficially innocuous chat about the hotel business and its ups and downs and one bold comment of Emmet's, buttressed by booming laughter (itself built on the solid foundations of Swiss *Kirschwasser* and Alsatian Riesling, compliments of Helvetair), to the effect that he'd always fancied redheads, Fiona's shaggy mane being of a pronounced auburn tint! "Really?" she'd replied, coyly catching on, her gaze, alight with the blaze of sensuality, locking with his, aglow with *Kirschwasser* and lust. Eventually—inevitably, inexorably—the public address system announced (trilingually) the end of their snowy tryst and Helvetair 101's prompt departure to Heathrow and Cork International, precipitating a scramble for the best window seats in the course of which (alas!)

the imaginary lovers were separated by a boozy row of North Country hoteliers loud on unlimited Cardinal beer and chasers; only her eyes were eloquent, above the Scouse and Geordie merrymaking (and consequent groaning, on the descent to Heathrow). Farewell, Fiona O'Malley, sobbed Emmet, overcome then as now.[6] Once a devotee of the Westport Music Festival, he no longer dared venture there, and the name F. O'Malley, inscribed in the register of Spudorgan Hall last Easter weekend, had brought on a seizure that confined him to bed for two days of near-delirium, fingers plucking feebly at the coverlet, tended by loving Roisin who suspected nothing, yet (in her wifely fashion) knew it all . . . .

That thought decided him. He would make discreet inquiries in person among the indigenous Fathers MacCarthy. Once he'd nailed the culprit, he'd tell him to go to blazes and take all his fellow Jesuits or Redemptorists with him, then he'd sit down and confess everything to Roisin: the extra pints at the pub, the gambling at Muldoon's, the false marmalade, the inflated hotel bills, that day in Geneva . . . *everything*. It was the only decent thing to do. One thing was certain: his conscience wouldn't give him a rest until he'd done it.

Emmet mentally reviewed his decision. Three days should be enough to ferret out all five priests, and Wolfetone Grey could take over the running of the Hall in the interim. This was an alternative that Emmet himself might not have chosen, but in the rigid hierarchical rules of the place as set down by Mr. Carfax, the Director of Catering was next in succession to the Administrative Manager (and yet, and yet! Emmet still had doubts about that Wolfetone article in his entirety: the voice, the morals, those prominent metacarpals so obsequiously handwrung): so that, in

---

[6]Aye. Poor Emmet. It brings to mind the final quatrain of Hoolihan's "Ode to an Unremembered Dame, from the third year of a five-year stretch for armed assault, Maryland State Penitentiary, 1901":

> Adhu, acushla, bonnie lass
> Imparfait ungentil knight am I
> Yet these travails too, must die
> In the jug, as in storied Lyonesse!

effect, was that.

"Aye, so 'tis," said Emmet, conclusively. His words were throttled by the ringing of the telephone. He answered with caution.

"Ah?"

The caller introduced himself as Thomas Maher, "but you may know me as 'the Greek,' heh heh heh."

"No, I can't say I do," lied Emmet testily, well aware of the man's reputation as a public malefactor and purveyor of polluted drink at his bar, Mad Molloy's; less than charmed by this opening gambit, however, still less was he likely to accept Maher's invitation to go "have a jar," as the other crudely put it, over at the very same Mad Molloy's, miles away on the other side of town, on a Sunday afternoon, with dinner yet to be eaten, and the *Sunday Recorder* still unread![7]

"Business," replied the Greek, when questioned as to his motives, implying sterling opportunities for such as Emmet Power —men, that is, of discernment and good judgement, not unlike himself (mirth brutally exhaled), further identifying himself as a land developer and estate agent of some prominence locally. Emmet yawned; the near-narcolepsis induced by the words *estate agent* threatened to plunge him directly into a coma. Alert as the salesman he was to flagging interest, the Greek became urgent, wheedling, seductive.

"All expenses paid," he said, with another resoundingly insincere laugh. "In other words, the finest Burgundies in the house on the house, Mr. Power. Or clarets, if you prefer. Power's whiskey, come to that, on the rocks or off, heh heh heh."

"Well, I'm not much of a drinker, Mr. Maher," said Emmet, virtuously. "And almost never on a Sunday, if you know what I mean."

"I do, I do. Tea, then? Or would it be coffee that catches your fancy?"

"Ah now you're tempting me, as it happens I did miss my

---

[7]And a good thing, too, if you want my opinion. The so-called *Sunday Recorder*'s nothing more or less than a screaming upper-class transvestite rag, fit only for the parliamentary side of my you-know-what (if that).

coffee this morning, and I'm always in a terrible state when I'm denied the old matutinal java, God help us."

"Well, then, what would you say to a drop of Arabica custom-ground mocha-lemon Belgian chocolate café viennois with burnt cinnamon undersling?" came the silken purr, invitingly.[8]

"Burnt cinnamon . . . ? Get out of that, Maher. Well, all right. But not in Molloy's. Divil the coffee they drink in that shebeen, with the whole cellar awash in poteen, as everyone knows—sure, don't they actually try to flog the stuff from the bar? No, let's say somewhere else, closer at hand."

"The Bay Window," snapped the Greek, and hung up.

---

[8]Yum, yum! Reminds me of bygone days at Bewley's on Grafton Street, when the three of us would get together after the flicks and pour ten or more helpings of sugar into one another's tea! What with poor Toby snuffing it of diabetes at age nineteen, and Stevie following soon after, I sometimes wonder if I didn't have a pretty close call myself, but I'm down to two tablespoons a cup now, and the doctor's quite optimistic (but not too).

11

The Bay Window's bay window commanded a sweeping view of the Parade, the Strand, and the gunmetal sea.[1] Kathy was in the window seat, ideal for admiring Cherbourg-bound ferryboats out of Rosslare and pintail and teal grazing on the waves and flights of herring gulls against the gathering clouds of a pigeon-grey sky, but the view began to take on a certain sameness after an hour and a half. She drew irritably on her Grand Pagnol cigarette and funneled the smoke upwards, away from nonsmoking Strongbow, sprawled at her feet. On the table in front of her, coffee things were arrayed (cup, spoons, sugar bowl, etc.),[2] adjoining a plate littered with biscuit crumbs. She was on her second cup of Mediterranean coffee and was readying herself to leave for the garage to reclaim her newly refenestrated Rover.

At the next table, sitting over cold toast, was an old woman, silent but for the occasional deafening bronchial manifesto, her reward for a lifetime spent in the moist air and smokiness of Ireland. An American couple of roughly the same septuagenarian age smiled placidly over scones and jam at the next table down, and at the end of the row was a solitary young man, bearded and pale, unfurling blue ribbons of pipe smoke from behind the *Sunday Other*. Across the room, on the other side of a pastry table groaning beneath a Bank Holiday bonanza of Vienna wafers,

---

[1] Beyond which lies nothingness, to the left and right of Eurasia.
[2] Tea? Sugar? Don't get me started, now.

gooseberry tarts and seven-layer muesli cakes, Emmet Power, Murphy's boss—Kathy knew him to nod to—was deep in conversation with another, ruddier man she'd seen here and there. The other fellow was obstinately (and rudely, in Kathy's opinion) wearing a cloth cap, as if to reinforce the initial impression he gave of being a first-class piss artist. This individual was doing the actual talking, and the other gent was watching him sculpt in the air the wonders of his subject, whatever it was.[3] Kathy cared not; Kathy was bored. She'd had more than enough time to think things over, but had only succeeded in plunging herself into a funk. Murphy had to be told, and the sooner the better, but she wasn't looking forward to it, because in her experience, men were more like women than vice versa—in other words, the view of women, common in the lower kinds of popular fiction, as fickle, panting creatures prone to melodrama when thwarted, better described the man who'd dreamed that one up than any women she'd known, bar an aunt or two.

Phelim had been a case in point, God rest him. She recalled incidents: the time he followed home a reporter who'd scooped him on some news story, bawling insults at him all the way to Ballsbridge, then brassily denying it had ever happened until the man's lawyers produced a video of the episode made by a passing busybody trying out his minicam. That instance of manly behaviour had made a five-figure dent in their bank account, exclusive of costs. Then there was the time when he'd accused their neighbour in Sandymount of being a Unionist for planting blue and white irises in the same flowerbed as his roses, coincidentally (or not, claimed Phelim) on the same weekend as the Royal Wedding; only for the intervention of Phelim's boss, the editor of the *Clarion* (ex-member of the city corporation and also-ran candidate for the Dail), they'd have had a fresh lawsuit on their hands. Admittedly, it was a delicious irony, and one savoured by Phelim to the point of nausea, that the neighbour in question had later popped up on the front page of the *Clarion* for having planted, not irises, but Semtex, at the foot of the Parnell statue on

---

[3]Something to do with property values, maybe? Oh, I'm way ahead of you here, sonny.

O'Connell Street, thereby simultaneously revealing his own Unionist sympathies and vindicating proud (also fickle, wrathful, not-to-be-scorned) Phelim Hickman.

"What'd I tell ya? What'd I tell ya? Well? Was I right or wasn't I? Oh, you lot were laughing your bums off, weren't you, but who had the last laugh, if you don't mind?"

No, he'd never been one for excessive self-criticism, not to mention the kind leveled at him by others, e.g., his own wife. This was another trait shared by the men she'd known: vanity. Not surprisingly Murphy had it in spades, only with him it blended into paranoia, the way it tended to with strugglers on the lower rungs of the social ladder, and he could be a nasty bugger whenever she tried to spare his feelings by giving him a dishonestly upbeat opinion of his career prospects (shaky, at best).

"Give over, darlin'. What do you know about hard work? Sod all. I'm all right, Jack, eh? Nah, I'll get on somehow, you wait and see."

Condemned as she was (it seemed) to repeat the mistakes of her past, all she wanted to do was forget the lot for a while, starting with Murphy, with the help of Strongbow (good dog! he'd always warned her against him), a readable book or two, and, most of all at the moment, her trusty satellite dish and television. Kathy was no TV addict, nor yet was she a snob: the tube was a pleasure, an escape, even a tranquiliser, used in moderation, with an eye peeled for crap. After all, the signals bounced off orbiting objects in outer space must have numbered in the hundreds of thousands, but fewer than a hundred of them made it through to her set, and of these perhaps three were worth the cost of the satellite dish (£500 initial outlay, followed by monthlies of £15.50 until the year 2006): the German Military Documentary Channel (SiegKanal, Zweibruecken), the Italian Game Show Channel (Canale *Boum!*, Milano), and the Costume Drama Replay Channel (Yorkshireman TV, Hutton-le-Hole, E. Yorks). It was to tune in the last of these that Kathy was suddenly impatient to return home. Starting at half-two that afternoon, they were repeating the entire *Dr. Menace* miniseries, one of her favourites. Few TV shows she'd seen (or films, for that matter) had left such fond memories behind. Dr. Menace himself, played by Tex

MacGroyne, was your standard stooped, greying, middle-class quack stuck in a dead-end gynecological practice in a back street in the Lower Falls, but his patients were a scream, especially the unemployed ones played by Randi Wadd and Titi Ben-Gurion— although, quite frankly, the coughing was so violent in their first episode that Kathy had been tempted to switch off for good, but before she knew it—in the twinkling of an eye (or two)—those loonies had had her on the floor, creasing herself and no mistake![4] Granted, it was a silly waste of time, and the intellectual content was about the same as that in *Glam* (in a word: nil), but for a good old chuckle, you couldn't beat it, and Kathy felt in need of a chuckle or two.

"Just the bill, please," she said, to preempt the waitress's hovering teapot. Sensing departure, Strongbow quivered with excitement. On the way out, he turned and jeered at the assembled company.

"WAAAF! WOOOF!"

"Come on, boy," said Kathy. Strongbow obeyed, eager for the olfactory kaleidoscope of the great outdoors.

---

[4] I remember it well. My favourite was the one where Dr. Menace goes looking for a wife and finds a harem on the East Side of the Shankill Road, half of them with rollers permanently implanted in their scalps— of course, the others were bald, poor dears (or as near as makes no difference). Boys, the laughs we had over that one! Why, the Da was still doubled up three days later, with the nearest chiropractor twenty miles away, and in that weather, too! Never mind. A smile's worth a thousand sobs, as the Chinese say.

12

"Feckin' dogs," said the Greek. "At your feet or at your throat, eh? Now take cats, there's a superior species altogether. My cat's a tom. You should see him at the mice when he has a chance! Go it, Super, I say to him—that's his name, Super—"

"Come along now, Mr. Maher," said Emmet. "I'd love to hear about your cat's exploits, but another time will do just as well for that."

"Very well, Mr. Power. Your point's taken. Did I invite you to this randy voo to discuss my cat? I did not, as you quite accurately point out. No, I wanted to discuss something quite other, Mr. Power. Something to do with—" here he paused, melodramatically, "redevelopment."

Emmet yawned politely, fist against mouth ajar.

"Over the phone, you said business," he said. "Redevelopment may be somebody's business, but it doesn't sound like mine."

"It's every man's business who wants to pad out his savings account a bit, and what man doesn't?"

Such was the Greek's enthusiasm when he leaned forward to explain that his eyes seemed to precede the rest of him by a measurable distance. Once he had himself under control, he took a deep breath and confessed that he wanted to pull down Spudorgan Hall and replace it with holiday bungalows, an even or baker's dozen depending on land prices and revenue.

"It's my dream, to be perfectly honest."

"Sounds like a nightmare to me," said Emmet. "Pull down

Spudorgan Hall, indeed. Who do you think you are, King Kong?"[1]

"Now, that's no way to talk. I'm perfectly serious. The only obstacle is Carfax, and when you've heard me out, you'll agree he's not that much of one."

"Oh, he'd be quite an old obstacle, I reckon. He owns the place, don't you know."

"So he does, but he's an embezzler and tax evader. Anyway, *he* lives in America. You're the manager, and *you're* right here in Killoyle."

Patiently, Emmet interposed a thumbnail sketch of his job, laying out the limits of his authority, these being identical (as he understood it) with the threshold of Mr. Carfax's ultimate say-so. Even from far Amerikay (not so far, after all, in the age of fax machines and computer modems) Mr. Carfax personally had to approve anything involving permanent modifications, or "capital improvements," and usually didn't.

"For instance, last year I wanted to knock down the dividing wall between the dining room and the bar and build a single through lounge." Emmet's inward gaze misted over at the memory. "The plans were laid, the blueprints drawn up, the contractors hired. We were ready to go. Then old Carfax rang up the day the job was due to start and handed me my head, right over the phone, for taking a decision on my own. Christ, wasn't he bawling loudly enough for a Japanese tour group to hear, and didn't they have a good old chuckle over it, the bastards?[2] Anyway, that's the kind of man he is, Maher. Not to be trifled with."

"Do you tell me so, now. The hard man, is he?"

The Greek's eyes withdrew into pouches of mirth. Hastily, he fished from his coat a cigarette case containing cigarillos.

"Dutch," he said. "Van Hoot Extra Mild Schimmelpennincks,

---

[1] A venerable Irish name, traceable to the like-named Barony, and Cross thereof.

[2] Undoubtedly. Just think: in a hundred years, from being inscrutable nutters with bouffant hairdos and dressing gowns, committing suicide and chopping one another up like nobody's business—with that ghastly music of theirs plink plank plunking in the background—they've come to where they are now, viz., scrutably mad, like the rest of us (bar the bowing, of course).

Gollogly's got in a shipment last week. I'm trying to switch from the fags, you see. Have one. How's your coffee, by the way?"

Emmet agreed to a refill and selected a cigarillo to accompany it, accepting also a light from the Greek's proffered Dunhill lighter (a trifle vulgar, like the man himself, thought Emmet). Briskly puffing to ignite his cigarillo, Emmet caught a glimpse through the smoke of a yellow gleam in the other man's eye, and found himself wondering if Evil[3] had any real meaning after all, apart from its religious, or biblical, connotations; in fact, he was on the point of asking the Greek his opinion of the matter when he realised that he, the Greek, was the very object of his speculations, absurd as it seemed—so absurd, in fact, that Emmet let out a loud guffaw, unrehearsed.

The Greek prided himself on being something of a mind reader.

"I see you appreciate the situation." He gave a sympathetic chuckle. "Carfax is an old gobshite, right enough. The question is, how do we diddle him out of his own property? Well, we might not have to. I've been making enquiries down at the Tax Office, where I've a contact or two, and you'd be surprised what I unearthed about your man's tax payments—or should I say, lack of same?—before he left the country."

Emmet was torn. Gossip about the boss always added spice to an employee's dull diet, but it was unseemly, in his view, to sit about like a nattering fishwife, dissecting other people's petty misfortunes or all-too-human mistakes.[4] It was spiritually akin to watching television during the day, or reading the papers,

---

[3] Horned devils, hissing demons, the urge to slap one's fellow man, etc.
[4] Scarcely the exclusive province of wives, to be fair. I mean, the worst blabbermouth I ever knew was a whacking great hurling player from Kilkenny who'd be on the phone with the latest lowdown on the personal habits of his teammates, their bank accounts, wardrobes, drinking, taste in cars, etc., before you could say Croke Park. The odd thing was, it was all a load of cobblers. That's right, he made it up. It cost his side a goalie and two centreforwards before they caught on to him, but turnabout's fair play, as they say: one of the ex-centreforwards exposed him as an adulterer and philanderer of the worst sort (convent girls, two at a time in the UC Cork exam halls). Last I heard, he was a warden at

wasting your God-given abilities on the stale and tawdry instead of taking a fresh look at life, trying for a new honesty with yourself and others; not accepting change, in other words, when change was needed, as now, with himself, more and more, ever since that blasted phone call . . . and here was this Maher bleeder, trying to get him to hand over the keys to Spudorgan Hall.

"As the manager, you're the legal administrator of the property, which means you're allowed to close the place down if you've evidence of malfeasance on the owner's part. That's the law, and you can look it up if you don't believe me," said the Greek, hotly. "You don't imagine I'd rush into this half-cocked? I've done my homework, so I have. My research uncovered all sorts of other muck, too, like nonpayment of property taxes, movement of funds through a mysterious investment company in the Channel Islands, numbered bank accounts in Liechtenstein—very dodgy, all of it. At the very least, it explains Mister Bloomin' Carfax's sudden emigration to America, I mean, it's not as if he hadn't the nicker when those payments were due. Did you know he won Haymarket two years in a row, '67 and '68—riding a horse called Belly Up, if you can credit it—with the purse both times running into the six figures? If I'd laid out for an accumulator on those races, I'd be buying up half the seafront property in Florida myself. Begod, Power, your man must have been walking around in 18-karat Y-fronts without the Revenue Service ever knowing, and a hundred thousand Irishmen trying to keep body and soul together on the Sosh! It's immoral!"

Oh, the glibness of the rug merchant, the crocodile tears of the Gombeen Man!

Still, assuming Maher was telling the truth, Emmet had to admit there was room for a little ethical tut-tutting, but this was an assumption he was willing to make only on the principle that it took one to know one.

"Well, I never thought Carfax was a paragon," he said. "Sure, don't half the country cheat on their taxes, one way or another?" As he said this, he realised two things: one, that *he* had never

---

Letterfrack, and that was a good wee while ago. Moral: keep your cakehole shut, except in self-defence.

cheated on his taxes, for all his failings; and two, that, in the face of villainy (was there another word for it? expediency, perhaps? or business?) he had just sounded the retreat—turned tail and fled—set a course directly for the hills—bowed ungracefully out—just like the cowering majority of shirkers and malingerers who wouldn't recognise the right thing to do if it ran up and bit them on the collective backside.[5]

He scrambled to retrieve himself, watched with scientific detachment by the Greek Maher.

"Not that I condone it, of course. As a matter of fact, now that you mention it, we did run across some irregularities in the accounts, a while back, but everything pointed to an employee we later sacked, a right caffler named O'Moon—I mean, good riddance to him, I'm not about to hire him back, but come to think of it the accounts *had* been approved by Mr. Carfax before we turned up the discrepancies . . . no, no, this won't do at all, at all."

By allowing himself to be maneuvered into indiscretion as easily as a child lured with sweets, Emmet realised he'd fallen prey to the chief tactic of businessmen and spies. Of course, he'd always been a rank amateur in the so-called arts of the business world—was he not a Power, after all, and were the Powers not men of honour first and foremost, even at the risk of their lives? As his rebellious ancestor, Edmund Power of Dungarvan (would-be Lord Chancellor in the prospective Home Rule Government of Tone, McCracken, Bonaparte, and Co.), had announced from the scaffold that wintry morning in 1798, "Power will have another day," giving the world an aphorism and the Powers a family motto.[6] Emmet, too, had always regarded himself as a fellow who stood up for the things he believed in, a decent old skin, a man

---

[5]The liver-lipped, hair-oiled, jewelry-wearing sons of bitches, with their Swedish massages and Italian suits. I've seen enough of their sort to last me a cat's lifetimes, mostly down by the Four Courts, or stuffing their greedy gobs with expense-account lunches at Le Phacochère— sweet suffering Jesus, don't they have mothers, too?

[6]"Beidh la eile ag an bPaorach!" in the original. Two ironies befell poor Edmund then, the first being the total absence of Irish speakers among the assembled officials of His Majesty's Government (although, happily for posterity, a secret Gaeltacht scribe was present in the cheering crowd

you'd trust with your wife, your daughter, or your life's savings, a sound man altogether and definitely not one to be conned by a pop-eyed shagger who wouldn't be admitted to a public jakes without a reference . . . !

"Now listen here, Maher," he said, firmly. The Greek shot a glance at the numerous dials of his gold watch.

"Half-one already? You know what they say about having fun, Emmet, but I'm running late, so let me just quickly lay my cards on the table, then I must be off."

The cards he laid on the table, face up, totalled £15,000 annual base pay *on top of* Emmet's current salary;[7] the title Vice President Emeritus of Maher Enterprises PLC, the perks to include car, driver, and monthly dinners at the Mariners' Club in Youghal; travel to luxurious foreign capitals several times a year; the opportunity to style himself Doctor . . . .

"Doctor?"

"Aye. Tradition among us property men, if you follow me. Doctor this, Doctor that. I'm Doctor Maher to half the estate agents in the southeast. Everybody else calls me the Greek, by the way. Anyway, do think it over."

"And what would you want from me in return?"

"Ah, not much at all. Your front-row perspective on the hotel's financial situation, of course—you know, evidence of fiddled accounts, et cetera. That way we'll smoothly pave the way for the tax examiners and from there—bingo! He'll have to sell up, and guess who's going to be in the front row at the auction! Emmet me old love, your fortune will be made, rest assured."

The Greek buttoned up his coat, tipped his cap to a debonair angle, and left. Seized with an uncharacteristic thirst, Emmet called the waitress over.

"Are you licensed, miss?"

"Yes, sir. Until two o'clock."

"A double Black Bush, then. On the rocks."

---

of market-day onlookers), the second, sadder one having to do with his own prompt execution that deprived him of any other days at all, unless it was the Day Without End on the other side he was thinking of.
[7]Italics his.

13

"Don't you have a liquor license?"

"Yes, sir. But not until six o'clock on Sundays."

"God, it's as bad as the blue laws."

Like most Irish, Milo felt himself to be part American, as the best alternative to being part, or wholly, British, this in spite of his unwholesome experiences in New York and the great number of obnoxious American guests, mostly of Irish descent, at the hotel. Of course, most hotel guests were, notoriously, at least as bad, only there were more Yanks than, say, Germans (the loudest) or Japanese (the tightest).

This one was American, but.

"Well, sir, as I recall, no beer or wine is sold before noon on Sunday in New York State, and there are certain states where—"

"Yes, but New York is a law unto itself. I'm from Chicago, in Illinois, or Illi*noise* as you would say. And defiantly in these days of nationwide hypochondria, I have a stiff Scotch every night before dinner, or even two. Now you're telling me I can't."

"Unless you wait twenty minutes."

"Fair enough. You don't make the laws. Hey, where are you from, Niles? It is Niles, isn't it?"

"Milo, actually. I'm from Dublin."

"Duh-ublin's fair city / Where dah guh-urls are so pretty"?

"The very same."

"I'm Italian, myself. Tony Mastronardi. This is Trish, my wife. She's the Irish half."

"Nice to meet you, Miles."

"Milo, actually."

And so it went, indistinguishable from a hundred other pseudo-acquaintanceships between affable headwaiter and hard-drinking customer that invariably led to the bar after dinner and a series of expense-paid doubles and braying conversation about great business opportunities somewhere or other and how green, or rural/cold, or mild/backward, or promising/beautiful, or melancholy (or all the foregoing) Ireland was, as well as—in the case of the American Irish—loud lamentations for the good old greener days before cable TV and two-car families;[1] also, what a cultured fellow Milo was, for a waiter. Why wasn't he married yet? Why was he stuck in such a dead-end job? Therefore: why didn't he send his CV to the head office in Atlanta or New York or London—or Chicago?

"Place called Elmwood Park, actually, just outside."

"Sounds great, Tony. You know, I lived in New—"

"Oh, I don't know, Mike. It's boring, if you want to know the truth. I'd relocate over here like a shot, if I could work it out."

"Over my dead body," said the wife, whose living body was, to Milo, well worth a sly hooded glance as she strode off to the ladies', blue-jeaned hips swinging; sensing the risk of husbandly scrutiny, however, he adeptly transformed his sneak reconnaissance into the raised eyebrows of cool enquiry at the sight of Murphy standing in the doorway of the restaurant, waving his hands like an interpreter for the deaf.

Milo excused himself.

"I'm knackered," said Murphy. "Could you take over for me when the bar opens?"

After tense negotiations, Milo agreed, as long as he could keep the tips. It was against the rules for the staff to swap jobs, but common enough practice on a Sunday, when Management was

---

[1] Aren't they just like our own tweedy greeny crowd, with me old enough to remember Dev's Great Economic War when all we heard was prattle about snug cottages and gleaming hearths and a dear wee fairyland of a chaste, church-going, peat-powered Erin (no mention of the poteen, mind). Well, that lot could kiss my arse then, and they can bloody well join the queue to do it now.

away and the tips from the Sunday drinking trade were generous. On that Sunday, however, Milo had hardly taken up position behind the bar, after reassigning all headwaiterly duties to his two subordinates, when Management appeared, in the person of Emmet Power.

"Evening, sir." Milo moved to one side of the bar, the way he wouldn't seem to be officially behind it.

Power snapped his fingers commandingly.

"Rogers, bring a pot of coffee to my office. Make it strong."

These were the last words spoken by Management that evening. Power accepted the coffee with a grunt and closed the office door in Milo's face. Burning the midnight oil (or at least the 7 p.m. variety) wasn't a common sight, mused Milo—in fact, it was the first time he could remember seeing the boss on the premises of a Sunday, or indeed out of hours at all, devoted family man (or housebound bore) that he was. Could the trouble be at home? Or at the Hall?

Milo returned to his post behind the bar and watched the telly addicts congregate in time for Eurosport Sunday.[2] The two Americans were gone, no doubt upstairs (he fought off visions of blue jeans lying in a heap on the floor) . . . well, anyway, it was no time to ask the man for an advance, that much was clear, although old Power's troubles, whatever they were, could have nothing to do with him, Milo assured himself smugly; sure, even if the place were on the verge of bankruptcy, or about to be bought out by Arabs, or due for demolition, he'd find a decent job elsewhere, if he had to—and he had to, sooner rather than later, if he wanted his existence to culminate in something a sight grander than professional subservience and Saturday nights without end.

---

[2] Elf TV Satellite Channel 6, Sundays at 7:15, live from Amsterdam (or is it Rotter-?). I know it's the number one TV show Europewide, but (a) I don't give a toss for popularity, and (b) I could never stand that cheapjack of a host of theirs, that Joop den Uyl character with his double-breasted blazers and mirrored sunglasses. He did the narration for *Teaching Your Dog to Fetch, the P. G. Wodehouse Way* (or is it Wood-?) on UTV 2, and of course his accent was so heavy they had to have subtitles as well.

He was, after all, a poet, *à ses heures.*[3]

A sharp-edged specimen in his late twenties—Burberry, burgundy pullover, slicked-down hair—bought a pint and a gin fizz for himself and his not bad-looking but (Milo reckoned) slightly loose girlfriend, that slight looseness being precisely the unbidden agent needed to spin the old song around the one track of his mind: *oh sex, where is thy stingalingaling?* Before long, inevitably, he was thinking of Martine, then—surprisingly—of a girl antedating that French connection, one Millicent from the Isle of Man, formerly a Dublin streetwalker (Baggot Street, the Quays, the Canal), known professionally as the Manx Minx, a Douglas Polytechnic graduate in (coincidentally) French Literature and Celtic Languages, now the co-hostess of a feminist radio show beamed westward to the benighted Gaeltacht—where abuse of one's spouse runs rampant, especially on cold Saturday nights—as well as southeastward to France, chauvinist redoubt . . . Millie, then, was going back a while, almost to cherry-picking season at age nineteen or so. Actually, a much older lady had performed that

---

[3]Not that *that's* any excuse, whatever it means. Oh, very well, if you must. Samples, please, samples, as the headmaster said! Here's one of Milo's sober efforts (and the two of us are after asking ourselves why the poor soul drinks?):

Insolence Chastised: An Homage to King Malcolm X
of Orkney and Shetland (1244-1312)

Och aye, Jimmy, said stout Malcolm the Thane
Of the silvery beard and mahogany tan,
Tam-Tam our jester's gone awa' to his grave—
By my royal hand. His penalty's paid
For doffing his breeches to brazenly wave
His wee withered willie in Her Majesty's face!

His jinks were soon over, he fell to my blade,
Begging forgiveness of Malcolm the Great,
As my queen she rose, and said with braw grace
(Mickle sweetness and licht, the Sassenach way):
"No mercy, my liege! By Saint Andrew, you saved
Your dear wifey's honour, this April Fool's Day!"

service: Edna Gallagher, from Balbriggan, then thirty-seven, nurse to Milo's ailing elder brother Tim (the building trade—rickety ladder—concussions galore).[4] Perhaps unfortunately for young Milo, when they first met, over tea and toast on a November Saturday in 1979, Edna had just finished reading the collected works of Don O'Liffey, in which every nurse, governess or lady teacher is portrayed as a raging nymphomaniac.[5] With too spotty an education to relegate the stuff to its proper subgenre—i.e., neo-Victorian romantic pulp updated to include nudity—Edna, like so many autodidacts, mistook fiction for fact, and she and Milo made the beast with two backs that very same day, and repeated the miracle every Saturday night for six weeks, until one day Tim sat up in bed and shouted for his overalls and trowel, fit as a fiddle.

Edna's zeal (or, as O'Liffey would put it, "her ardent amorizing") threatened awhile to stunt Milo's growth, or, at a minimum, lessen his interest in normal girls. Happily, in this it failed; indeed, as a result of his experiences with Edna, Milo became as nearly obsessed with girls of every age and complexion as a man could be and still survive outside the psychiatric ward—blondes especially, but also redheads and those with ink-black tresses

---

[4]Get away. Ladders had nothing to do with it, rickety or otherwise. The plain truth is, Tim was a drug addict. Concentrate of peroxide was his favourite poison, followed by pseudoephedrine, in easy-to-swallow gelcap form; hashish, smoked; a 7 percent solution of neat cocaine; and Thayer aspirin, 750 mg./hr., taken with lashings of black coffee and the cheapest possible whiskey. If you ask me, he got what he deserved, no more and no less.

[5]*The Nutmeg Man, The Vinous Vigour of Valentine V, A Billowing Man, The Ostrich Eaters,* etc. The effect of O'Liffey's novels on the reading public of the '50s was electric but negligible. By the way, he bought a garage near my uncle's place, with the intention of becoming the Midlands agent for Hispano-Suizas and Borgwards. On being informed by Uncle Mike of the long-ago demise of those noble marques, Don struck him with his blackthorn stick—he rather goes in for stage Irishry—and screamed insults in the broadest Brooklynese. The case came up before the Sligo Circuit Court last week. As we went to press, the jury were still sequestered in the judge's sitting room, admiring his prints, hurling trophies, first editions of Padraig Pearse, etc.

"like the curtains of midnight." Brunettes, too, had their charms, of course, and as for black Africans, well, hadn't he always regarded Queenie Sheba, the Oscar-winning actress and hereditary Princess of Ganda, as the *ne plus ultra* of femininity?[6] As for Edna, she put the experience to good use and went on to specialise in the sexual disorders of adolescent males, receiving an honorary degree from a university in Saskatchewan (whither she later emigrated) and publishing two best-selling books on the subject.[7]

"A Ricard, please, with ice."

Milo's brain snapped to attention. Standing opposite him was the Kathy or Kate girl, or woman rather (rather!), glancing from side to side, as if looking for—

"Murphy? He's gone home."

Milo busied himself with the drink.

"Did he leave long ago?" she asked.

"Ehhm, yes," he said. "He was feeling a little tired," he said, with a knowing near-wink. "*Knackered*, actually, was the word he used."

She ignored him and lit up, exhaling the pungent smoke of a foreign brand.

"Oh well. Thanks," as he placed the drink on the counter. She held it up, frowning. "Um—the ice?"

"Oh, sorry," said Milo. He grabbed at the drink just as she was handing it to him, spilling some on the counter, most on her blouse. "Jesus Christ Al-bloody-mighty. I *am* sorry." He thrust a damp dishtowel at her and made scrubbing movements with it in the air. "Here."

"No thanks. I'll just go to the ladies' and wash it off."

---

[6] I always thought that was something Parnell said, but never mind. Anyway, if you want my honest opinion, well over half of those so-called African-American people are at least as black as the Protestants in the Six Counties, if not more so.

[7] *All Together, Now* and *The Teenager's Handbook to Undressing*; she claimed a success rate of 98.6 percent overall, slightly less for chronic wankers and Peeping Toms. Still, the gell did her best, as the Da always said—oh, he was a great fan. Her photograph adorned the inside of his boot closet until the rats finally got at it, just before he passed on.

A reek of licorice rose from the dishtowel as Milo mopped up the spillage, cursing himself.

"Well," he said, under his breath, "that did it quite nicely, didn't it, mister. Oh, that was a grand display of tact and grace, so it was. Nipping it in the bud before there's even a bud to nip, you unbelievable feckin' . . . ."

Surprisingly, she returned.

"That's, ah, em, on the house." Milo plopped an ice cube into the refilled drink. She smiled, and, against all expectations, his lust took wing and became love.

"Never mind that," she said. "It's not necessary."

"I insist," he said, boldly.

"Ach, all right."

She shrugged and took her pastis to a table in the dimmest corner, away from the TV crowd—and as far as she could get from him, pondered Milo, nodding resignedly, certain that it was so. Women were like that, and it made no difference if you'd seen them as God made them or not—as he had, of course, he was quite sure, thanks to *Quest* (that nose, though?) and the poor girl's own undoubted financial need those many years ago, taking her clothes off for money and celebrating every hill and dale in full Kodachrome splendour; the slightly sad smile he already thought sweeter than the Mona Lisa's; the full blonde hair; the unexpectedly firm jawline serving to accentuate the soft tones of the skin! Ah (he sniggered, sotto voce, his fingernails digging into the palms of his hands), he'd score off that arsehole Murphy yet, so he would, with or without the documentary evidence: herself in the altogether, posing buff naked for lubricious publications—yet, at this suddenly purer stage in the evolution of his feelings, Milo felt mild disgust at the mere existence of such pictures, but this blended uncomfortably with surges of sexual desire that ruled out any precipitate action, e.g., returning the rag to Leo's closet, or simply chucking it away. Anyway (he argued to himself), his life was as empty as his bank account, so there was room to spare for this Rubensian beauty to whom only Rubens himself (or Botticelli—or was it Tintoretto?) could have done justice—apart from Renoir, of course, the one who captured so well the strawberries and cream of the boulevard belles—and possibly that other Impressionist chap, the one with the Santa Claus beard—Manet or Monet, or was it Gauguin (no, he was the one with the Hawaiian striptease dancers); Monet, of course, husband of the all-too-mortal grey-eyed Camille whose Athena-like wisdom lay in marrying a man with a talent Olympian enough to immortalise her in paint rather than in the pages of a soloist's fantasy mag![8]

Incidentally, did Kathy (or Kate) have grey eyes, too (or were they blue)?

"Hey, Mike. Can you whip up an Irish coffee for Trish, and get me a double Bushmills on the rocks?"

And so the dreary round of chit and chat began again, and this time the wife was deliberately flirtatious, more in an effort to embarrass her husband than from animal yearning for Milo's puddingy bod. He knew this, but he played along.

"Almost married, once."

Milo acted his part to the hilt, almost as if he were hearty Murphy himself.

"Aw! She let you down, Mike?"

"Milo, actually. No, she gave it up as a bad job."

Kathy left quietly, her absence unnoticed until Milo glanced over Trish Mastronardi's shoulder and saw the empty glass—vacated chair—twice-used ashtray. She'd gone to Murphy, he thought with a spasm of jealousy, outwardly feigning delight at Tony's stories of Chicago winters and bloodletting on the trading floor; then apprehension and desire clashed in his heart, and for a moment it was like the old days, waiting for Martine to say yes (or at least *peut-être*).[9]

---

[8]What the blazes is he on about? As far as I can make out, the creature only posed starkers for a sex magazine—she wasn't the blooming toast of Paris.

[9]Now, as for that Martine article, if you want my opinion of it she got no more than she was worth, ending up with six kids and a dicey ticker when God had given her the chance, after all—the regulation Knocking Up Opportunity so to speak—but she was too good for him, I suppose. Well, maybe she was, but look at her now.

14

Wolfetone Grey was in his favourite armchair, flipping busily through the pages of the Leonid Glossovich classic, *Up and Down and Round We Go*. A woolen nightcap, pajamas, dressing gown, and threadbare carpet slippers caparisoned his frame from top to toe respectively, and saliva born of pipe-sucking trickled down his chin, forming droplets that fell gently onto the well-worn flagstones in front of the fireplace. A haze of bluish smoke encircled his head like a halo. Except for the soft crumbling of the peat briquettes in the fireplace, and a distant lowing sound, as of an unmilked cow, from the direction of his wife's bedroom upstairs (they had maintained separate sleeping arrangements ever since Mrs. Grey declared her intention of ending each day with a handful of Supersleep tablets), the ambient silence was broken only by his muttering.

"Where is it, drat it?" His fingers scrambled impatiently through the pages. "I know it's here somewhere." He was looking for the part where Glossovich recalls his first telephone conversation with God, at age nineteen. Framed in once-red felt marker now faded to pink, the sought-for passage jumped off the page just as Wolfetone's distress began to translate itself into underarm sweat and accelerated heartbeat.

"Oh, the dear Lord be thanked."

With a sigh of relief, he settled back and slurped comfortably at his unlit pipe. The familiar, oafish informality of the author's style, and the unpredictable vagaries of the English translation, soon held him once again in their thrall.

It was in the course of the summer of '37, at my grandfather's tiny dacha in Komsomolgorodok oblast, that I first made contact with the Supreme Big Guy and his messengers, recounts Glossovich.[1] *I was nineteen at the time and studying reptilo-amphibian biology at the Lysenko Academy of Sciences in Omsk. I was, therefore, quite interested in experimenting on frogs, toads, newts and their friends, like lizards and what not. So! There I was, back in the long-ago summer of '37, with like ten each of all species in a series of unlabelled boxes, hoping to crossbreed and prove superiority of Soviet science (telling the truth, I was looking for a Lenin Prize, maybe by year's end). Anyway, when my grandfather raised objections I reported him to OGPU as a serious revisionist deviant and succeeded in having him placed under house arrest in someone else's house. Mamushka and I were therefore alone in the vast echoing corridors of the little dacha, but she had been dead for many years—since before the third Five-Year Plan, in fact—so there was nothing to disturb my concentration, except the frogs, toads, newts, etc., hopping and crawling about. I observed their social activity to be high, by and large, but sadly remarked that interspecies intercourse, i.e., reproduction, was practically nil. To be perfectly candid, I was frustrated, I felt like a failure; I even stood up and swore, using the then-forbidden name of "God."[2] All of a sudden the telephone rang. Now this in itself was hardly an exceptional event, as Grandfather was on a Party line and could therefore expect to receive phone calls night and day and in between from commissars, regional general secretaries, army corps commanders, party ideologists, etc. So when I answered, I at first took the rumbling voice on the other end of the line to be one of these nonentities and—annoyed at being disturbed at the moment that my experiment was coming to a crisis, as I had just noticed a toad*

---

[1]Oh, one more thing about the old spirit-sleuth: he married his own aunt—not for her fortune, which was confiscated by the Commies anyway, nor for her ample thighs, no ampler than those of so many Russian women: he married her, he said, because (a) she smelled of *kumiss*, viz. fermented mare's milk, and (b) she was psychic counsellor to Comrade Stalin, whom she always addressed affectionately as Goose, from his real name (Djugashvili). The trick backfired. Two days after their wedding, she denounced Glossovich as a religious lunatic and had him shot, but—mysteriously—the firing squad's rifles were loaded with blanks, so he escaped to Tadjikistan, or some such place.
[2]In English in the original.

mounting a treefrog, or was it vice versa—rather dismissively, I offered to hang up in (if I can remember exact phrasing) his "stupid hideous face that is a replica of a water buffalo's except for great big ugly nose like a tomato" (or words to that effect), but when my interlocutor only laughed, my blood froze in my veins. After all, Grandfather had been a classmate of Vladimir Ilyich at Kazan University, and fistfighter of the revolutionary boxing squad during both 1905 and '17 revolutions, later decorated five times in one day! Few would dare to laugh at the grandson of such a man, even if he had recently been exposed as a revisionist deviant, etc.! Very few indeed!! In fact, ONLY ONE!!!

But my first surmise was wrong. Our heroic General Secretary had a high, squeaky voice, in contrast to his bold mustache, and this was a booming baritone like the kind that might belong to a big guy with a long white beard—of course, I would have recognised all this instantly had I grown up in the effeminate West and seen Hollywood movies, say of D. W. Griffith or C. B. De Mille; certainly I would have recognised the modus operandi when he started giving me orders, using the second person familiar and very antiquated grammar, even for Russian.

"Thou shalt go unto the mountains, there to dwell alone with Me.

"Thou shalt come down from the mountains and gather around thee men, and women too, of families that are called by names beginning with G.

"Thou shalt undertake the conversion of the world to My cause, with thy unhappy nation as the first battleground."

At that point—I was just beginning to understand what was going on, and believe me suddenly I needed to go to the bathroom like very urgently—the lines got crossed and I could hear the great booming voice continuing to issue the commandments (for such is what they were) to the switchboard operator at the Twenty-Fifth of October Shoe Factory in Komsomolgorodok, who of course thought she was dealing with just another midlevel apparatchik with too much vodka in him and transferred the call to our local militia station . . . .

"Hell!"

This in response to a sudden cascade of brownish sputum directly onto the crucial passage. Wolfetone's nervous attempts to wipe it off only spread the stain across the onionskin page and corrugated it to near-total illegibility, except for one phrase that dangled tantalisingly at the very bottom:

. . . driving a fine Moskvich sports car stolen from the murdered cop, I finally left the huge rambling dacha with its memories of Mamushka and Babushka and dancing the Kazachok (Hey! Hey!), and set out for the wide world to preach the word of "Bolshoi Malchik," Supreme Big Guy of the Cosmos!

"Ah, Glossovich, you genius." Wolfetone shook his head, as much in amazement at the Russian's sheer brazen audacity as in envy of the man's all-too-evident spiritual hotline to the higher regions! Yes, that review in the Sunday paper had brought it all back: the ambition, the fire, the zest, the bittersweet aroma of cheap petrol wafting on the warm June breeze . . . .

"Ach, God," exclaimed Wolfetone, lost in nostalgia.

Suddenly, the metallic shriek of the telephone jarred the soft torpor of night. TRIIIIIIIIIING-TRIIIIIIIIIING! it declared. Wolfetone, slack-jawed in horror, released his pipe onto the floor.

"No, no, no," he whimpered, rocking back and forth in his chair.

"Answer the bloody phone," Mrs. Grey thundered thickly from the top of the stairs.

"Shut yer noise, woman. I'm in charge here. Hello?"

"Grey? Is that you?"

For the moment it was: Wolfetone remembered just in time that the call had been initiated by the caller.

"Yes? Wolfetone Grey speaking. That'll be you, Emmet, will it?"

Emmet Power hesitated, with an audible rattling of spoon/ cup/saucer.

"Emmet?"

Wolfetone briefly tasted his own medicine: a nocturnal call, the ambiguity of a half-familiar voice . . . .

"Grey, listen to me now," said Emmet, decisively.

Relieved, Wolfetone listened, and learned that, for three days—starting punctually at half past eight on the following morning—he was to be in charge at Spudorgan Hall, in Power's absence.

"Business. Unexpected, you know. Called away all of a sudden, like. You're second in command, so you're the fella, I'm afraid. There's not much to it, really. Make sure they all do their jobs, just. Ah, it'll be easy enough, sure it will. There won't be any actual administrative work, as such, and you'll be well compensated, overtime scale of course. I'll be taking one or two of the account books with me to look over, you see, best be prepared for tax day and so on, eh, haha?"

"What are you on about? Tax day's not for months."

"Well, well, I know that, Grey. Only Mr. Carfax sent instructions. New procedures, you see, getting ready for the new computerised whatsit. Network? Anyway, I'll tell you all about it when I get back, aha haha."

Laughing giddily, he hung up. Wolfetone swore. Trust Emmet Power to chuck his responsibilities without even consulting the Board, just so he could go off on a little jaunt, probably (knowing him) with his mistress (or girlfriend);[3] it was highly irregular, totally without precedent, plain wrong. Last but not least, Wolfetone had no idea what was expected of him. He only knew that he would feel painfully self-conscious sitting behind that huge desk in the manager's office, giving orders to people who usually made faces at him all day, or simply ignored him, or threw away his catering proposals whenever they felt like it, the cheeky buggers—of course, on the other hand (now that he thought of it), *there* was an advantage to this sudden elevation of status! People would have to take a little more notice of him as Acting Manager, wouldn't they, if only for three days? Of course, he would have to act the part, if he expected deference from his subordinates. Gathering his dressing gown about him, he drew himself up to his full height and practised commanding, managerial gestures: the lordly sweep of the arm; the upraised hand; the languid wave of dismissal . . . .

His rehearsal was cut short by the full-blown emergence of a nagging question: WHO WOULD SHOP FOR SUPPLIES!?

------

[3]Rushing to judgement, as usual. Typical, isn't it? The Peter Principle all over again, if you take my meaning. It reminds me of the number of times the lads over at the employment exchange put me down as an out-of-work travel agent, just because I admitted I'd taken the ferry to Holyhead once or twice.

Laying in the grub was no joke in a hotel the size of Spudorgan Hall, never mind if the dining room was rarely more than a quarter full. That quarter complement could be pretty unforgiving if the anchovies were off, or the cream curdling, or the bread stale, horrors routinely encountered in downmarket lodgings but inconceivable at the premier hotel in a district renowned for its cattle, hogs, breweries, lush grasses, pilchard hatcheries, etc.! To obviate customer displeasure, Wolfetone usually accompanied Jean-Marc Wenger, Spudorgan Hall's Swiss cook (Swiss Hotel School, Lausanne; two years at Le Cuspidor in Marseilles; assistant to Gaston LeFlatulet at Chez Hervé in St.-Etienne (Haute-Loire)) to the market stalls on Haughey Circle every Tuesday at dawn and supervised the purchasing strategy of the forthcoming week's supplies, leaving the tactical details to Chef Wenger, whose ingenuity was radical to the point of nausea. That week alone, for instance, the first drafts of his menu had included kippers with asparagus and meringue puffs; duckling in turkey sauce with cauliflower medallions; curried baron of beef; tamarind shells *à la mode genevoise*, garnished with parsley and beetroot; Belfast Lough prawns in Sligo gravy; Bern salmon Basel style; kedgeree and diced ginger soufflé; plaice cutlets in aspic; julienned cloudberry tart *en croûte*; etc. Pretty horrible stuff, in Wolfetone's opinion,[4] but the customers went for it, and there were even rumours of a star in next year's Michelin guide . . . anyway, Wenger could probably manage alone (barely), but it was so much like Emmet Power to scatter orders about like posies and never give a moment's thought to how they would be carried out . . . !

Wolfetone decided to call him back and demand details. With an ambidexterity born of experience, he looked up Power's number in the directory while simultaneously dialing it.

Unexpectedly, a woman answered. Her manner was curt.

"He's out."

Wolfetone was about to make the usual banal acknowledgments and hang up when inspiration flashed forth, illuminating

---

[4]He's not alone in thinking so. I'm just after staggering back from the privy myself.

the way ahead, like Paul's awakening on the road to Damascus, or summer lightning over the high meadows of MacGillicuddy's Reeks![5]

He reduced his voice to a trickle, suppressing the tremor of excitement.

"Could you tell him Father Patrick MacCarthy called, please?"

---

[5]High meadows? In the Reeks? Try the Alps, son.

15

Despite his millions, Luciano Pavarotti sang almost as well as Di Stefano, especially Puccini, especially the "Nessun dorma" aria from *Turandot* that had unexpectedly (and absurdly) shot to the Top of the Pops as the theme music to some silly televised football championship or other, a few years back; never mind, thought Father Doyle, better for the hoi polloi to get their culture through the locker-room door, as it were, than not at all. Anyway, Di Stefano was still the best: that voice, as strong and supple as a man's innermost longings—or was it only because he'd actually seen Di Stefano once, at the Teatro Santa Cecilia, swapping arias with Maria Callas, that he felt so righteous about it?[1] Odd, by the way, how the Roman audience had shown their affection in the rudest ways imaginable to a northerner accustomed to devoutly hushed concertgoers (the Protestant influence, no doubt): paper bags crackling, catcalls, even a chorus of hisses when the two stars embarked on the Love-death duet from *Tristan and Isolde*. Tancredo had joined in the ructions *con gusto*, priest's collar and all, somewhat unsettling

---

[1]Indubitably. I mean, better than Pavarotti's just not on. For a start, I've never heard of this Di Stefano, and what's more, in my opinion a gal singing a fella's roles is the next thing to flaming transvestism and I don't care who knows it. Call me old-fashioned, but there it is. Anyway, once you've heard Pav in *Cav* and *Pag* (try the IMI cassette/CD recording: Pav and Joanie and the Hyde Park Philharmonic under Sir Charles Coelecanth—or was it Colin?) you can pretty well tear up your lease and hand over the keys, if you know what I mean.

his *amico irlandese*, but as he'd explained afterwards, flushing bright red over a Galliano or so at their favourite *bar-gelateria* near the Stazione Termini, that particular music was simply too German, so soon after the war ('47-'48, or thereabouts): too damned Wagnerian, in short, with the usual, not yet banal, connotations of stiff-arm salutes, Triumph of the Will, mass murder, and so on. No Christian forgiveness for that lot, at least not until the war generation died out, said young Padre Tancredo, neck muscles flexing in his *passione anti-tedescha!* How the lad hated the Jerries, back then. He probably still did, unless all those years in Paris had smoothed the edges. The French were a compromising lot, weren't they, by and large, less given to sustained anger than the Italians (not that he knew many himself, but still) . . . in any case, such passion for things secular was something Father Doyle could never share, with his growing contempt for the everyday world as a stage for mediocrity and ignorance and venality of every sort, not excluding his own—for instance, the bottle he kept hidden in his desk along with the packet of Craven "A" (good name, that), both of them now softly illuminated in the smoke-veiled light of the desklamp—starting, in fact, with his own weaknesses, and building on that flimsy foundation to include hypocrites, meddlers, and busybodies from every walk of (ah yes) life; *life?* For most people, it was little more than the absence of death, to all appearances a mere repetition of comings and goings, enlivened by television. As much as he loved life's more bearable aspects, Father Doyle detested its overall cheapening, and television was the worst cheapener, after overt atheism, politicking, money-grubbing, and the like; it was the very soul of popular culture (or should that be *soil*, as in night-?) and few things aroused in him a keener sentiment of disgust and betrayal. Popular culture, indeed! What a sham. When he read the newspapers, or (inadvertently, or when they were showing a BBC costume drama) watched the idiot box, or listened to the radio (except for RTE 3's operas and symphonies, with a dash of Irish traditional), he felt naked and alone in a glaring arena of clamour and harshness and—worst of all—*fashion*, all of them enemies of spirituality and art and the eternal: Satan's work, to be quaint about it, being carried out quite well, thank you very much, by unthinking minions, unbeknownst to themselves—sure, they'd never catch on, they'd deny they were doing anything worse than providing for their families, or helping the national economy, or ensuring a comfortable retirement in the Balearics, or Torquay (or Killoyle); but Father Doyle was well-trained, his still-sharp eye saw through the counterfeit everydayness, the calculated banality, the so-called Real World that lulled hapless Mr. and Mrs. Everyman into their semidetached dream with all mod cons (two cars in the garage, cable TV, microwave)! *He* knew that underneath all that was the same old come-hither, more modern than the flamboyant horned and tailed galloping about of yore, of course, you couldn't accuse Old Nick of not being up-to-date, no, he'd studied us well, he'd learnt to ape our mannerisms, he'd metamorphosed into a myriad of scientists and television personalities and pop stars and journalists, and now—*voilà!* It was all going his way, viz., straight to Hell: churches emptying, crime on the rise, Hindu and Eskimo and animist and God only knew what other gods banishing the One True (the return of the pagans: Pan's revenge), sex turned into the reductio ad absurdum of all human desire, modern education become the funeral pyre of our hopes, beauty unknown, ugliness revered, everyone (in short) rushing pell-mell towards that spiritual wasteland from which they'd emerge only as reborn servants of the Fallen One!

Or so it seemed to Father Phil, in pensive mood.

He paused in his ruminations to add his voice to Pavarotti's in the next selection.

"Not now, Father," pleaded Mrs. Delaney, his housekeeper, from the next room. Loud thumps emphasised her point, but he defiantly soared to more ambitious, near-falsetto heights:

"OOO-na fooorteeeevaah LAH-cream-AHHH."

A cough loitered with intent. He stopped singing and, instead, emitted via the opposing orifice a sound similar to that a rubber duck might make, if trodden on heavily.

"Take that, Mrs. Delaney," he muttered.

How pathetic to be intimidated by one's housekeeper, for God's sake! Worse than being a henpecked husband,[2] because

---

[2]Than which there is nothing worse, unless you're a cockpecked wife.

there were none of the presumed compensations—presumed, mind you, but by no means guaranteed, from what he'd heard. Hadn't his own big brother Ronnie hauled his missus (a slip of a girl but stronger than she looked) up before the bench, accusing her of denying him his conjugal rights for six months at a stretch? And her excuse, poised on the cusp of a sob, had been that whenever Ronnie wanted . . . *that*, it was Saturday night and he'd a drop taken and was in no way fit to father more children, not on top of the five they already had, and she'd not be a party to bringing infant drunkards into this vale of tears, doing her level best to bribe the judge with tears of her own but failing to charm the jury, ten hard men and two harder women who returned a verdict of guilty as charged and got her to swear conjugal loyalty—in other words, spread 'em, girl! It was an injunction she'd evidently obeyed without delay, the outcome being Father Phil's new nephew Festus, born the exact length of one gestation period thereafter and raising the brood's grand total to six, with another said to be on the way; and during the week or so that followed the trial, wouldn't you have thought Ron was the King of the Great Blasket Island itself, what with his brays of triumph and hipwise swagger in all the pubs of the town?[3]

"God, what an arsehole," muttered the priest, through an exhaled thunderhead of cigarette smoke. He'd never much cared for his big brother, if the truth were known. Apple of mumsy's eye —bah! Their old man wasn't fooled, at least. He'd seen through his firstborn from the day he caught him behind the privet hedges at Brookeborough raceway, peppering horses' backsides with an airgun, the way he'd make the odd fiver from punters not too proud to give others' odds an extra handicap. Of course, Ronnie got his own backside nicely tanned after that episode, but devil the lesson it taught him; no, if experience ever spoke to a thickhead like Ronnie Doyle, it was in muted tones—sotto voce—or not at all, as with (to be honest) so many others as well,

---

[3]It's like the Da always said: a man's intellect should be measured in inverse proportion to how loudly he speaks—and never trust a fella that talks at a higher pitch than the noon whistle at the Guinness brewery! Do you know, the wisdom of that man beggars description, so it does.

when you thought about it, as Father Phil did, with unnerving frequency, not being in his opinion the aptest student of experience himself. The sum total of what he'd learned in his sixty-eight years (apart from the truth of the old Greek's remark that all he knew was that he knew nothing) was to believe in belief against all evidence to the contrary, thereby making the best of a bad bargain and shoring up the defenses against Satanic doubt, or belief in the unbelievers: *Lord, help thou my unbelief!* If only it were easier in the normal course of things, on a clear head, in ordinary streets, on an ordinary day, amid ordinary bustle. Some couldn't take it, Freddie Stripling for one, yelled at by unseen voices until he up and headed for the five-floor drop, restrained at the last moment by (who else?) his housekeeper. A sad case, but the monsignor was an austere and anguished man. He'd have done better to unwind now and then, put his feet up, have a cigar, watch television—*aha! how subtly doth he weave his web!*

Father Doyle's own nightly drinking and secret smoking (not so secret in the stale air of mornings after) were, he realised, symptoms of the same balancing act, as were his lapses, public and private. The dear knew he wasn't as young as he'd once been, but forgetting the better part of the sermon when he'd already delivered it twice—God Almighty, what would he do next? Wet himself during confession? He'd done it once, not recognising the sensation at first—taking it, in fact, to be either (a) gas, or (b) his hernia uncoiling itself (then the stain, the whiff, the shame) . . . and what else? Drop the next line of the Our Father? Not impossible: he'd learned his Paternoster in its grand and glorious mother tongue, after all, not vulgar *Sachsùn*.[4] Grope members of the congregation? Unlikely. This particular servant of Christ took his vows about as far as most priests did (or had ever done, piety being a relatively recent innovation in the Church, what with the Medicis and monastic orgies and popes like Leo X, the Henry Ford of the relic trade, who said, back in 1500 or so, "This myth of Christ has served us well," while cackling over the year's balance sheet: plenary indulgences in one column, relics in another) . . . and yet! What was the point

---

[4]Ir.: Saxon.

in abstaining from sin when the very notion was under siege? Abortion rampant, the sacred debased—everywhere, really,[5] but like most trends it got started across the Atlantic, where priests wrote best-selling pulp fiction and went about with one hand in their trousers and the other in the till . . . not that Ireland was free of such things, of course, with the nation's centre of gravity shifting to the cardinal's residence in Armagh every time there was a referendum, or a general election; so, as viable sins permissible to the muddled but rigorous priest that he was, that left whiskey and tobacco, tried and true friends of the friendless, boon companions of bachelor nights, mainstay of many a publican's fortune and soldier's Dutch courage, innocent failings for the most part, winked at by God and Man alike—sure, wasn't it the oldest of Celtic customs, going back at least to wild-haired Brehon days, to overlook a good man's only weakness, that good man more often than not being a priest, or bard, or mumbler of mumbo jumbo written or spoken, drunk or sober? In the words of Father Phil's own mother, invariably repeated on Saturdays and market days: "Yer dad's a fine and daycent man the way he is, and only for the drink he'd be a friggin' saint."[6] Could the same be said of the son? Sentenced by his calling to die childless, a disused locomotive parked on an overgrown siding, *off the main line of Life* . . . ? This image gave him pause. He reached for the bottle, poured, sipped; reaching then for the metaphor, he held it out at arm's length, turned it over, and examined it from all sides before recognising it as one among many items left over from his salad

---

[5]Everywhere, is it? Speak for yourself. I've been going to confession on and off since 1934 (mostly off, since '68), and if I've learned one thing in my life, it's that the Irish church is a hard man altogether.
[6]Isn't that just like dads and uncles? Take my Uncle Francis, for one: rumour had it he was in with the Opus Dei crowd. Well, maybe he was and maybe he wasn't, but he did always favour black shirts and pullovers, and one night I caught him saluting himself in the mirror, wearing nothing but black footer bags! Anyhow, after the video scandal, he led a retiring life, mostly in the olive groves around Seville, preaching to the shepherds and fashioning combs and toothpicks from fallen tree branches. They fetch quite a handsome price, now that he's been beatified.

days, the baggage wagon of youth hitched to yesterday's Belfast–
Dublin express, via Lisburn, Dundalk, and Drogheda . . . that
metaphorical siding's original, if memory served,[7] was somewhere outside Drogheda, and on the other side was a brick wall,
beyond which the chimney tops of a mansion, also brick, pro-
truded above the treetops like donkeys' ears. At the end of the
siding was a faded sign that read *Dillrea Manor Halt*—redun-
dantly, as nothing on rails had halted at Dillrea Manor since the
days of gaslight and hansom cabs. It was a fine place for a young
man's mind to people with ghosts, and a logical place to translate
into a metaphor for life's less-than-happy endings, in much the
same way as the statue of Henry Grattan on College Green—and,
by extension, the all-encompassing history of central Dublin,
from the Viking era (the Quays) to the Ascendancy (Grattan, his
parliament), via the Elizabethan age (the gates of Trinity, Trinity
itself)—appeared in his mind whenever the subject of history,
Irish or otherwise, arose in words or memory, although the
(admittedly infrequent) mention of H. Grattan, Esq., per se
tended, illogically, to evoke a pristine mental picture of the market square in Omagh, Co. Tyrone, hometown not of Grattan but
of Benedict Kiely the once-poor scholar; and on those rare occa-
sions when Ben Kiely was thought, or spoken, of, with a supreme
sense of comedy (Ben being quite a Nationalist) Father Doyle's
psycho-cinema ran a jiggling old reel of Union Jack-festooned
ferryboats setting out from Dun Laoghaire in the days when it
was called Kingstown and the Union Jack flew from every flag-
pole in Ireland, North and South![8]
   But when he thought of youth, he thought of Rome.
   Coincidentally, as Father Doyle's thoughts roamed to that
city, so did Pavarotti's, with the result that both of them, ignoring Mrs. Delaney, offered up "Arrividerci Roma" to the spirit of

---

[7]Your past is served, sir, as the Da used to say whenever bill collectors
came calling. Once he said it to Des Neeson the bailiff, who didn't take
it at all well and stood on the doorstep mumbling threats until it was too
dark to see; *then* he slapped him with an eviction notice! Needless to
say, Da slapped him back, but to no avail.
[8]Up the Republic, as my Uncle Mike always said, Sunday mornings
when I was applying the wet towels.

the Trevi Fountain, one of the few paganisms Father Doyle had ever permitted himself. How many pennies had he thrown in that fountain? More than a pound's worth, surely, over that year of nocturnal wanderings by the antic moon and daily walks in the imperial sun; yet—even with all that investment—he'd never returned, except, as now, in his dreams. It was ridiculous, absurd, unforgivable! Canada he'd seen, and America, and wretched New Nubia; Venezuela, and Surinam, and Brazil, too; of Europe's Catholic heart, he knew Alsace, the Rhineland, and Bavaria; Poland even, and the Valais, and the Limburg province of Holland; Belgium, as well, and Iberian provinces beyond the counting of them; but after a lifetime's roving hither and yon, not once in the intervening forty-odd years had he managed to extend his Italian wanderings below (say) Rimini, or Siena!

Still, if there was anything to that old fairy tale, he'd make it yet.

Pavarotti fell silent. To fill the void, Father Doyle sang the first words of "Three Coins in a Fountain," dressing his imaginary self in summer whites beneath a broad-brimmed hat (Pope Phillip I?) to stroll the sweet-breezed expanse of Piazza del Popolo in the light of a Raphael sky . . . .

"Three coy-ins in a fowan-tain," he brayed. Suddenly he cringed, partly at the concomitant thought of Italo-American crooners and their horribly bejeweled hangers-on,[9] and partly (indeed, mostly) because a brand-new pain chose that moment to put on a short but memorable demonstration. It skipped nimbly from his right shoulder blade to the approximate area of his liver, or greater pancreas region, en route lassoing his diaphragm with barbed wire and poking a red-hot finger into his chest, achieving its full effect when the lasso tightened momentarily and the fiery finger probed deep enough to bring out sweat on his brow. After a few seconds that stretched into micro-eternities,

---

[9]I know what he means. Once we went to Las Vegas, and the jewellery! I could hardly see my hand in front of my face, the glare was so intense. The doctor told me later that my symptoms were identical to snow blindness, and prescribed tinted contacts, or a corneoplasty to inflate the eyeball.

the pain slackened and vanished, abruptly and completely, except for a twinkling of residual painlets up and down his right arm— his *right* arm, mind you, so it wasn't . . . .

Father Doyle put down his drink with a hand that trembled ever so slightly.

"Baldy ballocks," he gasped.

Later, in bed, he spoke familiar words of comfort, to himself and another, hailing she who was full of grace. There was a church, he remembered, on the Via Bonifacio, near the Gesù, where beggars gathered, one of many shrines to the Virgin— Santa Maria del Cielo? Della Grazia? Santa Maria de something. The priest there—Bob Whalen, as he remembered, from the Irish College—was a good soul, utterly devoted to Mother Mary in an old-fashioned, pre-Vatican II way; in fact, he claimed she'd cured him of the malaria he'd contracted on mission in Central Africa, as well as of a number of lesser ailments: sinusitis, asthma, bronchitis—although that could just as easily have been the Roman climate by contrast to his native Donegal's (or was it Sligo?). He'd be in his late seventies or early eighties if he were still alive (*tempus fugit, irreparabile tempus!*), yet it was easy to believe he might be, with his unquestioning faith in the Holy Mother and the happiness she'd given him. Surely that was all the cure a man needed! Thinking of Bob Whalen at that moment for the first time in years, Father Doyle felt envy entering his soul, also for the first time in years, and he resolved to purge it by looking up Santa Maria de Whatsit and its pastor without delay, on his very first day back in Rome.[10]

---

[10]Rome the spiritual or Rome the temporal? Aye, it matters (see below).

16

Murphy was tired, but not too tired to respond to a pretty girl's smile, and although he might have his doubts about Doreen Grey's intellect, there was no doubt she made the most of her face and figure.

"I was on my way home," said Murphy. "Just stopped in for the one drink, like."

"Oh, come on," said Doreen. She was wearing a blue pullover, stretched rather tight for a Sunday. He tried not to look, until it became obvious that she wanted him to.

"You're looking well, Doreen. Getting lots of exercise?"

"Tons. Where've you been hiding?"

"Hiding? Not at all."

This duel of double-meanings was, of course, as old as deception itself. Murphy felt the weariness of the games-player descend on his shoulders, and for an instant all he'd ask from life was an armchair, a can of lager, and a good film in the video player: a moment of calm, in other words, a respite from the unending hunt, although he'd gone too far for that, as he would cheerfully admit (but not to a gal). It was what set him apart from the crowd. Once a Don Juan, always a Don Juan, even if, at some distant date, he officially quit the game for the sake of respectability and a better job in a proper city, where the game was high stakes and Killoyle's good-lookers would be Dublin's or London's backstreet bints![1]

---

[1] The big city, eh, where the fellas have shoulders broad enough to fill the dance halls and the gals are all legs from the hips down—or is it vice versa? Either way, I'll stick to the small-town life, thanks very much.

He bought her a g-and-t on the rocks. His was a pint—Murphy's, of course.

"Watch the head," he said, with stern authority. The curates behind the bar at Mad Molloy's had a thing or two to learn about well-poured stout.

They found a table in the corner next to the fruit machine, down from a vociferous group of regulars. Doreen presented a cigarette to the flame of Murphy's lighter, inhaled sharply, and exhaled the smoke in nostril-tusks.

"Good luck," said Murphy.

"Cheers."

She was a redhead, but without the freckles. Her eyes were large and blue and would inspire comparisons to a doll's, if their gaze weren't so liquid. Murphy stared back, frankly admiring, realising that he did quite fancy her, after all; granted, she was only a salesgirl at Woolworths, but like him she had ambitions, so it was natural for her to talk of them and equally natural for him to lend a sympathetic ear, and even talk of his own.

"We're big-city people, Doreen. Dublin's the only place for us in this country."

"Actually, to tell you the truth, I'd just as soon get out altogether," she said. "I've a cousin in Canada. She tells me there's lots of Irish out there."

"Wouldn't your family help?"

"Get away. My dad went mental just because I moved out of the house. He'd disown me if I asked him to pay for a plane ticket to Canada."

"Aye, he's a right old fruitcake, your da."

"I don't know I'd go that far." Miffed, she looked away.

"I only meant he's the bit of an eccentric, you know," said Murphy. "Nothing wrong with that. I'm all in favor of eccentrics—isn't it a grand old Irish tradition? Anyway, I'd take your da over any of the other higher-ups at the Hall, I can tell you."

Underlings both, they went on to complain about their superiors. Emmet Power wasn't too bad as bosses went, only a touch moody, said Murphy, and tight as a Presbyterian, whereas Doreen's manager was an actual Presbyterian from Cavan and about as keen on makeup, short skirts, days off, etc., as Oliver

Cromwell ("actually, that's what we call him behind his back: Cromwell"). This led them once again to measuring the mean boundaries of Killoyle by the unlimited horizon of their ambitions, i.e., faster living, fatter chequebooks, bigger cities, etc., which brought the conversation in a circular fashion back to their dreams of the future and another round, paid for by Doreen like a real sport.[2] When the closing bell rang, they were still so deep in talk on mutually sympathetic topics that it seemed logical to continue elsewhere—say her place (nearer; almost next door, in fact)? Or his (more spacious; no snooping landlady)?

These coy questions of geography were in no way inimical to the final decision. That had been a foregone conclusion from the moment Murphy entered Mad Molloy's, as both recognised. What only Doreen realised at this stage, however, was that a change of pace was in the offing for Murphy, and that it was somewhat closer at hand than he might have hoped.

---

[2]This round-buying will be the death of the Irish nation, you mark my words. Once I was conned into buying eleven in the space of a single wet lunch, with no one else in the bar!

17

According to the Meteorological Office, the first days of that final week in October were the warmest for the season in southeastern Ireland since 1898, owing to a low-pressure system that was moving in over the European landmass, stalling the Gulf Stream around the Western, so-called British, Isles and raising the temperature in Killoyle and environs to the record heights of 89.9 degrees Fahrenheit by Tuesday at noon. Bikinis were sighted on the Strand that day, and the pristine lawns of Parnell Parade were adorned by half-undressed bodies, some so blindingly white that Roisin Power, on her way to The Shops, blinked hard, bedazzled.

"Goodness me, it's like Spain," she muttered, reminded of their last long holiday, three years before. The beaches of the Costa del Sol had been one great mass of Hiberno-Britannic tourists slowly frying in the sun, with a good number of them on the critical list by the time the beer wore off;[1] indeed, deaths had been rumoured, and at least one attempted suicide. If these

---

[1]Watneys' Red Barrel, no doubt, known locally as *el baril rojo de Torremolinos*, a fine brew, and one I enjoyed quaffing in Shavian quantities, as you might say. Ah we had a grand old time, so we did, only there was one misfortunate occurrence that marred our visit to sunny Spain. Isn't it always the case? Wait till I tell you, so. On the last day but one, the Da was driving back from visiting the Blessed Uncle Francis in the olive groves of Seville when his motor—a rented Seat bus, just the thing for a real busman's holiday, in a manner of speaking—gave up the ghost just outside the village of Los Maricones (or was it Macarrones? don't hold me to it, now). Anyway, he tinkered with the wires and steering wheel

young people didn't mind out, she thought, they'd be red as lobsters, blistered, squirming like souls in torment! The image, icon-inspired (Sacred Heart, Saint Sebastian, etc.), was too much for her.

"I hope you're using sunscreen," she said to an undraped couple sprawled near the kerb.

"Great idea, lady, ya'd not have some handy, wouldja?" said the youth.

"You know, I meant to remindja before we left the house," said his girlfriend, a sloppy article with teeth that would grind barley. She had a tattoo on her arm, Roisin couldn't help noticing, that depicted four intertwined limbs, at least one of which was neither hand nor foot, but, rather . . .

"How disgusting," Roisin's voice trembled in a near-shout. "You've no respect, none of youse." They mocked her with shrill laughter as she hurried away, moaning: oh God, oh God, the horrid wee creatures, what made them that way, didn't they have any standards left? Then she remembered her own boy Sean, in the Maze these five years and still threatening a hunger strike if

---

and what have you, but nothing worked, so he stuck out his thumb, resigned to hitching a ride. Happily (as he thought) he got one right away (in more ways than one, if you take my meaning), and the icing on that cake was that the driver was to all appearances a real knockout: a gem, the princess he'd dreamed of meeting since dear Mumsy died! "Hello, big boy. Would you like to come to my bedroom?" she enquired, in the bold way foreigners have. Well! If she was offering him a cup of tea, doughty Da was on, right enough, so they repaired without delay to her penthouse room in a Moorish lean-to near Granada! Hardly had they entered her abode, however, than—without so much as a by your leave—she undressed and flung herself at him, revealing herself to be a man from top to toe, including you know what, and poor old Da only hoping for a quick cuppa! Boysoboys, he didn't stop screaming until we woke him up two days later, and you couldn't pronounce the word *Spain* in his presence after that if you knew what was good for you—or even words that sounded like it, like *Spam*, or *pain*, or even *Spillane* (our neighbours downstairs in the Northside days, tinkers it was rumoured, though no one ever proved it one way nor the other). Still, like I always say: with foreigners, a good insurance policy's the best policy.

the British Government didn't announce an unconditional with-
drawal from the Six Counties: good God, it made you wonder.
Why have children at all?

She was rattled at the thought, and considered going home
then and there, but the weather was lovely, and it was pleasant
enough to walk in the shade down Behan Avenue to the sunlit
Strand, with white sails on the horizon and the ice-cream man
jingling his bells. She breathed easier. The Strand and its sights
and sounds (and smells, especially) was a time machine that
whisked her away to a more distant past than the Costa del Sol,
as far back as one summer in Bundoran in '56—or was it '57?
The year, anyway, when her father had bought their first car,
a shiny new Morris Minor (black, with whitewall tyres and red
leather seats), the same year they'd moved into the new redbrick bungalow with indoor flush toilets and electric heating
range out Raheny way: gracious living in suburban elegance, as
Mam had so often, and so boringly, said, contrasting their new
life to the grey boiled spuds and daily drubbings of basement
living in the Liberties . . . ah, they were good times, thought
Roisin, nodding sagely, good times indeed, especially the holidays, that hard-earned annual fortnight in Bundoran for
Dublin's deserving ex-poor! Sure, she'd loved it by the ocean,
with the crested breakers of the Atlantic incoming, outgoing,
incoming, outgoing, forever and ever, in the words of the song
(Bobby Darin? Jimbo MacCloonichan? Elvis?);[2] the mewing of
the gulls and curlews blown about the windy sky like scraps of
paper; Dad stripped to the waist, fag in mouth, giving the car
yet another going-over with the wax and chamois; young Petey
with his forelock *à la* Fabian standing up like the mane on a
rocking horse; Sissy already half in love with Bob the house-

---

[2]Jimbo's the boy. I remember as if it was yesterday. "Incoming Out,
Forever": the hit of '57; you heard it in all the dance halls, even up
North. I spent a week at Portrush that year, and every night we were on
the tiles at the Seaview, with the jukebox playing that song about 732
times in a row. I wrote to Jimbo soon after that, but his secretary told
me he'd quit singing to join the army's much-admired *Privates on Parade* revue. What happened then is anybody's guess, but he never had
another hit single.

painter, later (and still, amazingly) her husband; sand castles and wading pools, and a lucky girl's first kiss (Tom Kennedy, the solicitor's son from Killiney: she remembered yet)—wasn't it that ideal summertime everyone was supposed to have had, as a child?

Except Emmet. He never spoke about his childhood unless she brought it up, and even then his only answer was a grunt, or a grimace.

"And now he's taken off by himself for three days and I've no idea where, or why," she said to Mrs. Delaney as they browsed through the vegetables at the Haughey Circle market. Roisin chose half a pound of ruby King Edwards; Mrs. Delaney, a turnip. Neither, however, had much hope that their menfolk would be in the mood for colcannon, or boxty.

"Father's consoling himself again," said Mrs. Delaney.

"Ah no. He isn't."

"Aye. Two bottles this past week that I'm certain of. Probably more, hidden away. And the way he carries on, at night, with that Eye-talian music of his. Stocious drunk, he was, last Sunday night. I'm just afraid the poor old fella's turning permanent, like."

"Now, my Emmet," said Roisin. "He went into the dumps about, oh, a week-ten days ago, and whenever I ask him what's the matter, he says Nothing or Leave me alone or worse. Once he even got up and walked out when I came into the room, just like a sulky little boy. Men get that way, you know. As if they were only waiting for the chance to prove what kids they still are. And now he's off somewhere, looking for someone, or something, and that's all I know about it, which is damn all. He gave me a phone number, mind you. The Bishop's Residence at Ballyduff, so I'm assuming it's not a woman he's after. Do you happen to know what bishop that might be, if any, Mrs. Dee?"

"I'm afraid not, Mrs. Pee. I've my hands full as it is, and he's only a parish priest."

Mrs. Delaney's devotion to Father Doyle was downright wifely, thought Roisin, not for the first time. Odd, how many of these old priests were in the same situation, as good as married to their housekeepers, bar the obvious.[3]

"Well, Father seemed on good form last Sunday," she said. "He gave us a right old cold shower of a sermon, all about sin and death and making your peace with God before you pass away. The appropriate death, he called it. It made me think, I can tell you. Actually, I found myself wishing Emmet could have heard it, the way he's been carrying on. But of course he doesn't go to church, hasn't gone for years, not since Sean got married, maybe longer."

Mrs. Delaney was hesitating between cabbage and green chili peppers fresh from Mexico.

"Father always speaks very highly of your Emmet," she said, homing in on the cabbage as an Irish, i.e., known, quantity, therefore less likely to be disdained. "He says he's quite a broadminded man for an unbeliever, he says."

"Is that so," said Roisin. "Does he say that, indeed?"

"Aye. Of course Father thinks any unbeliever's in a permanent spiritual crisis, and Emmet's no exception. But being friends with your confessor's like working for a relative, says Father. A bad idea for all concerned. If he's got something to get off his chest, best confess to someone he doesn't know. I'd guess that's what he was away doing, if you don't mind me saying so."

For a moment, Roisin did mind. Worse, she was taken aback. Mrs. Delaney's elliptical condescension seemed to imply still waters that not only ran deep but were choked with weeds invisible from the surface. Could it be true, she wondered; could her

---

[3]Rumour makes the world go round, eh? Sure, wasn't there even talk about Father Dunne, our priest in Colmcross, and Danuta, his twenty-five-year-old housekeeper and ex-Miss Poland? Mind you, I never took those old stories seriously for a moment. Father Dunne was a saintly man, even otherworldly. When that Mrs. Stallion from next door complained she'd seen Danuta doing the housework dressed only in an apron (if that), Father Dunne took the girl on a package pilgrimage to Lough Derg and Croagh Patrick that lasted two weeks, and when they came back, both with simply super tans, Danuta announced in her charming broken English that she'd decided to join the Little Sisters of Anguish, a cloistered order based in the Bogside. As for Father Dunne, he was a new man, and made bishop inside the year.

knowledge of her own husband be that superficial?

"You mean Emmet's gone away on a retreat and not told me? Freethinking Emmet, who's not crossed himself or said a prayer in twenty years? Well, anything is possible, Mrs. Dee," she said, coldly. "Only it's easier to spin a yarn than fine cotton, as the saying goes."

Her back was turned to any further conversation with Mrs. Delaney until the latter made an amends-making remark about the tremendous heat of their unexpected Indian summer.

"Oh, fierce," said Roisin, distantly. "Fierce."

"Ninety-three at Dublin Airport, I heard."

"Did you now? Ninety-three, my goodness. Eighty-nine's what I heard, of course that was locally."

Their bond forged anew, Roisin Power and Mrs. Delaney completed their rounds of The Shops together, Mrs. Delaney to assemble the ingredients of Father Doyle's tea, Roisin laying in supplies against her husband's return: the King Edwards, for mashing, boxty or chips; half a dozen jumbo eggs, grade A, to be beaten into a creamy omelette of jumbo dimensions; various vegetables and earth-grown fungi destined for that man-sized omelette; as appetisers, mixed nuts—including cashews, walnuts, and Brazils—and imported German pretzels, hand-dipped in German batter; 16 ounces of finely ground Ecuadorian coffee and a half-bottle of champagne to wash down the foregoing; a pound of ground Charolais beef for mince pie, or meatballs; and 11 ounces of Madame Charybdis imported Luxembourg choco-lates as dessert, a real luxury she'd normally not waste a penny on, but whatever it was that had driven her husband of twenty-five years out of the house, it had to be defeated, and his heart, like many another's, was soonest reached through his stomach.[4] Suddenly struck by the dimensions of the crisis—reminded of

---

[4]Ah yes, I know the feeling. If food be the music of love, play on, so to speak. It's well known that my only sin, if I had any (and modesty is as modesty does, as Mam always said), would be the sin of gluttony, especially at Christmas when they carry in the plum pudding; why, there was one time when I fell upon the old pud the moment it appeared in the doorway and had the whole thing in my mouth, flames, holly

Emmet by a ruddy man with a sideways expression emerging from the off-licence—she doubled her champagne purchase, watched wide-eyed by her frugal companion.

"Would you believe me if I told you I'd never tasted the stuff but once, at my cousin Artie's wedding twelve or was it thirteen years ago now?" said Mrs. Delaney. "God knows we're not tee-total up at the presbytery, but one thing I've never seen him drink is champagne. Of course, he's not one for putting on airs, ah no, he's never that, the Father . . . not that I was suggesting!"

"Musha, Mrs. Dee, nor did I for one minute think you were. It's just that whatever bee Emmet's got in his bonnet will be more likely to buzz off after he's had a bottle of bubbly at home by the fire than if he goes to the pub and boozes it up with the lads."

Roisin's observation, which she instantly regretted (when was the last time Emmet went boozing it up with the lads, for God's sake?), set Mrs. Delaney's ten-year-old widowhood to throbbing like a raw wound, so vividly did it call to mind her own departed Declan, as in a sepia-tinted photograph of the half-forgotten past, rolling down the lea on Friday night, pubward bound, all coarse laughter and racetrack gossip and too generous with his rounds for his own good,[5] as she'd so often tried to tell him, but she was of that archaic, Chinese generation of Irishwomen re-quired to defer to their menfolk in all things: politics, religion, and table talk, of course, but also (especially) their quirks and foibles, usually brewed and bottled. Unfortunately—or perhaps not so—booming, broad-chested Declan Delaney, although a public Lothario just this side of adultery, had in truth been as impotent as a stone, so she'd not been saddled with the standard-issue houseful of kids, and their infrequent conjugal forays had usually petered out into thunderous snoring (his) and silent cro-

---

branches and all, before they could drag me off! I've always been a terrible one for anything with sugar in it, as you know. Still, where's the harm, with only one life to live and, correspondingly (or perhaps not), one Christmas per annum?

[5] A bit too much like others I could name. This bloke sounds a right wet mother's git, if you'll pardon the expression.

cheting (hers).

"Aye, God rot 'em," she muttered. "Men."

"Oh, I don't know," said Roisin, as she gathered up her purchases into two clinking bags. "They only need to be told what to do and they're happy enough. Like dogs. Did you ever own a dog, Mrs. Dee?"

Mrs. Delaney had not. Declan could never abide them, and Father was allergic.

18

Emmet's little jaunt was coming to an end, and none too soon: freethinker, indeed! He was being nicer to these priests than most of their parishioners. Oh, it was easy enough to play the hard man and swear you'd go out and break heads, as he'd done before leaving, but how could he carry on like that when everyone treated him in a more civilised fashion than he probably deserved? After all, it was no everyday occurrence to have some strange bugger appear on the doorstep asking if you'd phoned him, like a butler in a play: You called, sir? To which the natural reply would have been something along the lines of Sod off, or No thank you, I don't want any, or at the very least, Why didn't you use the *telephone* to straighten it out? Why drive all the way out here?

But none had asked these questions, so far: politeness, he supposed, or simple Irish perverseness, like responding to like.

In any event, he'd crossed two of the five Fathers MacCarthy off his list, having visited one of them and heard news of the second, Father Pat, the ultratraditionalist of Youghal, lying stiff as a plank in a hospital ward following a series of strokes six weeks before; after conveying his sympathies to the Sister at the hospital (she shrugged, unsympathetically), Emmet took the others in geographic order, reading from SSW to NNE. The first name in the SSW quadrant was that of Father Paddy MacCarthy, the pastor of Ballymahone, who received him in the dusty parlour of his presbytery while packing his bags in preparation for a new assignment.

"Ballbelong parish, sir, in Queensland. Empty except for the kangaroos and a few hundred sheep farmers and their families to minister to. Some might call it a step down, but not me, I'm planning to enjoy myself. All that open space, and no bloody bogs, and, God willing, not an Irishman in sight. I've had it with our compatriots, sir. Had it up to here. Nothing personal, of course. Bless my soul, Mr. Powers, I've no idea who called you up, it could have been any ould caffler on for a lark. That's the Irish for you, all over. Pack of bogtrotters and haverils who don't know their parsnips from a hole in the ground, begging your pardon, sir."

Emmet's next stop, twelve miles farther on, was to see P. J. MacCarthy, the ex-Chinese missionary, now also an ex-priest—but not defrocked, as Father Doyle had luridly hinted. He'd simply lost his faith over the years[1] and retired from the priesthood to write his memoirs. Three decades in China had made no difference to his Liffeyside accent, or his Dubliner's crystalline view of the world's absurdities. When Emmet told him about the phone call, he cackled in pleasure.

"Shure and don't Oi wish Oi'd t'ought a dat?"

Over green tea, he launched himself into spluttering reminiscences of halcyon days up and down the mighty Yangtze Chang.

"Turty-noine toimes da soize a da Liffey, didcha know dat? No foolin', game ball. Ah, dose were de days, don't you know, ah yiss dey were dat, so dey were, ah yiss. Now, a course back in dem days, nobody owned a tellyphone achall achall, ah shure, God bless ya, day're quare wans, de yeller men, so day are, ah day are dat, aren't day now, ah yiss, but God bless da lotta dem anyhow and yerself, ay-men. Chroist, dis green tay's afful stuff. Woncha have some daycent Arl Grey?"[2]

Emmet spent a restless night in a hotel near Cobh. In the morning he called Roisin to tell her he'd be home that night.

"For Jesus' sake, what's the matter with you, Emmet?"

"Nothing at all, acushla. Don't fret yourself. I'll be back soon

---

[1]Nothing simple about that, boyo. Believe me, I know whereof I speak, with my Uncle Frank as an example.
[2]Well, close enough, although from a distance you might mistake it for Corconian, or Polish. I'll let it pass.

enough."

Ask no questions and hear no lies, he said to himself, only partly assuaging his conscience thereby.

After breakfast he dropped in on Padraig MacCarthy, the bishop of Derrymoyle. A thin-lipped old lady guided His Grace into the living room by one elbow. He was plainly on life's downward slope, gathering speed. His mouth worked labouriously for several minutes as he stared at Emmet like a baby at a new toy. When he finally spoke, he did so with a distinct lisp that a telephone conversation would have only magnified.

"Hello."

"Are you the inthurance man?"

"I beg your pardon, Your Grace. A small incident. I won't keep you long."

"Effie, who ith thith man? Ith it the car? Why ithn't he wearing a tie?"

He repeated the question about the tie and only gaped when Emmet tried to explain his business. The old lady steered him out again, pointing wordlessly to the front door. Emmet took the hint, with a sigh of relief.

That left Canon Patric MacCarthy, at Ballyduff, in north County Killoyle, an hour or so by the inland road through barren hills and green glens studded with black tarns and abandoned cottages from the 1840s and boulders stained brown by sulphur. Emmet hoped the drive might clear his mind a little. Although motoring around the countryside at the wheel of his late-model Peugeot 707TSI was relaxing and a better excuse in itself for getting away from home than the hunt for the midnight caller (which sounded like some kind of silly TV drama, for God's sake), there was a considerable matter weighing on Emmet's conscience, i.e., whether he should report his employer to the authorities. After spending most of the previous Sunday night comparing official (the Revenue Office's) and unofficial (Spudorgan Hall's) versions of the hotel's tax payments, his worst suspicions had been confirmed. Yawning discrepancies between the sums in the account books and the official tax returns, going back five years, were a clear sign that Carfax's adhesive fingers had been delving into the cookie jar for some time. It was shocking—in fact, it was only now dawning on Emmet *how* shocking (also immoral, venal, corrupt, etc.) the whole business was. Worse yet was the already-dawned realisation that for five years, maybe longer, Emmet Power—he of the sept of the Powers, tribe of the Gaels, father of three fine sons (*brave Sean! hearty Jim! clever Tim!*), husband to fair Roisin; that self-made man, freethinker and moralist—for all those years, then, E. Power, Esq., had been happily and stupidly toiling away in the service of a cheat—a thief—a tax evader—a Gombeen man to the nth degree! As he thought of this, his knuckles went white on the steering wheel, and he swerved from the path of a horn-blaring bus bearing tourists to Cashel.

He soon came to Ballyduff. Canon Patric MacCarthy, S. J., was a brisk and genial man in his late thirties, with a clean-shaven, pleasantly porcine face and vigorously expressed opinions on most things, including midnight phone calls.

"Travelling Redemptorists? Never heard of 'em. Tea?"

With pale priestly hands, Canon MacCarthy ushered Emmet into a gazebo in the garden of the so-called Bishop's Residence, a Victorian Gothic manor house and functioning school—actually a recently inaugurated branch of the Mussenden and Downhill Priests' Training College, of which Canon MacCarthy was, he averred modestly (head bowed over ice-breaking teacups) honourary secretary, i.e., (a chuckle) chief fund-raiser. The house boasted accommodation for twenty students and a fine view that took in the sun-dappled hills of north County Killoyle and, in the filmy distance, the many-spired city itself, engirdling its silver strand. At the foot of the nearest hill was a stone circle of the Neolithic period, a tourist attraction, Emmet remembered, because of one supposedly erotic stone image known to the ancient Gaels as a sheila-na-gig.[3] These old rocks, and the College building itself, were evidence that history had not despised Ballyduff.

---

[3] And not just the ancients, boy. I've known the name since I was knee-high to a dog's pizzle. By the by, "supposedly" is right, unless you go all squishy at the sight of a pie-faced (and possibly -eyed) Neolithic couple upside down on top of each other while somehow managing to be side by side at the same time, if you take my meaning.

Canon MacCarthy sprawled in one of the chairs in the gazebo, clearly enjoying the unexpected opportunity for a chat. Finest Darjeeling tea from the foothills of Assam was the lubricant of their discourse.

"You know, I'm inclining to the view that it was an impostor after all," said Emmet. He loosened his collar, rolled up his sleeves and raised his face to the unseasonable sun, unreasonably hot. He felt relaxed, confident, almost himself again. "Only, who would be such a bleeding John Thomas, begging your pardon, Father, as to ring me up at past 11 p.m., pretending to be you, or one of your namesakes, then phone again when I'm out and leave the same message with my wife?"

"Actually, Mr. Power, I'd wager the John Thomas in question picked both our names at random. I mean, mine's hardly original, is it, except the way it's spelled, I don't know if you noticed? Patric with a *c*, as I've had to repeat about ten times a day ever since I can remember. My folks saddled me with it to make me stand out from the crowd, I'd guess, and fair enough, you do run into the odd Patrick MacCarthy here and there in the holy land of Ireland, don't you? Especially in these parts. In any event, I've an alibi, Mr. Power. I'm hardly ever home. We academic S. J.s do a lot of travelling, you know, in fact you were lucky to catch me at all. I'm off to Austria in a few days, and last weekend—at the time the crime was being committed, haha—I was in a village in Italy called Chieti, up in the Alban Hills just outside Rome—ah, that place is like a vision of paradise, believe you me. Pine trees, lake, waterfall, Roman temple, the lot. What a holiday resort it would make! Of course, I wasn't just lolling about, they've quite an active training college and hotel next door—they're eager as all get out for a decent manager, you know. You wouldn't be available, would you?"

Emmet shrugged.

"I'd have to ask the wife, but I'd not mind moving to Italy, if there's a decent job going."

"I'll bear you in mind, so. They're also on the lookout for a director at the school, and with all the Irish College seminarians they get, they'd dearly love a real Maynooth Irishman running the place! Well, I was tempted, so I was—but I'll not bore you with shoptalk. Now, about your caller. My hunch is, some eejit with a skinful wanted to put the wind up a respectable citizen and, for reasons unknown, chose you. A drop more tea?"

Emmet consented, despite his fear that staying any longer might make him want to confess his sins to this amiable priest on the spot. He did confess, after another sip of smoky Darjeeling, that Father MacCarthy was about as much like the popular notion of a Jesuit as Ballyduff House was his, Emmet's, idea of a college.

"That would be a compliment on both scores, I'm sure," said the priest. "The one traditionally a redbrick horror, the other a whited sepulchre, eh? Well, I reckon you're not unique in that, Mr. Power. The Society of Jesus don't readily inspire confidence, I'd be the first to admit. But then, nor do priests of any stripe anymore. The West's going through one of its periodic anti-religion cycles, I'm afraid, rather bad timing with Muslims gearing up for jihads and what not, but there you are. Not much we can do about it, except wait it out, as we've always done in the past."

"But surely it's finished? Christianity, I mean?"

"My goodness, you can't be serious, Mr. Power. May I ask, by the way, are you a churchgoing, or should I say, believing man at all? No? Ah, I thought not. Only a nonbeliever, I said to myself . . . well, anyway. These are weighty matters."

Emmet put his teacup down on the sidetable and sat forward.

"No, no. If it's no intrusion, that is. I mean, I know I'm only a hotel manager, not exactly the level of intellect you're used to jousting with, I'm sure, but let's go on with the discussion a bit, if you don't mind."

"As long as you like. I've nothing on today before the governors' meeting at half-four. Why not stay for lunch? We can have it out here, in the solarium. Actually, in view of the weather, I rather fancy a salad, and they do a very good *salade niçoise*—say with a nice Vouvray?"[4]

---

[4]Actually, we always favoured Château Yquem ('45, '46 ,'50) for elegant luncheons in our house, or maybe a Lynch-Bages ('52, '56, '61–'64 at a pinch) if the occasion included the Da, home early from the Bus Aras— of course, he'd mix the claret with bottles of stout and short ones, no

"Ah—you wouldn't have coffee, would you?"

"Coffee to follow, of course. What sort of flaming barbarian drinks coffee with his meals? Honestly. It's worse than grown men sitting around drinking Pepsi-Cola all day, the way they do in America. No, I'd opt for a Vouvray, I think. I don't know if you've noticed, but Alsace wines do tend to have a somewhat cloying aftertaste on a warm day."

Emmet didn't know if he had ever noticed this, not knowing what Alsace wine was, exactly (Al's ass? did that mean arse? was it a joke?), but Canon MacCarthy, seeing his hesitation, made curvaceous gestures in the air to describe smallish bottles with slim necks, then spoke the word *Green*, bringing it all back to him: that day in Geneva Airport with Fiona O'Malley, compliments of the airline, an elegant green bottle with a gold label and a fruity taste that went straight to his head!

"Oh yes. I *had* noticed, now that you mention it."

"I was sure you had, as the manager of the renowned Spudorgan Hall."

Emmet studied his host narrowly, alert to condescension and/ or sarcasm, but Canon MacCarthy, he decided, was that rarest of men, a plain speaker. This was confirmed when they resumed their discussion and the priest humourously but with the utmost sincerity dismissed Emmet's arguments and those of all "heretics," as he called them.

"Sorry about that word, Mr. Power, but there's really no way around it. If you publicly espouse beliefs contrary to Church doctrine, you're a heretic, full stop. I'm afraid it's that simple, unless you hold with cutting your cloth to suit the fashions of the day, and I most emphatically do not."

"You believe in excommunication, so?"

"Of course. But only as a last resort, after the priest does his priestly duty and tries to lead the errant member of the flock back to the fold, which can take a while, sometimes a lifetime, but you'd be surprised how often it works out, in the end. Needless

---

matter how hard we tried to stop him, more's the pity. Still, it was worth a try, as a certain Mr. Bonaparte said on his way home from Moscow.

to say, in the face of serious, organised defiance, or downright schism, you give them their last chance, then—yes, you wheel out the big guns, Mr. Power. What more can you do? How else keep the Church intact? Persuasion? Bribery? Mind you, it's not as if those methods haven't been used in the past, and excommunication itself was as common in bygone days as it is uncommon today, in the late Middle Ages, for example (so much so that entire provinces in Central Italy found themselves excommunicate because of some silly territorial dispute with the Pope), but then I'm not arguing that the Church hasn't made mistakes, oh no, far from it, in fact it's spent a good deal of its history cocking things up."[5]

"I'd not disagree with you there."

"No, I'm sure you wouldn't, but I know what you're thinking, that that's just one more reason not to believe, eh? That's part of the freethinker's argument, isn't it, that because the Church isn't perfect—and how could it be, administered as it is by mortal men—we might as well give it up, isn't that it? Pisherogues, man. Why not give up going to the supermarket, or the betting shop, or the pub, on the same grounds?"

"Ach, it's completely different, Father, surely. For a start, the betting shop doesn't tell you you'll burn for eternity if you don't follow house rules."

"Oh but it does, in its own way. Jail is a kind of temporal hell, isn't it? And that's where you end up if, say, you hold the place

---

[5] Well, I never said so, although I'm not denying I've thought it, once or twice. Uncle F. was a case in point, of course, but it doesn't stop there, not by a long shot: what about the ex-cardinal of Cracow, a man with a keen mind who still can't see farther than the end of his own eyelashes? Or the Knights of Iona, spending two million quid on an extension to their dance hall in Lisdoonvarna? Or the American archbishop who sounds like a member of the Trotskyite wing of Fine Gael, bleating away about gay birth control and the oppressed masses and the Church's duty to preach politics along with that boring old catechism and Bible? God help us, I had more fun yawning over debates at the Trinity Student Union when Milo was there (e.g., "This House Believes That Husbands and Wives Should Be Exactly the Same Height and Not an Inch More or Less").

up, or embezzle funds, or fiddle with the accounts, eh? At least in theory."

The Carfax crisis suddenly loomed like a boulder in the way of their philosophical—not to say Jesuitical—train of thought, from which Emmet disembarked without warning.

"Speaking of embezzling, Father, there's something I'd rather like to—well, if you don't mind. It *is* a bit of an intrusion, I know."

Canon MacCarthy's boyish face fell, then settled into a placid priestly smile, as if—good Jesuit that he was—he regretted that their duel of beliefs had come to an end, while at the same time—good priest that he tried to be—he thought he recognised in Emmet nothing more heretical than a layman's vain struggle against the urge to confess.

He pushed aside his teacup, symbolically.

"Shall we go indoors, then?" Noting puzzlement, he explained: "It's not really customary to hear confessions in a gazebo."[6]

"Confessions? Steady on, Father. Where'd you get that idea?"

Relief intercepted disappointment in the canon's soul: so the man was a hard case after all! He reached for the teapot as Emmet, holding out his cup, racked his brains for eloquence—in vain.

------

[6]Although the cardinal used to, all the time, rain or shine! In fact, rumour has it he caught the chill that ultimately killed him one night towards eleven, while sitting in his gazebo listening to Uncle Francie's confession over tea, biscuits, Smarties, etc.

19

She noticed he was bantering in the way men did when they thought they were flirting urbanely: avoiding the leer as such, but laying on the innuendo.

"With a name like that, I'd guess they only hire glamorous women of the world, eh? I mean, well-rounded women like yourself, aha ha?"

"Hardly. Glamorous? You should see the features editor. She usually looks like she spent the night under a hedge."

"But the actual writers, they'd be a pretty, em, cosmopolitan lot?"

"Well, I've been abroad a few times, and they do have correspondents in relatively far-flung places, like New York and Milan."

"Paris, too, I expect?"

"Of course. And there's a man in Geneva who covers Central Europe and the south of France.[1] But I don't get away from Killoyle much."

---

[1] Ah, grand places, noble cities, venerable names. Tell me honestly now, is there a finer way to spend a summer fortnight when young than to stand by the side of a tree-lined road in France (outside Rheims, say, or hard by Dijon) with the scent of cow dung and car exhaust in your nostrils, as you thumb a ride to points gloriously southwards? Seeing for the first time a legendary name on an everyday sign: Carcassonne, or Avignon, or Dubonnet; then, once there, glanced at, glancing back, in a crowd, or on a café terrace . . . holy saints above, how time *does* fly, as the old priest said!

"Don't you? Bloody hell, he's bitten me. Ah—could you get him off?"

"Oh no. *Bad* dog."

Strongbow's punishment for gnawing the heel of Milo's left shoe —drawing attention, alas, to its scuffed surface, and the archipelago of stains that darkened one side—was a sharp slap on the muzzle and the timbre of reprimand in Kathy's voice. The dog cringed obediently, fearing the worst, but a scant five minutes later all was well, in a dimly lit and wonderfully redolent corner of Magilligan's Lounge on Pollexfen Walk. In token of reparation, Kathy offered to buy, and Milo gazed at the back view of her white jumper and black denims as she stood at the bar waiting for the drinks, admiring the amplitude of that prosaic yet poetic culmination of a woman's curves so alluringly captured in the paintings of Boucher (or was it Renoir?) as well as in the photo pages of naughty mags, one in particular; but there was a time for slobbering and a time for action, he reminded himself sternly. Opportunity had knocked, in the guise of coincidence, directing their steps to the same spot (the Parade, corner of Pollexfen Walk) at the same time (6 p.m.) for different reasons: his, that it was a short cut to Magilligan's, cheapest boozer in town; hers, that it led directly to the prime dog-walking territory of the Strand.

Yes, he had to rise to the occasion, or forever live in regret.

(She was having a pint too, he noted, approving.)

"You lived in London, then?"

"I did, yes. How do you know that? Did I pick up an accent?"

"Ah. No. It's just with the magazine and that—one associates London with that kind of life, if you know what I mean."

"Our friend Murphy was gossiping, so. God, and women are supposed to be the ones. Well, you're right. I was there for a while. Six months in a Kilburn bedsit and two years in a semi out the Finchley Road. Do you know it? London, that is?"

Enormously well, asserted Milo's sagely nodding head. They raised their glasses and spoke the same word in unison.

"Cheers."

Milo tilted his pint to the angle best suited to the drinker's ritual of first-one-down-in-one, then remembered the circumstances and reluctantly lowered his glass, suppressing the standard sigh of satisfaction. Bemusedly, he looked at his pint for a second, as if he hadn't quite got the hang of this drinking caper. Kathy observed the routine and correctly interpreted it as a sham. Bloody Irishmen, she said to herself, also observing Milo's desperate struggle to heave off the dead weight of silence. Milo, for his part, noticed her noticing him. This made things awkward, for a moment, then he flung himself into the fray with small talk about London and the infinite treasures of that splendid city, where, he declared, a "goodly" part of his youth had been spent ("or misspent, ahaha?"), much of it in and around Russell and Soho squares, mostly (of course) in the Reading Room of the British Museum, but also—in his spare time—in the museum itself, admiring the Elgin marbles, Titian's *Seasons*, Houdon's *Voltaire*, etc., as well as various artifacts of Assyrian manufacture; then, after tea on a normal day, he'd be off with springing step and light song on lips to the Lamb on Lambs Conduit Street, one of the great pubs of London (did she know it?), with those frosted-glass window-panes partitioning off the bar and the wonderful cashew-flavoured Shepherd Creame they had on tap—real ale, never mind if it went for two quid a pint (she stared blankly, unshocked)— not that he'd spent that much time at the pub, of course, with such powerful rival attractions as the museum and the Inns of Court and the shops of Oxford Street only stones' throws away![2]

"Ah yes," he said. "London." Daringly, he seized his drink and swallowed it in one gulp; yet guilt, or prudence, forbade any exhalations of pleasure. He was beginning to realise that having a jar with the woman of his dreams was a balancing act that called for a clear head and a nimble tongue, drawing the line between the discretion of being a gentleman (i.e., say nothing risqué but get nowhere), and the overt desirousness of staring eyes, twitching lips, etc., this being, as he knew, the danger inherent in too many pints of Magilligan's excellent porter. Furthermore, he felt a perverse resentment at fate for arranging this rendezvous and depriving him of his malodorous (stale beer, tobacco) yet mellow

---

[2] I know for a fact that the wee hypocrite no more went to the British Museum than I'm his granny, and the sum total of his London expertise could be contained on the scratch side of a box of Swan Vestas.

few hours of masculine pub torpor, that Tuesday night institution of playing darts, reading the same news in three or four different newspapers, ogling squint-eyed from afar, smoking ten to fifteen cigarettes (or more: enough, in any case, for a fine morning chest rattle), soaring into the empyrean of the mind on flights of boozy fancy, solo or in the company of other tippling dreamers; then, around nine, stopping at the Koh-i-Noor on O'Connell Square for a Vindaloo and calling in at Mooney's off-license for a carry-out after that, to wind up the evening armchair- and television-bound, drifting beerily off at about midnight, an unambitious but pleasant routine now shaken to its foundations in the traditional manner, with the arrival of Woman on the scene.

The good part was that she seemed pretty regular, not hoity-toity, and even said yes when he volunteered a second round.

The dog growled when Milo got up.

"Good boy. Irish terrier, is he? I'll bet he's well-fed."

Strongbow lunged, but fortunately for Milo's feet he was held back by his lead and Kathy's choice words of domination.

"Bad. Sit. Stay."

She watched as Milo did a nimble two-step to avoid the dog's jaws and went over to lean on the bar. His back turned to her, he exchanged words of recognition with fellow regulars, mostly old-timers with cigarettes clutched in nicotine-stained fingers and noses blooming red and purple with the drink. A couple of them glanced furtively in her direction and turned away to conspire in coughing guffaws.

"Stick it in your nose, Cyril," said Milo, to his credit—but loudly, as if intending her to hear. Kathy chuckled. He was a recognisable type, she thought, one more common in Dublin or Cork than in a small place like Killoyle: the student or semi-intellectual down on his luck, professing indifference to appearances while carefully grooming the image of Behanian bohemian, hard-bitten by borrowed cynicism, a deep drinker and incessant dreamer, not much concerned with love except when he'd had a few[3]—if he were true to type, in fact, he might not even admit

---

[3]Ah, she's a wee bit off the mark, God bless and keep her all the same. Milo, like so many young layabouts, has the one thing on his mind, and

that love was of any importance to him at all. In the undying words of another mass-produced Irishman, her brother Jack: "Women? Nah. As long as I've me pint and me fag I'm all right." Admittedly, the difference there was that Jack had the brains of a mince pie and this Milo character showed some signs of wit, or minimal literacy, anyway (Elgin marbles, Voltaire, etc.): he was, at the very least, no threat, the way the Jack (or Murphy) type might be, or pretended to be, with exaggerated machismo and no real pleasure in the act of love except as a means of dominance, a notch on the belt, a conversation piece over drinks with the fellas . . . well, this guy certainly wasn't like that, it would clash with his arty-boozy image. On the other hand, as the headwaiter at Spudorgan Hall, he was hardly much of a step up from the bartender at the same establishment, and he was a bit too generously padded (no doubt for the usual beer-drinking, curry-eating bachelor reasons) to kindle her animal passions. Not an Apollo, then; more of a young Dionysus, like that statue in the National Museum in Athens, sozzled yet cunning—or would his role (if any) be that of cuddly teddy bear, arousing maternal rather than sexual instincts? But she was letting her imagination run on ahead of reality, as usual. Funny, how she'd just been thinking what a relief it was to be on her own, after formalising the split with Murphy (one valedictorian drink at Spudorgan Hall, just to be polite about it, easier than she'd hoped, admittedly, never mind that he'd not even offered it her on the house, the cheapskate), and here she was, already stroking a fantasy again, only this time reality was a fat squirt who worked in a restaurant, no prize for anyone, least of all himself, judging by his appearance: corduroys worn paper-thin at the seat and his torso enveloped in a once-elegant but over-sized tweed jacket with (inevitably) patched elbows. Strongbow, of course, had pointed out the shoes, which in turn had underscored the argyle socks, in need of mending, anklewise.

---

you can't entirely blame him for it, in a society with little else on *its* collective mind. Sure, when *I* was growing up, if we mentioned sex organs, or exposed our own, we had to recite enough Novenas and Acts of Contrition and Hail Marys for an all-expenses-paid air-conditioned trip to Fatima and back!

He was something of a slum on legs, to be blunt about it.[4]

The servility had vanished, at any rate, no doubt the moment he'd walked out the door of the restaurant, and thank God for that: having him flirt was bad enough. Not that he was obsequious, exactly, but she'd always felt awkward with waiters and wine stewards and the like, having been a waitress herself, for a while, in a London bistro. She pretty much instinctively thought along There-but-for-the-grace-of-God lines whenever anyone in a restaurant called her madam, or bowed and fluttered as if she were the blooming Empress of Japan just because she'd be leaving a tip, poor bastards.

Bartenders were different, of course. They were like priests, in more ways than one.

"Murphy's a real beauty, isn't he," she said, involuntarily. Milo handed her a fresh pint and put his own down as the table started vibrating with the rumbles of a dog on the *qui vive*.

"Your dog?" he said. "Yes, he's a fine specimen. Terrier, isn't he?"

"No, not him. Hey! Be quiet!" The growling stopped, momentarily, then resumed, modulated to a lower volume. "I'm talking about Murphy, the bartender at the hotel. Your colleague."

"Ah! Himself! The hard man, is it? Good old Murph! My colleague, your je ne sais quoi?"

He stiffened, alarmed by his own impudence. After all, the woman was still a customer, and the policy at the Hall was no different from that at any other establishment devoted to making money, i.e., if the boss was Jesus Christ, the customer was God, pure and simple. Of course, being Jesus Christ was quite enough, if an employee drove a customer away—as Milo's predecessor in the headwaiter's job had allegedly done by making a habit of loudly and repeatedly belching out the word *Ballocks* while serving dinner (the Japanese had been especially upset)—

---

[4]Well, now, people in glass houses, wouldn't you say? Drinking that so-called coffee and smoking those putrid French cigarettes all night isn't my idea of style—not that she's a bad one, altogether. I like a girl with spirit.

or, worse, if customer complained to management. Yes, word might get out. What if he alienated her with his sloppy smiling and clumsy chatter? He'd be called onto the carpet; Power would do his nut; Murphy would have the laugh of his life; and as for Leo Gomez . . . !

Bugger the lot. He'd get a new job, and about time too.

Anyway, she only laughed, and gave him the first real woman-to-man look of the evening (aha! her eyes *were* grey—or less blue than they'd seemed in the photo spread, at any rate).

"Je ne sais pas," she said, charmingly. "Not anymore. That wee fling's over. I assume you knew all about it?"

"Well. Not all. But."

"How could you avoid knowing, with me coming in there all the time and him carrying on like the answer to a woman's prayers? Which, by the way, he isn't, at least not to mine. And that's all I'm going to say on the subject. I'm sorry I brought it up. I don't believe in public postmortems."

Milo agreed heartily. United in approval of their own good taste, they naturally turned the conversation to others' lack thereof, and Milo took the lead with reminiscences of hotel guests, usually tour groups, frequently German, notably one from Hamburg, six months before. On that occasion the Rentokil bills had come to over a thousand pounds, he recalled, and few if any of the staff had escaped fumigation.[5]

---

[5] That reminds me of the trip we took to dear old Deutschland back in '71 (or was it '72?). Da and the others wanted to spend the day in the Hofbrauhaus, naturally, while I opted for Dachau. Well, once I got there, the first thing I saw was a horrid wee hop-o'-my-thumb relieving himself against a tree, just outside the Autobahnhof, or train station. I struck him with my umbrella, but the wretch resisted, accusing me of belonging to an inferior race—Jew or Turk, I don't remember which—and promptly set about trying to pick my pockets. Naturally, as soon as I felt those clinging hands in the outer reaches of my topcoat, I lost all reason and struck out, then called the rozzers, or *Polizei* as they quaintly style them over there. Guess what? You're right: they sided with your man and put me on the first train back to Munich. Of course, when I got there, the sight of the family's silly faces peering out from between the legs of their new German friends drove the unhappy incident clean out of my head—until now, that is.

"Then there was the hurling crowd in from Carlow for the semifinals who went boozing in the fields all night and next morning thought it quite fitting to let loose a cow in the dining room during breakfast. God, the smell. Mind you, Daisy was happy enough. The other diners fed her bits of toast and marmalade, and she only unleashed on the floor twice. On the other hand, her owner wasn't best pleased when he found out where she'd gone. Being of a litigious disposition, like most Irish farmers, he threatened to take the whole blooming hurling team to court. I'm not sure if he ever did, but I do know they lost the match, in the end."

The combination of womanly propinquity and beer—daringly, he'd bought another, while she was still on her second—was loosening Milo's tongue and easing the tension to the point of sociability, if not actual relaxation. His anecdote—*echt Irisch, mit Schlag*—further thawed the chill. Kathy laughed; sensing the general relief, Strongbow fell silent and settled down to contemplate smells, tastes, and high-pitched sounds, many of the latter emanating from an invasion of boys and girls in the terminal stages of adolescence.

"Behold youth, in all its squalor," said Milo. "Hard to believe we were young once, eh?" He hastily backtracked. "Not that I'm implying . . ."

She waved a dismissive hand.

"Never mind that. I try not to be coy about my age. There's nothing I can do about it, is there? I'm thirty-nine, and that's that."

"It's a good age. Isn't life supposed to begin at thirty-nine?" said Milo, cheerily.

Give him his due, she thought, that was nice of him, not that it made any difference. Regardless of fashion, or good manners, thirty-nine was the point of no return, the last year of youth and the first of middle age, when maturity, so long sought after, could turn traitor and become a woman's worst enemy, not just as despoiler of smooth skin and firm muscle, but (far worse, in Kathy's opinion) as an almost religious self-absorption of the kind that kept magazines like *Glam* in business. Little columns like hers had no inherent justification; they were merely hitching a ride on the backs of the countless how-to articles about urine diets or hand-jogging or sex after ninety or any of the other illusions of endless youth that fed the conceit of the modern woman, whoever she was—and whoever she was, she would never give away her age to a fella, just like that! But Kathy had no regrets; in that sense, she was a thoroughly unmodern woman. Anyway, such frankness served as a warning to younger fellows—Murphy for one, and a couple of the suitors of her early widowhood, and maybe Milo too—who'd be happier running with fast fillies like the young ones who'd just come in. It was also, of course, a cue for Milo to be equally straightforward about his age, but he ignored it, instead mentally calculating how old she must have been when she posed for *Quest*. Mid-twenties, he reckoned, and the intervening years showed. She looked like a different person entirely: the eyes, for one thing, the nose, for another. Not that she was less attractive, quite the contrary. Just different. Not kittenish, more statuesque. But thirty-nine wasn't so bad, not at all. Hadn't some whiskered luminary—Shaw, was it, or Havelock Ellis—commented on the ripeness of that particular age in a woman?[6] He was fed up with *young* girls, anyway. They were always angling for success, if not their own, then yours: nag nag nag, in other words, and it took its toll. Now, a real woman wouldn't give a toss about that, especially if she'd had more success than the man in her life; a woman of a certain age, as the French so tactfully said, a real woman with experience to match or even surpass his own! It was exciting, daunting, a challenge, and never mind the nose.

After all, hadn't he'd always fancied Barbra Streisand, alongside whom this one had no hooter at all, to speak of?

---

[6]Not those quare old crocks, the one chaste as a pin and the other ploughing only the furrows of his bedclothes, and that with wild abandon—what would the likes of them know about normal relations? Benjamin Franklin, the clean-shaven Yank Romeo, did say that a lady's anterior and posterior amplitudes (I apologise for the language, but it could be worse) were the last parts of her to reflect advancing age. I had that story from Uncle Mike, the old libertine. Sure, isn't the time he hid in a hedge and shouted dirty words at passersby still the talk of Co. Kerry (funny; it happened in Roscommon)?

"How old are you, so?" she said, taking the offensive.

Milo was overcome with impishness.

"Thirteen," he squeaked.

She forced a smile.

"Really? You're awfully mature for your age. You mean thirty-one, I suppose?"

"That's it. I always get the numbers in the wrong order. Last year I went about telling everyone I was three."

He shuddered with self-approbation. She merely shuddered, noting the slippage in courtesy since he'd started on his third pint. He was sitting tactlessly, legs apart, arm flung over the back of the banquette behind her, a lank lock aslant his brow. Some of his pals at the bar had been glancing in their direction, so she supposed he was trying to convey intimacy, even owner-ship. Well, she wasn't having any. It was well past seven and she'd had nothing to eat since tea. No doubt about it, the third pint was the decisive one, as she knew from a lifetime's associa-tion with her male compatriots. It led beyond the still-habitable borderlands of "a couple of drinks" into the howling wilderness of intoxication. After number two you could go home unscathed, but once you'd had the third you were probably a fixture until last orders, and Milo was nothing if not typical—indeed, just like Jack, he seemed quite happy to drink his beer and stare into space.

Kathy got her things together.

"Well, I think I'd better."

Unexpectedly, Milo shifted to bully-poet mode: eyes aglitter, hand on chest.

"*There was never a man less embraced / By ambition; to win the worldly race / Was not his fancy, nor did he seek / Fools' approval to scale his peak,*" he declared, stoutly.

"Nice. Yours?" she said.

Gaping, he looked more like a Portuguese man-of-war than Dionysus.

"Um. How did you know that?"[7]

---

[7]The liar. Actually, it's from "Me," Jasper Hoolihan's autobiographical

"Ach, get away. It was obvious, wasn't it," she said, at ease again, at least for the duration of another Grand Pagnol. He lit it for her with an elegant flourish belied by his green plastic lighter, smilingly speaking words made inaudible by sudden jukebox noise that sounded like compressed-air construction equipment (e.g., the pile-drivers on the building site he'd worked on in Queens, New York—all puff and no go, as the Donegal-born foreman always used to say).

"How's your drink?" he shouted.

She made gestures of sufficiency and pointed to the door. He hesitated. It was a gamble, and he'd hardly the cash for it, but he had to make the gesture.

"An Indian?" he bawled, miming a turban, beard, flames emerging from mouth. After rapid mental calculations relative to Milo's solvency, character, and morality, Kathy decided her column could wait another night, and as there was nothing worthwhile on television except an old propaganda film on the SiegKanal—but she'd seen them all, and that ghastly Rudolf Hess was bound to pop up sooner or later, he always did—another hour or so with Milo was worth the risk. He was a bit immature but harmless, even funny in spite of himself.

Confident, then, that a single biryani was just that and committed her to nothing more, she yielded.

"Yes, OK, why not." She mouthed the words above the din.

The ensuing dumb show comparison of watches (his Swass in plastic blue, displaying a pair of crossed alpenhorns in lieu of hands; her Tissué, black roman numerals on a white face, rimmed in gold) set the rendezvous for eight o'clock at the Star of Bihar, the new Tandoori house on the Parade—the Koh-I-Noor being, Milo decided, too familiar with his usual shambling and slurred homeward-bound self to be a place where his

---

sonnet, written on his bedroom curtains the day before they took him to the Ismay P. Stark Memorial Penitentiary in Outhouse, Montana. It was found by the next guest, a melancholy country-and-western singer who used it as inspiration to commit suicide. Eventually, it made its way into *The Albatross Book of Modern Verse* (Heathrow, 1967).

presence would command respect.[8]

"Eight o'clock, then," he bellowed.

After she left, he went to the bar for a refill to celebrate, if not success, at least not failure, and not-failure was enough to feed his dreams for an hour or so.

---

[8]Commanding respect's rich, so it is. None whatsoever's what he gets and none whatsoever's what he deserves, so long as fawning over the rabble's his bread and butter. God in heaven, if the Da knew what he was about, he'd take a poker (or tongs) to him and no mistake! "We kiss the arse of neither man nor beast" were his nightly last words before lights out.

20

G Day, Wolfetone decided, had arrived. He scanned the roster. There were eleven people at the Hall with surnames starting in *G*.

"Mrs. Gallagher," he murmured into the intercom (twelve! *Perfect!*). "Could you please tell the following people I want to see them in my—I mean, the manager's office, immediately?" He read out the list.

"Certainly, Mr. Grey."

While he was waiting, Wolfetone gloatingly imparted his secret to his Confidant ("God Almighty, so what do You think of that then, eh? Eh?") and perused the relevant passage in Glossovich once again.

Some of us have names most pleasing to Him, Whose Own pronunciation of His Name, as He told me, is most nearly akin to the Saxon tribes'—English, German, Friesian, etc., to wit the hard glottal G—as in (for example) "Golbkiy'"—and most definitely not the elided, slovenly Latino-Sanskrit D, as in (for instance) "Dagenham," nor the Arabo-Turkic dropped-labial Uhl, as in (say) "Uhl." By the way, the noble Slavonic B, as in "Bog," is a balm to Him, but only when repeated twice the number of times it takes a Buddhist to say the holy syllable "Om" before full relaxation of the sphincter, pelvis, lower part of legs, and feet (seventy-five, by latest international estimates).

Anyhow, being serious here. How did I find this out, I hear my honest, simple-minded reader asking in a multitude of voices, some high, some low? OK, so it was like this. You know I lived for many years (how many I don't remember, but believe me it seemed like a whole lot)[1] *in a leather hut ("yurt") on top of Mount Five-Year-Plan in Tadzhikistan. Well, one day I realised I was very much under the weather, especially after two solid weeks of heavy raining and icicle storms and the sky breaking loud wind in my eardrums. I wanted to go somewhere, see green (or bluish) things, wear T-shirts and drink iced drinks—yes, this happens even to holy-type men, or guys such as I. So, with rich cursing at the elements (containing no sacred words, mind you, just references to functions we all perform, like it or not, even queens of England, popes, your sister and so on) I left my yurt and went downtown to the biggest travel agency in Ulan-Ude, a government branch with twelve employees. They were all very happy to see me, as usual, and immediately pinched their noses in the traditional Tadzhik gesture of respect. Hey! I said, boys and girls, how are you today? OK, Daddy-o, they said. Hey! I said. Are you going to tell me about cruises on the Black Sea—Sevastopol, Sochi, Yalta, Odessa, whatever you've got (maybe I was sinfully thinking about spending some holiday time on beaches, flexing muscles, getting a tan!)? OK, Daddy-o, they said, and gave me brochures. Suddenly I was noticing two things at once, one after the other: a strange orange light coming from everywhere and nowhere simultaneously, and that good old booming voice from up-stairs. Of course, I pretended not to hear at first, which was very clever because He was talking about the employees in the agency, their per-sonal habits, where they lived, how much they made (and believe me, that was a joke, and a pretty funny one too), names of their kids and so on, saving the best for last, the way He likes to.*

"Hey, Leonid! Thou, guy! Ask thyself each and every one the name by which his or her family or clan is called," He said, very loudly, so I stopped pretending not to hear and asked everybody their family names as they backed slowly away from me in the traditional Tadzhik sign of respect.

"Gorky," said one. "Gogol," said another. "Goncharov," said a third. "Glinka," said his neighbour, and so it went on, yea, unto the twelfth that was named Gorbachev, and he bore the mark of the Chosen on the bare skin of his noggin.

"Lo," He said, when I was done. "Guess what?"

---

[1]Fifteen, give or take (see above).

Naturally, I was soon putting two and two together, making twelve, so then I fell to my knees and praised Him in the highest. It was a maximum day. The state of grace had arrived; I had found my first followers; I was anointed and ready to begin my journey across the parched Kazakhstan-like wastes of Life.[2]

With a sigh, Wolfetone put down the book and leaned back in his—or more properly, Emmet Power's—swivel wingchair. He stared aloft, but his millennial thoughts were blocked by the sight on the ceiling of an Ulster-shaped damp patch in the embryonic stages of formation (the Six Counties minus Fermanagh and parts of Tyrone, filthy sods), next to the overly ambitious chandelier that struck something of a meretricious note, he thought, especially in combination with the wall-to-wall leather sofa at the other side of the room and the doubleknit doilies draped over everything like Dalian dream watches.

"Whores," he hissed, lighting his pipe. He swivelled around and tossed his match through the open window. At least the view was decent, even admirable (reading from top to bottom): Uphill Street and the MacLiammoir Overpass snaking down to the boat-studded blue amphitheatre of Killoyle harbour, with the long silver line of the Strand at one end and the antennaelike spires of St. Oinsias' on the other; to the north and west, the great white unribboning of the "Irish Algarve" in its blissful entirety, and in the darkling distance: Hawaii! Well, the North Killoyle Hills, actually, but they were of the jagged, basaltic variety featured in the film version of Mr. Michener's blockbuster,

---

[2]One more note about the old jiggersnapes. He snuffed it last year, you know, and they gave him a right royal sendoff: troika ride through the park, state lying-in at Lenin's Tomb, televised two-finger salute and what have you, but when they were shifting the stiff, one of the pallbearers looked down and noticed it wasn't your man at all, but an old granny in a plastic mac and blue-rinse, holding a red handbag! Well, you can imagine the ructions. This lot said he'd been taken up, that lot claimed he'd been abducted, the government issued an all-points bulletin in five languages; the truth is, of course, nobody knows what happened. Believe you me, he could turn up any day and request another funeral at taxpayers' expense, then pull the same trick all over again. It would be like *Finnegans Wake*, in prime time.

as well as in the musicals and stage plays *Bali Hai, Kon-Tiki, Easter Island Bunnies*, etc., all one-time favourites of Wolfetone's; finally, illogically—at least to his sketchy notion of gravity, the tides, geophysics, etc.—the sea towered above, half hiding the sky, an unsettling, not to say dizzying, phenomenon, even considering that Killoyle (back in the days when it was a humble Celtiberian settlement called Cuìll gHuaìll, long before it acquired its Ascendancy and post-Ascendancy names of West South and Quille L'Oisle, respectively) had actually been built on land reclaimed from the very seabed itself (or so rumour had it)!

At the summit of this watery horizon floated the Quimper-Rosslare ferry, no doubt full to the gunwales with French products, e.g., Geiger counters, cheese, wine, TVs, Peugeots and/or Citroëns, cognac and Frenchmen (and -women). Setting out from Killoyle harbour, in the lower left-hand corner of the picture, was a white ketch Wolfetone recognised as the *Gutta-Percha*, owned by Joe Jim Glasnevin, a reserve colonel in the North Meath Fusiliers who had briefly rented the Greys' basement some years previously and had moved out, cursing with a soldier's fluency, the morning after Wolfetone paid him a late-night visit to read out selections from (coincidentally) the works of Glossovich. The estrangement was doubly unfortunate because the colonel had a keen ear for voices and brutally derided Wolfetone's subsequent telephonic claim to be his—the colonel's—Australian second cousin, Bruce.

"If you ever call me up again, you ghastly little speck of sputum, I'll horsewhip you from here to Christmas" had been his exact, unforgettable words, but Wolfetone reckoned he'd banjaxed him with his retort: "Bloody dinkum bugger off, cobber," sounding (to himself) as Down Under as you could get without being the real thing. Aye, that had brought the old hardnose up short, right enough. There'd not been much for him to say then, except stammer the usual boring threats of police, jail, the law courts, etc.—fancy threatening to take a man to court for something as harmless as that! Some people (most of them, to be brutally frank) had no sense of humour, or adventure, not to mention education . . . as he rested his chin on the windowsill and watched the *Gutta-Percha* swaying and bobbing like a nutshell on the sea's heaving breast, Wolfetone became ever more enraged at the thought of Reserve Colonel Joe Jim Glasnevin and his ilk: the ignorant swine! The swaggering, overbearing know-it-all know-nothings! The gutter rats! The cheats! The bloody Philistines . . . !

THE ATHEISTS![3]

"I hope you drown, you bastard," he shrieked. A diplomatic cough insinuated itself into his consciousness. Wolfetone's pipe trailed a comet tail of smoke and cinders as he slewed around to confront the intrusion, himself confronted by overweight, horn-rimmed, ever-disapproving Mrs. Gallagher with, in the doorway behind her, a spectrum of flesh tints ranging from the pinkish white of the majority to Ragu Gupta's deep bronze, via the olive drab of Leo Gomez. Instantly debonair, Wolfetone greeted the assembly with a bow.

"Good afternoon, Mr. Grey."

They said this with no sniggering; nor, he was pleased to observe, did anyone make a face. Expansively, he motioned them to the sofa. It was a tight fit, mostly thanks to the overlapping thighs of eighteen-stone Finbarr Gilhooley, the head porter days and weekends, but they managed, by dint of squeezing their knees together like schoolchildren.

"Galhern, P., Gargnan, M., Gavigan, K., Gavin, M., Geoghegan, P., Gleason, N., Gilhooley, F., Gogarty, J., Gomez, L., Grimes, R., Gupta, R., and of course Gallagher, D.," recited Wolfetone. "Have I got your names right?" Nods and grunts. He beamed. "Good. You're all sacked."

---

[3]My goodness, he *is* a bit of a head case, isn't he—but then so many of these God Squadders are, aren't they? I mean, the idea of going about telling everybody they've got it all wrong and *you're* the one who's somehow sussed out the Big Secret! Now, don't get me wrong, I've never called myself an atheist, that leads to all kinds of long-haired, hare-brained, polysexual rubbish I'd not tolerate for an instant under my roof. No sir, call me an agnostic, if you must, but the sum total of my position vis-à-vis God is as follows: maybe He's there and maybe He isn't, and how the blazes am I supposed to know? You might as well expect a fat, sleepy tabbycat to suddenly wake up and start explaining the Heisenberg uncertainty principle, whatever that is. I mean, honestly.

His was the only laughter that ensued, and there was a high cracked note in it that brought expressions of concern to several faces.

"Eh, Mr. Grey," said Mrs. Gallagher. "Could you tell us what this is actually about? We've all got jobs to do, you know."

"Of course. Forgive me, Mrs. Gallagher. I apologise. Just my little joke."

Wolfetone sat back and knocked out his pipe in the ashtray with a series of ceramic clinks before laying it bowl upwards on the desk, as gently as if it were spider-spun of cobweb silk. Clasping his hands, he smiled with avuncular ease while (paradoxically) assuming the pose favoured by dynamic executives and vote-seeking politicians: out-thrust jaw followed in ascending order by mouth, nose and beetling brow and the last, pathetically brilliantined outcrops of a once-luxuriant *chevelure*.

"Now. When I read out your names just now, did anyone notice anything?" he inquired, scanning his audience. "Leo?" The Spaniard shifted uneasily, bookended as he was by Mrs. Gallagher and Finbarr Gilhooley.

"Hi no no. All nays are espell wit' *Yee*, maybe?"

"Bravo, Leo. All names are indeed spelled with *G*, as you say. You see, ladies and gentlemen?" Wolfetone sat back, smiling, hands outspread. "It sounds foolish, even idiotic, but our simple friend—or should I say *amigo*?—our *amigo*, then—*el Señor* Gomez, haha—Leo's just put his finger on the reason why I asked you all here on the last day of my provisional tenure as your manager. I'd go so far as to say that Leo's inadvertently stumbled on a much larger reason, that of life itself, even perhaps the very meaning of our presence on earth. Oh yes indeed." He lowered his eyes pensively to his hands. "Some of you may find this a bit hard to swallow. Well, let me tell you I know exactly how you're feeling, haven't I been going through the same thing myself?" He raised anguished features in time to intercept a sequence of worried looks. "Oh, drat. I'm not getting through, am I?"

Mrs. Gallagher cleared her throat with loud and precisely enunciated hoots, like an actress in a play by Sheridan, or Wilde.[4]

---

[4]Or Shaw, at a pinch. Some Prod or other, anyhow—which reminds me.

"Mr. Grey, if I might interrupt for a second, I think I ought to point out that except for Miss Grimes here—of course I can't speak for Miss Gupta or Mr. Gomez, but as for the rest of us, I'm fairly confident I won't be contradicted if I say they—we—well, I think we're all good churchgoing Catholics, or most of us anyway, and I only bring this up because I've the distinct impression that you've called us in to participate in some kind of a revivalist meeting, if you don't mind me saying so."

"Oh course I Cat'olic," said Gomez. "Jew saying maybe I you?"

"You me? I'm sorry, I don't—"

"No, no. You!" Gomez equipped himself with the unseemly token of a giant nose, or trunk, fashioned with a cupped hand from the air.

"What the—oh, you mean Jew. Oh dear. No, no, Gomez, I only meant—"

"If you ask my opinion, Grey's stone mad altogether," announced Mr. Gilhooley.

"Now, Mr. Gilhooley, was that a helpful thing to say, at all?" Mrs. Gallagher stood up, eliciting gasps of relief from unlocked diaphragms. "Mr. Grey is only doing as he thinks best, I'm sure. I'd not be at all disappointed if you chose to apologise to him, you know."

Hues of red and white alternated on Wolfetone's face, blending slowly into vermilion.[5]

When you think about it, doesn't something in our once-ascendant Protestant countrymen seem to favour them lolling about taverns and tea shops, in spite of being geniuses of one kind or another? I mean, just think of old Jonathan "Coffee Shop" Swift, and Larry "Cheshire Cheese" Sterne, and Oliver "Mine's a Pint" Goldsmith, not to mention the infamous tandem cyclist O. Fingal O'Flahertie "Bottoms Up" Wilde and his kinsman Georgie "Anyone for Absinthe?" Moore, and (of course) our old rave fave G. Bernard "I Don't Smoke or Drink or Eat Meat, So There—And by the Way, Isn't Adolf Great?" Shaw. Then there's Bishop "Where Am I?" Berkeley, and the sublime Roger Boyle . . . I could go on, and *my* crowd's been RC since the days of An Uaimh! All credit to the Prods, but: they may spend longer in the jakes than we Papes, but by God they've a brain or two among them, so they do.

[5]God preserve us, that's cardiac itself or I'm a Dutch person named Edo

"Mad, is it?"

"As old King Sweeney, *mo chara*."

"Mr. Gilhooley, it's an apology you'd be owing Mr. Grey, after those offensive words."

"No, no, that's quite all right, Mrs. Gallagher," said Wolfe-tone, straining to recover. After considerable effort, his normal pallor returned, with a dash of orange. "I quite understand Mr. Gilhooley's confusion, and of course the allusion to Sweeney establishes him as a man, shall we say, learned above his station . . . but listen to me, youse cafflers. I know you have things to do, tight schedules and so on, jobs you're obviously longing to return to, God knows why—but that's the point, isn't it? Jobs, work, the way you spend your lives: God, in short. Maybe I can take it from that angle, then. So let me ask you, one by one: why?"

Gingerly, warily, Mrs. Gallagher approached the manager's desk, atop which were two telephones, one red, one black, the red one boasting a direct connection to Garda Headquarters on Haughey Circle—seldom used, but a reassuring presence in the event of holdups, unlawful entry, and threats of physical violence to the person of the manager (or others).

"Why what, Mr. Grey?"

"Why are you all so bloomin' eager to go off and sweep the stairs or carry bags or answer phones or whatever it is you do? I'll tell you why: only because you get paid for it, right? Well? Una, don't you agree?" He aimed his question at Miss Grimes, the entertainment director, but she ducked it with ease, being one of the few staff members suffering from ambition.

"Far from it, Mr. Grey," she said. "Speaking for myself, I can

---

de Waart. The vermilion hue—why, it's the Da to a T, every morning between the eggs and bacon and his third filterless Carrolls Deluxe or Woodbine Full-Strength (but after he'd finished his second pot of Earl Grey, nine sugars a cup). Oddly, it wasn't the ticker that got him in the end, though—it was eruptions on the Isles of Langerhans, of all places, producing effects identical to those consequent to the uncontrolled mutation in the DNA of the mature Antipodean Kangaroo Rat, i.e., utter exhaustion; or so the quacks told us afterward, and your guess is as good as mine as to what the frig they were on about.

honestly say that my goal as entertainment director is to make Spudorgan Hall the premier family resort hotel of the southeast."

"Cobblers," said Gilhooley.

"Oh—you!" Miss Grimes' exasperation shrank her already-pinched features into the mask of a badger, or other burrower.[6] "No, I daresay not *you*, Mr. Gilhooley, I mean you've been here for twenty-odd years, haven't you, and from what I hear the only progress you've made in all that time is going from sitting at Reception letting the customers carry their own bags to swanning about the Porter's Lodge ordering young Gargnan and Gleason here to do it for you. A grand career, to be sure!"

"Aye," said young Gargnan.

"Lolling about, is it? Fifteen years I lugged them bags," roared Gilhooley, with whistling intake of breath. "Fifteen years giving myself hernias and slipped discs, but it was honest labour and now I've made head-bloody-porter days and weekends and I don't have to set here and be insulted by some jumped-up secretary—"

Wolfetone stood up and raised ecclesiastical hands, imposing a hush.

"Come along now," he said. "That's enough."

Silence fell, after limited whispering and grumbling. Unused to such obedience, Wolfetone hesitated; then, prodded invisibly by an Almighty Finger, or his own sense of mission, he started talking and, much to his surprise, was soon explaining with relative fluency and confidence that the great Russian spirit-sleuth Leonid I. Glossovich had made several crucial discoveries about Man and Society, discoveries that had not only changed the way he, Wolfetone, looked at the world, but had also radically altered his own "self-image," as he put it. His eloquence celebrated the apogee of that moment of glory when God, Grey, and Glossovich were, briefly, as one.

"You see, what we call the air, or atmosphere, is really a curtain of impenetrable but invisible and odourless marsh gas," he

---

[6]Mole, ferret, etc.

said, oblivious to the sidelong glances and squirming in his audience. "Behind this curtain lies the 'Near World,' or what Glossovich calls 'Next Door,' of the 'Great Ones' or 'Big Guys.' These are fellas just like you and me, only better, a bit like our own little people—the leprechauns, clurichauns, and so on, don't you know. Now, in fact, these Big Guys are the chosen, or 'Favourites' of God, His booking agents, as Glossovich says—ah he's the one for the *moe joost*, isn't he, you should read this book, by the way—" displaying back cover with photograph of glowering Leonid—"anyhow, as I was saying, through these booking agents, you or I can book enlightenment, the way you'd book a theatre seat, or make a dinner reservation at a fine restaurant. Mind you, it *is* a pretty exclusive club, you'll be happy to know. Enlightenment isn't available to just any old Tomdickharry or Seamus, oh no! The world beyond the curtain belongs to an elite group of 104,000 mortals, all of them bearing surnames beginning with G. They alone are empowered to find the 452 gaps in the curtain and pass beyond. All clear so far?"[7]

Mrs. Gallagher was edging nearer the desk. She nodded, as in understanding, even approval.

"And Leo spotted it, of all people," exulted Wolfetone. "Well done, Leo! It's all in the Gs, you know. Let me put it simply. According to Glossovich, certain names beginning with G are sacred and those who bear them, although they may not know it, are anointed by Him to be the Finders of the Gaps and His special representatives on the other side of the Curtain."

After a brief recapitulation of the marsh-gas theory, Wolfetone enhanced his pose to a stern-jawed, arms akimbo likeness of the Great Leader stance, Peking-Pyongyang version, in vain anticipation of question time. Feet and bottoms were shuffled, youth (Gargnan, Gleason) sniggered, and Gilhooley hastily converted a belly laugh into a cough that overwhelmed shy tittering from athletic Miss Gavigan, the assistant receptionist (weekday afternoons/evenings) and milder expressions of mirth and/or disbelief from the others, except Miss Gupta, who only stared.

---

[7]Crystal. My only question is, where was the KGB when we needed them?

Wolfetone sat down, sensing that his moment had passed.

"Well?" he snapped. He felt drained, exhausted, put upon. "Is it clear or not? Speak up, you mongoloids."

"It is very interesting," said Miss Gupta. "I am thinking of Mahatma Gandhi."

"Yes, all right, but, what about Goebbels?" said Mrs. Gallagher.

"Who?"

"Goebbels. And Goering, come to that. That Nazi shower."

"Aye," said Gilhooley, belly ajiggle with suppressed laughter. "And what about Jungles Con, speaking of Mongoloids?"

"Oh, I see." Wolfetone beamed, revived momentarily by the parry-and-thrust of honest debate. "You mean, what about right horrible bastards who just happen to be G-named? An excellent question. Well, it's very simple. There are two explanations, perhaps more. One, certain names that appear to begin with *G* may actually begin with *H*, and vice versa."

"Like, Hoebbels?" said Mrs. Gallagher. "And Hoering?"

"Exactly. Actually, Herring is a quite common name among the fisherfolk of the Baltic, as well as in the—"

"And Hitler, as long as we're at it?" interrupted Miss Grimes. "Are you saying that his name was really Gitler?"

"In Russian, yes." Wolfetone leaned back and placed his fingertips together, like a college don. "But Glossovich explicitly excludes the non-Slavic *H*, which in Russian is really a false *G*, you know. Gitler, as you so rightly point out; also Galifax, Gemingway, Gooligan, et cetera. But we're not Russians, so we don't have to worry about that."

"That *is* a relief," said Miss Grimes.[8] The faint sneer of sarcasm on her face transformed itself into a semiotic eyebrow wiggle for the benefit of Mrs. Gallagher. That lady, having drawn discreetly parallel to the manager's desk, barely hinted at a frown and a shake of the head.

"Then of course there are the other false *G*s. They have perfectly genuine God-names but they've been sent among us to sow

---

[8]Isn't it? They're a queer lot, aren't they—a bit like us, come to think of it (best not to).

confusion by You Know Who."

"Aw, Christ, I've had enough of this," said Gilhooley.

"Maybe you should be listening more hardly," suggested Miss Gupta.

"Listening to that blether? 104,000 chosen ones? Names starting with *G*? It's all yer fanny, Ragu darling. The man's a nutter."

Crimson with rage, Wolfetone slammed his hand onto the desk. Sweat beaded his brow; veins throbbed in his neck.

"Clowns like you are the exceptions that prove the rule, Gilhooley," he said, in a strident near-shout. The faint tinkle of the phone went unheard in the ambient din of his anger. "You will not be taken up with the 104,000 chosen ones, so there! What do you think of that, then? Eh?" He took a deep, therapeutic breath and counted to three before continuing, then rose slowly from his chair, menacingly, with an unblinking stare. "You're a fool and a Philistine, but I thank you all the same for successfully illustrating Glossovich's Third Principle: never assume all G-names to be God-given. On the other hand," and here his basilisk sternness collapsed into gentle chiding, as if the spirit of forgiveness[9] had ridden through the window on the soft October breeze, "it is never too late, Finbarr, my friend. Remember, you have the great—the inestimable—advantage of being G-named, so no matter how lowly you are in His sight today, you are also on the springboard of eternity: aye, today you may fall, but tomorrow, how high may you also rise!"

"That's right. Spudorgan Hall. Thank you." Smiling the blandest of smiles, Mrs. Gallagher put the phone down with a merry ding.

Wolfetone turned sharply.

"Who was that, Mrs. Gallagher?" His eyes narrowed in suspicion.

"Delivery persons, Mr. Grey. Arriving shortly."

"Delivering what?"

"Oh, this and that. Delivering things, you know."

"Delivering fiddlesticks, Mrs. Gallagher." His shoulders ruefully aslant, Wolfetone looked at her as Caesar did Brutus.

---

[9]Or schizophrenia.

"You've called the guards, haven't you? You think I'm raving."[10]

"Ah, not raving. Not at all, Mr. Grey. You're just a little over-worked, that's all."

These mild protests failed to persuade, but Wolfetone was soon indifferent, at best; at worst, the strain of the experiment had cleared his mind, and the realisation of its failure—utter, absolute, ignominious—sent shivers down his spine and rendered his thigh muscles useless, as after a night's poteen. Leglessly, he slid to the floor, repeating "how high."

"My goodness, poor Mr. Grey. I am feeling very sorry for him," said Miss Gupta.

"He's stone bloody flewtered," said Gilhooley. "No wonder he

---

[10]You can say that again. Speaking of raving, I knew this carry-on reminded me of something: my cousin Ferdia D'Alton, notorious for a week or so a couple of years back as the man who bit Owen Parsley. Ferd was a top-hole motor mechanic (Talbots, Reliants, Daimlers), but after a night on the town (Magherafelt: Tuesday, November 6th) he woke up to find a fella glaring at him that, one way or another, he worked out was God; anyway, he soon got religion, only in his case it was a curious subspecies called Anglislam. Now, as far as I can make out, they're a pretty orthodox C. of E. (or I.) lot, except for their belief in Sufi dervishes and an all-knowing holy class of fella called the Hidden Vicar, who's supposed to pop up just before the Day of Judgement and sort things out. He's such a gas the true believers spend all their lives looking for him, silly buggers. Anyway, one day at a Red Hand rally outside Portrush, the Rev. P. was winding up one of his usual tirades against the Whore of Rome and the Common Market and "the pseudo-Romans," as he calls them, i.e., Jews, Muslims, Marxists, and everybody else, including Anglislamists, who'd been making a few too many converts from Owen's own Wee Frees (proving what I've suspected all along, that one thing both sides up North have in common is Codology on a grand scale); well, Ferdia by that time was a bona fide crusader without a trace of subtlety left in him, so, feeling called upon by Godallah to avenge these insults, he threw himself at the Right. Rev. as he was leaving, freezing onto (as I recall) his arse. Security hammered him to a pulp, of course, but he wouldn't let go, poor chap, sacrificing his left eye and several metacarpals to the One True Faith. Last I heard Big Owen was still in a potty-cast, but Ferdy was out of the jug and on the mend somewhere in the kingdom of the blind—or was it the Shetlands?

was talking such shite. Why the hell didn't he say he'd a drop taken?"

"Because he hadn't, Mr. Gilhooley," said Miss Grimes. "His kind don't need it. They're high on God, you see."

"How high," mumbled Wolfetone.

21

He began, as he always did, by putting on the amice, like a hand towel with white strings attached, at the nape of his neck. The alb followed, floor-length, togalike.

"Salve, Philohippus," Father Doyle said to his mirror-self. He looked better in the alb, he thought. It was plain, neutral, and pure, a blinder on the world's prying gaze. After knotting the cincture around his waist, he paused and leaned forward to inspect his reflection more minutely, assessing his clean-shaven, if somewhat shockingly denuded, cheeks and jawline. The absence of a beard, after seventeen years, made him look fatter, or topless, or something; completely different, anyway, and not necessarily better. Peering, he discovered a blemish on his jowls revealed by the razor, reddish-purple grog blossoms that from a distance might mimic the ruddiness of vulgar good health but were a beacon of over-indulgence to any who cared to look closer. Fortunately, few did. The altar boys wouldn't know the difference, but Skelly the curate was giving him odd looks now and then—did he suspect? Did he know? How much did he know?

What was the difference? Sod the sod, anyway.

He kissed the embroidered cross on his navy blue stole and hung it round his neck. Lastly he inserted his head through the neck-hole of the chasuble and sprang a beardless grin on his unsuspecting reflection. The chasuble was burgundy, with white lines. He stepped back and admired the full effect. In his regalia, he had once seen himself as a delegate of divine mystery, an earthly angel; now he reckoned he looked a bit like a carnival barker, even without the shrubbery.

Roll up, roll up! Come one, come all! Roll up and see the Miracle of the Host!

It was mid-morning Wednesday and the pastor of North Killoyle parish was preparing to celebrate a special Mass for the twenty-fifth wedding anniversary of Ted Nugent, Garda Chief Superintendent for the Southeastern Region (and Youghal) and his wife Moira, a well-known and widely admired local do-gooder, active in Fabfam, Lockjaw Charities, Green Cross, etc.; although it was a grand and happy occasion for the happy couple and their five strapping sons,[1] the strain of being courteous and priestlike all day was a dreadful prospect for Father Doyle, and he would have let young Skelly do the honours if the Mass had been for anybody less exalted than the town's Top Cop. To be sure, Ted Nugent was a decent enough fellow, but he would bring in his wake the entire upper echelons of Killoyle society, notably such eminent flotsam as Ben Ovary, the Mayor, and his simpering wife; Mr. O'May, the pharmacist, and whatever doxy was currently his fancy; big Tom "the Greek" Maher, the estate agent; Oliver MacSmarmey the lawyer and his skeletal wife Smeagòl; Dr. and Mrs. Stan O'Drossa, proprietors of the Kilmainham Clinic on the Waxford Road; Danny Doheny-Nesbitt, the television personality,[2] and too many more such *arlecchini* to put up with, without the benefit of a stiff one. It was

---

[1] An insurance salesman, two computer technicians, a golfer, and a lorry mechanic—ah, lovely lads they are, so they are, especially Stevie the golfer: such impeccable manners he even blows his nose with an Oxford accent!

[2] A self-important bore given to denim outfits and lectures on subjects like the erosion of Ireland's peat bogs and the dangers of infection from handling grimy banknotes; I know, I spent a dreary afternoon with him on the Enniskerry bus. I seem to recall he had a TV quiz show back in the '70s called *Your Wig, My Lord*, featuring such brain-teasers as, "Name the Fine Gaelic backbencher who unexpectedly made moist vibrating mouth-music halfway through Jack Lynch's maiden speech in the Dail. Hint: he later ran off with a barmaid named Nuala." I remember that one for obvious reasons, I was properly ticked off to hear my dear old auntie described as a barmaid. Although she may have pumped the odd pint, she was always an ecdysiast at heart (and much, much more).

an emergency, after all (the infallible excuse). The only question was: where had he stored the stuff? He looked cautiously round the sacristy. The bookcase? The wardrobe? The steamer trunk?

THE WINDOW SEAT!?

It had long been a favourite retreat, with its leaded windows framing a yellowed vista of the car park, Behan Avenue, and a sliver of the sea. He threw aside the cushions, raised the seat, and looked inside. Sure enough, nestled beneath a stack of long-un-read mystery novels—Dino Carr, Betty Sprue, J. B. Gaskett, et al.—and a tarnished Gaelic football trophy dating to the late '40s (Philly Doyle, king of the goalposts!), between his Maynooth scarf of emerald green, edged in yellowish egg white, and a pair of periwinkle-blue bath towels nicked from the Hotel Terminus et de la Gare, Lourdes, lay a bottle of Red Tory Japanese Single Malt, three-quarters empty; or, as Father Doyle hopefully saw it, a quarter full. Either way, it exuded the promised solace of a holi-day, or the first hours of hard-earned unemployment, its amber contents sloshing quietly as he lifted it to the light and looked round for a glass before dismissing the thought on the grounds that a straight slug from the bottle would be the best disinfectant for Mrs. Delaney's breakfast that was lying on his gut heavy as two pregnant ewes—Heaven knew it had worked before, often enough (in fact, he could, and did, blame his wee indulgence on her cooking, as God was his witness he'd never had more than two in a single day, maybe three at the outside, before she started forcing her saucepan scrapings down his throat); accordingly, he took a long pull from the neck, leaning back slightly torso-wise but well-anchored on his feet until, without warning, a jolt shot through his body. His stomach buckled and heaved—his frame shook—his tongue thickened—his eyesight faded, briefly. Hic-cups followed, to an acidic power of magnitude, then, climacti-cally, a stream of buff-coloured puke rushed forth and was depos-ited without further ado in the sink.

Father Doyle wiped his eyes and swore.

"Shitebaskets. That's not whiskey."

After soaking his face in cold water he remembered. It was the old dodge: the bachelor's bedpan, putting your empties to good use, the way you'd not have to go running off to the jakes every ten minutes when you were well into a good solo session, say at home in bed, or in the sacristy, as he'd done (he remembered now) last April, round Easter, relaxing in the window seat after a hard Holy Week . . . so the bottle must have been there since then!

Ah, he was in grand shape for a Mass.

When, presently, he emerged from the sacristy, reeking of soap, his torso vibrating with tiny retchings, the chimes were sounding from the belltower, the congregation were assembled, the altar boys were at their posts. The anemic autumn flowers in their altartop vases, illuminated by a single dusty shaft of sunlight from the Non-Norman Altar Windows, implied a funereal spectacle that reminded Father Doyle of his (and everyone else's) final end. He handed the cruets and censer to the altar boys and faced the congregation, trying to ignore the dual nausea of stage fright and the toxicities just swallowed.[3] It was a fairly good turnout, too good for his liking, with fully one-third of the pews occupied by celebrants ranging from the happy couple in the front row—Superintendent Nugent uniformed and bemedalled to the nth degree, his wife a vision in silk and twill—to their anticipated fellow luminaries, themselves leeched upon by stragglers and sundry human marginalia, social fag ends hoping for free drinks, a foot in someone's mahogany door, or a discreet gorge at the buffet table: lawyers, writers, building contractors, and the like. It was an intimidating sight, or would have been, had the altar been a stage, the church a theatre, the congregation an audience, but Father Doyle reminded himself—as he always did whenever the jitters threatened—that in the dear old, pre-Vatican II church he'd grown up and been ordained in, and to which he was still loyal in his heart (partly from nostalgia, mostly from conviction), his back would be turned to the congregation, thereby cancelling the stagey element. In any event, the only

---

[3]Did you know, by the way, that that particular brew's said by some Hindus to be arch-effective in countering cataracts, tinnitus, bleeding ulcers, and asthma? And would you be surprised to learn that, like you, I'd be willing to take their word for it from now until the sacred cows come home, or Judgement Day, whichever one's later?

spectator of consequence was He Whose Mysteries imbued each and every Mass, and a priest's calling—indeed, his life itself—was, like it or not (and how could you *like* it?), a sacrifice on that heavenly altar; why, the Taoiseach could be there, or the Holy Father himself, both capering about naked as the day they were born, and in the eyes of God it would be as the faintest stirrings of the merest grub under the mouldering compost at gutter's edge . . . *or less!*

Father Doyle shivered, and raised his eyes to give thanks to the source of his faith and fears. In the organ loft, Dairmuid the organist brought the organ to climax, sending the Respighi Toccata in D roiling and rolling up and down the booming vaults of the old church. The Respighi was a real virtuoso piece, chosen by Father Doyle to lift the spirits and give Diarmuid a proper workout, after all that modern rubbish he and Skelly were so keen on. The music settled his stomach and buttressed his heart, and by the hymn-singing he felt no worse than mildly hungover, with none of those dodgy pains in the right arm; in fact, he was beginning to feel quite good, reasonably fit, almost himself (he thought, worriedly) . . . .

In due course, all sat for the sermon, painstakingly constructed on the premise that there was a parallel between faith and marriage (wrinkled smile kindly bestowed on Mr. and Mrs. Nugent): in one, the spouse our helpmeet, in the other, the Lord, *idem*—in other words, in both you needed to set aside your momentary fears and doubts in the interest of the greater love that was eternal.

Speaking of doubts, said Father Phil, a certain parable came to mind.

"The Gadarene swine—you all know the one I'm referring to, of course. Thomas? Matthew? The two of them telling our Lord about the fella near eaten up by his demons? Aye, that's the one, sure you all know it, who doesn't, but have you ever looked at it as a test of faith? I'd used it in my sermons for years before it struck me. Think about it. Our Lord goes to the man and casts out the demons, causing them to enter a herd of swine, who become maddened, rush into a river, and drown. Your man recovers nicely, and gives thanks to his Saviour, as you'd expect, all well and good—only hang on a moment, I don't know about you, but suddenly I found myself wondering: what price the poor swine? Couldn't our Lord have simply sent the demons straight back to hell? And how did the swineherd feel, seeing his prize hogs charging off the cliff?"

He glared at the congregation, baiting them with his own makeshift doubts.

"Now, if we stop there, the whole thing does seem rather unfair, doesn't it?" he continued. "Here's the score sheet: one man saved, fair enough, but another man's livelihood's up the spout and a herd of harmless old piggies are wiped out, just like that. A fine old three and fourpence, you'd be saying—sure, where's the justice in it, at all?" he shouted, spotting a head in the third row lolling in sleep, or boredom—it jerked upright, awake, or suddenly engrossed—"but that's what makes this story a parable, which is to say a moral lesson in anecdotal form, not just a yarn for the lads at the local. It tests our faith, it shows us the limits, it makes us take notice, and we need all of that, for without faith, brothers and sisters, nothing makes sense, not the parables, not the miracles, not the story of Our Lord's suffering, not life itself, unless you're an atheist, or a pagan, or a hopeless case altogether. So the true Christian must see setbacks, when they come, as part of God's infinite wisdom, not just as a bad hand at the card table—in the same way that we must believe Our Lord saw beyond the transitory pain of those old pigs and their owner to greater reasons unknown to humble sinners like you and me."[4]

He drifted dreamily on, in pursuit of other parables—the loaves and the fishes, the walking on the waters, the prodigal son, all of them (he maintained) traps for the faithless, to a greater or lesser degree—and concluded his sermon with a neat contrapuntal flourish in which the ideal principle common to marriage and faith, that of lifelong (or even eternal) fidelity, was contrasted to the real-life, practical slogan of a certain outlaw institution

---

[4]Well, to be quite honest about it, I've been harking to that priest's palaver since I was a nipper, and it hasn't really helped on long trips quite as much as a nice hot Ovaltine, or a good old bit of fiddling on the radio (ideally both)—but that's probably just me.

up North allegedly dedicated to long-term virtues by means of short-term vice, viz.: *once in, never out!* The analogy was appreciated by the congregation—after all, Killoyle had once been a Republican stronghold (pre-1923)—and loud was the laughter when Father Doyle said, "Now that I've spoken my piece, I'll come quietly, Superintendent."

"You're entitled to one phone call first, Father," retorted Superintendent Nugent, and so raucous was the mirth consequent to this fine instance of Irish wit that the solemn veil of the Mass lifted, briefly, to reveal a Mayfair salon, *circa* 1890, with footmen circulating silver trays among ladies and gentleman of unimpeachable style, Messrs. Wilde and Shaw themselves being the guests of honour! The illusion vanished, however, when Father Doyle cleared his throat with unmistakable significance and the congregation rose to sing "Our Lord Is a Genial Host."

After the Mass, the newly re-weds presided over a reception and sit-down champagne luncheon in Spudorgan Hall's Balsa Room, venue of many of the town's premier social events. *Le tout* Killoyle banded together in the middle, while the socially covetous circled them like hyenas. Father Doyle, as a member of neither group, repaired to the outskirts, nursing a light Chablis—white wine being the ideal compromise between the false abstemiousness of a soft drink and the excessive booziness of, say, a double malt—and was surprised to be approached by the Greek Maher, cap aslant, sipping a Ballygowan on the rocks.[5]

"Grade-A sermon, Father," said the Greek. "You know, I don't believe I'll ever look at that old parable quite the same way again, thanks to you."

"Nor you will, Mr. Maher," said Father Doyle. "And nor will I."

Maher gave him a penetrating look that reminded Father Doyle, quite spontaneously, of the eyes of Michelangelo's devils

---

[5]That's a mineral water, in case you were wondering, Ireland's answer to Perrier, minus the kerosene—or is it benzine? Sounds to me like old Maher's a young Pioneer, just like my Uncle Francie, before the visions started.

in the Sistine Chapel.[6]

"Smallish crowd in church today, eh, Father?"

"About standard for a weekday Mass I'd say, maybe a little larger than—"

"Oh, right enough, but I mean generally, like, with the old folks snuffing it right and left and the young ones the way they are, business is thinning out a bit, wouldn't you say?"

"Well, if you mean, are people coming to church in the numbers they used to—"

"What I'm getting at, Father, is this. My sources tell me St. O'Toole's down the way's been doing a deal better than dear old Oinsias'. St. Pee and Ell's the coming church—the society church, they call it, because as you know it sits on a very desirable site adjacent to the marina and the new dog-racing grounds. I even heard they're getting some smart young curate in down there to replace Father Whatsit, you know, the old hoor that did the swan dive out the window—"

"I take it you'd be referring to Monsignor Stripling."

"Right, absolutely. Whereas over at St. Oinsias' you're not really adjacent to much, are you? Bugger all, if you ask me, begging your pardon, apart from the MacLiammoir Overpass and those old shops the Corporation condemned last year. Mind you, things could change, what with the new dual carriageway from Waxford and the revised Concordat Gar Looney's been pushing through the Dail, not to mention the sort of view you'd have from thereabouts—from St. Oinsias', that is, with a few minor modifications, like a spot of demolition . . . aye, I've no doubt of it. Do you credit it, Father"—as he breathed closer, preparing for

---

[6]And wouldn't I take a Killarney jaunting car round the world itself to avoid having dinner with those johnnies! Only it struck me, the first time I saw them (mind you, it was a school trip, and I was in the lower third at St. Saviour's at the time, but even then I had a reputation as being a hard one to cod) that they'd the class of build on them you'd expect to find, quite frankly, gracing the centrefold in *Muscular Person Singular*, or *Glam*, or one of those rags, rather than the gates of Hell! I suppose you'll be calling me a Philistine and an art-hater next. Well, *ars gratia artis*—or, as Da always used to say, round Waxford Festival time: The arse scratches the artist.

a confidence, his eyes bulged almost[7] clownishly—"I've been hearing some shocking things round town."

"Have you, indeed?"

"I have. I've heard, for instance, that Ben Ovary's being investigated by the attorney general."

"Well, that's Ben's business, surely. Or the attorney general's."

"Not necessarily. I've also heard very interesting things about our Lord Mayor and his Southeast Asian investments."

Father Doyle was getting irritated. It was like being back in school again, on the playground with some lout like Sticky Muldoon (commander-to-be of the Bogside Brigade) trying to organise an expedition to the girls' changing rooms.

He stepped sideways, but Maher lunged like a moray eel.

"I've also had a nugget or two about this noble establishment"—eyes uprolled, indicating their surroundings—"and"— he downrolled his gaze, bringing it into focus on his true target— "I'm sure you've heard the news about St. Oinsias', as long as we're on the subject."

"You're on the subject, Mr. Maher, not I. What news?"

"They're planning to close down your operation and make St. O'Toole's the pro-cathedral."

Father Doyle spluttered into his wine.

"What do you mean, operation? What do you think I am, a heroin dealer?"

"Ah, now, that would be between your conscience and your God, Father. But do you mean you've not heard about it?" Maher smacked his lips, savouring the moment. "I suppose I could have been misinformed, but between you and me—"

"And who's 'they'? The Curia? The Mafia? The Killoyle Hurling Team?"

"Well, in a normal line of business it'd be head office, and as your GHQ's in Rome I'd guess it would be the men in the Vatican who call the shots. Sure, amn't I the humble layman, just, and aren't you the one in Holy Orders with all the inside info fresh from the *Observatory Romano*, haha? All I know's what I

---

[7]But not quite.

read in the paper, as the man said. Actually, if you want my opinion, Father, I'd say business is business, whatever you're selling,
and in business, if there's one ironclad law, it's no demand, no
supply. Eh? Aha, there he is. Me hard man!"

He suddenly seemed sloshed, a sloppy smile spilling across his
face at the sight of the approaching Superintendent Nugent—
seemed being the operative word, thought Father Doyle, because
in reality Maher was as cold sober and calculating as any Church
bureaucrat (could they seriously be planning to do the dirty on
him, the sods?), as his subsequent actions implied: deciding he
was outgunned by the Garda, at least for the time being, Maher
was plainly trying to disarm potential opposition with the age-
old Irish countryman's stratagem of playing the buffoon.

"God bless and keep ya, Superintendent tharlin'—and wasn't
Oi just afther sayin' to meself, Misther me man, if da craychur
don't getcha, da rozzers will."

Booming gusts of laughter honoured this peerless display of
stage Irishry, in which others—Dickie Doheny-Nesbitt, the
Lady Mayoress, O'May the pharmacist—joined with gusto. Feeling faintly nauseous, Father Doyle was preparing to leave when a
wine bottle wrapped in a serviette thrust itself under his nose,
followed by the unsvelte person of headwaiter Rogers.

"More wine, *Monseigneur?*"

Father Doyle was tempted, but resisted, steeled by the thought
of the greater temptation he could yield to later, in the privacy
of the presbytery—real whiskey this time, in an unopened pint
measure, snuggling up to his socks and shirts in the laundry bas-
ket, the perfect hiding place, unless that old cow was snooping
again; she'd a nose on her like a bloodhound when it came to
finding his supplies, so maybe he should stop and buy a back-
up pint on the way back, just in case—no, he should go home
and change first, he couldn't risk being seen going into the off-
license in full church clobber[8] (but that would mean running into

---

[8]Bless you, that never stopped the cardinal, in the old days. Prince of the
Church robes and all, he thought nothing of going in the back way at
Feeley's Bar after-hours and carrying out a paper bag clinking with
"liquid parishioners," as he called the Magog's Gold Malt and James

Mrs. Delaney) . . . .

Racked by doubts and fears, he left unobserved, except by the poet Rogers (and God).

Johnson's Deluxe Multi-blended he always favoured as aids to his beauty sleep. One night he ran into the Da coming home from work and without being asked reached into the bag and pulled out a bottle of JJ's and two glasses, and didn't the pair of them make a right old night of it, "on the chirping slopes of Cahill's Hill / beneath the rubbery moon" (Hoolihan, *Verdant Verses*, canto 3)! Mind you, they said later that was when His Eminence caught the chill that killed him, God rest his soul, and not from that day to the last one of his own life did the Da look at a bottle of James Johnson's again, but he was quite enthusiastic about wine, and the new Bushmans line of raspberry-scented whiskey liquors.

22

Swiftly and silently as the star of some appalling low-budget horror flick, the Greek maneuvered his bulk into dimly lit Oxtail Yard, blocking the view of Spudorgan Hall and the MacLiammoir Overpass looking north, while commanding the southward one of Oxtail Corners, his least favourite housing estate. In one hand he held a plastic carrier bag from Brown Thomas' of Grafton Street;[1] in the other, car keys jangled on a Daimler-Benz key ring. On his head, instead of his trademark Donegal cap, was a wool bonnet pulled down to eyebrow level. A casual observer might have noticed that he was dressed entirely in the nocturnal shades of the New Zealand rugby team, the better to melt into the background. It was eleven p.m. and the neighbourhood was as still as a Sunday in Coleraine,[2] apart from the hollow booming of a television in no. 7b. The Greek cackled quietly as he padded up to the curtained windows.

"Hahahaha. Heeheeheehee."

Outside no. 7b, he risked a peek through a gap in the curtains and was rewarded by the unappetising spectacle of that wanker Rogers in his undershorts, in the act of hoisting a jar. The Greek could even see the bobbing of the fellow's Adam's apple as he swallowed his drink—probably a Triple X, like the poteen-laced

---

[1]Flaming overpriced den of snooty jackanapeses. I once paid £50 for a wool muffler there, but even so I had to cuff the salesman about the ears when he looked me up and down and said, "Ha!", the cheeky bugger.
[2]Try Randalstown, Co. Antrim. A man was arrested there last year for coughing too loudly on a Sunday (suspended sentence, £50 fine).

Hyper Ale they served the head cases at Mad Molloy's—while at the same time reaching into his Y-fronts to scratch himself, thoroughly and vigorously, with a grimace of pleasure. The Greek assaulted him with several consecutive disapproving glares through the chink in the curtains. The miserable hand-jobber, lolling about half-pissed in front of the television! What kind of tenant was he, at all? He lived like a pig and never paid his rent on time, so whatever he got, he deserved, and what he was about to get was: EASI-FERT!

In other words: liquid concentrate of cow manure, widely marketed to the farming trade as a shortcut to longer growing seasons. Sprinkled liberally throughout the cellar, it would, the Greek was confident, be more effective than a mere dead dog in driving home his message to no. 7b—and, by the way, it would be no great misfortune if no. 7c, that bartending berk, and no. 8, the Pakis, were likewise motivated to up stakes and move on. With the whole block empty—and if the manure method didn't work, there were other ways, short of your actual eviction notices and the law courts (always risky): cousins Tiny and Stan, the fast-knuckle artists from the Archway, for a start—demolition could begin, and what a swish approach Oxtail Corners (renamed Maher Place, with the cooperation of the town council) would make to the Spudorgan Hall and St. Oinsias' sites, once he'd done a proper job[3] on them as well (Dr. Thomas Maher Esplanade?)!

The key barely chirped in the lock as the Greek let himself into the cellar. He gingerly closed the door behind him and stood motionless for a moment, waiting for his eyes to adjust to the darkness before setting about his task. He removed the sloshing container from his carrier bag and probed the floor with the toe of his right shoe to ascertain flatness of surface, not wanting to pour the liquid into a hole where it might stagnate—fester—impregnate the foundations—breed mosquitoes—stink up the place permanently—even drive down property values (city-wide)! After a brisk trot round the cellar, satisfied that the floor was level, he propped open the door with a handy brick, clapped a handker-

---

[3]Job, is it? Well, you can't say I didn't warn you.

chief to his nose, and started the irrigation, moving in a rapid crouch as nimbly as a gorilla, or Groucho Marx. At first, the odour was merely obnoxious, but it soon seemed to double in intensity every second (or less); by the time he had covered half the floor area of the cellar, he was choking on the fetid air, despite the modest ventilation from the door—but the door, he realised with a cold inward swooning, was now at the far end of the cellar . . . !

Worse yet, the tiny draft that trickled through was ushering the fumes inwards, rather than drawing them out . . . .

"Feckin' hell," gasped the Greek.

The stench was soon so monstrous that he found himself involuntarily emitting loud and persistent groans similar to the belling of a stag. His reek-steeped handkerchief was no longer any kind of defence, and his hands were swarming with the scent of methane. The neck of his pullover was cut too low to cover his nose, leaving his face hopelessly exposed. Prodded by panic, his mind raced, outraced by the fiendish stink. It was a desperate situation. It was clear that his only hope of avoiding asphyxiation (sudden bowel-loosening death, himself discovered facedown in the muck) was to bleeding well bugger off without a second's delay; accordingly, coughing boisterously, he threw down the container—which emptied its contents onto the floor with the comfortable gurgling of a draining bathtub—and stumbled out the door, moments ahead of oblivion. Never had the innocent night air smelled so sweet. Gagging and heaving, the Greek staggered into the road like a maddened bear and made a crashing ursine exit through the privet hedges and thornbushes.

Lights went on up and down Oxtail Yard, and it wasn't long before the first resident (not Milo), took a tentative sniff and said, "Phew! What's that horrible stink?"[4]

---

[4]All these olfactory high jinks bring to mind—yours as well as mine, I daresay—our chum Jim Barnacle of *The Haunted Overcoat* fame. Well, I'm happy to report they finally had their first night at the Peacock Theatre, but—alas—the critics were merciless. "Feces," barked Omar Hogg-Davies of the *Times*. "The way Barnacle writes, you'd think he was a solicitor's clerk or something," pouted Sheridan Pyle of the *Independent*. "Where's my bucket?" mournfully inquired Jupiter O'Brady of the *Longfordian*. It isn't all bad news, though; Jim won't necessarily have

to go back to sitting in a stoop-shouldered posture at the law office, grovelling and fawning and nursing his ulcers. Word on Abbey Street's that a deal's in the works with New Zealand TV for a five-part mini-series starring Claudia Fiammiferi and Jock MacHooter.

23

Emmet and Roisin lay back and looked into each other's eyes like feral lovers from the forests of Arcadia, half-stunned by the realisation that it was yet possible, at ages fifty-four and fifty-two respectively, to jointly ignite the flame of sex.[1]

"How long was it—three months?"

"Ach, get away. More like four."

"I was a bit distracted, acushla. One thing or another had me going. I don't know, I was feeling out of sorts."

"I noticed, Emmet. I'm not blind, you know."

"Of course not. I only meant."

Sweet suffering Jay, moaned Emmet inwardly, why was it so difficult to put into words, even at a time like this? He reached for the champagne she'd unaccountably laid in while he was away, and sipped disdainfully, an unwilling orgiast.

"I meant I was going through a sort of moral crisis, I suppose you'd call it."

"You mean that's what your friend the Jesuit priest would call it."

"Well, he did say something along those lines. But he said he reckoned it was a healthy sign. The sign of the true Christian, he

---

[1]Undoubtedly. There are those who say it gets better with age, although I'm not one of them. Personally, I never enjoyed it that much to begin with, except the Irish way (half-undressed after a quick fumble, with the soft pitter-pat of rain on the roof and the faint aroma of bacon in the air).

said, is hesitation in the face of choice, because it means you're figuring out the morality of the thing. Actually, what I think he was getting at was fellas like Carfax—or even Maher, God help us—plunging right in whenever they see the glint of gold and not giving a toss about the moral angle. Mind you, Father Pat went easy on the evangelising. He knew he was dealing with a hard case, but he said the whole business showed I was at least thinking about these matters, you know, not glossing them over, or finding convenient excuses."

"You mean the embezzling and that."

"Well, yes, but that's not all." A belly-deep sigh warned of impending solemnity. "There's things I've done to you, acushla, behind your back, like, that I've not told you about. Things I'm heartily ashamed of."

"Such as?"

Propping himself on one elbow, Emmet winced, suffering; yet luxuriating, too, in the martyrdom of the moment. Roisin stared at him, puzzled. When he got to the Geneva Airport episode, after the ersatz marmalade and brief memory-sojourns in Muldoon's Betting Shop and various pubs on the other side of town —squandering hard-earned money like (to hear him tell it) a ne'er-do-well, and soaking up the drink like (in his words) "a sea sponge"—she began to laugh.

"You're such an old ninny, Emmet. Why don't you go out and actually *do* something wicked, if you're so keen to own up?"

Momentarily peeved, he turned his back and sipped more champagne, but in her practical womanly way she soon steered him back to the dominant issue.

"The embezzling, dear."

"Aye. Right." His gaze was frank, unclouded, uxorious. "Well, it's funny, isn't it. It's not the embezzlement itself that bothered me overly—I mean, right enough, I'd not be in favour of giving Carfax a medal for services to the nation, but it was more the fact of being let down by your own employer, you know, here's this bugger who's been paying my salary for years and suddenly I discover his hand's been in the till all the time. His own bloody till, for Christ's sake."

"What will you do about it, so?"

Ah, that was the question Father Patric had failed to answer, except obliquely, by reminding Emmet, as he was about to leave, of that useful distinction drawn in the Gospels between what was Caesar's and what was God's.[2]

Emmett drove to work the next morning thinking about this and allied matters, like his own blinkered judgement in appointing Wolfetone Grey to fill in for him, despite well-formed misgivings. "Time you started using a dash of common sense, Power me lad," he told himself, ruefully.

The journey to the Hall took longer than usual, as the entire North Side had been sealed off by the Garda, jamming traffic onto the MacLiammoir Overpass. After sitting for ten minutes behind a car from Germany, Emmett rolled down his window and summoned a lounger.

"What's up?"

"Don't you smell it?"

True enough, the air was faintly flavoured with flatus, but Emmett's first inclination had been to attribute it to his interlocutor, a dodecephalic itinerant in his mid to late fifties, with the vein-patterned eyeballs of an addict.

"They had to evacuate a whole street down near the church," said the man. "The guards say it was a gas leak or something like an overturned lorry full of old socks or Jesus Christ Almighty can you catch the hum off it an entire brigade of men with unwashed oxters itself."

It was, at any rate, not a bomb, and that was always a relief, in the Ireland of then.[3] There were enough loonies about without bombers to boot, mused Emmett, dispatching his Peugeot in slow pursuit of the Mercedes from Essen, by means of clutch depression and a quick shift into first; logically enough, the thought-

---

[2]It's what's in between that worries me—or are we supposed to assume that what doesn't belong to one must belong to the other? What if a third party lays claim? What about the endless back-and-forth lawsuits that bedevil the Irish countryside? What about dogs, or bonfires, or the cooing of the courting woodpigeon (the sweetest sound of all to me, that is)?

[3]I.e., last October.

topic of lunacy invoked a mental image of Wolfetone Grey, and this lured him into a brown study, from which he only emerged to supervise the forward motion of his car as far as the familiar, dreaded gates of Spudorgan Hall that customarily ushered the motorist into one of two car parks, left for staff, right for guests. Emmet eased his Peugeot into the manager's space and went inside. Mrs. Gallagher was waiting in his office.

"I spoke to Mrs. Grey earlier, sir," she said. "She said he's been lying in bed for about twelve hours, hardly moving."

"Dead, God save us?"

"No. Apparently he'd been talking on the phone quite a lot."

"Ah."

An unanswered question hovered, buzzed, nipped, and was swatted away.

"Then there's Rogers, Mr. Power. He won't be in today."

"What happened to him? Too much wine, I'd bet."

"Eh—no, not exactly. He's in hospital with a powerful case of nausea, the doctor said. His house is right over the source of the gas leak, you know—oh, perhaps you didn't . . . ?"

"I saw it, just now. They've closed off the upper roadway. Nausea, is it? Poor old Milo. Still, it won't be exactly an unfamiliar sensation to him, will it? Call him later, Mrs. G, and ask if he wants Grey's job."

"Milo? Catering supervisor?"

"Why not? He's a bright enough fella. Anyway, Grey certainly won't be back now. We can work out some early retirement dodge. Good God, we can't have senior staff going about ramming their own nutty beliefs down the employees' throats. It's outrageous."

After the door closed behind Mrs. Gallagher's broad beam and slowly shaking head,[4] Emmet pondered the extent to which Wolfetone's proselytising was indeed outrageous—intolerable—impermissible—scandalous, etc.; and not just because it was some new religion (Russian, as he understood) he was peddling, either. Father Patric MacCarthy would be the first, Emmet was

---

[4]Understandably; the poor creature's had a shock: MILO? CATERING CHIEF!?

sure, to discourage such hamhanded and unsubtle attempts at conversion, even of unbelievers by devout Catholics.

"You see, Emmet," he'd said (having led the way to the smiling uplands of first-name terms), priestly hands scuttling between cigars and coffee—and bloody good coffee, too: Brazilian arabica, rich and black—"it isn't my mission to convert the heathen, although of course as a Jesuit I belong to the order that Christianized half the world, from the headhunters of Timor to the Guarani of Paraguay; no, my mission's right here, with the young priests we're training." Two such had joined them for lunch, and had retired soon afterwards, with murmured apologies: clean-shaven, well-spoken young men, thought Emmet, a welcome change from today's run-of-the-mill yobs—assuming they weren't secret self-molesters, or gay buggers even, as was known to occur among those sworn to lifelong avoidance of women—but those chaps were surely too ascetic and bookish for that (still, you never knew) . . . "*they're* the ones who'll be going out there and holding off the enemies of the Church," continued Father Pat, "while I sit here on the sidelines and cheer them on. Mind you, if I see the chance of winning back the occasional lost soul, then I'm certainly willing enough to throw myself into the fray."

"Forget it, Father." Emmet spoke with beaming candour to this most beaming and candid of priests. "I'm not the errant sheep you're looking for."

"But you are, Emmet. You are indeed. You've a good brain fitted with a moral compass, and that's rarer than you might think. You're a loyal husband and father and, I've no doubt, a fair boss, yet you're restless and dissatisfied. Naturally, as a priest, I'd attribute that to the void within you, symptom of the searcher."

"No void after that spread," proposed Emmet, patting his belly and thereby overreaching wit to grab at the obvious. Father Patric grunted and pursued his point.

"A spiritual void, of course. Now, as an unbeliever you'd no doubt find a euphemism for it, probably one borrowed from psychoanalysis, something like dysfunctionality or male menopause or midlife crisis or some such—by the way, a fine substitute for religion that's turned out to be, wouldn't you say? Providing all the miseries with none of the solace and charging an arm and a leg for the privilege? I speak not as a eunuch in the matter, in case you were wondering, but as a former lover of the mind science, in fact at Louvain I was the student of Bishop Joachim Schindler, who himself studied under a pupil of Adler's, in Zurich."

"Is that so? Actually, it never caught my fancy. It always struck me as the ultimate form of self-abuse, a bit like renting Croke Park just to wave your willie at the punters. Anyway, I could never see myself blethering away about my own worries to a total stranger. Sure, if I wanted to do that, I'd go to the pub."

"Solid Irish sense. Freud, you know, said we were the one race he always found impossible to get on the couch."

"Did he now. Very sound. Equally difficult, I should say, to *have* one of us on the couch, too, if you follow my . . . ?"

"Sexual innuendo. There you are. If that's not the Viennese influence, what is?"

"Just my dirty mind, Father. My marital relations aren't great, these days."

"Well, that ought to be easy enough to remedy. How's your coffee?"

Excellent, excellent, the best since the underslung burnt-cinnamon at the Bay Window, that day with Maher—a propos of whom . . . .

Emmet sat up, as if stung by the hovering thought of a moment before. How odd people were, the way they went through life ignoring the obvious! Heads buried in the sand when they weren't turned away in disdain, like pouting kids refusing to eat their spinach: death, for instance, seldom prepared for, never really expected; ditto deception, disappointment, betrayal; ignorance likewise, and madness, and superstitions that might, in themselves, be a refuge for the culturally uninformed—religion's great appeal, after all, was as a substitute for all the stuff that takes too much time and effort for the average blowhard—hang Beethoven, sod Rembrandt, up Plato's, I'll take Rod McIdiot and Brainless Boyne and *The Late Late Show* and let God manage the rest, after all He churns out such great art, doesn't He? Notre Dames, Sacred Hearts, Pietàs and what have you—read books? Me? I'd love to, mate, but I haven't the time, I'm far too busy writing computer programs/trading dollars for yen/painting houses/repairing cars/managing hotels . . . .[5]

Well, there you had it. A little learning was a dangerous thing, especially when blended with frustration and failure and all of today's commonplace confusion. Result: Wolfetone Grey, or some other poor benighted sod declaring he and he alone had stumbled on the secret of life; on the other hand, combine virtually no learning at all (or rather, the shrewd, survival of the fittest variety of basic mix-'em-up education, i.e., everything's money so nothing really matters) with the conscience of a crocodile, and presto! A Carfax was born—or a Maher.

Emmet swivelled in his chair and took in three views: that of the harbour, sparkling in the morning light; that of his office, whitewashed by the reflected sun; and that, internal, of his mind, still clouded by doubts. He focused on the latter view, hoping to see more clearly. What he saw, as the fog slowly lifted, was very much like the interior of his briefcase—indeed, it *was* the interior of his briefcase, which, although at that very moment slumping against the desk like a tired racehorse, yet totally preoccupied his thoughts, hence the image, mind-as-briefcase; in any case (briefly), the object itself contained three ledgers, each one stuffed with enough information, cross-referenced to actual income, overheads, gross capital expenditures, average tax payment for hotels in the same category, etc., to uphold Maher's charges and indict Carfax for tax evasion and embezzlement of funds— or, at the very least, embarrass him into permanent exile. It was a powerful weapon, that briefcase, but Emmet had to make sure it didn't blow up in his face, in a manner of speaking. It very well

---

[5]Didn't they make books portable so you *could* read them on the bus, or at the lunch counter, or in the bath—I mean, it's not as if you were being asked to lug the blooming *Book of Kells* about, is it? There's always time to read. Take me, for instance: when I was swotting for my Guinness clerkship (second class), I'd drive in from Roscommon every day of the week, and in my left paw, next to the steering wheel, was a slim volume of Plunkett. On the return journey, every night, that same volume was in my right hand, and in my left was a Carleton, or Harrington's latest. In between was my head; adjacent to that, the wheel. It was tricky, but it worked. Try it yourself sometime.

might, if he called Carfax's bluff and made the information public—ah, then he could just see Maher himself popping up like a jack-in-the-box, all wind and blarney, demanding his pound of flesh, waving transcripts and chits and counterfoils from those banks in Liechtenstein and the Isle of Man . . . but of course *that* bit wasn't illegal. Any businessman with more than three quid in his pocket was trying for a numbered offshore account these days. No, it was what was inside the ledgers that would do the trick, one way or another.

Emmet suddenly, urgently, longed to scarper, to take his Roisin with him to the storied south, or the golden east, somewhere with distant snowpeaks like crumpled wastepaper on a vast horizon, beneath the blue bowl of the universe, with the scent of resin and honeysuckle on the air . . . ![6]

Clenching his fists, he made groaning noises akin to those associated with bowel blockage and raised imploring eyes to the Wales-shaped damp patch (minus Anglesey, Glamorgan, and parts of Dyfed) on the ceiling that came between him and (say) God:

What, then, must I do? he wailed at (e.g.,) God, via Wales.

Throw them ledgers away, boy bach, replied "God" through Wales, with a Gallic shrug. *Then quit yer job and piss off.*

Yes, but there was the future to think of: Roisin, their savings, his pension. He'd need another job, and at his age they wouldn't be handing them out on the street corners.

With the impeccable timing of desperation, Emmet suddenly remembered that Father Pat might, unwittingly, have supplied the answer—not the bit about rendering unto Caesar, etc., although he'd said that with just the right amount of ironic emphasis on the word *God* to make it clear where his sympathies lay, but before that, when he was (as Emmet had thought at the time) rabbiting on excessively about his travels: didn't he say they needed a *manager* at that seminary-cum-youth-hostel place in

---

[6]Ah, that'll be the Knockmealdowns, as seen from Ballybunion, or the Twelve Ton Strand. There's a fine wee b.-and-b. near there: "Beelea," run by my Uncle Francie's ex-wife Nuala, she of the lowered profile and lifted face.

Italy? Or was it a Maynooth priest?

OR BOTH!?

Emmet was reaching for the black phone (direct lines to Directory Enquiries, Front Desk, Night and Day Receptionists) when the red one (direct lines to Garda HQ, *Bord Failte, Bord nà Mona*, etc.) rang. The subsequent voice identified itself as belonging to Teddy Egan of Blemished Kiddies Rescue Worldwide, and indeed there was a throbbing earnestness in it that might have convinced someone who had never received a call from Father Patrick MacCarthy of the Travelling Redemptorists; but now, at last, Emmet knew he had his man.

"Is that you, Grey?"

"Egan, Mr. Power. Teddy Egan's the name; kiddie rescue's the game. Did you know, sir, that the fate of forty thousand severely blemished children may be hanging in the balance? You heard me right, sir: forty thousand, in this country and abroad, poor abused kiddies with no one to turn to, and all because of the blemishes they were born with, sir. That's correct, sir, I said blemishes. Did you know that in some cultures, God save and protect us, such as the Fulani of West Africa and the Cherokee of Oklahoma, birthmarks on the nose and cheekbones are regarded as the fingerprints of the Devil, or Beelzebub himself, especially when visible by night?"

"Ach, for God's sake, Grey."

"Egan, sir. Now I wouldn't be invading your precious schedule, sir, without very good reasons, and they are as follows: primo, our organisation's trying to raise a hundred thousand pounds Irish by the end of this month to cover adoption costs for the latest boatload of blemished kids from Africa and the West Indies; secondo—"[7]

---

[7]Actually, now that you mention it, the O'Hares next door adopted one of those wretches, a Hindu girl from Trinidad named Indra Pal. Her only flaw was a scimitar-mark extending from the left nostril-wing to the edge of the right jawbone; otherwise, she was a dish, and made sure everyone knew it, too, going on to change her name several times and winning scholarships to beauty institutes in Berlin, Paris and Milan; training as Joan Fondell's understudy in the Oscar-nominated film

"Primosecondo yourself, Grey: (a) you're sacked; (b) if you make any more of these damned phone calls, I'll be making one myself, to Superintendent Nugent."

"I'm sorry you have to take this attitude, sir. My name's Egan, Teddy Egan."

"Well, fuck off, then, Teddy Egan. You're sacked too."

Confident that he'd demonstrated grace under pressure—i.e., genius—Emmet boastfully recapitulated the incident some minutes later for Mrs. Gallagher, when she came in with his mid-morning coffee, but instead of the expected murmurs of approbation she looked him up, down, and sideways and exclaimed, "Not Teddy Egan, Mr. Power? Why, he's an angel in human form, so he is. Do you know how many poor black babies wouldn't be alive today without that man's selfless dedication? And white babies too, some of them Irish I've no doubt, exposed on cold mountainsides because of a birthmark or a freckle in the wrong place? Oh, I've always donated to Blemished Kiddies. It's one charity that actually seems to do something, you know? Mr. Power, I don't mind saying I'm quite surprised at you."[8]

Queen of the Vinegar Crisps; appearing on the covers of such publications as *Glam*, *Tibetts*, *Ostrogoth*, and *Spume*; giving master classes at the Anglo-Trinidadian Institute, and of course authoring the best-selling *Loving Your Birthmarks* under the name P. Pears. It was thanks to her guidance that the Birthmarked Persons Task Force forced legislation through both houses of Congress and Parliament, and when the first openly birthmarked Head of State, a Russian named Gorbachev (or -chov?), resigned through no choice of his own, Indra, under the name P. Ploughperson, filed an antidiscrimination suit on behalf of the Birthmarked Persons Task Force, in the World Court at The Hague. Between you and me, she's being talked about for the Nobel Prize in the same breath as Lord Irons, Father Mark Cuspidor, Lola Managua, and Omar Ben Salaad.

[8] Well, that might seem a trifle, but surely it's no worse than the Fulani using interlocking brass nose rings during the mating season, or the Inuit painting their backsides green to confuse the polar bear. Believe me, sonny, I've studied a good number of primitive peoples, including my own, and you wouldn't believe the heights of idiocy human beings can reach without even trying. Just spend a July 12th on the Ormeau Road, or an Easter Monday at Bodenstown—or look at Lourdes, for the

With a toss of her perm, she sailed superbly out. Emmet puckered his lips and cooled his coffee with short, intense exhalations. To his freshly minted resolution to burn the ledgers (after telling Carfax what he knew) and resign his job (after finding out from Father Pat about that manager's position in Italy), he added another: to write a cheque to Blemished Kiddies Rescue, nothing overly generous, of course, a quiet three figures, maybe four . . . and yet! He could have sworn!

THAT VOICE!

Emmet seethed. Why was it still so hard to tell the difference between life and farce, at the age of fifty-four?

---

love of all that's holy (so-called)! Desiccated oldsters who should have been in their graves years ago, feebly twitching under starter's orders in the bath chair Grand Prix, each and every one of them seriously expecting to finish the race not only as a non-invalid, but deeply tanned and twenty years younger into the bargain, with money in the bank and a vacation home on the Costa Brava! Honestly. Even Glossovich seems halfway sane by comparison (well, maybe not, but you take my point).

24

"Catering Supervisor."
"CHIEF CATERING ADMINISTRATOR?"
"*DIRECTOR OF CATERING SERVICES!*"

Milo, deep in bed, rolled the alternate honourifics round his mouth, along with the breakfast croissant to which he was entitled as an official (if short-term) resident of Spudorgan Hall. Mentally and intestinally, he was at peace. Far from having the managerial boot applied to his corduroys, as he'd feared,[1] he was, *au contraire*, being promoted—raised—elevated—actually put in charge of ten or more people, including (and here he shivered, partly from the fading aftereffects of *nausea tremens*, partly in delight) MURPHY!

"Murphy?" he bawled at the walls, in a croissant-clotted voice. "You're through! Pack your bags! Vamoose!"

As an artist, of course, he owed it to the Muses not to take such paltry honours too seriously, much as Evelyn Waugh had turned down his O.B.E., and Beckett his Nobel. Still, the fact that old Power's secretary had called to make the offer with Kathy standing at his hospital bedside trying to kick off their first conversation since that Vindaloo evening at the Star of Bihar—well, women liked the man with prospects, although the difference between head waiter and catering supervisor was, admittedly, a bit of a fine point to an outsider.

---

[1]For no good reason, needless to say, beyond being Irish and therefore deeply suspicious of things in general—especially inedible things with no walls or branches or places to sit, like jobs and promises.

"Oh, that's good," she'd said. "Congratulations. Listen, will you be OK now? I must dash."

Milo, remembering, converted an oily chuckle into a quavering burp, flavoured with aftertaste of croissant. Poor thing, she'd really wanted a fag, that was the plain truth of it! Of course, he wouldn't be surprised if she quite simply had an aversion to hospitals, like most other (fertile, non-lesbic) women he'd known, and not a few men (mostly smokers), but as far as he was concerned, with the state footing the bill, an overnight stint in a semiprivate room in the old Mater Misericordiae was a welcome break in routine, and—once the initial retching, thrashing ghastliness of the Great Stink had subsided, thanks to the hereditary luck of the Rogers clan and the swift intervention of a passing sergeant in the Gardai—there'd been pretty good crack in the ward, what with the thrill of survival and Kathy's visit and the old duffer in the other bed, one Jams Fogarty, retired trawler captain out of Youghal and (allegedly) ex-scrum half for Ireland in the 1959 Five Nations Tournament. Something of a poet was old Jams, or at least a top-notch reciter of others' verse, if you could ignore the gale-force cough. His favourite, he said, was Allingham: pithy and to the point.

"The poet launched a stately fleet: it sank. / His fame was rescued by a single plank."

"Lucky poet, eh? Most of us would settle for a splinter," he'd remarked, poignantly, before yielding to the mucal dissonance of chest music. Alas, there was no doubt about it, poor Jams would be dead inside the month, God rest his soul! On the other hand, to hell with the old pisser (snarled Milo, inwardly)! Wasn't that the way of it for those whose thirst outlived their livers? What more could they expect? Immortality? Liver transplants? A SECOND CHANCE? Ye shall reap, etc.: fair enough, most of the time. For instance, based on his own current predilections for beer, curry, and ciggies, Milo resignedly foresaw his life winding down (or up) between the ages of fifty-nine and sixty-three or so, like Philip Larkin's, in a poetic welter of regret.[2]

---

[2]Easy enough for him to say now. Ask him again when he's hit four-score, like me.

He replaced his empty teacup on its saucer on the bedside table and lay back with loud lip-smackings and deep gut-chortlings of the grossest variety. It was still early enough (0835 GMT) for a prolongation of his short lie-in, a well-deserved self-indulgence after these many months of harried misery and four-hour nights. Cradling his head on the pillow, through lazy lids he contemplated the quadrangular, paisley-wallpapered room management had agreed to let their future catering czar use while atmospheric tests were underway at Oxtail Corners: facing south, it directly opposed the northward-aligned, therefore inward-pointing, giant gargoyle on the window ledge (a disconcerting effect at first, as of an intruder or cat burglar about to spring, but architecturally of a piece with the rest of Spudorgan Hall: eclectic, with a pinch of kitsch). Piney *frissons* rippled through the grove of evergreens outside the window, implying wind. Through the shifting branches, the spire of St. Oinsias' stated a theme forcefully reiterated by the twin spires of SS. Peter & Laurence O'Toole's, towering above the Lower Town, below. On the watery horizon, out of range of Milo's bed-bound vision, ferryboats placidly plied their way to Wales, France, etc. Closer at hand—in fact, directly across the room from Milo's pillow-supported head—was a reproduction of Millet's *Angelus*, of the same size, quality, and tint as its million or more mates in living rooms and parlours across the island of saints, scholars, and Millet-lovers. There'd been one in the kids' bedroom in Drumcondra when Milo was growing up, another in the headmaster's office at St. Barnaby's School, and even one in the Porter's Lodge at Trinity (or was it over the gents' in Mulligan's bar?) . . . his memories blurred as, dozing, he slept; sleeping, he dreamt.

It was a vivid dream-drama, furnished with stage decor left over from a Restoration play—oil portraits of cavaliers, wood-paneled walls, filigreed fittings—and reassembled under the roof of the well-known dream-personality Mr. Watts O'Wacker, a heavy-jowled, bewigged member of the indolent class who, it transpired, was engaged, while himself asleep, in the composition of a bildungsroman in which the main character, Myles (or Milo) Rogerson-Quay (né Rogers), a sleeping ex-waiter (or head-writer-to-be), was in turn writing a roman à clef about Mr. O'Wacker's waking life, involving bustle, deception, lechery, money changing hands, etc., a state of affairs so dramatically at variance with the Cartesian harmony of Mr. O'Wacker's self-image, asleep or awake, that mortal enmity between them was assured, and the contest to be the first with the lowdown on the other was a bitter one indeed; for example, the future writer's (or quondam waiter's) book, when completed (announced a tiny voice offstage), would be bound in leatherette of a Tara blue hue, in sharp contrast to Mr. O'Wacker's oeuvre, destined to appear between covers tinted as green as emeralds, or envy. The battle was joined. As Milo himself tossed and snored in an agony of Morphean creation, Mr. O'Wacker, also sunk in profoundest slumber yet busily writing all the while, heaved and flopped on the reinforced mattress of his massive handcarved four-poster, looted from the besieged Zarzuela Palace shortly before the outbreak of the War of the Spanish Succession. At his bedside was a small Louis XIV escritoire, atop which an ever-dwindling quire of paper measured out Milo's life as Mr. O'Wacker, using an old-fashioned feather quill, wrote fluently and automatically with his right hand, pausing only to dip his nib in the inkpot and tuck his nightshirt between his knees. His latest scoop was the time back in the late '50s when the above-named Myles Rogerson-Quay, Esq., holder of four O levels and a gentleman's degree from Trinity, had publicly, and at knifepoint, commandeered a bus—the 12A, O'Connell Street to Donnnybrook—and forced the female passengers to retire to the upper deck for "protection," while leading their male fellow riders on the lower, nonsmokers' level in a chorus of "Mack the Knife," "Helter Skelter," and other hit songs of the aggressive variety; taking over the controls of the bus (ironically, from his own father), the madman then drove them all at great speed into the foyer of Jury's Hotel, Ballsbridge, where Des O'Driscoll was performing choice scenes from *Camelot* and *Man of La Mancha* to an international police convention. Royal flush for the rozzers—curtain—*ende unsere gesichte*. O'Wacker's imperturbable sangfroid in (so to speak) dreaming up this calumny maddened Milo/Myles and drove him to take desperate measures, including the bold insertion into his own magnum opus of a shady episode implicating a devious and scheming international financier named Wackwaters; Abdul Greenhouse, a corrupt Judeo-Arabic oil tycoon; and several American congressmen, all of whom were led away in chains (and disgrace) by FBI agents in white suits, a tableau clearly inspired by (a) Rodin's *Burghers of Calais*, and (b) too much TV news. This merciless ploy left Mr. O'Wacker no alternative but to sit up in bed and reveal his true, waking identity, exposing sharklike teeth in a slobbering grin, opening pink-rimmed eyelids on bulging yellow-tinted eyeballs, and—with the effortless transformation of his Charles II wig into a Donegal tweed cap—metamorphosing into none other than THE GREEK MAHER, brandishing his quill pen above his head like a dagger![3]

Milo lurched awake, sweating, appalled.

"The bastard," he gasped.

It was time to face the day.

Rude hisses and laughter, and a distinct raspberrying sound, greeted his foray later that morning into the labyrinth of management-labour relations. He described the experience to Kathy over a lunchtime pint at Mad Molloy's.

"It was like being back at school. Yobs taking the piss, you know. Except the Swiss chef, mind you, oh he was very polite. 'Oui monsieur, non monsieur.' I reckon he'd be the one to keep an eye on, right enough."

"Not Murphy?"

"Nowhere to be seen. Actually, I'm feeling a bit let down. I was looking forward to ordering him about, not that he'd've put up with it, of course, I mean all credit to him, whatever his faults he's never been a crawler, has he? But now that you mention it, I think he's gone, at least I've not seen him in a day or so—anyway, I was reading out the roster, you know, as part of my

---

[3] Odd, but this little number reminds me of a charming comedy of manners by Brian O'Brien—or was it Flann O'Nolan?—teeming with pookas and fairies and nocturnal characters writing one another in and out of existence; its influence on the greatest book in history, *The Chapelizod Chronicle* (aka *Here Comes Everybody*), should be clear to all but the thickest illiterate.

new duties—the school analogy again, only this was a bit like being a frigging prefect, minus the respect—and he was absent both times. Mind you, there was talk of him running off with some girl who worked at Woolworths . . . oh, sorry. I didn't mean to, you know."

Kathy glowered fetchingly.

"Listen, Milo, what Mister Bloomin' Murphy gets up to from now on, and with whom, is his own business. I've relinquished all claim or interest."

Milo's smile registered dual approval: of her vehement indifference to the once-formidable Murphy, and of his own aptitude in drawing this sentiment out.

"Another quick one?"

Kathy declined, with a brisk shake of her head. One drink was more than enough at lunchtime, and it was certainly more than she'd have allowed herself in the old days—*the pre-Milo days?* No, that wasn't quite right, because that implied some kind of emotional frontier dividing her life into pre- and post-Milo eras, and that was absurd, of course. Nothing had happened between them yet, and as far as she was concerned there was no guarantee anything ever would. They'd very likely just stay mates, meet for a drink now and then, give each other moral support, even advice, but nothing heavier, or more physical, than that, although naturally he'd think otherwise, being a man—and of course nothing was impossible, it was just the timing that was a bit off at the moment, particularly *that* moment, as he was on duty in the catering manager's office at Spudorgan Hall (thank goodness he wasn't a waiter anymore, anyway), and she wanted to stop in at the tobacconist's for her monthly shipment of French cigarettes before delivering her latest column ("Irishwomen in the Workplace: A Quiet Revolution") to *Glam*.

After she'd paid for the round in honour of Milo's promotion, they parted, his eyes dimming in disappointment at the businesslike handshake that preempted the hoped-for kiss.[4]

---

[4]Fair enough. When I was a nipper, the only way you could get kissed was to lie down on the banks of the Grand Canal, close your eyes, pucker up, and hope for the best—and believe me, there were precious

Kathy smiled briefly at the thought of the unchanging nature of men as she made her busy way through the town's misty streets of cobblestone and October chill. Oddly, she felt an obscure exuberance, and this (paradoxically) worried her, suggesting as it did that the changed circumstances of her life were responsible—and what could that mean, only the absence of Murphy, and/or Milo's arrival? She sighed, spleenfully. Had she been given to self-chat aloud, her words would probably have been along the lines of "Ach, snap out of it, girl," or "Wake up, for God's sake," for, in most respects, she was a normal Irishwoman—of somewhat higher than normal intelligence, certainly, but otherwise typical of the species in her gritty, fatalistic, life-hardened way. High spirits (to such as she) were a luxury forgivable only on feast days—Christmas, birthdays, anniversaries—or when she'd had a piece accepted by a reputable magazine, or if they were showing three *Dr. Menace* episodes back to back on the TV, or (and this worried her, somewhat) when romance was imminent and the unreasoning heart anticipated change, even improvement. Otherwise, this Celtic maid was more or less permanently on her guard, on the principle that you couldn't be too careful when you had life to contend with.[5]

At the corner of Casement Street (W.) and Pollexfen Walk (E.) she turned right and headed to the Parade, past the pealing bells, shiny cars, white veils, and black ties of a wedding at SS. Peter & Laurence O'Toole's. The deep-breathing sea was pewter grey and empty except for the white flecks of bobbing gulls, a colour scheme reflected in the mirrored ceiling of the sky. On the barely visible line separating them, restless whitecaps licked their lips. The wind along the Parade was unwelcoming and cold, like a Presbyterian breakfast, but The Shops were as bright and hearty as a Catholic Christmas, and Gallogly's the tobacconists had an unusually rich Bank Holiday display of smoker's arcana in their old-fashioned oriel window: meerschaum pipes, a hookah,

few who fancied doing that of a Saturday evening, unless the stakes were really high.

[5]You know, the moment I clapped eyes on her I knew she was a solid class of gal, French fags and all.

onyx cigarette cases, gold and platinum Jacques Duclos lighters, seventeen-inch Havanese *Flor Finas*, etc. Kathy paused to admire all this before entering, in the aftermath of a loud door chime that distracted the pipe-smoking near-midget behind the counter—the eponymous Gallogly—from a nose-focused discussion with a customer, also pipe-smoking, decidedly taller than Mr. Gallogly yet somewhat more wizened, with overtly declarative facial extremities tipped with droplets of sweat, despite the chill. In one hand he held a book, familiar to its author's fans as the best of its genre; in the other, a pipe reamer of shining brass, shaped like a small trowel. His eyes were fixed beadily on this utensil, like a scientist with a new specimen.

"Do you have any bigger ones than this, Mr. Gallogly?" he inquired, loudly.

"I'll be with you in a moment, Mr. Grey. Yes, madam? Ah, Mrs. Hickman. You'd be in for your Frenchies, would you?"

"Good afternoon, Mr. Gallogly. Yes, please."

Mr. Gallogly came over to Kathy, spreading his hands into obsequious fans. "We did have some small delay this time with the shipment, Mrs. Hickman. Something to do with that war out there, those old Swiss or Turks or Corsicans or whatever the blazes you call 'em—Balkans, is it, Mr. Grey?"

Typical, thought Kathy. Ignore the woman and ask a man—any man (just listen to this one hemming and hawing: Um, Um, he hadn't the foggiest); sure, after all, God bless and keep the poor creatures, when it comes to serious matters like world affairs, why should they bother their pretty heads . . . ?[6]

---

[6]She's spot on here. It was one of the Da's few faults, if you ask me. Whenever Mum, or one of the girls, volunteered an opinion on (e.g.) national politics (mostly Fianna Fail), he'd stand up, put his hands on his hips (or in his pockets) and drown her out with an amazing variety of noises: theatrical laughter, terminal-intensity coughing, forced farts and/or hiccups, long, sustained vowel sounds (usually *aaaaah* or *uuuuuuh*), tongue-clucking, violent expulsion of air between lips and teeth alternating with sudden, howling inhalations, etc., etc. On the other hand he was convinced the country would be better off with an all-female government: God keep and protect him, it's true to say that like all great men he was rich in contradictions.

"Occitanians, actually, Mr. Gallogly," she said. "They've been fighting the Corsicans and Draconians. As my order originates in Marseilles, I expect there were delays at the airport."

"Ah? You're well informed, aren't you, Mrs. Hickman."

"Well, I *am* a journalist."

"Ah, are you, now?"

"A journalist?" interjected Wolfetone Grey (yes! it was he). "With what paper?" When told, he plucked his pipe from his mouth and made a face. "*Glom*? Pah. Never heard of it. Does it have a religion page?"

"Not as such, no," said Kathy. "But there is a priest who answers readers' questions, once a month."

"Pah. Pah! Priest, eh? Let me tell you something, young lady. They know sweet damn all, the priests. Sweet bloody damn all."

"Well, I suppose that would be a matter of opinion, wouldn't it? Not that I'd totally disagree with you."

"Would you not? My name's Grey, so. I beg your pardon . . . ? And yours would be?"

"Mine? Hickman, why?"

Crestfallen, he put his pipe back in his mouth and began sucking, moistly and smokelessly.

"Married, or . . . ?"

"It's my married name, yes."

"Beg pardon, may I ask—that is, your ah, maiden name? Gee, is it, or . . . ?"

"Well, MacRory, if you must know."[7]

"Aha! All right, right. I had a cousin, you see—never mind. MacRoar? Very good! Carry on."

Kathy gave him the once-over with narrowed eyes that widened slowly as the pipe-drooling from his netherlip downwards became more manifest; yet, astonishingly (to her way of thinking), he didn't even seem to notice. She was in a quandary, as with foreigners mangling the language, or an acquaintance sporting encrusted nose hairs: ought she to mention it? Would it be rude? Should she drop a hint by rubbing her own lower lip, say, or ostentatiously brandishing a hankie? Non-involved by

---

[7]*Anglice* Rogers, by the way.

nature, she decided against, and turned away from the spectacle so dispiritingly reminiscent of village life in Co. Louth, where public drooling was eternally in vogue,[8] to the more cheering sight of the tobacconist bearing her order under one arm: four amphora-shaped cigarette tins, bound in stout Provençal rope.

"Thank you, Mr. Gallogly."

She offered payment, accepted change, and lost no time in leaving, watched with melancholy detachment by one pair of eyes, mercantile satisfaction by the other.

"Shite and rubbers," she said, under her breath. "Some people."

After handing her manuscript over to the editing people at *Glam*, she hurried home to King Idris Road (W.), there to per-colate hearty Mediterranean coffee and subdue the tail-wagging frenzy of Strongbow. When the brew was ready, she kicked off her shoes and lit up a Grand Pagnol, then—scowling in distaste —another, then another, her face registering a widening array of hostile emotions. Simply put, the fags had come through battle lines and across a thousand miles of Europe for nothing: they were stale, and burnt like tapers. The prospect of being stuck with Virginia tobacco for the next month depressed her unutter-ably, and Turkish was worse. Not even her daily trot to the Strand and back with Strongbow, and an unexpected old favour-ite on SiegKanal (*Triumph des Willens*, L. Riefenstahl, 1936) could raise her spirits. She sat down at her word processor and tried a line or two of graveyard verse, but found herself beset by *O*s, as in *"O, the very drains themselves / Speak to the depths of this dundrear day,"* and *Ah*s, as in *"Ah, the insomniac nightingale / Hurtles like a bogallen 'neath the unmade sky."* Brahms, who usu-ally soothed, only vexed ("teeh-TAH-teeh-TAH-teeh-TAH— Christ!"). Once-loved novels (*Murphy* (!); *Strumpet City*; *The Brothers Veen*) had all been plucked clean, like carcasses on the veldt. In short, boredom was manifest.

---

[8] True for you again, girl. In Colmcross townland, in my days of hope and vigour, there was a rutted boreen known as Dribble Alley for the amount of saliva discharged thereupon by slow-witted farmhands and aging pipe-smokers (one and the same, more often than not).

At a quarter to five, with the rainbow glow of the autumn sky dying in the west, Kathy picked up the phone and dialled Milo's number with studied indifference to repeated self-accusations of IDIOT!

"He's in hospital," said a female voice.

"What? Again?"

"No, not the same thing as before. Oh, are you the lady from . . . ? He was stabbed in the neck, dear. In his office—well, he'd just settled in, hadn't he? Nothing serious, apparently. A flesh wound, they say. His assailant was the man he replaced, you see, resentful at being given early retirement, *he* says, but if you want my frank opinion he's miles round the twist—oh, we'd had one or two problems with Mr. Grey, certainly, but we never expected physical violence."

"Did he have a knife, yeah?"

"No, it was some kind of pipe-cleaning tool."

"Pipe cleaning . . . ?" Kathy, horrified, remembered: Gallogly's, the dribbling . . . .

"Aye. You know. One of those wee gadgets they use to clean out their pipes. Quite sharp at the end. Well, sharp enough, I'd guess. Ah, it's terrible. You know, I said to Mr. Power, the day after we had Mr. Grey removed from the premises when he tried to convert the staff—or at least the ones with names beginning with *G*, if you can believe it—I said, Mr. Power, we ought to have him committed, so I did . . . hello?" But by then Mrs. Gallagher was addressing the dial tone, alone.[9]

---

[9]Well, now, it doesn't look as if they're going to let us in on the actual drama, does it? A bit like those boring old plays we had to read at school, where some masher in a toga or cross-garters was always charging in with news of the really interesting things that were going on off-stage. Anyway, to fill you in on the details, here's a clipping from the *Killoyle Clarion* of October 21st:

MAN RUNS AMOK WITH PIPE REAMER

KILLOYLE CITY, Oct. 20—Wolfgang Graves, a recently retired Director of Catering Services at the famous and historic Spudorgan Hall Resort Hotel, was remanded in custody at Garda Station 6 this afternoon on charges of having willfully, and with malice aforethought, carried out a physical assault on his successor in the post of Catering Services Administrator, one Milo Rogers, 34, in the latter's office at Spudorgan Hall, by stabbing him in the neck with a pipe-cleaning implement. "He's a wee whore's get and he stole my job," said Graves, by way of explanation. Rogers is in satisfactory condition at the Mater Misericordiae Hospital. A former colleague at the Hall, Peter Murphy, 29, interviewed in a public house near the scene, said, "I always thought the poor old fellow was a bit of a head case. Things were never good at home, you know." Murphy is said to be affianced to Mr. Graves' daughter, Doreen. Other eyewitnesses say Graves—whose ludicrous attempt to proselytise on behalf of an obscure Protestant sect at the Hall had led to his sudden resignation the day before—was dishevelled and appeared to have been drinking when he arrived at the Hall shortly after 14.30 this afternoon and demanded in a loud voice to know the whereabouts of several people unknown to those whom he questioned, including Ragu Guptu, 56, who claimed to have sensed "that danger was about to lurk." Suddenly, Graves burst into the office he himself had occupied for eleven years and according to Priscilla Gallagher, the executive secretary—who has an adjoining office—hurled insults of a deeply personal nature at Rogers, challenging his legitimacy and accusing him of being mad, atheistic, lecherous and so on. He concluded by throwing himself at Rogers and embedding the tip of a brass pipe-reaming implement in the nape of Rogers' neck as the latter was attempting to call for assistance with both hands, thereby neutralising his retaliatory potential, as it were. The sound of the scuffle soon reached the neighbouring ears of Mrs. Gallagher, who informed her superior, E. Powers, Esq., General Manager. When they arrived on the scene the two men were grappling, with the pipe reamer as the evident object of their struggle. The Gardai arrived on the scene shortly thereafter along with the emergency ambulance from Mater Misericordiae Hospital and performed their respective functions by taking Rogers to hospital and Graves into custody. Lawyers for the accused are preparing a defence of Not Guilty By Reason of Insanity, which could result in incarceration in a psychiatric institution, with early parole in mitigating circumstances.

A press statement issued by Milo Rogers from Mater Misericordiae read, in full: "Bugger Gray" (sic).

25

"Arrah," declared the Greek to himself, through a mouthful of blackened rasher and egg. "Yerrah. Arrrh." Mascara-lidded from sleeplessness and the preying on his mind of anxieties inherent in his situation, he doggedly chewed his third successive breakfast of the morning and watched Mrs. Tierney next door align three flapping pairs of boxer shorts and four singlets on her washing line, along with a T-shirt bearing the slogan *¡Watneys, la cerveza brava!* and six sky-blue pairs of frilly knickers quite unsuitable for an ample, not to say bloody lardaceous, cow like herself, with an arse three cheeks wide and legs that would hold up the GPO . . . !

The subsequent thought-association, fatal to lust but provocative of mirth, caused the Greek to snort with such violent derision that charred shards of bacon and fried albumen were abruptly vacuumed into his nasal/sinus chambers from the epiglottal region, blocking normal respiratory functions and resulting in a shrill, even high-pitched coughing fit of furniture-shaking and window-rattling intensity. Superman the cat fled in alarm out the kitchen door, and Mrs. Tierney, draping a lace antimacassar and matching doilies over her washing line, smiled and nodded in grim satisfaction at the sound of it, for it was the sound of human mortality, especially in Ireland.[1] When it was over, the Greek hid his crimson face in a handkerchief of match-

---

[1] True, true, it is that—the cigs, of course, with a touch of the pipe, our national failing *par excellence*, so to speak, bar none, and forget the booze. Did you ever ride the no. 11 or 12 on a weekday morning, say

ing hue and blew a nasal trumpet peal, like a musician dazzling his audience with an encore. Throat-clearing followed, and cavernous sniffing, and another cup of sweet black tea, and at the heel of the hunt the ultimate reward: a smoke. Thin silvery wheezes drifted up from the tattered remnants of the seizure, but all in all his fag tasted grand and sharp and the treat almost set him up for the day. He still had his worries, of course, some of them quite prejudicial to peace of mind: for one, four days after the Oxtail Corners disaster, the afterpong off him was so pungent that Superman was still leery of coming too close; and for another, his wife had left to stay indefinitely with her brother and his kids in the Shannon Industrial Development Zone.

"Thomas," she'd said that night, in a near-shout, arms on hips like the prizefighter she had once been, "the dear knows I'm called on to endure much in this life of mine, fool that I am, but I WILL NOT stay in the same house with a walking tub of cow dung and that's the end of it."

She'd gone, so. Since then he'd been lying low and had opened the door only to the fumigators—not the local lads, but a crack team from his old regiment, the Offaly & Leix Light Infantry. To seal their lips, he'd made extra payments under the table, or tables (kitchen- and side-, crowned with bottles of Bushmans single malt), accompanying these gratuities with a punter's wink and a sly forefinger laid alongside the bridge of the nose, familiar and well-loved gestures that charmed the company beyond the telling of it and, he was sure, guaranteed their discretion. As long as official investigations were underway, such discretion (not to say downright secrecy) was the Greek's sole desire, perhaps taken to the extreme of actual disappearance for a while, i.e., a well-deserved holiday in the sun, or emigration itself, that

---

about 7:30, and the hacking and retching on the upper deck so colossal the old bus was rolling back and forth like the Holyhead ferry, damned near veering off the Irishtown Road into the Ringsend Gasworks, or Dublin Bay itself? It's a wonder we ever learn—of course, there are those, your father among them, who'd say a pint of stout's never the same without a good smoke to smooth the way, and the lot of them after washing down the same pint with a double Jameson's, no ice, a small Peterson's on the side! What a country.

time-honoured Irish practice. Truly, his preoccupations were as multitudinous as the massed saints of Heaven! No wonder, then, that his brain was ajangle with alternative plans and the feverish plotting of moves, countermoves, and their kin.

He sighed, exhaling smoke and a faint after-rattle that echoed in his fingertips and coalesced briefly into a phlegmy ball, soon squelched. Wincing, he turned to behold Mrs. Tierney's broad thighs hurrying after the rest of her through her kitchen door, with the billowing semaphores of the Tierney family wash left behind to dry in the episodic October sun. The Greek ruminated, over a final deep pull on his fag. Not being one for excessive, or even moderate, humility, he hated to admit it, but the plain truth of it was that he'd made an imperial haimes of the whole business, in his eagerness, even greed; and what was the upshot? Not only were the tenants to be allowed back with 11 percent downward adjustments in their rent—including Milo Rogers, the spalpeen bawn—but (according to his inside source at Mansion House, viz., Ben Ovary) as the landlord, he, the Greek, stood in grave danger of being formally charged with (a) proprietary negligence; (b) failing to abide by housing standards (that was a laugh—*standards!?*); (c) creating an insalubrious environment; and (d) aiding and abetting through deliberate disrepair the natural forces of erosion, aging, and dry rot, i.e., assisting God in acts of God . . . actually, God was the only one who knew where it might end, just as only He knew the truth behind the affair, and for the time being that was how it had to stay, between the Greek and his Maker (if any). He was fairly sure he'd guaranteed his own anonymity on the night in question, at any rate, what with that shoe-wax makeup and the All-Black rugby gear. No one, he hoped, would speak his name to a Garda supergrass number, or point a trembling finger at him in a lineup. Most importantly, because of his spurious but widely announced bout of "flu," no one in authority had yet come within sniffing distance, a real bit of luck, because if they ever caught a whiff of the intractable Easi-Fert, his very liberty might be in question, his good name dragged through the mud, his bank accounts seized . . . still, there was no getting round it: damage had been done to his reputation, and therefore to his marketability, at least in Killoyle. *Maher the slumlord! Boycott Redux! BOYCOTT MAHER!* He shuddered. Clearly, Oxtail Corners, as a potential redevelopment site, was a bit of a write-off, for the time being. There'd been no word from Power at Spudorgan Hall, either, and with things being generally dodgy, Maher Enterprises PLC might have to beat a strategic retreat—regroup—withdraw to lick wounds and bruises —readjust priorities—streamline operations—sack a few people for appearance's sake—etc.

Ah, things had changed since his salad days, that was certain.[2]

On the other hand, there was, eternally, Europe!

Summoned by the melody of his dreams and the caffeine/tannin stimulus in yet another beaker of black tea (his fourth), that imagined—yet real, Church-owned—mountainside in the south of Italy rose up again in his mind's eye, once carpeted in soughing forests but now, in the ideal, Maherian future, shaved, razed and—as the jargon of the trade had it—"developed" with access roads and lay-bys and stucco (or pebbledash, for that homey look) holiday chalets (double-glazed, 1 up, 2 down, carport, satellite TV and sauna included, Jacuzzi and IMAX screening room optional) catering to the Irish holidaymaker at play in the Mediterranean sun, a stone's throw from the sparkling sea. This image was enhanced by an entire mental Cinerama of imagined stacks of those Italian banknotes that looked like oil paintings: the pot of gold, all right! Best of all the Eye-ties were an accommodating race, grand ones for the odd bonus off the books, or a phone call after hours to the right ministry at the right time. Oh, that was it, so it was. He'd been wasting his time, all these years, counting on Killoyle's growth and future fame as the Irish Estoril or Palm Beach or whatever the blazes the promoters were calling it.[3] Europe was the place for him.

---

[2]Not enough. The landlords still exploit honest men and women to pay for a box at the opera, or airfare to the Caribbean, or a *cave* of overpriced plonk. Pity Vatican II did away with Hell; a lot of those gents could use a season or two in the toastiest corner.

[3]The dear knows how they planned it, with no casinos or strip joints, and precious little in the way of tourist sights excepting The Shops (especially Beano's) and the silvery strand. I mean, one dreary little

He drummed his fingers excitedly on the kitchen table.

"Not that there's not *potential* in the owld place," he explained to Superman, who was tentatively retracing his steps to his milk saucer in the corner, tail erect. "Oh, there's *potential* right enough, amn't I after proving it? Only for the way things turned out the other day, I'd be pulling down St. Oinsias' and Oxtail Yard at one and the same time. But it's time for a wee holiday, Super. Time to start investing in the dear owld European Union, eh?"

Presently, wreathed in smiles and smoke, he was slumped against the wall in the hallway, conversing on the phone with Father Patric MacCarthy, S. J.

"Yes, Father. Best to let them know I'm coming, eh? Ah, God bless you, Father, old Dad Doyle's on his way out anyhow, where's the harm in warning him, man to man? Fair enough, I've a Corkman's tongue in my head, I apologise. Arrah, get away, you know I'm strict TeeTee, Father. A Pioneer from way back, so I am. The important thing's keeping a sober eye open in this den of thieves, wouldn't you agree? Wisha, the place is crying out for development, from what I hear. Not far from Rome, as I understand? Fee-yoo-mee-chee-no? Is that the Jap fella who . . . ? Oh, the airport. Grand, grand. You'd want that in the adverts, like, fifteen minutes from Fye-you-mee . . . from the airport, that kind of thing, ah bless you Father of course it's all me willie, that fifteen-minutes-only stuff, a right load of owld shite, eh, more like an hour and a half, but by the time the eejits are on the spot, like, they'll be that taken with the foreignness of everything and trying not to be hit by mad Eye-talian drivers they'd not notice the coming of the Second Coming itself. Now, this hillside's the property of the college, you say? And they'd be willing to negotiate ownership terms under the right conditions? Through the Banco dee . . . ? Ah, right, *L-A-V-O-R-*—grand, grand. I'll have

---

sheila-na-gig thirty miles away's not going to bring the tourists in droves, is it (see below)? And as for the shrine of the Invisible Virgin, well, you'd be drawing a somewhat elderly, not to say geriatric, class of tourist there, not like the spry hypochondriacs who haunt the vicinity of Lourdes and its cathedral, which, by the way, they hid away underground because it's so blooming hideous.

the money transferred right away."

Presently, he arrived at Mad Molloy's and let himself in through the side door. Bucko, the manager, was on the premises, but the Greek sent him on an errand to nonexistent wine suppliers in Weterford, thereby ensuring solitude for the next half hour, at least until opening time. He waited until the gurgling of Bucko's vintage two-stroke 1961 Auto Union DKW had died away,[4] then, with a brisk rub of his carefully gloved hands, he embarked on a rapacious inspection tour, trawling a faint waft of manure from the curtained gloom of the lounge to the still-shuttered public bar to the fluorescent-lit committee room upstairs, rank with the stale cigar smoke of the past weekend's Killoyle Lion Cubs Club. Each room boasted a till, in each of which he found a sum approximating a week's takings, awaiting transfer that very afternoon, in payroll form, to various bank accounts—*his* bank accounts, he reminded himself, just as Molloy's was *his* place (67.4 percent of it, anyway), and the money, therefore, his as well, to do with as he chose, and he chose not to waste it in paying salaries, electric bills, and so on. They were incompetent arseholes anyhow, the lot of them; he'd leave them severance pay, say £10 each, and inform them via fax or phone that they'd been sacked by order of the Board, i.e., himself.

"Feck 'em," he growled, shivering with inner laughter, or another coughing spree. Inside ten minutes he'd emptied all three registers. Combined with the emergency sum sitting in the safe in the manager's office, he'd totted up £3991.14, £2500 of which would go off directly to the Italian bank, with the blessing of Holy Mother Church—or, at least, the Mussenden and Downhill Priests' Training College, Italian branch.

Sordid as it seemed, this was the crowning moment of a glittering partnership with pious overtones. The Greek Maher and Father Patric MacCarthy had known each other at least since Father Pat's return to Ireland at the behest of the Secretariat of Property Holdings and Territories, the arm of the Church dealing exclusively with the buying and selling of land, deconsecra-

---

[4] A grand motor. No front seats, but quick pickup.

tion of churches, building of seminaries, etc.; it was traditionally run by the Society of Jesus, as the most worldly and agile of the clergy and the best able to attract the middlemen, mostly lay, required to ease the way and occasionally to grease the palms of Caesar's minions. In Father Patric's mind—and a keen mind it was—when an up-and-coming land merchant from Killoyle named Tom Maher staked out a decrepit sawmill and former bishop's residence as the ideal site for his Priest's Training College, pointing out its location adjacent to the Rosslare ferries and Weterford airport and the utter tax exemption compatible with its status as a religious institution, it was proof enough that he, the Greek, fit the bill as their go-between in Ireland's southeast. Since then, discreetly, the association had flourished; and if SS. Peter & Laurence O'Toole's—"the society church"—was the coming place, as the Greek had blandly yet boldly told Father Doyle, it was no more than the truth, as purveyed by H. E. the Secretary of State of Property Holdings and Territories in the Vatican itself, no less.[5] Now it was time for the payoff, and none of your guff about it being easier for a camel to pass through the eye of a needle than for a rich man, etc., self-chided the Greek (himself chided fleetingly but chillingly by the ghost of his churchgoing past); sure, if that were true, there wouldn't be a churchgoer alive with a respectable bank balance.

Moving with all the speed and nimbleness of a bear on roller skates, he filled a shoulderbag with the money, turned off the lights and stepped out the side door. Minutes later, he was in the Allied Irish Bank on O'Connell Square.

"That's right, ducks," he said to the young woman behind the counter. "Like it says. Your guess is as good as mine. Eel Banco Dell Lavoratory, eh?"

The teller wrinkled her nose slightly in the country-scented gust of laughter that followed, but the Greek, mistaking her expression for one of amusement, only winked and complimented

---

[5]An instructive intertwining of limbs, albeit fictitious. Some enterprising reader with a strong stomach and contacts in the underworld might care to research the topic further; I know I wouldn't, thanks all the same.

her on her fine Donegal wool pullover, having wrongly identified as such her Taiwan-made polyester cardigan.

"Well, thank you, sir. And that's a cool cap you've got."

The Greek tilted his cap forward, like Cary Grant in *Royal Divorce*, and blew her a kiss on his way out the door, as does Cary, to Jennifer Haddock, in the opening scene[6]—indeed, for a moment he *felt* like Cary Grant: suave, ebullient, with a dash of malice.

All three of these attributes governed his dealings with the travel agent, an effeminate young man easily banjaxed by the Greek's oaken manliness.

"We're not supposed to sell Alitalia connections through Paris, Mr. Maher. London or Milan's all I can manage."

"Bugger that, Cedric, if you'll pardon the expression. Here's an extra twenty quid that tells me you'll find a way—and I want a hotel in the centre, mind, not one of your fleatraps in the suburbs, although I understand they make ideal trysting places for delicate gentlemen of a certain persuasion, eh? Like Lime's Motel, out on the Waxford Road? What is it they call it now? Gomorrah Gardens?"

On his way home, the Greek took time out to exhale smoke under the beech trees on Behan Avenue and allow himself a moment or two of blind self-approbation: his courage, his daring, his sheer old-fashioned Irish brass!

"Arrah, you're a class bloody act and no mistake, Thomas me owld son," he cooed, his voice as unctuous as whiskey aged twelve years in the wood. "There's precious few would've thought of this caper. Precious bloody few. And that's a fact."

At home he packed his bags and attached £25 to a note to Mrs. Tierney, ensuring that Superman would be fed until his wife's return, or the cat's own emigration.

"How would you like to be an Eye-talian cat, Super, eh? Ciao,

---

[6] I thought Cary Grant wore a topper in *Royal Divorce*. Mind you, he might have popped on a cap during the parts I slept through, i.e., the first and second halves—and anyway, this sounds more like an amateur production of *Babar's Birthday Bash*, if you ask me.

or should that be Miao? Ah haha?"

Shortly thereafter the house was surrounded by Garda and the Greek was under arrest as an accessory to murder, handcuffed and bundled into the back seat of a Ford Fiesta limousine between a lady sergeant and a wiry inspector not a gentleman.

"Listen, yez feckers. I demand my rights. I never murdered anybody."

"Up your friggin' rights, fattie," said the inspector.

The motorcade sped away, watched by Mrs. Tierney as she was taking down her doilies from the washing line. Mildly intrigued yet unsurprised, as by a TV drama, she shook her head in the hard-earned wisdom of her sixty-six years.

"I'd have locked him up long since," she muttered to Superman. Sensing a change in administrations, the cat pranced at her legs, back arched, tail hopefully upheld.

At Garda HQ the Greek loudly demanded to see Superintendent Nugent, and backed his request with bulky gestures of intimidation and the casual mention of names in high places.

"Ben Ovary, no less. Danny Doheny-Nesbitt, as well. Emmet Power, I'm sure you know who he is. And there's one or two I could name at the Vatican, including—and this is between you and me—a secretary of state."

"Aw, shaddup," said the inspector.

Later, Ted Nugent stopped by the Greek's cell.

"Sorry, me old love, but you can't go on selling that Hyper-Ale of yours and expect to get away with it. One of your customers died of a pancreatic embolism last night and the autopsy revealed sixteen ccs of the stuff in his gut. We've just had it analysed. Fat-free and no artificial preservatives, right enough, but it turned out to be 89.7 percent pure wood alcohol, with added anisette. No denying your man was a soak, but selling the stuff makes you an accomplice."[7]

"God bless an' keepya, Teddy boy, and as the sweet Mather Mary's me witness Oi never had the faintest idea them lads was

---

[7] Well, if you believe in justice, here's your chance. Speaking for myself, I don't buy it, personally.

floggin' that class of pie-son under me own nose, like, but wait till Oi tellya, Bucko Heffernan's the man you want, may God erase the day Oi set eyes on him, the sore louse that's in it, sure, didn't Oi give him the job out of the kindness of me heart, just, and his poor owld mather me own dear wife's auntie that died in the great flood of '84, and wasn't she a very saint in her limbs and accoutrements and wouldn't she be interceding for the two of us at this very moment, up there at the right hand o' God . . . ?"

"Knock off the blarney, Maher. We've talked to Bucko, right enough. He'll be the State's chief witness. And speaking of your dear wife, she's brought separate charges against you in Limerick County Court. *She* says you went out one night last week dressed like a Ninja and when you came back, according to her, there was such a stink of fertiliser off you she had to leave the house. Could be a coincidence that was the night we had to evacuate Oxtail Yard, but on the other hand. Actually, I fancy you've still a dollop of that perfume on you—or is it my imagination?"

The moves and countermoves the Greek had busied his mind with earlier that day were mere tiddlywinks compared to the mental chess game he played that night in his cell, while staring at the opposite wall, the snot-green monotony of which was broken only by a reproduction of Millet's *Angelus*.[8]

---

[8]Let me just say, as long as you seem to be making a point of it, that I'd rather spend an entire Bank Holiday weekend alone with that painting in an attic than five minutes with any of your Picassos or Jean Dubuffets or Joop den Uyls in the finest gallery in the world: five minutes, do you hear, AND NOT A SECOND MORE.

26

At first, Father Doyle's heart leaped, and he basked briefly in sunlit memories; then he recalled the ominous words of the other night, and tore open the envelope from Rome with the palsied fingers of the alcoholic he was.

The letter was from the Pope.

Most beloved and esteemed Father Philip Doge, brother in Christ!

Yes, a loyal and hard working servant of the Church you have been many years. Like you, few exist. I am aware about your work for the poor, the needy, the Irish, &c., and so this opportunity was good, with excellent timing, to inform you of many things, dear Father Doge, how you are the best of our priesthood and a roll model to inspire youngs, like priests, seminarians, &c.!!!

Missionary work was yours also, many years ago in most difficult situation of ignorance and povertys' vice. Alas, today's case is like these, also. Even in your blessed country which I call Beloved Daughter of the Church I know congregations are small, only smaller. At Maynooth our Precious Jewel the registration is diminuated. In your parish staying home is done, not churchgoing, or even dancing, holidays, &c.—yet Killoley has nine churchs of the Faith, biggest of them which are your St. Oinsias and the noble O'Toole which now recently is having more and more congregations, yours less. Unfortunately the large matter of moneys therefore rises as a question for disputation, dear Father. Churchs funds are lower, and lowest ever. Maintenance of these such properties is falling on us with always harder force in these days of abstinence of nothing when concentration and Faith in God we need mostly (in Latin America, last year, 978,000 converted good Catholics to Protestants, bad news universally, except Africans are going more and more churchgoing because ADS as you know and Islam, &c.). At your esteemed age of life, dear Father, the time perhaps is coming any way for plannings of peaceful retirement with sweet thoughts of God and if these are true of course you may always turn to Your Church with absolute confidence for help in brotherly charity of . . .[1]

"Christ," said Father Phil. "I've been sacked."

He looked up phone numbers of significance in the Church directory, but no bishop was available to take his phone calls, let alone the cardinal; not even a monsignor could be had. All the half-hearted compromises of his life seemed to underlie the single, repeated phrase: "I'm sorry but he's not in just now. May I . . . ? Father Who?"

Father Doge, aka Nobody!

Mad Begg was brazenly clamouring, but Skelly was somewhere about, and anyway it was only Tuesday (and Vespers, at that). Ignoring the elfin pains that skipped lightly up and down his right arm—as they did regularly now, especially when stress pressed hard—Father Doyle changed into his everyday clothes and strode out of the presbytery into the matchless insolence of the outdoors with firmly set jaw (newly stubbled in the lower reaches, signifying a regrowth of beard, itself significant). He was muttering imprecations under his breath, but on his way across the lawn he realised he was navigating almost exclusively

---

[1] Typical. When Uncle Francie passed away, they beatified him, right enough, but would they give us the time of day otherwise, or help out with the colossal dry-cleaning bills (£175,000, according to recent studies) he ran up in those last weeks of his life, when he was living at the Marbella Hilton and escorting the likes of Gina Gadd around on his arm? Not on your nellie. All *they* ever did was make obscure threats in Sicilian (or was it Calabrian) dialect and—rather insistently, I thought—insert their right thumbs between the middle and index fingers on their left hand, leering all the while (e.g., wiggling eyebrows; rolling eyes once left, once right; tongue darting over the lips in a suggestive, lizard-like fashion—and mind you, I'm talking about bishops, at the very least!).

by instinct, owing to an unexpected mist of tears in front of his eyes that left him momentarily flustered—uncoordinated—confused—disoriented, like a bull beset by picadors.

"Ballocks," he snapped, with a sniff. He wiped the dew of sadness from his cheeks and pressed on, head bowed, anonymous in his anorak and leather workman's cap. As he walked he brooded, acerbically, almost agnostically, like an oft-rejected artist: so they'd done their worst, the vultures! Now there was nothing left but resignation and a rapid decline into senility and acute cirrhosis in a Church-run nursing home for derelict priests, probably that Stella Maris place near Cobh with the cartoons on the video player in the evening after tea and parlour games every afternoon and the Father Superior's Rottweilers trained to bark all night, thereby guaranteeing heart attacks and a constant bed vacancy rate, i.e., a profit for somebody . . . . Father Doyle started violently at the thought, and glanced round to discover that he had left the church behind and was halfway up Uphill Street, no doubt en route to Spudorgan Hall's public lounge and its fine view of the harbour, the sea and the ferryboats.

Once there, as expected, he sat on his customary stool at the southwestern corner of the bar, requested a double Bushmills of the dour Spanish barman[2] and fell into his habitual pose of indifference to the quality or nature of the beverage being dispensed, indeed frankly ignored the whole operation to stare fixedly over the heads of an American tourist party (who looked up nervously to reassure themselves that the pale visage turned towards them intended no threat) in the direction (did he but know it) of Cardiff, Swansea, and Aberystwyth; yet all he could see, in the darkling twilight, were the interlaced necklaces of amber-coloured streetlights, and even they were blurred, not through tears, but as a simple consequence of advancing age, possibly a cataract or two, or distortion of the retina, although his vision grew sharper, as it always did, after a drink.[3]

---

[2]Gomez, L.
[3]And isn't Ireland the land of the keen-eyed men!

Hunched over in the pose of one hard done by, he ordered another, and started at the sound of a voice nearby.

"That's you, is it, Father?"

Emmet Power was leaning on the bar from the tending side.

"Ah, Emmet. How's yourself?"

They batted pleasantries back and forth like Wimbledon champions until Father Doyle, exhausted, dropped out of the exchange and confessed (a) depression and (b) the cause there-of.

"By janey," said Emmet, concern scrawled legibly across his face, "I never knew they could forcibly retire a priest who wasn't —that is, who was still *compos mentis*, so to speak."

"So to speak, aye. Well. It happens all the time. Never a year goes by without them sacking some old priest or other. One or two of the ones I told you about, for instance, like His Grace the Bishop of Derrymoyle, he of the dazzling intellect and razor-sharp wit—did you ever see those fellas, by the way? The Pat MacCarthy brigade?"

"I did, Father, and I'm that glad I did, actually now that you mention it, let me tell you—"

"What a gang, eh? Who's the dimmest of the bunch, do you reckon?"

"Well, you know, you won't believe it—in fact, I had a hard time believing it myself—*me*, an alleged freethinker, haha!—but—"

"Bloody Ned Skelly'll be pleased. Now he can get out of Killoyle and find himself a fashionable parish in England like Hampstead or Highgate, someplace with about ten R.C. congregants where he can ignore the sacraments and Gospels and all that boring crap and get down to the serious stuff like holding guitar masses and giving sermons on the oppressed peasantry of Peru or some such ballockheaded blather."[4]

---

[4]Why doesn't he try Nannygrove, left of Hampstead? The last I heard, their parish priest had changed his name from Donny to Dishy and moved in with Joe, the Television Transvestite, with whom Dishy was proud to be publicly seen, especially on safe sex demos and Ban the Family sleep-ins.

"Your curate, is it? Nice for him. Now, I've a proposal for you. There's a small—"

"Not to mention the la-de-dah upmarket oh-so-trendy Saints bleeding Peter and Laurence's, the local religious fashion shop, the designer label *du jour*, the ones with fat wallets and slim morals, ah they'd be in line for a nice gleaming late-model priest, I reckon, power steering power windows power brakes power brain . . . ."

Emmet snatched away his drink, firmly placed it beyond grasping radius and folded his arms in a show of decisiveness. Father Doyle's shoulders sloped in disappointment, then rose and fell ataxically as cigarette tremors struck, tickled by the dancing elves of pain.

"What the blazes are you about, Emmet Power? I'm over age and it's after opening time."

"Just fasten your gob for a sec and hear me out, Father, if you please."

It was a matter of some urgency, explained Emmet, with the job postings—like all job postings, they were likely to evaporate at any minute—but there did actually appear (he said, hesitantly) to be, temporarily anyway, a pair of average-to-well-paying positions open in a priest's training college, one for a manager of the adjoining hotel, one for director of the actual college, preferably a Maynooth graduate (which he was, wasn't he?)—at least that was what he'd heard from Father's colleague Father Patric MacCarthy, S. J., who definitely knew about these things ("oh, definitely")—it sounded like a right decent place, too, up in the hills, with a spring or two gurgling away and sunshine most of the year and even an eighteen-hole golf course, they said.

"Sounds grand. Near Killoyle, is it?"

"Ah. Not really. Italy, actually. About fifteen minutes from Rome airport, he said, although I had a look at the map, and it would be nearer an hour, if you ask me—but still."

"God have mercy. Italy? You're joking."

"Well, I understand it's a bit far to go at a moment's notice, like, but we're all in the dear old Community together, aren't we, all Europeans and so on, and the weather's nice, and by God they've grand grub, the Italians. Then there's the old vino, of course, if you like that kind of thing."[5]

Was it really possible, wondered Father Doyle?

Could he accept that such things happened without believing them to be some kind of divine loan, or credit, on guaranteed future setbacks on the installment plan?

And what combination of forces, divine or malign, had placed him at such a juncture, at that particular point in his life, to balance reversal with good fortune . . . ?

ITALY!?

There had to be a catch—several catches, in fact. For a start:

"Your man's a Jesuit? Dodgy, Emmet, very dodgy. Sly sods, they are. Fingers in every pie, you know that."

"I do. Which is how I found out about this in the first place."

"No adverts? No contracts? No tours of the premises? In other words: no proof?"

"I've checked with our Foreign Ministry and the Italian Embassy. The place exists, it's earning money, and they need a new manager. True bill, Father. So I'm off."

He outlined his decision to quit Spudorgan Hall, barely hinting at the cause—barely, because he was unsure himself how much he was motivated by moral scruples and how much by the simple human desire to live a better life in a warmer climate, and whether the two, in this case, were connected, and if so, how closely. All he knew was he'd chosen well; he wanted it; he had Roisin's vote on it; and enough was enough (which clinched it).

"My boy Sean's coming back from the States to take over the house."

"Now hang on there a second, my son, old son. Did you say it's a Maynooth priest they're after to run the place?"

---

[5]Not to mention the greatest history, the gassest cars, the grandest (a) churches, (b) motorways (great undulating rivers of concrete), (c) towns, (d) squares, (e) restaurants, (f) (for the fellas) gals, (g) (for the gals) fellas, (h) music, (i) paintings, (j) sculpture . . . I could go on (and will, if you're buying). As you may have gathered, I'm something of an Italophile (if that's the word). The only problem is, the Eye-ties themselves *know* they're the best, just like their cousins the Froggies, who also have things pretty well worked out, and they can't both be right—unless Corsica and the Riviera are the answer, after all.

More tolerant of the clergy than he had once been, Emmet patiently reiterated. As he was unaware of Father Doyle's near-tribal attachment to *la bella Italia* (or at least to his memories thereof), he presumed a need to persuade, even cajole. Rome itself, he suggested, the Eternal City, etc., etc.—a mere twenty kilometres distant—might well be appealing for a man of the cloth, and if not, well, he threw in Rome airport, and easy accessibility from there to Ireland, as an added, even decisive, attraction.

"Sure you're only an hour and a half from Cork International, so if homesickness strikes—bingo, ring up dear old Aer Fungus and you're on your way."

Father Doyle clasped the bar counter to support himself during the ensuing unshaven cadenza of smoker's and whiskey-drinker's laughter. For the second time that day, tears welled—invoked, ironically, by opposing emotions, despair in one case, relief in the other.

"Ach, Emmet," he said, stuttering slightly, "do, do you know I've been dreaming of getting these old bones back to Rome for twenty years and more? Man, if ever there was a Godsend, this is it." He stared disbelievingly at Emmet, inviting his lifetime's experience to trample over the garden of his joy. It obliged; he frowned. "Of course, there's no guarantee they haven't given the job away, or even that your man the Jesuit—Canon Patric, is it? The sharp one he is, from what I've heard, just the sort to give the order a bad name—or a good one, depending on your morals—who's to guarantee the job's on the level, by the way? Director of a training college? Me? What the blazes do I know about directing colleges? I'm a parish priest, full bloody stop—or rather, I was, but after booting me out of that, they'll probably veto letting me back in at all, at all."

"Don't be talking, Father. The place is a bona fide seminary and it's a Maynooth man they're after and it's my opinion you'd be tailor-made for the job."

As eloquently as he was able—and wondering, parenthetically, why he was making the effort, if the old badger was so set on being a royal p. in the a.—Emmet knotted together the strands of Father Phil's virtues into a Jacob's ladder of goodness, expounding on the necessity for, and rareness of, this particular priest's combination of experience, wisdom, compassion, humour, knowledge, and education; he was, in short, a bloody treasure trove of talent, he said (delicately averting his gaze, inner and outer, from Father's failing, that good man's weakness so common among celts and their cousins).[6]

"Spare my blushes, Emmet." Father Doyle, weary of doubt, was almost prepared to hope. "Do you think so, Emmet? Do you really think so?"

"I do, Father. Will I tell him you're on, then?"

The priest looked out the window and saw the threaded street-lights of the town sparkling as clearly as a diamond choker in a jeweller's window, saw the ruby-red aft light of the late-night Cherbourg ferry moving out to sea, saw the steady stream of car headlights flowing along the MacLiammoir Overpass, saw the washed-out fluorescent deadness in the faces of the passengers on the no. 17 bus toiling up Uphill Street, saw the neon sign advertising Dunphy's Lager winking above the dimly lit doorway of Mad Molloy's on the corner, saw the bright new clockface of SS. Peter & Laurence O'Toole's hovering like a beacon above the rooftops of the Lower Town, saw—finally, contrapuntally, decisively—the dusky orange glimmer of the old clock of St. Oinsias', like a harvest moon on a cloudy night above the stone-strewn fields of West County Derry (or over the Appian Way, illuminating ghosts of the pagan past and the tall marching poplars pointing to the Christian Heaven to come) . . . .

---

[6]Well all right, they *did* take the odd drop, I won't deny it. But if you ask me things were better then, booze and all. That's right, I'd take the old Ireland with its good manners and style and the clip-clopping of milk horses over the cobbles and the cairns of their dung steaming in the morning light and the Good morning Madams and Sirs of the police-men and a good fifteen years of innocence and rigorous education for the kids—along with, admittedly, a certain narrowness of outlook, as well as a poppylike profusion of red noses on Saturday nights and con-comitant shrunken livers and D.T. cartoons like the *Book of* blooming *Kells* itself—I'd take all that, as I was saying, over today's Eurovapidity and sterile unisexmindedness and two-car ranch houses and Des O'Connor look-alike contests in every suburban lounge bar in the greater Dublin area, God save us.

"Aye. If he's on, tell him I am too, so."

"Right. I'll give Father Pat a buzz. Never fear, *an t-athair*. We'll be young again in the Italian sun."

Magically, Father Doyle's taste for whiskey was gone, although he yearned for a cigarette as he yearned for redemption, i.e., heart and soul. With the formal manners of a vanished era, he thanked Emmet elaborately, shook hands and left, zealously inhaling the damp night air, mixed with the smoke of a Craven A, as if it contained the aroma of a thousand Roman memories: cappuccino + *Strega/Galliano*—exhaust fumes + dank Renaissance stones, danker medieval ones, luminous stones of golden antiquity—honeysuckle in the Forum—wild speedwell + the sun-baked vineyards of Frascati—midsummer in the Campania, silver-green fields shimmering in the heat haze and on the horizon: Vesuvius!—grass + lavender + persimmon—the murky cloacal Ostian shore—daffodils + tulips at Easter in St. Peter's . . . !

He was summoning the past dangerously close, forcing it to reassert itself in his life; his youth was made flesh once more, but only to mock his old age from the shadows, like a villain in Plautus—or was it Petronius?[7]

Walking down Uphill Street with the church in view he was reminded of the walk from the Villa Borghese down to the Piazza del Popolo, with the compass needle of the obelisk in the middle of the square. He remembered the faded elegance of those residential streets, lined with dusty trees limp in the summer heat, resonant with the chortling of cars and mopeds and the rattling of the black-and-green trolley cars that lurched along where the Roman Army had once marched (bearing like the legions the imperial emblem SPQR).

And now it seemed that the past, too, had the power of rebirth. WAS IT POSSIBLE?

Or was it another of the Devil's deceptions?

This had always been one of the hardest of life's many conundrums, to Father Philip Doyle: identifying who was behind what, and where it might lead. Similar dilemmas, he suspected (having

---

[7]Fellinius, actually.

observed, and been confessed to, or at) confronted the layman, and this was surely what gave monotony its appeal, the reassurance of repetition, the known familiarity of sameness, the certainty that one's office desk or pulpit or kitchen contained no hostile spirits, no Devil's familiars, no demons conversant in the tongue of a strange place plotting among themselves in that, or other, tongues; routine was next to godliness, in other words, and change was the Devil's work. Nonsense, of course, for the most part, but as a race we still remembered the uncharted forests and seas, where monsters were called into existence for the sole purpose of falling upon the hapless Christian traveller voluntarily uprooted from his kind (for good, i.e., missionary work, or ill, i.e., brute profiteering) to rend him limb from limb . . . .

Moving to Italy *would* be a change, of course, a wrenching violent in its essence, a complete alteration; but leaving Killoyle, and Ireland, would be easy enough. For twenty-eight years he'd walked Killoyle's streets, eaten in its restaurants, chatted with its residents, ministered to its believers, consoled its bereaved, congratulated its newlyweds, and (increasingly, of late) frequented its pubs; yet for all those years he had been *in* it, not *of* it. True, he liked the countryside beyond: the brown rocks of the North Killoyle hills, the old stone circle at Ballyduff, the wild bogland studded with bluebells in the spring, the white seastrand, the Elizabethan harbour at Youghal, the shrine of the Invisible Virgin at Ballymahone—the only shrine (as far as he knew) to a non-event: the Virgin had been expected to appear there, but never had. The faithful still waited, and always would, and that was comforting, somehow—indeed, it made Ballymahone Father Doyle's favourite shrine, one built and maintained solely on faith (without which he wouldn't give a fart in his chasuble for life, or music, or whiskey, or anything else), yet even his favourite shrine was only a scribble on the palimpsest of the Holy Mother's everlasting glory and the vastness of the world![8] There were other shrines, other churches, other sanctuaries, like that one near the Gesù, the one run by Father Bob Whalen, the man from Sligo (or

---

[8]Whatever you say, but I'll stick to the classifieds myself.

Donegal), the one whose name he'd been trying to remember: Santa Maria de . . . ?

Des? De la? Too French.

Della?

Dell' Abondanza, that was it. Santa Maria dell' Abondanza. It would be his first stop in reconquered Rome—*Roma reconquista* —well, his second, after the obvious (thank you, Your Holiness, for your dismissal) and a long visit with Tancredo, *Monsignore* as he was now—and that trattoria near the Stazione Termini . . . .

Earlier than usual that night the duet of sandpaper baritone and Pavarotti took wing from the bedroom window upstairs.

"Ah-ree-vee-derchi Roma-a-a-a."

Is it truly better to journey hopefully than to arrive? Let us hope so, for Father Doyle's sake. The next morning, Mrs. Delaney, venturing into his room upon receiving no response to her shouted—indeed, screeched—summons to the telephone (Father Patric MacCarthy, S. J., with the bad news Father Phil had initially, and accurately, foreseen), found him in bed, nude and dead, one arm cushioning his head. Around him yellow-tinted snapshots were strewn, of himself and other seminarians (Fausto, Tancredo, Seamus) in Rome, 1949. No bottles were in evidence, but an ashtray full of Craven A cigarette ends was at the foot of the bed, and on his face was a smile, almost a smirk, as if the secret, whatever it was, had been worth the wait after all.[9]

---

[9]I, for one, suspect it was mere rigor mortis, but we must allow room for the poet, so-called, to display his license, as it were, to the authorities (so to speak).

27

The ambulance taking Wolfetone Grey and two nurses from Killoyle Garda HQ to the Nutterburke Institution in Co. Waxford was hijacked on the main Killoyle–Waxford road, just outside Ballyduff, by Wolfetone's daughter Doreen and her fiancé, P. X. Murphy, using antiquated but still effective Libyan-made Akhakh neo-Kalashnikovs purchased after hours at Mad Molloy's, the night before its final closure. The couple—their identities hidden under woolen ski masks, one blue, one mauve—claimed to be acting on behalf of the Bodenstown Irregulars, a Republican splinter group, but all they really wanted, as they explained to groggy Wolfetone, was a down payment of £5000 on a Tudor-style semidetached in Terenure; and with Murphy out of a job and heading for the dole, Doreen reckoned they needed the loan before Wolfetone went away to serve his three years for aggravated assault (with mitigating circumstances, i.e., a verdict by halves: half guilty, half not). With her mother refusing to advance "a single frigging blasted penny, do you hear?" from her end of the family bank account, Doreen felt, reluctantly, that coercion in the guise of political action was their only choice.[1]

---

[1] I didn't follow the Wolfetone saga as closely as some—not until he became famous, that is—but I'd not doubt this part at all. Sure, when you get right down to it, isn't Ireland the place that produced Buck Whaley, who walked from Dublin to Jerusalem and back on a bet, and Lord MacAnnan, who chained his stroppy old dad to a bear, and of course in our own time Sean Nò Beàn, famed nationalist kidnapper of

Wolfetone's reaction to these events was unambiguous. He had been allowed books from the prison library, and preferred to hide his nose in one of them (*So What! The Autobiography of Blessed Leonid Glossovich*) rather than (as he put it) "watch life imitating television."

After drubbing the ambulance driver and the two nurses lightly about the ears with the butts of their Akhakhs, Doreen and Murphy turned the three of them out onto the road. Murphy took the wheel and, siren howling, they continued on their way to Waxford across the rainswept Nearside hills.

"So, why'd you do it, Dad?" inquired Doreen. "Stab the fella, I mean."

"Right enough," said Murphy. "Old Milo. Good chum of mine, he is, or was. A bit of a hard case maybe, but there was no need to go after the poor sod with a knife."

"It was a pipe-cleaning tool," said Wolfetone, distantly. "A Reamer. I couldn't help it, as I told the judge. Being given the sack was one thing, seeing that Milo of yours behind my desk quite another. He's a horrible fat alcoholic get with the morals of a Barbary ape."

(Wolfetone was paraphrasing the section in chapter 10 of the Glossovich autobiography, in which the great sage fulminates against those who had incarcerated him in psychiatric prisons deep in the Soviet heartland:

Big fat alcoholic guys with behavior like zoo animals, and same smells and education too, like gorillas in Africa, or the apes on old Barbary coast, also in Africa. All this I explained politely to them, with illustrative hand gestures and sounds, not to mention translation into their native Uzbek, Ukrainian, Kazakh, and so on, but the effect was no more than if I had been scratching my bum, or tying my shoelaces (forbidden, in case you were wondering—too easy a way out, or route to Hell, as per our belief structure). One outstandingly stupid guy, named

---

paintings (including Bowell's *Fish Hatchery* and the Sputacello *Allegory of Migraine*) supposedly at the behest of the Belfast Brigade, but in reality for himself and his villainous Uncle Vic? In this country, one thing's sure: in this country, nothing's sure.

Fiat after the small but big² Western car that brought so much hope and opportunity to the banks of the Volga region (and believe me when I say stupid, like there was a Nobel or Lenin Prize for having no brains AT ALL, Fiat Maximovich would be the one walking away hands down, world if not cosmic champion), took me by the labels and placed his giant face the shape and size of a Karelian beetroot pizza (flat; approx. 2 metres 21 cm. across) across mine sideways, with loud threats to dismantle me piece by piece like a Mekhanov set because I was a dirty revisionist reactionary anti-Marxist occidentalist running dog of unknown but mixed species!

Hey, girls and boys, and all you others too—even you guys with names of other, non-chosen, non-G denomination—remember, in moments like this, turn your mind off and upward to the Great Guy in the sky (or somewhere like that) and pray, pray, pray! That is what I did, with fists crashing all round my head but never scoring a hit—part of subtle KGB-type torture technique, like when you would swear that Fiat, or another massive moron in an East German suit, is emptying his Skoda machine gun straight at you but it turns out it's nothing personal, there was a cockroach on the wall behind (not anymore, after 167 rounds!)—and devilish refinement of such punishments as fashioning cuffs on your trouser legs when they know you hate trouser cuffs, filing their fingernails right next to your ears while you're taking a nap, ironing silly-looking wigs all night until you want to scream or even agree to dance the kazachok (hey! hey!), etc.; in Russia, nothing was easy, then, but everybody believed, because they weren't allowed to. Nowadays, everything's easier, but belief gets shaky. What kind of religion is that? If you want my advice, get on the blower to the Big G NOW—TODAY—PRONTO—RIGHT AWAY, and have a unilateral conversation, like a summit conference call! Maybe it will take you a while before He comes to the phone, but when He does, you can recognise Him immediately by the sound of his slippers (shuffle, shuffle, like Ukrainian potato pancakes on your Babushka's griddle) as well as his extremely deep bass voice and antique, even old-fashioned, way of

---

²Small but big? I don't know Russian, but I know English when I see it, and if you ask me this is neither. Try "great." If it works, write to the publisher (q.v. *supra*); if not (better still), chuck the silly book out the window.

speaking—and by the way, He doesn't like to be interrupted, so listen to Him, but keep your pierogy-trap shut. Remember: He was around when you were wiping ice cream off the buckles of your plastic sandals, and even before!

It is, truly, my truly dim but earnest reader, the only way out, and anyway if you believe this stuff, others will too. I found that out myself, even in Pskov Psychiatric Hospital no. 116B I spread the Word, and trust me, the Word got around! In the end, even horrid Fiat Max-imovich fell to his knees and accepted me as his globkoy, or booking agent of God; thus, in this way did he become the first 'bolshoi stariy', or Big Old Guy of the Glossovian Church!

Yes, yes, I hear what you're saying, in a wide variety of tones and accents, some major, some minor: he was like Saint Peter to my Jesus, right? OK, OK, but not as bright, do you know what I'm saying? But listen: if you're trying to contact me, and you can't get through, try Fiat. He's always home, usually in the garage!)

Wolfetone closed the book and looked through the wrought-iron bars of the ambulance window at the rain slanting over the grey bogland and the road's gleaming belt across the bulging wasteland beyond. Despite this mournful view, for the first time since his agony began he felt the inner darkness lifting. Glosso-vich's words, so prismatic, so luminous, shone in upon his gloom like glimpses of the Other Place through the gaps in the great world-curtain of gas. After all, he, the Master, had undergone the same trials, or worse; he had been humiliated, mocked, physi-cally abused; many years had gone by without the faintest hint of success, or hint of future greatness; reptile-brained ignoramuses had jeered at one whose mind encompassed all, much as Wolfe-tone himself had been pilloried and derided by fools. No doubt, there were parallels, and in that light what was losing a job? What was a bit of a stint in a mental home, compared to the ultimate reward? He should feel honoured to be tested thus by the opprobrium of the stupid, the indifference of the unin-formed, the hostility of the non-G-named; honoured, to be exiled to his own wilderness. What did it all mean, if not the moulding of a new leader, the forging of a new pontificate, the anointing by God of a successor to the great Glossovich, now conversing eternally with the Almighty on the static-free phone lines of Heaven?[3]

It all fell into place, ruminated Wolfetone, nodding in accordance with his thoughts and the van's bumping and rolling over poorly patched potholes. His hips, too, were swaying rhythmically from side to side, as in an involuntary belly dance. Both motions put him at ease; he felt relaxed, released, relieved—in short, confident once more.

OF COURSE THERE WAS A PLAN!

How could there not be? He mentally reviewed the evidence: the long years of misery and drudgery at Spudorgan Hall; the chance rediscovery of half-forgotten Glossovich in the newspaper one mundane Sunday morning; the revelation of Truth by degrees, over the phone, and through the mesmerising prose of the Great One; the ill-fated assembly of the G-named and his consequent dismissal by the heathen Power; the vile Milo taking his place and receiving his due reward. Seen from the vantage point of time and distance, it was a pattern on the most seamless of garments, woven by the Master Craftsman on high and destined to be worn by . . . .

"Me," said Wolfetone. Spontaneously, he rocked back and forth, hugging his knees.

"Look, there's a bank," said Doreen. "I reckon you can turn off the siren now." When Murphy had done so, it was silently and unnoticed that they coasted into Ballyhamlet, a village in the Otherside Hills of south Co. Waxford. It boasted the standard-issue half-dozen pubs, pair of rival betting shops, Shell service station, notions shop, Spar minimarket, ham-and-egg cafeteria, news-agent/tobacconist, and—in between the Tir-na-Nog hair-

---

[3]Well, that's what he *would* think, of course, but there's already at least one Society for Glossovich Spotters coordinating reports of sightings coming in from all over the world. A fortnight ago a retired bus mechanic from Swindon claimed to have seen the old urine merchant hang gliding in the Chilterns; the week before, three German tourists ran into him on the Mall in Lahore, with a former prime minister of Pakistan on his arm; last month, according to a reporter on the *Racing Times*, he won the Monaco Grand Prix under the name Wellington Zappudo. Stay tuned; it can only get worse.

dressing salon and O'Hatter's haberdashery, in a Georgian-style former Methodist chapel (1826)—a branch of the Allied Irish Bank.

Murphy parked the ambulance across the street.

"Come on, Dad," he said. "Let's get this over with."

Wolfetone's face assumed an expression proper to a personage of substance offended by the *lèse-majesté* of underlings.

"Eff off," he barked. "You ugly bugger. You look like a monkey, did you know that, Murphy? And don't call me 'Dad.'"

"Aw for the love of Jesus, give over, will ya?"

"Why should I let you have a penny of my hard-earned money? You were a lousy barman and you seduced my daughter when I wasn't looking and anyway your name's all wrong. Murphy, indeed! Ha!"

"Let's not start all that, all right, Dad?" implored Doreen. "The money's for the family, not just him, so off you go to the bank and get it, if you don't mind."

Wolfetone shook hands with himself in an access of smugness and bile.

"Can't," he chuckled.

"Why not?"

"Because, my darling, I have no cheques, no chequebook, no account with that bank over there, no current account with any bank anywhere, no letters of credit, no credit, no automatic banking card, no wallet, no folding money, no coins, not even fifty pee in my pocket to buy an ounce of Cavendish for my pipe, if I had my pipe, which I don't, because they took it away, along with everything else. Sorry, colleen bawn. You're out of luck with me, as usual."

Doreen's sky blue gaze darkened to reflect inward frustration coalescing into rage. A shadow passed across her pseudo-virginal face and her rosebud lips tightened to a thin red line.

"Now you listen to me, you old shagspot. Murphy and I've gone well out on a limb to pull off this caper. Either you go into that bank over there and get a cashier's cheque for five thousand quid, or—"

Murphy chimed in, brightly. "Or we'll go across and get it ourselves." He picked up his Akhakh and made childish strafing

sounds with his tongue.[4] "Why not? They'll blame it all on the
Bodenstown Irregulars, whoever they are."

Indeed, the midmorning torpor of Ballyhamlet was so complete that (as Wolfetone observed, entering into the spirit of the
enterprise) an entire regiment could take over the place and no
one would raise an eyebrow. Doreen pondered for as long as it
took her to smoke a cigarette.

"To hell." She flicked the fag end out the window. "Got the
masks?" Murphy replied in the affirmative, holding them up as
evidence.

"Then let's go."

So they went, and so goes crime: with a slack moral code,
built-in greed, and a grudge against authority, it takes only moderate luck and one successful bank raid before you're hooked—
and hooked they were, with eight thousand quid in their Switzers
of Grafton Street carrier bags, after that fifteen-minute stopover
in Ballyhamlet.

On the way north, in a speedier but less ostentatious car (a
Rising Sun Trenta TI) prised from the grasp of a young man
readying himself for a big win at Noonans' the bookmakers,
Wolfetone, reclining in the back seat, expansively asked Murphy,
at the wheel, whether his mother's maiden name might not begin
with *G*. When it transpired that it did (Ginty), Wolfetone soft-
ened to his future son-in-law to the extent of reaching forward to
shake his hand, thereby temporarily causing a wild zigzag course
across the road that nearly culminated in a collision with an ar-
ticulated super-Eurolorry transporting hogs from Monaghan to
Brest.

"Feckin' bloody hell."

The car's trajectory was soon restored, however, and all was
once again well. In token of their recent success, and newfound

---

[4]That's right: the tip of the tongue repeatedly striking the palate just
behind the incisors, with a voiced vowel sound—*a* or *u*, preferably—to
supply aural verisimilitude, as our father always said. Mostly he enjoyed
doing it during sermons in church, or at work when the boss was on the
phone brownnosing at long distance, or even at home after dinner, with
a jigger of malt at his side. It's fun! Try it at the office sometime.

family harmony, the trio sang, in disharmonious unison, "The
Soldier's Song" and other favourites of yesteryear, including
"Wann Mein Schatz Hochzeit Macht," "The Old Triangle Goes
Jingle-a-Jangle," "Blowin' in the Wind," "The Ballad of Roger
O'Hare," "That's Amore," and "La Vie en Rose." Two hours
later they were across the border in Co. Armagh, one more nutty
splinter group among dozens, a drop in an ocean of bank-rob-
bing patriots and trigger-happy dreamers.[5]

---

[5]Here's an update for you, if you're interested. Our young couple's
house-buying dreams were shelved for the nonce, or good. The
Bodens-town Irregulars were born again under the name the
Glossovians, spiritually led by self-styled Divine Guide (or Guy)
Wolfetone Grey, who in short order acquired authority over his followers and mythic status in the roadside car dealerships and isolated software outlets of the West Midlands and the rocky hills of Sligo and
Donegal. Tales were told of his wandering yet hypnotic gaze, his fawning yet decisive manner, his dull yet instructive past, his matchless fund
of folklore and his knowledge of ancient wisdom, including fluent Russian and the secret to the universe; thus was the legend of "God's Grey
Wolf" born. The lonely, stupid and/or sexually regressive became his
followers, generally by eagerly entering into conversation with anonymous callers over the phone, or by responding to cryptic messages on
their e-mail screens. Meetings were held in the unlit storage rooms of
pubs, with faces averted, or outdoors, masked, under the nighttime sky.
Soon the Glossovians swelled in numbers to become a nomadic church,
a mobile sect of God-fearing bank robbers, all with surnames beginning
in G, crisscrossing the south Ulster borderlands and striking at housing
societies, banks, and churches of all the old denominations. The last I
heard, they had a politician or two in their ranks, and were lobbying the
government to become an established church with tax-exempt status—
and oh, by the way, Doreen and Ginty (né Murphy) just had their first
child, a boy named Leonid. Congratulations? I think not. Who knows
what he'll turn into, with that kind of a start in life.

28

In the end, Milo was quite simply left holding the bag, from which (as it were) the cat had long since been ousted: Managing Director of Spudorgan Hall he might be, at least until the Board put the matter to a vote, but there was little joy in it, with government examiners poring over the account books and computer records in the director's office twelve hours a day, and reporters snooping round from half the dailies in the country—notably one especially persistent lady journalist from *Glam*, the fashion magazine, now, at least in part, a periodical of distinctly crusading, not to say muckraking, bent, thanks to Kathy's first article on the Carfax Affair and the subsequent rise in readership—or "upward trend," in journalese.

"It's got all the elements of a best-selling trash novel," she said. "Fame, money, sport, the ponies, Swiss bank accounts—well, not Swiss, Liechtensteinian, which is much the same thing, of course. Actually, the only thing that's missing is sex. Can't you find out what old Carfax gets up to in bed?"

"Mrs. Carfax, I reckon," said Milo. His innards were crawling with excitement. "By the way, ah, Kathy?"

This unfinished exchange took place in the living, or television, room at Kathy's house on King Idris Road (W.), on the first Friday evening since Milo's apotheosis. Positioned diagonally across from Kathy's forty-one-inch Nippotron DeLuxe Ultra-Screen television, he was half-sprawled on the sofa rather than fully recumbent because (a) the still-throbbing wound on his neck, concealed by a thick bandage, minimised spinal articulation, and (b) he was, after all, visiting a lady. On the television, SiegKanal

Zweibrücken's Friday night *Zum Goldener Oldies* show was displaying the swarthy, un-Aryan mugs of Hess, Goebbels, and their Führer, staring sternly through a drizzle of white dots, holding up their right hands like Boy Scouts about to take the Scouting oath. Their jaws were working in an awkward joint rendition of "Deutschland über Alles"; behind them were banners; on the banners were swastikas; behind the banners, shafts of light probed the horrible night sky of Naziland.

"Ah, that'll be Nuremberg. 1938. The Cathedral of Light," said Kathy, with the easy confidence of the expert. Blue-jeaned legs slung over one arm of her armchair, she was at the upper right-hand corner of a hypotenuse triangle formed by herself, Milo and the TV. Next to the chair Strongbow lay lionlike, muzzle on forepaws, glaring, and occasionally growling, at Milo.

"That was Albert Speer's invention, of course, the Cathedral of Light. Kitschy but clever. It wowed the crowds, anyway."

"Bloody Nazi bastards," said Milo. His voice shook slightly, an indication of strong emotional undercurrents that had nothing to do with the plug-uglies on the television. Rather, he was trembling on the threshold of that most crucial transformation in the acquaintance of man and woman:[1] the metamorphosis of the casual chum—the fraternal friend—the Platonic pal—into suitor/paramour (at worst), even boyfriend/lover (at best)!

This Milo was about to do in his characteristic style, quaveringly, with irony, and a touch of rudeness.

"By the way, Kathy."

Kathy took her eyes off the hated Hess.

"God, what a hideous bastard. Doesn't he look like a baboon? Hmm?"

Milo ignored Hess. His heart was battering as he reached simultaneously into his recent past and its immediate future to yank out the question he had wanted to ask from the outset.

He stumbled twice, started again.

"Have you, ah?"

---

[1] I'll scrub round this, thank you very much. There are some things I'd just as soon never know—but mark my words, they'll be making a TV miniseries out of it soon enough.

It was amazing, the other day he was looking through a, shall
we say, men's magazine . . . .

In other words, had Kathy ever posed for a photographic so-
called essay, in an English men's mag, oh, about eight or ten years
ago, over in London? As one of numerous Irish country girls
seeking their fame and fortune in the Big Smoke and making a
few quid on the side in ah unorthodox ways, somewhat chilly in
Blighty's dampness, ah haha?—and before she answered, he hastened to add that no *arriviste* arrogance towered behind his question, no moral judgement dangled therefrom: he was motivated
merely by friendly interest and the deep personal, emotional . . .
well, she knew the rest.

Didn't she?

"I *beg* your pardon?"

Her tone was cold, possibly hostile. Milo suddenly wondered
if he hadn't got the whole thing wrong, misread the signals,
presumed too much, as he almost always did, with women—of
course, it was their fault, wasn't it, for being so cute about it, for
being too bloody subtle for a thick galoot like him and not spell-
ing things out from the start; but on the other hand (sweet suffering Jesus!), what was he supposed to think? Any dispassionate
observer with one eye and half a brain would have said they were
getting on like stout and oysters, judging by the events of the
previous fortnight. Hadn't the creature come to see him at the
hospital twice (no, three times, including his first layover after
the Great Stink)? And hadn't she damned near moved into Spudorgan Hall after Emmet Power's letter arrived from Italy de-
nouncing Carfax and elevating Milo to the succession by default?
And hadn't they spoken on the phone five, no six, or was it seven,
times? And what about those two Vindaloo dinners, and the several pints they'd shared at Magilligan's, the night of his second
discharge from the Mater Misericordiae . . . ?

His ganglions rang with the tangle of signals. Bugger it, so. If
she took this the wrong way, she'd keep on taking things the
wrong way, and there was no future in that for either of them.

"I saw you in a sex mag, posing starkers. That's all."

"Oh, that. You mean *Quest.*"

"Aye."

Had it been another woman—Martine, say, or Millie, the Minx of Man—Milo would have described her expression as a simper, but Kathy wasn't the simpering sort, nor was she given to coy come-hithers; still, there was an unprecedented gleam in her eye, and her mouth was unmistakably fashioning a smile. Her feet, too, joined in the general excitement, jiggling up and down, and she arched her back in a feline stretch that conferred redundant advantage to her bosom. Strongbow growled, accurately suspecting Milo of a conspiracy to spray the scent of the human male far and wide.

"Quiet, boy," said Kathy, with a firm hand on the dog's collar.

"So it *was* you," said Milo, in a hoarse countertenor. He blasted through the huskiness with a series of semi-coughs. Strongbow barked, and was exiled to the kitchen.

"It was," said Kathy, on her return. "Simple, really. I needed the money. Times were hard for country girls, and this country girl in particular. Like, I had to get away from home, and everybody was going to London in those days, not just the traditional Paddy neighbourhoods like the Archway and Kilburn but as far out as Barnet and Hammersmith there were whole areas where you heard nothing but Irish accents—but of course you know London, don't you."

"Not really," said Milo. "I've been there once or twice."

Kathy stared, remembering their first drink together: the Elgin marbles, Houdon's *Voltaire*, the Inns of Court . . . .

"Ach, get away."

Anyway (she continued), things were rough, back then, but she'd faced up to them, and in doing so she'd faced them down—and, by the way, she'd long since made her peace with herself about the *Quest* episode: yes, yes, when you thought about it, it was a kind of one-way whoring, wasn't it, taking off your clothes for money and arranging yourself in uncomfortable poses for the second-hand delectation of anonymous men.

"Pretty horrible, I admit. But no one laid a finger on me, and anyway it's in the past, where all our mistakes are safe. Where on earth did you find that old magazine? I mean, that was ten, twelve years ago."

"Oh, a friend was cleaning out his box room. We naturally had a glance at one or two, boys being boys, ah haha."

She gave him a solemn look, eyes wide.

"What did you think, then?"

"About what?"

"About what, he says. About me. If I remember correctly, they asked me to wear a garter belt and fishnet stockings for one of the shots. Very sexy, they said. A bit of a cliché, I thought. What did you think?"

Milo felt a dryness in his throat and a gentle pulsating that was simultaneously disturbing—elevating blood pressure, bringing out the sweat—and the greatest thrill imaginable, summoning images of sensual delight beyond compare, and well beyond the hopes of a bachelor long accustomed to his own company. It was the crucial moment, the last frontier, the Rubicon; he remembered, now, what it was like (not since Minnie the Minx had he . . . !), but there was the extra burden, in this case, of love (true? Or false?).

"Well, I. Of course, I only paged through it, you know. I'm not much interested in that kind of thing. It's illegal in this country, theoretically, isn't it? And there's a reason for that, isn't there? I mean, let's face it, not everything the Church supports is rubbish, after all."

She glared, accurately suspecting trumped-up outrage.

"What are you on about?"

"Pornography. Sex mags. Peep shows. You know."

"I thought *Quest* was in relatively good taste, for that kind of thing. I wouldn't call it pornography."

"Oh, right. Definitely not."

"So what did you think? You're ducking the question."

Milo, maladroit swain, licked his lips and clasped and unclasped his fingers several times, harrumphing with nervous coughs; then he threw his hands in the air and laughed, almost convincingly.

"I thought you were dazzling. Venus in the flesh and no mistake."

"Did you, so? I'm flattered. That was a while ago, but. What do you think now?"

This led, naturally, to Milo's protesting that he had no direct comparison to set against the photographic evidence of the magazine, delicately conveying his lack of fulfillment, of honest experience, not having seen more of her *au naturel* than the standard, socially acceptable (indeed, expected) hands, ankles, face, etc., and therefore being in no position to judge—although he was quite sure the work of the years would have if anything enhanced the qualities in evidence, fully ripening, as one might say, fruit formerly half-ripe . . . .

"Well, there's one way for you to find out, isn't there?" she said.

She aimed the remote control at the television and banished Hess, Hitler & Co. to the oblivion they deserved, then stood up and walked out of the room, leaving Milo to follow.

He did, so.[2]

---

[2]Well, to be perfectly honest, she seemed a bit much, even to Milo, with her French cigarettes and jodhpurs and Nazi TV programmes, not to mention that sodding dog, but her articles on the Carfax caper had made her a bit of a minor celebrity in her own right—you should have seen the way the waiters grovelled at The Bay Window (she hated it, though, I'll give her that!)—but at least Milo was at ease in her company, for once not getting sloshed all over the place and playing the wild rover or mad genius or touching everybody for money or doing any of those other juvenile things he used to bore us all with! Of course, he was happy enough that he didn't stay Managing Director at Spudorgan very long; in fact, after a couple of weeks they got in some johnnie from an accounting firm in Dublin, and last I heard Carfax was being indicted in Florida for gross naughtiness or something. Anyway, Kathy got Milo a minor editing job of some sort at *Glam* and guess what: his first collection of poems, *Gobbing into the Gutter*, came out last week—and yes, we're all very proud, although as the critics said the influence of Hoolihan is plain to see and he's got a bit to learn about controlling his metre. Still, it's a start, and that's more than we'd have once said he deserved, eh?

29

If the carved lintelstone above the front door had it right, the Powers' house in Chieti (pop. 27,000; 43 km. SSE of Rome, 212 km. NNW of Naples) was built in 1672, and was therefore a historic residence, not to say a bit of an old pile, but its interior had been whipped into shape in the early '90s by an economics professor from Bocconi University and sold consequent to *il professore's* being promoted to *la presidenzia*. As a result (after a two hour flight from Cork International to Rome Fiumicino, and an hour's drive by hired Fiat on the Autostrada as far as the Frascati exit),[1] Emmet and Roisin found a house humming with the most mod of cons: central heating, washer, dryer, microwave, multideck stereo, 25" television with 1400-channel capability, computer-ready outlets, etc. The whitewashed walls gleamed inside and out, and the dining room window immodestly flaunted a view across the Pogginarno valley and the plain of Lazio Inferiore, a yellow-brown carpet of naked vineyards and stubbled wheatfields stretching to the bulky hills of Campania, pachyderm-gray in the clear November air. The bedroom upstairs commanded a more limited perspective of the vegetable garden behind the neighbouring Casa Comunale, with a glimpse of the fifteenth century belfry of the church of Sant'Angelo above the red-tiled roofs. Birds chirped outside; cats mewed in

---

[1] Exit number, please? Mileage? Model Number, Year and Performance Data of said Fiat? Availability of service stations? Ladies' and Gents' conveniences? Three-star restaurants in vicinity, yes/no? Come on, boyo, you're falling down on the job—or should that be *giobbo?*

the courtyard; mopeds clattered in the street beyond; bells chimed, distantly.

"It'll do us, eh, acushla?" said Emmet.

"It will, as long as there aren't rats in the cellar. You can never tell with old houses. Do you remember my great-auntie Teresa? Gram's sister? The one who shaved every day? She lived in an old house outside Longford, if you recall—the Athlone road, was it, or Sligo—and there were more rats in that old place than hairs on her face. Every time she sat down to dinner, it sounded like Amiens Street Station at rush hour with the bustling of the creatures, and once when I was a girl I remember actually seeing three of them lounging about at the head of the bed, waiting for me to get up and fetch their breakfast."

"Aye," said Emmet. He had discovered a set of keys hanging above the kitchen sink, and was eager to match them to their respective locks. "Best mind the snakes, but."

"Snakes?"

The shocking idea brought a momentary Medusan glare to Roisin's gentle features.

Father Patric MacCarthy, as nominal head of the College Foundation—which oversaw the Albergo del Collegio, as well as the Collegio itself—had arranged for Emmet to assume his duties as *Direttore* of the hotel immediately, rather than just fill in until the tourist season, as had been originally planned; funds from Ireland, explained Father Pat, had made this possible.[2] In any event, Emmet reported for work early the first day after a frugal *prima colazione* of espresso and buttered roll in the Gran Caffè Romano on the Piazza Garibaldi, the town's sloping main square. The Collegio, he discovered—after driving aimlessly through echoing streets and shaded squares—was a short way outside of town, hidden behind a double barricade of poplar trees and a brick wall. It revealed itself to be a renovated but genuine sixteenth-century *palazzo*, flanked on one side by a chapel (San Bettino, 17th cent.) and on the other by the Albergo, a mock-Romanesque annex about half the size of Spudorgan Hall, with

---

[2]Surprise, surprise! Don't say I didn't warn you (*qv. supra*)!

tremendous vistas of the countryside (green, yellow, brown) and a fountain or two plashing in the gardens behind. Dario, the *sottodirettore*, was an impish-featured young fellow with the pallid complexion of a hearty indoorsman. He welcomed Emmet in Italianate English laced with casual obscenities, showed him round the hotel, and generally made him feel slightly worried. For one thing, the duties of the director appeared to be nominal; although Emmet had a modern, well-appointed office and a desk in that office with a nameplate bearing the name *Sig. E. POVER*, there was little or nothing to do, according to Dario, except meet once a week with the members of the faculty.

"All speak English. It's OK."

"But what else do I have to do?"

"Ah, not too much. Talk on the telephone. 'Ave dinner with some important *prelati*. Focking cardinals, even the Pope, 'oo knows? Go sometimes to Rome, make arrangements for more focking priests to come 'ere. Maybe at Easter, Christmas, you're busy. That's all." He shrugged, Italically. "Never mind. If they give problems, send them to me. Relax, Maestro. OK?"

Emmet looked the fellow up and down and received in return a grin that, while hinting at impertinence, also conveyed utter confidence that this was the way things were, *amico mio*, and there was no point pretending otherwise.

"OK," said Emmet. *"Va bene."*

In response to Emmet's linguistic trial balloon, Dario switched to his muscular mother tongue *con gusto*, but Emmet could go no further, except for the usual restaurant pidgin and the necessary instructions for filling the petrol tank, finding (and flushing) the toilet, telling left from right, sidestepping sexual innuendo, etc. Fortunately, the slack schedule of his new job afforded him more than enough time to converse in loud half-witted tones with Inlinguaphone cassettes and wade through *La Stampa*, declaiming *Buon Giorno, Signore Paor* (the Irish version of his name proving more Italianisable than the English) into his office mirror. Roisin resisted all such foreign chatter, at first, but once the house had been put in order—prints of Armagh and Killoyle hung on the walls, cutlery installed, rugs laid down, Irish magazine subscriptions sent off—she realised she was beginning to resent Emmet's growing coherence on the telephone and in the *pasticceria* and *salumeria*, while she was reduced to the mock-idiocy of incomprehension, or the pointing finger of the deaf mute. Accordingly, they settled on an hour's daily practice and sat at the dining room window identifying things in the lucid syllables of their new second language: *la chiesa; le fiume; il campo; le monte.*

"*Guarda! Un uccello nel cielo,*" announced Roisin one memorable day, as a crow flapped by overhead. Emmet chuckled.

"By janey, you've arrived, acushla. *Molto bene.* Break out the Asti Spumante, *subito.*"

As Dario had predicted, Christmas was somewhat busier than the rest of the year, but even then, *il direttore* had to be present only from half ten or so to around four, reassuring, soothing, cajoling, or answering long-distance phone calls, just like Spudorgan Hall—unless there were ecclesiastical guests (or "more focking hass'ole priests," in Dario's version—ironically for the *sottodirettore* of a seminary hotel, he was anti-clerical to the point of staring eyes, waving fists, etc.) to be wined, dined and generally fawned over. On St. Stephen's Day, one such was Father Patric MacCarthy, in transit from Malta. He and the Powers luxuriated over a three-hour lunch in the hotel restaurant. A dusting of snow had bestowed the cliché appearance of a Christmas card on the umbrella pines and box hedges in the hotel garden.

"If Ireland's the Blessed Daughter of the Church, Malta's at least her Blessed Niece," said Father Pat. *Linguini alla Napolitana* and accompanying Frascati wine rumbled happily through his guts. "Ah, Malta's a potential bonanza, believe you me. Just like this place, only more of your standard tourist attractions: azure seas, white sands, picturesque ruins and so on. Also, for some reason I can't fathom, Malta's chock-a-block with young lads who want to join the priesthood—and not just the priesthood, but the Society of Jesus, believe it or not."

"This college-cum-hotel dodge is turning into quite an industry, eh, Father?" said Emmet. His lolling posture subtlely spoke to the Jesuit of a new arrogance that time or circumstances would inevitably check—whereas, in fact, Italy had merely worked her magic on Emmet Power, as surely as she had done on previous generations of Northerners, and his managerial qualities had taken second place in his soul to more human ones: ease, confidence, living in the moment, peace of mind . . . . [3]

"Well, now, I'm not sure you'd call it an industry, much less a dodge, Emmet. What we've done is combine two ancient Church traditions, hospitality and pedagogy; and if there's a quid or two to be made in it, well, rest assured it won't go amiss. *Ancora una grappa?*" He held up the bottle. Emmet shook his head. "Mrs. Power?"

"Oh all right. As long as we're not driving. We so rarely do, any more, and that suits me, the way these people drive. Actually, that's a big advantage to living where we do, Father. Emmet can walk to work. At nine o'clock he steps out the door and at half past he's behind his desk, aren't you, dear?"

Emmet nodded.

"Right," he said.

There was no compelling reason for Roisin to know that his daily habit was to spend an hour or so at the Gran Caffé Romano on the morning-lively Piazza, reading *La Stampa* and the previous day's *Irish Times* (delivered in bulk every evening for the eleven Irish subscribers at the Collegio) before strolling to work, rarely arriving before ten, on most days. There was nothing deceitful or adulterous in this, but Emmet had come to accept the need for a clandestine interlude, away from the enclosure of his domestic life, and the fact that the Gran Caffé Romano was frequented in the morning exclusively by men of his own age and class suggested that some Italians, at least, had come to this conclusion long since.[4]

The conversation ensnared itself in sudden awkwardness.

---

[3]Very Chinese, that, or French—or Italian, actually, before they all started rushing about in Lamborghinis and getting oh so very bloody chic and up-to-date. "Peace of mind," as the da used to say, "is worth every cow in the Midlands of Ireland, and their milk, uncurdled." *Mar na beidh ar leitheidi aris ann:* God bless him and the face he wore to his grave!

[4]And not just among the Italians, boy. Take my Uncle Mike, now. As a

Roisin disentangled it with a lament.

"Poor dear Father Doyle," she sighed. "Such a good man."

Father Pat raised his eyebrows.

"Well, yes," he said, "but from what I heard the old chap was a bit of a bottle man, don't you know. As a matter of fact, it was well-known in the parish that he'd been pickled for years."

"Still," said Emmet, "I can't help thinking he'd have slowed down if he'd made it over here. There's different kinds of boozing, Father."

"In other words, if he'd taken the job here, he'd have become a new man," said Father Pat. "That's what you're saying, is it, Emmet?"

"Well, I was only remembering the expression on his face that last night in the hotel bar, when I talked him into applying for it. He looked—forgive the expression—transformed."

"And what about poor Mrs. Delaney?" interjected Roisin. "She was transformed, wasn't she? Transformed to the dole

---

newlywed he was, to all appearances, the ideal husband: punctual, devout, and hard-working, but behind the scenes, i.e., between the hours of six and eight o'clock in the a.m., he was a right royal tearaway, up in the freight yards behind Connolly Station, usually with his old railway mates on the Donabate local, long acknowledged to be the world's slowest train (*Cf.* Guinness Book of Records, 1995 edition). The lads would bring in the cards, of course, and the tongue sandwiches, lashings of rashers and sweet black tea, as well as dominoes and even nature magazines straight from Holland (or was it Sweden?), and have themselves a proper old stag party, and that every blessed morning of the week—then, one day, by a fluke, Eileen had to take the 7.11 to Donabate to interview a nurse for the twins, and whom did she see clicking over the points in the opposite direction only her own dear hubby, cards in hand, a cigar clenched in his teeth, his eyes round as wrens' eggs with the goggling and nothing less than pictures of half-clothed Swedish (or Dutch) bathing beauties being goggled at, and wasn't he hemmed in by the roughest class of scoundrels this side of Stonybatter! Well, I don't need to tell you, it was in the guise of a sadder and wiser man that he went home that day; and if, ultimately, he buggered off (to America and Roscommon), I reckon he had no one to blame for that narrow lonely bed but himself. He made it, and he lies in it yet.

queue, that is. Poor old Father D. was like a second husband to her—spiritually, of course, Father—and the dear knows she devoted long enough to taking care of him."

"She'll be well looked after," said Father Pat smoothly. "The Church doesn't forget those who labour in her service."[5]

"Except old Philly Doyle," said Emmet.

Father Pat bristled.

"That was a purely administrative decision," he said. "St. Oinsias' just wasn't taking in the congregants any more, and that's the honest truth, Emmet, and however much we'd like to be spiritual and loving all the time, we're not in it as a losing concern, either. Believe you me it's given me sleepless nights. But in the end my superiors simply decided St. Oinsias' wasn't pulling its weight, and the same was true of North Killoyle parish generally. Oh, Father Doyle managed to scare up a decent turnout now and then, for weddings and baptisms and so on, and he had his loyal parishioners right enough—like you, Mrs. P., and may I say it does you credit—but St. Oinsias' was losing miles of ground to Saints O'Toole's and the south parish every day, especially now that they've installed that quadrophonic sound system and IMAX superscreen over the altar—that was Monsignor Stripling's idea, you know, first day back on the job, now there's forward thinking for you."

"Right. A miraculous recovery," said Emmet. "Only if you want my opinion old Stripling's a raving nutter—yet he's back in harness, isn't he, but Father Phil was an old soak, so they said, so no Italian job for him—and he a Maynooth man, by the living Jesus! Incidentally, I haven't noticed too many candidates at the College with Maynooth backgrounds, Father."

"Ach, get out of that, Emmet. This is Italy. We can't go about

---

[5]Will you hark at the fellow? The brass of them, the sanctimonious pseudo-salvationists! It brings back the Blessed Uncle Francis fiasco. Thanks to that crowd, we're still paying off his debts. Let this story be a lesson to you, boys and girls. Believe what you must, but never assume the next man to be holier than thou—especially if he's wearing one of those collars.

appointing Irish to every vacant position, however much we'd like to. The fact that we managed to squeeze you in at all involved a fair old amount of genteel arm-twisting and knees delicately applied to cobblers, I can tell you."

"And Emmet appreciates it, don't you, dear." Roisin laid a pacifying hand on her husband's arm.

"He does, he does, I know, Mrs. Power," said the priest. Confident of a small but significant victory over the forces of dissent, he drained his glass and sat back, sated. Geniality gradually gained ground, and Father Pat slapped his thigh in token thereof, quivering with anticipatory laughter.

"Did youse hear about old Tom Maher, now?"

As Emmet put out his cigar, self-willed relief forced out concern from his freshly-tanned features: Father Doyle, R.I.P.![6]

"Maher?" he said. "The dreaded Greek of that name?"

"The very same. Or Doctor Maher, as he likes to be known in the trade."

With a near-squint of delight, Father Patric MacCarthy regaled his companions with the picaresque Greek's travails in the civil and criminal courtrooms of Killoyle: after pleading guilty to charges of willfully damaging his own property, he got off with a mild caution and handshakes all round because the judge and three members of the jury owed him favours financial and electoral as well as back rent on various shops and brothels and the odd empty parcel of inferior farmland. Officially charged two days later with being an accessory to murder in the second degree as the owner of Mad Molloy's—purveyor of HyperAle to the late Kenneth O'Moon (notorious addict)—he succeeded in convincing the jury, through the use of photo slides, newspaper articles and expert mimickry, that (a) the world was a better place *sans* O'Moon, and that (b) HyperAle, taken in small doses, did no harm, in fact aided sufficiently as an inducement to sleep to have been prescribed as a cure for chronic insomnia by three West of Ireland doctors, one of whom (the one who'd put up ten acres of

---

[6]Oh yes. And life must go on, blah blah blah. God, it makes me *sick*. Will you excuse me half a tick while I . . . ?

Galway grazing land as collateral against a stingy loan from Maher to cover his losses on the ponies) took the witness stand in the Greek's behalf and even heartily swigged the stuff prior to falling into a deep sleep, proving the case for the defence. The Greek was acquitted and all charges against him dropped. Another man, one Bucko Heffernan, was convicted and sentenced to six months in prison on charges of gross negligence and found heavily suspect in the embezzlement of some £3000, give or take, from Mad Molloy's, with an upshot totalling two years' probation, consecutive to the half-year in the clink. After that, the only charge outstanding against the Greek was his wife's allegation, made in open court at Limerick beneath the stoic beak of the Beak, His Honour Lemuel E. Fant, that T. Maher, Esq., was the bane of her existence and, incidentally (but crucially) the sole perpetrator of the Easy-Fert outrage; but with no witnesses and little, if any, legal precedent, the case promised to dander its way round the courts for years . . . . Among the Greek's well-wishers at the courtroom door, post-acquittal, had been Ben Ovary, the Lord Mayor, Dickie Doheny-Nesbitt the television guru and Superintendent Ted Nugent of the local Gardai.

"And yours truly. Well, what choice had I in the matter?" said Father Patric, in querulous tones. "Of course the fella's a bit rum, but he knows the real estate business, and he can smell a rotten deal a mile away. Actually, I've arranged for him to fly out to Malta when his legal troubles are over. He's just the man to give us the appraisal we want, and he won't bugger about, or give us a phony price."

"And that's the important thing, of course," murmured Emmet.

"Who's to say, Emmet?" said the priest. "Who's to say—bar Him?" His index finger indicated God's traditional whereabouts.

That evening Emmet took his coffee (Yucatan Arabica blend) at the dining room window and watched the shadows sweep the Pogginarno plain.

"Christ," he growled. "Italy, eh?" The accuracy of his observation awakened plaintive inner longings: that sky; those smells; that language . . . *sweet mavourneen!* But they might never go back to Ireland. They'd become semi-Ite, if they worked at it; gibbering anomalies, latter-day colonials, if they didn't. Still, going native wouldn't be a total disaster, if he and Roisin made a friend or two. Dario's English needed cleaning up, that was certain, and Signora Grilli, the widow next door, was always bringing over books and magazines in English with ill-comprehended passages heavily underlined in lipstick red. If Emmet kept his job, things would be grand—but Father Patric would, ultimately, decide that part of it—and that was enough to wind a fella up, of a night. Emmet had always set great store by a man's instincts, his and others', and Father Pat gave the impression of being motivated less by instinct than by ambition:[7] hadn't he flicked aside the memory of old Father Phil like snot off his thumbnail?

Emmet frowned, beset by thoughts of the dead priest.

"Ah, never mind. He'd have loved this place but hated everybody in it," he muttered. "He's probably better off dead."

Shock leapt within, briefly, at the heretical idea. It was hard to concede that someone was better off dead, but there were those who hated the turmoil and unpleasantness—and most of all the *imperfection*—of life so much that the only break they ever got was death, after a certain point—say seventy years, and Father Doyle had been nearly that, hadn't he?[8]

"Aye," self-seconded Emmet, sagely. "Poor bastard. And of course he couldn't top himself, being a priest."

---

[7]And not at all a bad thing, if you ask me. I'll take ambition (the Pyramids, Handel's Messiah, Neary's Bar) over instinct (Rover fetching the ball 749 times, tumescence leading to the unnamable, fisticuffs in coatrooms and alleyways) any day of the calendar, thanks very much.

[8]Too true, too true. Look at me, I'll never see fourscore again, and there are some days when I look at my ghastly crumpled-up old mug in the mirror and think of the creaking, groaning, smelly efforts I had to make just to get out of bed, and I sometimes wonder: where's the nearest .45, or box of rat poison itself? But the mood soon passes, and in the blink of an eye I'm in the kitchen belting out "Carrickfergus" and swilling the full-strength tea like nobody's business; then, before I know it, my legs are positively trembling in their eagerness to carry me off to the shops at maximum speed! It just goes to show: wait a bit, and things change. *Plus ça change, plus ça change*, is what I say (and I hope you're impressed with the parlayvoo, you superior buggers).

But E. Power, Esq., was a happier man than those life-haters. In fact—he recoiled at the thought, then eagerly embraced it—he was quite probably that rarest of creatures, that butt of jokes, that enemy of modern culture, that lost cause:

A HAPPY MAN.

And why? Because, all in all, his conscience was clear, he'd acted according to his lights, he'd not stained the family escutcheon: *Power would have another day!* Oh, right enough. He'd told the truth about Carfax; he'd up and left a place and a job he'd become heartily sick of, and in so doing he'd given young Milo Rogers an opportunity, one way or another, to do with as he chose; he'd handed his boy Sean the keys to the house, if not the kingdom, and a haven back in Ireland after long years of Yank exile (providing he washed his clothes, fed the meter and made no enemies at the Garda station); and he and Roisin had settled in Italy, in *this* place, in *this* house, with *this* view out the dining room window (from their dining room in Killoyle: the O'Mearas' potting shed, part of a lichen-grown wall, a slate roof) . . .

Roisin came into the room and saw her husband slumped, brooding, staring out the window. She put on the light.

"What's the matter, dear?"

Emmet grunted.

"Ask me in Italian and I'll tell you."

"Ach, Emmet. That's not fair, is it. Well, all right, let me see, what would it be, now. *Che . . . che c'é, caro?* Is that it?"

Emmet turned with a grin sloping across his face and threw open his arms like a lover in the *opera buffa* style.

"Nothing's the matter, *carissima!*" he said. *"Niente!* I'm feeling grand. Let's go for a walk."

"You go, dear," said Roisin. "I've a touch of headache."

"Headache? *Malatesta,* ah haha? OK, acushla. *Ciao.*"

Emmet left. From the hallway Roisin watched him stride past the Casa Comunale into the semi-night; then, surreptitiously as a footpad, she stole into the bedroom and withdrew a book from under the mattress of her bed. She saw no harm in her little deception, for deception it was: she had no more of a headache than the clouds in the sky, or your own backside. It was only a book, after all, one old Signora Grilli had come across in an out-of-the-way-but-up-to-date bookshop in Rome (Popinglese, 44A Viale Nerone), and had recommended highly to her new *amica irlandese* Roisin Power—especially when *la Signora* learned, via family albums, faded wedding announcements, etc., that Roisin had been born a Gavin! Of course, Emmet would go spare if he found out, but boysoboys! It was "a terrific read" (Erskine P. Grogan, *Hog Farmers' Weekly*); a tale "told by a hoarse, melancholy, vodka-voice from the steppes" (Pierre-Alain Geutweiler, *Gazette de Lausanne*) against "the plangent urgency of a dozen wailing balalaikas backed by the throbbing of a hundred tractor engines" (Dan-Gus Guzman, *San Angelo (Tex.) Whiplash-Times*) . . . she was on page 143, just before your man heads East.

"*I really wanted to see White Sea Canal. Hey, that's great, I hear you saying, but why, Leonid, you ask (in all your voices of differing timbres and ranges)? Well, so, just let me tell you why. Back in those days all you heard about everywhere, on radio, in streets, under covers, over your shoulder, I mean EVERYWHERE, was: White Sea Canal, White Sea Canal, WHITE SEA CANAL and so on (and believe me you better listen or that's one single to Siberia coming up faster than an Antonov light transport), so when this NKVD person hits me somewhere between third, fourth rib area and says, 'Hey, Glossovich, we got room for one more guy on White Sea Canal cruise—I mean chain gang,' well, there I am signing on the bottom line, you can believe that! Hoping, I don't need to tell you, that out there in our beautiful wide Soviet hinterland there was going to be lots of ways to bring up, you know, Him, and sacred stuff, etc., as well as all kinds and shapes of ears to talk into—not knowing, of course, that White Sea Canal was great big White Elephant Canal in middle of Big Guy-forsaken tundra where it's always the middle of the night, or more like 3 a.m., and it's minus 72 outside, with crazy two-meter-tall machine-gun-carrying malchiks ready to turn you into Ladoga blackberry jam whenever it fits in with their busy schedules . . ."*

In Naples, a month to the day later—that is, early in the next year, green with false promise—fleeting congruity of the world's oldest and newest professions was symbolised by a fortyish woman of the streets in miniskirt and fishnet stockings patrolling the pavement outside the Software Superstore on the scooter-loud Via Malta, perpendicular to the National Museum of world renown.[9] As the day waned, traffic, automotive and foot, intensified, and the whore's potential customers became more numerous, but this particular pro was discriminate in the extreme. Indigenous prowlers passed and repassed, like steam irons; they ogled, beckoned, whistled, blew kisses, were ignored, to a man. A drunk bore the brunt of her disdainful glare. A masher in a white hat and double-breasted suit sidled over and sculpted in the air poses in which he, she . . . only to be banished from her presence by an imperious raspberry ("BRRRRRRRRPPP") and the horned hand *("Cornuto, va!")*.

For a moment, she was alone.

"Aie, Dio," she sighed. Would no *stranieri* come? No *americani, inglesi*, even *tedeschi* . . . ? Then, from the direction of the port, eclipsing the westward orb of the setting sun, riding a momentary crescendo of Fiat-music, a foreigner loomed, shadow cast hugely, lengthwise: a big boy, *inglese* by the tilt of his cap.

"Coocoo, Coco," cooed the courtesan. "You *gigante*, you Inglish? You pretty big, Gianni, hey? You wanna come with me, now?"

"Nun parlow like, eye-taliano, darlin'. Eh—listen, I need the railway station. Stats he owny?"

"Stazione? Si, chiaro, I know it. Come with me and I tell you, okay?"

"I really don't have time to dander about. I'm on me way to a place called Kye-etty, do you know it at all? C-H-I-. . ."

---

[9]Aye, I made it there once. I'll not be returning soon. Nothing in the place but statues of Greek bumboys wearing eyeliner and lipstick, as God's my witness—and I shouldn't be at all surprised if the raddled old slut who came sashaying up to me outside the jacks was one and the same as she here. You know, this goes a long way toward explaining why so many of us, when given the option, choose Bundoran or Lisdoonvarna—or Killoyle, come to that—as the ideal holiday venue, rather than Abroad, which, although rich in culture, foreign languages, hotels and what have you, always has a surprise up its sleeve, usually simultaneous with the wandering of its swarthy hands over your nether regions, if you take my meaning. At least in Bundoran a pint's a pint, and Eff Off carries some weight.

"Chieti? Si. So? Is near Roma. Is too far tonight, Gianni. Plenty of time for fun 'ere in Napoli, no?"

"Fun, is it. Aha. Feckin' prossie, aren't ya? Listen, I don't fancy a shag just at the moment, so point me in the direction of the stats he owny and we'll say arreeveederchy, how's that?"

Sycophancy turned to contempt, acid-tipped.

"*Va fa'nculo. Coglione. Finocchio.*"

"Right. Piss off yerself."

So, with the grim inevitability of childhood ailments, or taxes (or death)—or the volcanic lava that coursed from time to time down the slopes of Vesuvius hard by—Thomas Fingall Wellington Casement O'Malley "The Greek" Maher, on his first venture abroad (not counting Blackpool, Stranraer, and your average Paddy's standard stint in the Kilburn and Hammersmith districts of London) made his way to the Stazione Centrale and—after awkwardly yet effectively communicating his travel plans—from there (via Capua, Caserta and Ferentino) to Chieti, that once-peaceful resort in the hills.[10]

---

[10]Now that the horrible git's away, will peace come to once-turbulent Killoyle? Don't count on it. It just goes to show, as the Da said at "Eyes" Molloy's funeral: "You never know what's coming round the next corner, or who's just gone round the last bend." By the by, as long as we're on the subject, said "Eyes," the young brother of an old Republican acquaintance of the pater's from Armagh, went so far round the proverbial bend he ran into his own taillights, so to speak—but wait till I tell you. A sad case, so it was. "Eyes," like so many, spent his undergraduate years in Crumlin Road on a scholarship from Her Majesty's Government and later went on to graduate with honours from the Maze. Once out in the world again, he headed South and found a job through the Greater Dublin Republican Prisoners' Sinecure Scheme as a Time and Motion Advisor to the Ministry of Prisons. He was assigned a work carrel containing a desk, a wheelchair (he was a martyr to the arthritis, and the wardens at the Maze would insist on taking bone marrow samples—very politely, mind you, but still!), an imitation aspidistra, and a typewriter. It was cosy enough, but your man could never stay in one place for more than fifteen minutes, for fear of arrest (years of Brits and their Ulster Protestant running dogs barking in your face day and night, that'll do it every time). He preferred to quietly maneuver his wheelchair down the hallways and pull into other carrels behind

their seated occupants and announce his presence, after a few seconds, with loud stage laughter followed by direct conversation, with no further preamble, along the lines of (say): Was the blister on his bum a pimple or an insect bite? Why didn't the pre-1972 Ford Escort have an unsynchronized first gear? Do moths have brains? Which animal has the most muscular rectum (his candidate was the cow, of course, with all those tummies emptying out)? In short, a sundry congeries of items so ludicrous that he was soon an object of widespread resentment, even horror, and in short order found himself returned to the dole queue despite his loud protests and threats to mail a hundred milligrams of Semtex to every man Jack in the place . . . aye, poor "Eyes."

But it didn't end there. He next turned up, wearing leg braces and astonishingly thick glasses, working as potboy at Mountjoy's Bar in Longford, and held pretty steady for a year or so before his temper frayed and he dashed his pots to the ground. After that he did no work. He preferred instead to stand outside, arms akimbo, and make suggestive faces at passersby, a no-no in the catering trade. (Witnesses reported that among his favoured grimaces—the one that gave him his nickname, no less—was one in which the eyes are wide open and slowly rotating, as per B. Karloff, *The Mummy*, 1932: a suggestive detail, in light of events to come.) Handed his marching papers again, and being a deft class of a man in the car line, "Eyes" got himself a job—despite his leg braces and the two-inch-thick tinted prescription eyeglasses he was now sporting—as assistant driver to Lord Steamer, down Ballygowan way. It was, on the face of it, nothing less than a cushy number, considering the quantity and quality of Jags, etc., in his lordship's holdings. "Eyes" even struck up a deep acquaintance with Ginny Penrod, the sous-chef, herself a sufferer from chronic myopia; for once, things seemed to be working out, but that was before the luck of the Irish started in on him. Wouldn't you know it, the day "Eyes" was assigned to fill in behind the wheel—peaked cap, striped trousers, silver piping, the lot—was the very day the pookas plunged him into the jigs for good: on his maiden drive, five miles or so along the road, with Lord S. perusing *The Pink 'Un* in the back seat, "Eyes" became aware (or so he claimed) of flights of winged mice alighting on the rims of his spectacles; with an oath, he set about swatting the creatures with both hands, and climbed onto the bonnet to get a better view of the incoming swarm. Well, you'll hardly be surprised to learn that the first words to come out of his lordship's mouth in the hospital were offensive and had to do with "Eyes"—not that poor "Eyes" gave a tinker's, what with both legs gone west and a growing conviction that the rims of his spectacles *themselves* interfered with his sight: he saw them, he said, even in his dreams. After he left hospital, contacts were fitted, but they only succeeded in bringing his nose into obnoxiously clear focus. One day at the roadside he plucked the lenses out, with a cry of anguish. To make a long story short, the jigs took him over completely and he ended his days at home, humming about in an electric wheelchair and staring at the precise point on various ceilings at which his vision was least encumbered by ambient facial features; soon, naturally, he'd become a bit of an expert on this angle of vision, and fancied writing a monograph about it, but of course every time he lowered his eyes to the paper his nose hove into view, followed by everything else. It was a bind, right enough. In the end, there was nothing for it but (a) blindness, self-willed; (b) family-size sunglasses, black; or (c) despair, in the fullest romantic sense. The subsequent discovery (by Ginny Penrod, poor lass) of his body floating in the Suir face up, wearing a business suit and sunglasses and garlanded with flowers, suggested a neat cocktail of (b) and (c), with a dash of the Pre-Raphaelite. To Ginny, and to the world, "Eyes" had left a farewell note, clumsily handwritten (his eyes, as we can imagine, being elsewhere), even eloquently so: *I've had enough Cheerio.*

DALKEY ARCHIVE PAPERBACKS

DALKEY ARCHIVE PAPERBACKS

STEPHENS, MICHAEL. *Season at Coole* 7.95
WOOLF, DOUGLAS. *Wall to Wall* 7.95
YOUNG, MARGUERITE. *Miss MacIntosh, My Darling* 2-vol. set, 30.00
ZUKOFSKY, LOUIS. *Collected Fiction* 13.50
ZWIREN, SCOTT. *God Head* 10.95

FICTION: BRITISH

BROOKE-ROSE, CHRISTINE. *Amalgamemnon* 9.95
CHARTERIS, HUGO. *The Tide Is Right* 9.95
FIRBANK, RONALD. *Complete Short Stories* 9.95
GALLOWAY, JANICE. *Foreign Parts* 12.95
GALLOWAY, JANICE. *The Trick Is to Keep Breathing* 11.95
HUXLEY, ALDOUS. *Antic Hay* 12.50
HUXLEY, ALDOUS. *Point Counter Point* 13.95
MOORE, OLIVE. *Spleen* 10.95
MOSLEY, NICHOLAS. *Accident* 9.95
MOSLEY, NICHOLAS. *Assassins* 12.95
MOSLEY, NICHOLAS. *Children of Darkness and Light* 13.95
MOSLEY, NICHOLAS. *Impossible Object* 9.95
MOSLEY, NICHOLAS. *Judith* 10.95
MOSLEY, NICHOLAS. *Natalie Natalia* 12.95

FICTION: FRENCH

BUTOR, MICHEL. *Portrait of the Artist as a Young Ape* 10.95
CÉLINE, LOUIS-FERDINAND. *Castle to Castle* 13.95
CÉLINE, LOUIS-FERDINAND. *North* 13.95
CREVEL, RENÉ. *Putting My Foot in It* 9.95
ERNAUX, ANNIE. *Cleaned Out* 10.95
GRAINVILLE, PATRICK. *The Cave of Heaven* 10.95
NAVARRE, YVES. *Our Share of Time* 9.95
QUENEAU, RAYMOND. *The Last Days* 11.95
QUENEAU, RAYMOND. *Pierrot Mon Ami* 9.95
ROUBAUD, JACQUES. *The Great Fire of London* 12.95
ROUBAUD, JACQUES. *The Princess Hoppy* 9.95
SIMON, CLAUDE. *The Invitation* 9.95

FICTION: GERMAN

SCHMIDT, ARNO. *Collected Stories* 13.50
SCHMIDT, ARNO. *Nobodaddy's Children* 13.95

DALKEY ARCHIVE PAPERBACKS

FICTION: IRISH

CUSACK, RALPH. *Cadenza*	7.95
MAC LOCHLAINN, ALF. *The Corpus in the Library*	11.95
MACLOCHLAINN, ALF. *Out of Focus*	7.95
O'BRIEN, FLANN. *The Dalkey Archive*	9.95
O'BRIEN, FLANN. *The Hard Life*	11.95
O'BRIEN, FLANN. *The Poor Mouth*	10.95

FICTION: LATIN AMERICAN AND SPANISH

CAMPOS, JULIETA. *The Fear of Losing Eurydice*	8.95
LINS, OSMAN. *The Queen of the Prisons of Greece*	12.95
PASO, FERNANDO DEL. *Palinuro of Mexico*	14.95
RÍOS, JULIÁN. *Poundemonium*	13.50
SARDUY, SEVERO. *Cobra* and *Maitreya*	13.95
TUSQUETS, ESTHER. *Stranded*	9.95
VALENZUELA, LUISA. *He Who Searches*	8.00

POETRY

ALFAU, FELIPE. *Sentimental Songs*	9.95
ANSEN, ALAN. *Contact Highs: Selected Poems 1957-1987*	11.95
BURNS, GERALD. *Shorter Poems*	9.95
FAIRBANKS, LAUREN. *Muzzle Thyself*	9.95
GISCOMBE, C. S. *Here*	9.95
MARKSON, DAVID. *Collected Poems*	9.95
ROUBAUD, JACQUES. *The Plurality of Worlds of Lewis*	9.95
THEROUX, ALEXANDER. *The Lollipop Trollops*	10.95

NONFICTION

FORD, FORD MADOX. *The March of Literature*	16.95
GREEN, GEOFFREY, ET AL. *The Vineland Papers*	14.95
MATHEWS, HARRY. *20 Lines a Day*	8.95
MOORE, STEVEN. *Ronald Firbank: An Annotated Bibliography*	30.00
ROUDIEZ, LEON S. *French Fiction Revisited*	14.95
SHKLOVSKY, VIKTOR. *Theory of Prose*	14.95
WEST, PAUL. *Words for a Deaf Daughter* and *Gala*	12.95
WYLIE, PHILIP. *Generation of Vipers*	13.95
YOUNG, MARGUERITE. *Angel in the Forest*	13.95

Dalkey Archive Press, ISU Box 4241, Normal, IL 61790-4241
fax (309) 438-7422
Visit our website at http://www.cas.ilstu.edu/english/dalkey/dalkey.html